The Shiksa
Barbara Bartlett

William Morrow and Company, Inc.
New York

Excerpt from *Pleasures and Days and Other Writings* by Marcel Proust. Copyright © 1957 by F. W. Dupee and Barbara Dupee. Copyright 1948 by Lear Publishers, Inc. Reprinted with permission of Doubleday Publishing Group.

Excerpt from "The Choice" reprinted with permission of Macmillan Publishing Company from *Collected Poems* by W. B. Yeats. Copyright 1933 by Macmillan Publishing Company, renewed by Bertha Georgie Yeats.

Excerpt from "The Dead" from *The Collected Poems of Rupert Brooke.* Reprinted with permission of Dodd, Mead & Company, Inc.

"The Fire Sermon": From "The Waste Land" in *Collected Poems 1909–1962* by T. S. Eliot. Copyright 1935, 1936 by Harcourt Brace Jovanovich, Inc.; copyright © 1964 by T. S. Eliot. Reprinted by permission of the publisher.

Excerpt from *The Cocktail Party.* Copyright © 1950 by T. S. Eliot; renewed 1978 by Esme Valerie Eliot. Reprinted by permission of Harcourt Brace Jovanovich, Inc.

Cartoon by Jules Feiffer quoted with permission of Mr. Feiffer.

Excerpt from "The City" by C. P. Cavafy, as translated in *Justine* by Lawrence Durrell. Copyright © 1957 by Lawrence Durrell; renewed 1985 by Lawrence Durrell. Reprinted by permission of the publisher, E. P. Dutton, a division of NAL Penguin Inc.

Excerpt from *Nightwood* by Djuna Barnes. Used by permission of New Directions.

Library of Congress Cataloging-in-Publication Data

Bartlett, Barbara T.
  The shiksa / Barbara T. Bartlett.
    p.   cm.
  ISBN 0-688-04389-5
  I. Title.
PS3552.A7652S5   1987
813'.54—dc19   87-12526
                                                    CIP

Printed in the United States of America

First Edition

1 2 3 4 5 6 7 8 9 10

BOOK DESIGN BY MARK STEIN

For P.T. and P.B.

To my editor,
Pat Golbitz,
for her perception, patience, and great good humor,
I owe an incalculable debt of gratitude.

Contents

Part Three

Part Four

Prologue

Listen, Alexander Portnoy, were you aware, while you were complaining and jerking off in New Jersey, that all over America adolescent girls of a certain type were huddled in confessionals preparing for you? Not for their fair-haired Christian male counterparts, but for someone just like you—dark, brooding, brilliant, insecure, funny, and Jewish. At least it seems likely this was happening everywhere; it certainly was in Rochester, New York.

Katherine Winterhaus may have been the only one with this predilection at the Convent of the Sacred Heart, that Gothic mansion on Prince Street where a community of elite nuns consecrated their lives to turning Catholic girls into soldiers of Christ, but there must have been others in Ohio, say, and Kentucky, California, Mississippi.

We know who we are—a kind of secret society: certifiable, card-carrying masochists driven to expiate personally the two thousand years of suffering endured by our love objects; forsaking families, sanity, dangerous sports, and country clubs to cleave unto our addiction, the Jewish male.

Poor Portnoy. If only you had known. What comfort you would have derived, there in your bathroom, from contemplating the Shiksa Syndrome.

Introduction:
Adolescence

"Bless me, Father, for I have sinned. It has been one week since my last confession. I was disrespectful to my mother six times. I neglected my homework once. I was lazy and disobedient and I told a lie and lost my temper twice and I committed a sin of Pride and three uncharitable acts and . . . uh . . ."

Out of breath and venial sins, Katie knelt there, a slim growing girl in a green gabardine uniform, racking her brain to postpone telling the Big One. Old Father Keneally waited behind the grille, his right hand cupped to his ear. In preparation for confession, she had studied the Examination of Conscience in her daily missal and exonerated herself of gluttony, drunkenness, doubts as to any article of faith (the Trinity was a hard one to understand, even using the metaphor of the three-leaf clover, but she didn't for a minute *doubt* the three distinct Persons of the Godhead), worship of graven images, consulting fortune-tellers, and those twin transgressions against the Holy Ghost, presumption and despair.

"Is there anything else?" the chaplain murmured.

She cleared her bangs from her forehead in a nervous gesture. "I broke my silence four times during the retreat. . . ." Face burning, ears ringing, at last she blurted, ". . . And I had Impure Thoughts."

There. It was out. She took a deep breath and prayed that the priest would not ask her to be specific. According to Mother MacDowell, the rangy nun who taught Christian Doctrine and basketball to the Junior School, the Devil put such thoughts into your head when you were idle, off-guard—like getting the ball past an inattentive opponent on the court. "Idleness is anathema to a true child of the Sacred Heart," Mother MacDowell would say in a register suitable for Gregorian chant. One terrible Tuesday, she'd charged out of the locker room, her habit pinned up, the ball tucked in the crook of her elbow, the large silver cross that hung around her neck clinking against a referee's whistle, just as Katie raced in to the gymnasium, late as usual for sports. The collision that occurred knocked Katie off her feet and caused "Foul" MacDowell to sway like a reed in the wind. Without the round, metal-framed glasses that she always removed for basketball practice, the nun resembled a nighthawk. From the mysterious region under her capelet, she'd fished out a pocket watch, glared at it, and proclaimed, "Katherine Ann Winterhaus, you are a dawdler and a dreamer. What's more, you are habitually late for everything except *goûter*. Woe betide you if you fail to correct this character flaw!" Then she'd turned and dribbled the ball down the court, her gauzy veil flying in her wake.

"Foul" MacDowell was right. In fact, what Katie looked forward to even more than the afternoon snack of milk and cookies (called *goûter* in convent lingo) was lying in bed at night deep in romantic reverie. For a long time her daydreams had been harmless ones about turning into a ravishing beauty at eighteen and having someone like Todd Babcock, the blond Adonis who taught sailing at the Yacht Club, fall in love with her at a ball. Then, during Christmas vacation in New York, her parents took her to see *Guys and Dolls,* starring Robert Alda as Sky Masterson. His black hair was sleek with brilliantine; his suit had pinstripes and wide lapels; his rough voice addressed women as "Babe." When he rattled the dice and sang, "Luck, Be a Lady Tonight!" Katie got a queer, melting feeling in the pit of her stomach, and her fantasies took a different turn.

"Impure thoughts," echoed Father Keneally, shifting his weight behind the grille. A fusty odor emanated from his cassock. From the shadows he whispered, "How many times?"

I can't say "Constantly," Katie thought. I really cannot, with that long green line of girls snaking through the chapel waiting their turn, give him an estimate of seventy-eight! She scratched at a spot on her uniform sleeve and mumbled, "About five, Father," thinking, Another lie.

"Now you wouldn't want to let weeds grow in a lovely garden, would you, child?" he said in his quavering brogue. "Your mind as well as your body is a temple of the Holy Ghost. Vigilance! We have always to guard against the temptations of the Devil, who roams through the world seekin' the ruin of souls . . ."

Katie had straight A's in Christian Doctrine. She could quote Mother MacDowell and the Baltimore Catechism verbatim on the subject of free will, which was automatically activated at the age of seven, when a person becomes liable for knowing the difference between Right and Wrong. The Devil's no excuse, she thought, bowing her head before the chaplain.

"For your penance, say the five sorrowful mysteries of the rosary and make a good Act of Contrition."

"OmyGodIammostheartilysorryforhavingoffendedThee. . . ."

"Dominus noster Jesus Christus te absolvat . . ."

". . . I firmly resolve with the help of Thy grace . . ."

". . . deinde ego te absolvo a peccatis tuis . . ."

". . . to confess my sins . . ."—through the grille, she saw him raise his hand in a blessing—". . . todopenance . . ."

"InnominePatrisetFiliietSpritusSanctus. . ."

". . . andtoamendmylifeAmen."

"Amen."

It was a trick to finish together.

With clasped hands and downcast eyes, Katie went from the cubicle to the front of the chapel, past the wooden pews and the nuns' Romanesque seats under stained glass windows depicting scenes from Our Lord's life; past old Sister O'Rourke scrubbing the floor on her hands and knees, skirts caught up with a clothespin, her cheerful peasant's face framed by a flat, starched wimple instead of the teaching nuns' crimped bonnet; past the *surveillante*, Mother Manning, an El Greco figure standing in an arc of light from the sanctuary, her cheeks aflame with Divine love, her arms outstretched like His before the Twelfth Station of the Cross; past the tabernacle and along the marble railing to the side altar, where the plaster statue of the Sacred Heart wore a crown of thorns that spilled ruby droplets onto that tortured, aquiline, supremely Semitic face. She made the sign of the cross. Behind her, she could hear the shuffling of oxfords as the line for confession inched forward. She mouthed the words to the Confiteor: "I confess to Almighty God, to blessed Mary ever Virgin, to blessed Michael the Archangel, to blessed John the Baptist, to the holy apostles Peter and Paul, and to all the saints, that I have sinned exceedingly in thought, word and deed"—

with a small fist, she struck her breast thrice—"through my fault, through my fault, through my most grievous fault . . ." and raised her eyes in adoration to Jesus.

The Son of God. Handsome, persecuted, omnipotent. Every Catholic girl's first Jewish man.

CHAPTER 1

Goldilocks and Bagels

The last year that Katie remembered the four of them living together as a real family was when she was eight. Her parents gave up the apartment in town and bought a vast English Tudor house in Brighton, which her mother said would take the decorator months to finish, so they stayed all year round at the lake, miles from anywhere, their property secluded behind a low stone wall at the end of a private road shaded by giant elm trees. A snapshot from that summer showed Katie standing outside the wall dressed in a pinafore and saddle shoes, a ribbon in her blond hair and a cocker spaniel at her feet. Every afternoon at four-thirty she would swing back and forth on the little iron gate, listening for the clang of the Good Humor truck, waiting for her father to return from the city. By mid-December, snow lay like an eiderdown over the rock garden, the tulip beds, the boathouse roof, and the lawn that sloped in terraces to the beach. Under the apple tree, a ceramic elf still stood grinning crookedly, but now his pointed cap dripped with icicles. The other houses along Rock Beach Road were boarded up, all but the one across the railroad tracks belonging to the caretaker, old Fred Spencer, who people said had gone a bit off living so far from civilization. Only the whistle of the milk train pierced the silence. The Winterhauses' white summer palace was transformed by billowing snowdrifts and frozen currents into a great ghost haunting the shores of Lake Ontario. Katie's mother complained bitterly of the cold, and fifteen-year old Margot wailed that no boy in his right mind would drive all the way down to Irondequoit to pick her up. "Sell the place!" her father grumbled, but secretly he agreed with Katie that it had a touch of magic in winter.

On the snowy afternoon that the convent let out for Christmas vacation, Katie took the bus as usual down East Main Street and got off at the Mercantile Building. Bypassing the creaky elevators in the arcade, she clunked in her galoshes up the service stairs and into her father's world. Bold black letters on the glass doors spelled out TAYLOR-RIDLEY & CO., MEMBERS, NEW YORK STOCK EXCHANGE.

Here a steady buzz of activity was underscored by the click of the ticker tape; dour-faced men in three-piece suits hooked their thumbs in vest pockets and tipped their swivel chairs backward, mesmerized by figures that marched across the top of the big board; clients wandered in and out like gamblers in a bookie joint; secretaries and telephone operators sat in a glass-enclosed area—good-natured, middle-aged women whom brokers called "the Girls."

Katie waved to Cliff, the sixtyish board boy, who was chalking up quotations on the big board, and went down the hall to her father's office. Looking up from his charts, he said with a big grin, "Hi, Skeezix. What'd you learn in school today?" She loved to see him this way: in his shirtsleeves, the gold pocket watch strung across his vest on its chain, his head bent over a graph book as he meticulously recorded the day's rise and fall of stocks.

Douglas Winterhaus was not a customer's man; he was an independent trader with an account so large that Taylor-Ridley provided him with its only private office, a back room stuffed to the ceiling with filing cabinets, one grimy window overlooking a parking lot. As far as Katie knew, her mother had never set foot in it, nor, from the looks of it, had it been graced with any woman's touch. It was a male preserve, and the child guarded her position there jealously—that was *her* chair next to the walnut desk stacked with market reports and *Wall Street Journals*. She propped her elbows on the edge and told her father about her day.

Her earliest memory was of his hand. The tips of his right thumb and little finger had been blown off in a fireworks accident on the Fourth of July when he was twelve. She remembered putting her four-year-old hand into his as they crossed a sunlit plaza in Miami on the way to the brokerage office; nothing she did during that vacation—not birthday parties at the Pancoast Hotel or even riding her pony at the ring—compared with walking to work with her father. Now, through her eyelashes, she studied the blunted thumb holding the pencil and tried to picture him as a child lighting a firecracker. It was impossible.

The telephone at his elbow rang: Uncle Gerry, asking for money or advice, Katie supposed, and went outside to the main office to watch the ticker tape, then wandered downstairs to browse in the arcade shops. When Douglas was ready to leave, he found her across the street at Tucker's Religious Store, staring through the window at a miniature electric altar on display, her small features superimposed on its marbleized tiers studded with twelve tiny candles. For her eighth birthday, he'd given her a wooden crucifix with a secret compartment (useful for concealing jewels or private documents); now, more than anything in life, she wanted that altar. She pictured herself kneeling before it in her bedroom with a black lace veil covering her head, like some doomed queen—Mary, Queen of Scots, for instance. She raved about it all the way to the parking lot.

Every year her father got a new Cadillac, even though her mother complained that the fins were ostentatious and garish. This one was maroon. On the way home, as usual they listened to *Lorenzo Jones* on the radio. The program about a failed inventor and his wife, Belle, bored Katie stiff, but because it made him chuckle she pretended to enjoy it. Douglas was a master of the shortcut. Where the average man, traveling the main route, took half an hour from downtown to Irondequoit, he pared the time to fourteen minutes by twisting through back streets that he called "the colored section."

Emerging from an underpass near the railroad station, he turned onto a garbage-littered alley lined with ramshackle buildings, and put on the brakes at a stop sign. "Judas Priest! Look at this mess," he muttered. Katie cleared a space on her frosty window with a mitten. Outside a dry goods store, a Negro boy of twelve or thirteen leaned on a snow shovel, his eyes fixed on the Cadillac's chrome fins; as Douglas accelerated, the chained tires spat slush at him. A familiar depression descended upon her.

"It's a disgrace the way these people live," her father said.

"They can't help it if they're not rich," she retorted.

"Huh," he groused. "Let me tell you something, young lady. The Irish had it just as rough when they came to this country, but they pulled themselves up by their bootstraps. There's no excuse for the colored people. You give them a house in Brighton and in six months they'll turn it into a slum."

"Really? How does anybody know that, Daddy?"

"I'll tell you how. Mr. Truman takes more and more of our money to give to them, and where does it get 'em? Right back in the ash can. Take the Italians—they've managed to make something of themselves."

"That's different."

"How so?"

"I don't know . . . it just is." Katie felt her leg muscles tense under the fur lap robe. They'd had this fight a hundred times; she wished he'd take the long way down Lake Avenue. In silence they listened to *Portia Faces Life*. Walter was still blind and Portia was distraught.

Just past the railroad tracks, Douglas turned onto Rock Beach Road and drove slowly underneath a canopy of snow laden branches, past the shuttered estates to the bottom of an icy incline, where he stopped the car, got out, and raised one of the garage doors; it rumbled on its tracks. A blast of wind made him turn up the collar of his storm coat. Katie remembered how the clerk in Tucker's had asked if he were her grandfather. She hoped he hadn't heard. Patches, the black cocker spaniel, had been cooped up in the garage for hours, and ran rings around them as they tramped across the lawn in the growing dusk, their galoshes carving craters in the deep snow. "Too bad you can't make up your mind what you want for Christmas, Snooks," Douglas teased, his eyes crinkling above what his wife, Emily, called "that big German nose."

On Christmas morning, Katie awoke with the sun in her eyes. A lemon sliver appeared above the rim of the lake, swiftly brightening over the crusted waves, showering the ice with golden beams that became, as she sat up to watch, phantasmagoric figures floating toward her window, crystalline and faintly androgynous—a word she had looked up after seeing Risë Stevens in *Der Rosenkavalier* at the Eastman Theatre.

Stirrings below. She jumped out of bed and scrambled down the staircase in her flannel footed pajamas. The dining room had French doors that opened onto the long lakefront sunporch, and was separated from the living room by a library table and a chintz couch, on which Margot was collapsed, waiting for the opening of the presents. Across from the fireplace, glossy packages were piled beneath a gigantic blue spruce shimmering with lights and a cascade of tinsel. In a flash Katie registered the array, then turned away, crushed—none of the boxes was the right size. She went to kiss her mother, a vibrant presence at the breakfast table in a burgundy velvet dressing gown with amber buttons, lighting her first Chesterfield of the day. Her brown hair smelled of Fleurs de Rocailles and smoke. Relieved to see that she was in a good mood, Katie looked beyond her to the sunporch, where her father sat hidden behind the funnies; from the way the paper was shaking, she could tell he was reading "The Katzenjammer Kids." He peered over the top; she followed his gaze and there, gleaming in a shaft of sunlight on the coffee table, was the altar. She let out a shriek and ran to plug it in.

"Ho, ho, ho!" he chortled. "Too bad Santa Claus didn't bring you what you wanted this Christmas, Skeezix."

Margot raised her head on her elbow and looked over at her mother. "It doesn't bother you," she inquired archly, "to be raising a religious fanatic?"

"Don't be such a smart aleck, miss," Douglas retorted.

Religion was a sore subject between them. Margot prided herself on the fact that she had gotten out of Sacred Heart and into Greenvale, a private Protestant day school, by the ninth grade, before the nuns could subvert her with their bizarre notions. Skepticism had entered her soul on First Communion day; her teenage attitude was that anyone who believed in Catholicism was mentally deficient. The year before, when their parents had sent Katie to board at the convent while they were in Florida, Margot had predicted, "She'll come out a basket case."

Each morning, minutes after the rising bell clanged at six, Mother MacDowell would make the rounds of the sleeping alcoves with holy water, and woe betide the child who was still in bed. While boarders put on their uniforms in the frigid dormitory, the mistress said the Angelus; then, with veils covering their hair, they filed in a silent rank down the marble staircase to meditate in the chapel before Mass. The permanent boarders were half a dozen South American girls in the Senior School, unfortunate sugarcane and tobacco heiresses who went home no more than once a year and were allowed to speak Spanish only during the evening recreation period. They did the latter relentlessly, driving seven-year-old Katie to the chapel, where she shed tears of homesickness in the front pew.

It was silent as a crypt at that hour. A flickering vigil light cast shadows on Our Lord's terra-cotta robe. Even though her knees started killing her after a few minutes, she loved to kneel at His feet and pour out her heart to Him. She told Him everything: how lonely she was for her parents and Patches; how much better it had been when Margot went to the convent, too; how depressing the weekends were at her grandmother's, where, long after Gram and Aunt Steffie had gone to bed, she would lie awake in her father's old room, staring at the huge red roses in the wallpaper. All the while, Jesus looked down at her from His pedestal, His bleeding heart exposed, His soft brown hair falling to his shoulders, His face a mask of compassion in the reddish glow from the sanctuary lamp. How she loved Him! More than anything she wanted to be worthy of His love, maybe even dedicate her whole life to Him. By the time her parents came back from Palm Beach, Katie's devotion to Our Lord rivaled that of Mother Manning, whose lustrous eyes followed her daily Office as if it were a love letter. Douglas saw no harm in Katie's religious fervor, but Emily, leery of all forms of passion, considered expressions of extreme emotion unladylike, and Margot thought her little sister was deranged.

In looks and temperament, Margot favored her mother: both were dark and vivacious; both sought a niche in society, courting such arbiters of acceptance as country clubs, debutante committees, and the Junior League. And being of the same dissatisfied nature, they found it impossible to get along. The quarrels between them had grown so bitter that Margot had launched a campaign for boarding school despite the prospect of the new house she had wanted for so long. Kept secret was the fact that she intended to shed her religious background like a tree snake's skin the minute she got away from Rochester. Catholicism had proved to be a social and academic liability: a boyfriend named Ramsey Harrington had broken off with her because his mother disapproved of Catholic girls, and Thelma Beaver, Greenvale's redoubtable headmistress, had advised her not to set her heart on either Bennett or Bradford junior college because both had a quota.

From behind the cushion at her back, Margot extracted a box of maple sugar, unwrapped one, and gnawed at it as she watched Katie pull a wisp of tulle across the tabernacle door.

"What d'you want to be when you grow up, Kate?" she inquired.

"An actress or a nun," came the prompt reply.

Margot shot her mother an I-told-you-so look.

Emily inhaled sharply. "Over my dead body."

***

On Emily Winterhaus's list of Fates Worse Than Death for her daughters, becoming a nun ranked just below marrying a Jew. Not that opportunities for the latter were rampant in Rochester in the forties. There were no Jews in the summers at the lake house— certainly not on Rock Beach Road—nor were they even allowed to own land in the Barnard tract of Brighton. This information came to Katie's attention at the dinner table in the huge new house when she was eleven.

She had turned into a spindly adolescent with a pale complexion and dirty blond hair. Her red cardigan was buttoned down the back (the way Margot had worn hers when she was home for Christmas vacation), and she had on knee socks and penny loafers. One look at the dimes wedged in the front had made her father start talking about inflation again, and her mother had told him for the millionth time that he was penny wise and pound foolish.

They discussed the "scandal" during the first course, while Katie silently drank her consommé. It seemed that a Jewish couple had tried to buy the house across the street, using their Gentile lawyer's name as a front. When members of the Barnard Tract Association had discovered the ruse, they applied genteel pressure until the deal fell through.

"How mean," Katie commented.

"It's an unwritten rule," Emily said, twisting the stem of her crystal water goblet.

The pantry door swung open, making the prisms of the chandelier tinkle like wind chimes. The chandelier was Katie's favorite thing in the room; everything else about it—the linenfold paneling, the Regency furniture, even the screened sunporch overlooking an acre of lawn and birch trees—she compared unfavorably to the coziness of the lake house. Doris, the cook, entered bearing a silver vegetable dish. Emily took the fork and spoon from her and said something in a low voice about using a tea towel instead of oven mittens. Doris had on her black uniform with the lace collar; the night before she'd worn the white one, and Emily had commented sotto voce that she was getting slipshod. Two other cooks had come and gone in the last three years, and Katie was betting that Doris wouldn't last, either.

Douglas's ear was cocked to a portable radio at his elbow. When Doris had served the spinach and left the room, Emily frowned at him, her eyeglasses flashing in the candlelight. From seven to seven-fifteen, it was almost impossible to get his attention, since the early part of each evening's meal was accompanied by Gabriel Heatter's sepulchral tones. The newscaster's "There's good news tonight" was as punctual a summons to the dining room as Doris's tremulous "Dinner is served."

"Personally," said Emily, raising her voice to be heard over the morbid drone, "I can't imagine wanting to live somewhere I wasn't accepted. Don't you agree, Douglas? Can you understand resorting to such underhanded methods to buy into a restricted community?"

"Well, that's characteristic of them," Douglas mumbled philosophically, and turned up the volume.

"What does 'restricted' mean?" Katie inquired.

"There's an old saying: 'Children should be seen and not heard.' Finish your milk, please." Emily said firmly.

"I hate milk."

"Don't say 'hate', dear. You *dislike* milk."

Katie chewed a morsel of calf's liver, pondering the meanings of *restricted* and *them*. Heavy brocade draperies were drawn across the French doors, but she could still hear the wind whistling in the rose garden. The thought of Patches confined to the basement made her sad; she stared glumly across the table at Margot's empty chair. Dinnertime was when she missed her sister most.

Since Margot had gone away to school (after two years at Concord Academy, she was now at Briarcliff), Katie had suffered the pangs of an only child, retreating into the world of her imagination, making up plays and acting Shakespeare scenes in the attic, memorizing poetry, studying the *Books of Knowledge* in her room. The more she immersed herself in literature, the further she removed herself from the interests of her eight convent classmates.

"Sit up straight, Katherine," Emily said suddenly. "Your posture is atrocious. Imagine a string going from your neck to the ceiling—that helps. Tomorrow, you are getting your hair cut. Mary Jo Prentiss has such a neat, tidy hairstyle. I'd like to see yours that way—off your neck."

"I'll look like a giraffe, Mother. Mary Jo Prentiss is a geek."

"Don't contradict. A long neck is a sign of beauty. Take your elbows off the table, dear . . . left hand in your lap."

Gabriel Heatter said sadly, "We'll have more for you tomorrow on the reaction to President Truman relieving General Douglas MacArthur of his command in the Far East."

"Bosh!" Douglas exclaimed, banging his fist on the arm of his chair. "First he packs the Supreme Court with liberals, and now this! Mr. Roosevelt started something, all right. You mark my words: this country's headed for the ash can."

"Would anyone care to hear what happened to me today?" Emily inquired, as Doris dispensed the finger bowls.

"What's that, Em?" Douglas asked.

"The Garden Lovers Club asked me to be president next year."

"Whoops! Well, what do you think of that?" he crowed, turning off the radio as Heatter concluded his report.

"It's quite a compliment," said Emily.

"Humph! They'd be lucky to get you. I'd steer clear of too many duties, though. You don't want to get overtired."

"That's terrific, Mother!" As much as Katie dreaded detailed reports of Emily's two clubs—the social Garden Lovers and the Bernadettes, a group of Catholic ladies who serviced the altar at Our Lady of Lourdes Church—she was impressed with this evidence of her mother's effectiveness outside the domestic realm. "Are you going to do it?"

"I haven't made up my mind. For one thing, the house isn't finished, and then I have to be here when you come home from school."

"No you don't. Doris is here. And the house is never going to be finished."

"Don't be saucy, Katherine."

"This young lady has plenty of homework to keep her occupied after school," said Douglas. "No more ninety-eights this term, Skeezix. I want to see that missing two percent!"

Emily waved a cigarette between her second and third fingers to indicate that she needed a light. "Do you have much homework, dear?"

"Tons," Katie groaned on her way to the sideboard. She clicked the table lighter until it ignited and held the flame to her mother's cigarette. "May I please be excused?"

"No, you may not. My, how you Winterhauses love to rush through a meal. I prefer to dine, not merely to eat," said Emily, expelling a stream of smoke.

Katie slouched back to her seat. Interminable minutes ticked by before a second cigarette was ground into the tiny silver ashtray and Emily indicated to Douglas that he might pull out her chair. He rushed to comply. Observing the ritual, Katie vowed that never, not even if she became a total *invalid*, would she allow a man to open a door for her or pull out her chair, let alone go into a revolving door and *stand* there, the way her mother did, waiting for someone to push her through.

"Can I blow out the candles?"

"*May* I," Emily corrected.

"I'm going to set up the card table in the living room, Em," said Douglas. "After we play a few hands, I think I'll lie down and have a short snooze."

There were certain ineluctable facts about the Winterhaus life-style: six-thirty cocktails, postprandial gin rummy, and the need to arouse Douglas from napping on the couch to go to bed.

On her way up the staircase, Katie looked out the tall leaded window on the landing. Windsor Court Road had recently been plowed, and snow was banked four feet high at the curb. Through the whitened balsams on the front lawn, she could see glimpses of the massive, vacant Preston house. A white elephant, her father called it. It had been on the market for over a year; you'd think the neighbors would be glad someone wanted to buy it.

Upstairs it was dark as pitch. Going down that long corridor at night gave Katie the willies; as she lighted the lamp on the antique writing desk outside her mother's dressing room shadows darted across the Flemish tapestry where maidens and unicorns gamboled in a woven wood. Too spooked to breathe, she closed the door that led to the third floor, where Doris slept, and in spite of her father's frequent reminder that he did not have stock in the Rochester Gas and Electric Company, put on all the lights in her sister's bedroom as well as her own.

Seated at Margot's mirrored dressing table, she raced through her assignments, then got undressed and climbed into bed, stashing a forbidden radio under the covers to listen to *Lux Presents Hollywood* and *Living with Tessie*. Along with photographs of stars like Hedy Lamarr, Lana Turner, Rita Hayworth, and Christabel Rivers that crammed Katie's scrapbook, was one of Irene Miller, who played gorgeous, dumb Tessie, gazing adoringly at the show's creator, a man named Jed Bernard. The evening's episode opened with Tessie and her boyfriend, Sam, a renowned tightwad, arriving at Union Station. "Let's get a redcap, Sam," Tessie chirped. Sam replied, "I'll carry your bag, chicken. Why tip strangers?"

Katie squirmed with laughter. As she listened to the familiar voices in the dark, she forgot the wind rattling the windows, forgot the quarrels with her mother, forgot her loneliness, forgot the mysterious threat of "them" moving in across the street.

The blizzard that occurred in May of that year took even upstate New York by surprise. On the day it thawed, Katie went shopping after school with Emily to I. Frankel & Co., Rochester's swankest department store. A fine needle rain was falling and the air in the cosmetics department was tinged with the scent of damp wool. Katie was undoing the snaps on her red slicker when she heard Emily exclaim: "Why, Eddie Frankel! Hello there, stranger!"

A tall man with wavy brown hair and a cornflower in his lapel was smiling at them. "Good afternoon, Mrs. Winterhaus. How's my favorite customer?" he said. Button eyes and the way he tilted his head to one side made him look like a scarecrow, Katie thought.

"Very well, Eddie. You're not snubbing us up here in the sticks, are you?" asked Emily in a gay, girlish voice Katie had not heard before.

"Never!" Eddie said. "If I forget Rochester, may my right arm wither!" The scarecrow eyebrows lifted as he peered down at Katie. "And who have we here? Not another beautiful Winterhaus woman!"

"This is my baby, Katherine," said Emily. Katie cringed.

"Margot I know—I call her Warmth," he said with a chuckle, "but how come nobody's ever introduced me to you, Goldilocks? Are you married?"

"No, silly," Katie tittered. "I go to school."

"Silly?" he echoed, one hand spread across his chest. "You call me *silly*? Obviously you're not studying to be a diplomat."

"This is Mr. Frankel, dear. Don't let him fool you that he's the floorwalker . . . he's actually a brilliant attorney." Emily's eyes sparkled mischievously behind the bifocals; her tone bordered on the coy. Katie studied the man who had wrought such a change.

"Your mother's a great kidder, did you know that?" he said, nudging Katie.

She shook her head slowly.

"Listen," he went on. "She was a big comedy star before you

were born. You ever hear of Fanny Brice? A *nobody* compared to Emily Kelly!"

Emily laughed. "No, no, Eddie. Katie's the star in the family. Bishop Kearney saw her in *Alice in Wonderland* at school and said she's a born actress."

"One of the great critics, Bishop Kearney . . . a regular George Jean Nathan," remarked Eddie, putting his hand on Katie's shoulder as they walked toward the escalator. "Don't tell me you're going off to finishing school like your sister, Goldilocks."

"Who, me? I haven't even started!" she said, hoping to make him laugh. When he did, she felt as she had after sneaking a glass of champagne on New Year's Eve.

"Katie is staying right where she belongs—at the Sacred Heart Convent," Emily interjected.

Eddie twirled Katie toward him. "Of course! I knew I recognized you in that coat—it's Little Red Riding Habit!"

Katie dissolved in giggles. She was acutely aware of the warmth and pressure of Eddie's hand. At home there was hardly any physical contact; Margot positively shrank if anyone made a move to hug her, and the only touching Katie had observed between her parents was when she came upon them standing in a stiff embrace, patting each other affectionately on the back. Douglas did not share the master bedroom in the new house; because of his snoring, he'd been banished to the upstairs study, where he slept on a pullout couch, under a sepia likeness of Our Lord.

At the foot of the escalator, Eddie said good-bye and shook hands with Emily. "Watch out for this one, she's gonna be a heart-breaker!" he added, giving a playful tug to Katie's bangs. "With those eyelashes, Goldilocks, you shouldn't settle for anything less than a prince. On the other hand, you could become a famous model."

Emily waggled her forefinger. "Now Eddie, don't go putting wild ideas in the child's head."

"Motherrr! He's kidding," Katie said between her teeth.

"I've never been more serious in my life," Eddie replied, and disappeared into the shoe department.

Emily scrutinized Katie as they rode up on the escalator. "You look quite flushed, sweetheart. You shouldn't wear your coat in the store. I hope you're not coming down with something."

Katie peeled off her slicker; she did feel warm, and the perfumed air was dizzyingly sweet. "Gosh, he's nice," she said.

"Don't use slang, Katherine," Emily admonished, but she agreed, "Yes, Eddie's a peach."

Katie folded her slicker over her arm and hugged it to her, thinking, He's so . . . *different.*

"I must say, they do have something, Douglas," Emily remarked at dinner. "That Eddie Frankel could charm the birds from the trees." She smiled at Katie. "Our little girl's developed quite a crush."

"That's all I need," Douglas griped, sawing the lamb roast. "Haven't I had enough trouble from that element for one lifetime?"

"What element is that, Daddy?"

"Your mother knows what I'm talking about."

"You're not going to bring up that man at the dinner table, are you?" Emily asked.

"Okay . . . never mind. Forget it," Douglas snapped.

Katie looked from one end of the long table to the other like a spectator at a tennis match. Her mother's cheerful mood had vanished; the big vein in her father's forehead pulsed dangerously. Uh-oh, he's got that look, she thought. The one that means he's brooding about Sol What's-His-Name, Winterhaus Enemy Number One, a man whose last name had so far eluded her because her parents spoke it only in whispers.

Not that this was out of the ordinary. There was a list of words Emily never said aloud: sex, for one; and rape, pregnant, cancer. Just last week, for the first time she'd said "menstruation" audibly, forced to it by the matter of Marilyn Toohey, Katie's classmate, who had discovered blood on her underpants in the convent lavatory and become hysterical, convinced that she was dying. The next day Mrs. Toohey was on the line to the mothers' grapevine, and that evening, so that her daughter should not be caught unaware like Marilyn, Emily had gone to Katie's room to explain the delicate matter. After a botched attempt, she suggested they look up the word in the leatherbound dictionary downstairs. Their arrival caused Douglas to put down his cards and beat a hasty retreat to the fruit cellar; whereupon, with Emily standing by, tongue-tied for once, Katie read silently that what Marilyn had experienced and she must anticipate was "a monthly displacement of the sun in longitude caused by the moon's revolving round the center of gravity of moon and earth." She pondered this scientific phenomenon; somehow it caused women to bleed. "I understand," Katie lied. Looking greatly relieved, Emily sent her mystified daughter up to bed.

A similar cloak of mystery shrouded Sol What's-His-Name, that nemesis out of her parents' past. And Emily was part of the puzzle. Years before, according to family lore, the Winterhauses had lived in New York in a Park Avenue triplex, from which Margot, baptized Margaret Mary, was chauffeured to the convent at Ninety-first Street, and Katie, born at the Lying-In Hospital, was wheeled by her nursemaid to the park in an English pram. That she remembered none of it was a source of frustration to Katie; that her mother did something to bring this enchanted existence to an end and cause them to return to the sticks upstate stuck in her father's craw, and bound Katie to him in mutual resentment. Nor did she know the exact nature of Sol's villainy, only that he was Jewish and had caused her father untold anguish.

"You're well out of it," Emily was saying. "I've never changed my mind about it for a minute."

"It was none of your—" Douglas broke off with an exasperated, "Aw, what the hell."

Katie bit her lip. Only the greatest duress caused her father to swear. To distract him, she said, "Mr. Frankel's the funniest man, Daddy. He turns everything into a joke."

"Huh! See how funny you think it is when he bilks you out of—"

"How did Mr. Frankel bilk you, Daddy?" Katie interrupted.

"Not him personally. But probably just because I never gave him the opportunity." He pulled at the knot of his necktie to loosen it. "Listen, I've got nothing against Eddie Frankel. He's a good egg. And a smart cookie, no doubt about it. But they're all alike—they get points in their religion for putting one over on a Gentile."

"How do you know Mr. Frankel's Jewish?"

"Huh! Didn't you see the sign on his face?"

"Could we change the subject, please?" Emily requested.

CHAPTER 2

The Chosen People

Katie cracked the spine of her French reader, propped it against a pile of books on Margot's dressing table, and stared at it, unseeing. Her mind was on Eddie Frankel and what he'd said about her becoming a model. She examined her face in the three-way mirror. Compared to the golden beauty she was in her dreams, reality always came as a shock: an overbite, eyes startlingly blue but too small, hair the color of twine. What does he *see* in me? she wondered.

The revelation that Eddie Frankel was one of "them" added a tinge of adventure to future shopping expeditions. Alone or with her mother, Katie would find herself searching for him in the aisles, her heartbeat quickening in anticipation of the teasing and the jokes and the way his eyes lighted up at the sight of her. Once he took her with him on his inspection of the main floor, punctuated with roguish remarks to the salesladies, many of whom were in their sixties. His jokes unglued Katie; when he imitated Jerry Lewis in *That's My Boy*, she laughed until her sides ached.

"You're one of the great audiences, Goldilocks," Eddie told her. "If you were twenty years older, I'd marry you."

"You could wait," she suggested.

"It's possible," he said with a scarecrow smile.

Eddie would disappear for weeks at a time, off on one of his mysterious, solitary business trips, from which he would return with reports of the latest Broadway opening and what women were wearing in New York and how Brenda Frazier had looked in a backless Fortuny dress at El Morocco. He was Katie's lifeline to the glamorous world from which ill fortune had snatched her in the cradle and where she believed she was destined to live when she grew up. During one of Eddie's absences, she was alone in the house on a winter evening (Doris had quit, and Emily and Douglas were playing in a canasta tournament at the Chatterbox Club), doing her homework in Margot's room with music blaring from the radio. Suddenly an announcer interrupted with a bulletin:

"One of Rochester's leading citizens died today. Edward Frankel, owner with his two brothers of the exclusive I. Frankel & Co., was discovered late this afternoon in his room at the St. Regis Hotel in New York City, the apparent victim of a heart attack. He was fifty-six years old. Mr. Frankel is survived by his mother, Mrs. Rose Frankel of Rochester, widow of Rabbi Maurice Frankel, and two brothers, Leon and Irving, also of this city. Born in Odessa, Russia, Frankel came to America in 1912 . . ."

Sound blurred; the wan face in the mirror crumpled. Katie got up and moved toward the radio; halfway there, she fell to her knees, sobbing. Her parents found her when they came home, curled up on the rug sound asleep, her cheeks still wet with tears.

Perplexed by her grief, Douglas made light of it. "You should have seen the way Katie carried on when Eddie Frankel died," he would say to people. "Ho, ho, ho! She had quite a case on him."

It haunted Katie that Eddie Frankel, the jolliest and most gregarious of men, had died alone in a hotel room. She asked the nuns to pray for his soul; they did, but Mother MacDowell told her that if he hadn't been baptized, he couldn't go to heaven. Katie protested. He was a kind, wonderful man. Where would God send him? Limbo, she was told. With the *babies*? she asked skeptically.

School prayers, once recited by rote, took on new meaning. "Almighty and everlasting God," Reverend Mother Telemacher would intone at First Friday Benediction, and the nuns' voices would respond like altar bells: "You do not refuse your mercy even to the Jews: hear the prayers which we offer for the blindness of that people so that they may acknowledge the light of your beauty, which is Christ, and be delivered from their darkness." Although Katie continued to include "the perfidious Jews" in the litany during Mass, from then on she was alert for negative comments in Doctrine class. Her monitoring failed to unearth any of the name-calling prevalent at parochial schools, slurs such as "Christ-killers"; at the Academy of the Sacred Heart, where, as Bishop Kearney often pointed out, "girls were still ladies," Jews were perfidious and to be prayed for. That was all.

Unlike Margot, Katie showed no inclination to leave the convent. Hers were the instincts of a double agent, working within the system to effect change. More than once, contentiousness earned her a brown *Assez bien* card at Monday morning *Prîmes,* while more docile classmates received a blue *Très bien* from Reverend Mother. To Ann MacDowell, R.S.C.J., Katie at twelve was the scourge of Christian Doctrine class.

"There are three states of holiness in this life," Mother MacDowell trilled one morning as she balanced at the precipice of a raised wooden platform, conviction causing her to vibrate like a beadle out of Blake. "Holy orders, single blessedness, and matrimony."

"In that order?" Katie asked from the front row, her assigned seat since she'd been caught with a copy of *Men Are Like Streetcars* behind the New Testament.

"Foul" MacDowell crossed her arms under her capelet. "If you wish to contribute something, Katherine, raise your hand. Do not speak out." As her eyes flickered over the class, she rocked back and forth on her heels.

Once during Benediction, after Katie had been gazing for a minute at a candelabrum on Our Lady's altar, hypnotized by the molten orange flames, without any apparent reason it tipped over and crashed to the floor, setting fire to the altar cloth. The experience had jolted her, put the suspicion in her mind that she had mysterious hyperkinetic powers, and now, to prevent Mother MacDowell from plunging off the platform, she switched her eyes from the nun's face to the blackboard behind her where the hierarchy of beings, preternatural, supernatural, and natural, was diagrammed. Angels were the highest order, which was why Lucifer's fall from grace was particularly devastating to God. Sympathy for the Almighty was a major tenet of religious instruction at Prince Street; Katie often thought of Him as "poor God."

"Can you tell us, dearie," said Mother MacDowell, and Katie followed her wolverine gaze to Angela Jo Contaldo, a heavyset girl with orange hair, who wore strapped across her chest a pink grosgrain ribbon, a coveted prize for comportment. "From your reading of yesterday's Scripture assignment, what were St. Paul's views on the third state?"

Angela Jo pushed her glasses up onto the bridge of her nose. "It is better to marry than to burn," she responded, unable to resist a smug look at Katie, who, although she was the youngest, had been unchallenged as the class brain before Angela Jo transferred from Our Lady of Lourdes in the fall.

Katie's hand shot up.

"Yes, Katherine?"

"Is he really saying, Mother, that if you don't have a vocation, you're better off spiritually as an old maid than as somebody's wife?"

Beneath the black forehead band, Mother MacDowell's eyebrows twitched a warning. "That is St. Paul's opinion. No Pontiff has declared it a matter of infallible dogma. Can you give me another way of putting that, Katherine?"

"It's not *ex cathedra*."

"Correct. Now, has anyone else memorized the passage?" the nun inquired, toying with a piece of chalk.

Katie doodled interconnecting boxes in her spiral notebook. It's one thing to have a vocation, she brooded. That's at least a choice and even sort of romantic. But a *spinster*—like Aunt Steffie! A shudder went through her. "Mother?" she said, raising her hand. "Since what St. Paul says isn't infallible, we can disagree with him, right? So if we don't put it on the test, will you mark off?"

The chalk snapped in two. "Katherine Ann Winterhaus!" Mother MacDowell seethed. "You are taking up valuable time with these irrelevancies. You will go to the blackboard and write twenty times: 'I will not interrupt the class.' "

Matters worsened. The following year, in First Academic, Katie's midterm report card was marred by a D in theology. Aghast, Douglas requested a meeting with her teacher, Mother Veronica Graves, Mistress General of Prince Street. On the appointed day, he asked Katie to wait in the front hall after school, and when she got there at three, the elderly portress greeted her with a plate of cookies, informed her that Mother Graves had just gone into the visitors' parlor, and retired to the pantry to read her breviary. The corridor was empty. Katie edged closer to the parlor's curtained doorway and peered through the crack. Emily and Douglas sat side by side on the claw-footed sofa whose purple nap had been worn thin by generations of concerned parents, while the Mistress General had chosen a straight-backed chair against the window. The winter light at her back gave her even more of an other-worldly air; when she raised her translucent blue eyes, she reminded Katie of a paint-ing of St. Sebastian, serene despite the arrows piercing his flesh. Hers was one of those classic faces enhanced by a wimple and veil; the perfection of her features had inspired Katie to start a rumor that, in spite of the interdiction against nuns looking in mirrors, she kept in her cell a secret one of which she nightly inquired: "Mirror, mirror, on the wall, who's the fairest nun of all?" Exaggerated enun-ciation that hinted at a sacrificed acting career made her voice carry: "Reverend Mother has asked me to convey to you once more, Mr. Winterhaus, our gratitude for your generous donation of the Oriental rugs for the chapel."

Whatever Douglas replied made her smile and finger her cross. "You know, Mr. and Mrs. Winterhaus, what a lovely child Katherine is, and how intelligent—more than she wishes to admit, I fear. How-ever, she needs to channel her capabilities in the proper direction. It's not that she fails to grasp the material; far from it. Her deport-ment is the problem. I have had to reprimand her repeatedly in class."

In a tone turned chilly at this implication by an outsider that her daughter was less than perfect, Emily inquired, "Do you mean that Katherine has been discourteous, Mother?" Loyalty was Emi-ly's strong suit.

"Discourteous is not precisely the word. It is more a question of wasting other people's time." Mother Graves raised her hands in steeple fashion, tapping her fingertips together with the mesmeriz-ing precision that had earned her the sobriquet "Ladyfingers." "Last week," she continued, "in preparation for Lent, the curriculum was the Passion of Our Blessed Lord. I was reading aloud from the Gos-pel of St. Matthew when Katherine interrupted to say that as far as she could see, it was the Romans who crucified Christ, so it was completely . . . the word she used was 'illogical' that the Jews were ordained by the Bible to wander homeless until the end of time for something that was out of their hands. You see, she is full of spe-cious arguments."

"How did you answer her, Mother?" Emily asked.

"I cited the passage in which Pilate offers the Jewish rabble a choice, and theirs was Barabbas. 'They had free will, dear,' I re-minded her."

Douglas nodded in vehement agreement.

"Bold as brass," Mother Graves continued, "Katherine replied,

'If the purpose of Christ's Incarnation was to die for mankind, and He chose to become a Jew and therefore be crucified by them, how can we possibly blame *them* for something that was *His* idea in the first place? Isn't that what the Chosen People means?' "

(Katie recalled the nun's vexation at THOSE questions: she had plunged her hands into the sleeves of her habit and turned bright red.)

"Mother Manning says that Katherine is the most exceptional student she has ever encountered in Logic class," Mother Graves reported. "One hopes that she will learn to channel this aptitude in a constructive manner. But I was obliged to give her a D for attitude. Argumentativeness is only detrimental in Doctrine class."

(Indoctrination class, you mean, Katie thought.)

Emily cleared her throat. "Katie is very softhearted, Mother," she said. "She tends to identify with the underdog. For some reason, the plight of the Jews is a pet subject with her."

"So I gather," said Mother Graves. "However, it's all very distracting for the others. Certainly *my* train of thought was disrupted."

In the corridor Katie heard a swish of skirts punctuated by the clacking of a rope of rosary beads. She darted into the pantry. The portress sat on a high stool, her finger tracing lines in her breviary, her lips moving silently. Minutes later, the silence was pierced by three long bells and one short. Recognizing the Mistress General's signal, Katie knew that she would rise in the graceful, boneless manner that was a trademark of Sacred Heart nuns, and make her excuses in order to prepare for Benediction. The portress kissed her prayer book and closed it. When they went out to meet her parents, Katie caught a glimpse of Mother Graves rounding the corner to the cloister stairs, where no civilian was allowed to venture.

The acrid odor of incense permeated the front hall. Emily's high heels made a worldly racket on the marble floor as she and Douglas and Katie followed the portress to the door, passing under the portrait of St. Madeleine Sophie Barat, which bore the inscription: "If I can save the soul of one child, it will have been worth it to found the order."

"My, but it's drafty in those halls," Emily remarked as they got in the Cadillac, a green one. "No wonder you're always coming down with a cold."

Douglas coasted down the driveway and through the wrought-iron gate that bounded the cloistered world of the Sacred Heart.

Drawing the lap robe up to her neck in the back seat, Katie recalled the last time she'd been summoned to the Mistress General's office; on that occasion it was to be reprimanded for immodesty because someone had reported falsely that she'd worn a strapless dress to the winter dance at the Chatterbox Club. Katie had denied it, adding that, in any case, her chest expansion was hardly sufficient to incite lust. "It's the *idea* of what holds the dress up that is provocative to boys," Mother Graves had responded sternly. Odd how much contempt she felt for many of the nuns' theories, Katie mused, while retaining a passion for religion. The nun she most admired was Mother Manning, who had confided to her once during Holy Week, "Some mornings when I wake up inexplicably happy, I think perhaps it's the anniversary of my death, when I'll be united with Our Lord at last." It was a thought she kept to herself, she'd admitted, for fear of being considered morbid; but somehow she'd felt Katie would understand.

"Thank goodness Katie gave up that silly idea of becoming a nun," Emily said to Douglas in an undertone.

"I always told you she loved the world too much for that, dear," he replied.

"What *is* this fascination of hers for the Jewish people?" Emily asked.

"Just a phase. She'll get over it."

"Katie's problem," Emily continued (as if I weren't here, Katie thought irately), "is that she confuses sympathy with love. It could cause her to do something foolish one day. She takes after you in that, Douglas. Only an old softie could have let a man like Sol get away with—"

"Let's not go over that ground again," Douglas interrupted gruffly. The traffic light turned yellow; he put on the brakes fast, so that the tires spun in the slush. Drumming his gloved fingers on the top of the steering wheel, he said over his shoulder to Katie, "I learned one thing in life the hard way, Snooks. The only thing that counts is a man's family."

It was what he said, she thought, whenever he was brooding about Sol What's-His-Name's betrayal.

Various suppositions on the nature of Sol's perfidy had occurred to Katie as she was growing up, fabrications based on her active imagination, overheard snatches of conversation, and the gossip of relatives, who were less discreet than her parents. Thread by thread she wove, as children will, an impressionistic tapestry of family history before she was born; by now, people and events were stitched in bold outines.

Low, insistent, Emily said, "You have nothing to blame me for on that score. Sol was the very worst sort."

Without looking at her, Douglas said evenly, "So you pointed out at the time."

CHAPTER 3

Katherine's Tapestry

The time was the late thirties. One balmy spring morning, a thirty-four-year-old German immigrant presented himself at Douglas Winterhaus's office in the Mercantile Building. A dilapidated wooden suitcase weighed down his right shoulder. His name was Sol Levant. He was almost dwarflike—five feet four with an oddly shaped head. Since his arrival in America a few years before, he had settled in Philadelphia, where his wide range of interests and glibness had earned him a reputation as a dilettante in the business community he sought to infiltrate. His braggadocio put people off, preventing them from perceiving the caliber of his innovative mind. Although he was still young, there were bitter lines at the edges of his mouth, marks of frustration at intelligence thwarted by poverty. Above all, he was a survivor. Unlike many of his countrymen, he had perceived very early on the danger for Jews under Hitler and had fled to the United States. The meager living he made peddling cigars kept him going while he attempted to market a string of inventions that had so far proved worthless. During a sales trip to Rochester, a lawyer named Ray Harris told him, "There's only one fellow I can think of with the know-how, the cash, and the gambling spirit you need. He's got an iron stomach for the commodities game. His name is Douglas Winterhaus. He's pretty much of a lone wolf, but then so are you. The two of you might just hit it off."

"How do I get to him?"

"His door's open to everyone. That's the kind of man he is."

It turned out to be the most important lead Sol had ever gotten.

Douglas Winterhaus's integrity appeared to be unimpeachable. Tales were told of his phenomenal mathematical ability and various killings in the market. The idea of a self-made man who had achieved success without stepping on a lot of toes was impressive; Sol entered Douglas's cramped office at Taylor-Ridley with heightened curiosity. An astute judge of character, Sol relied on his first impressions; he sensed that he was in the presence of a shrewd, scrupulously honest man. "Even back in Philly," he flattered Douglas, "folks say Doug Winterhaus is the smartest operator around."

"To tell you the truth, Sol," Douglas said, "I've got a soft spot for inventors. You ever listen to a show called *Lorenzo Jones?*"

Out of Sol's valise spilled formulae and diagrams: a self-cleaning impeller for industrial pumps, a coolant for a dental drill, a riveting hammer; but what interested Douglas was a sample of synthetic rubber that Sol had brought with him from Germany, the product of his work with a chemical engineer in Berlin.

"This is more advanced than anything our companies have come up with," Douglas said.

"Once we abandoned the search for chemical equivalence," Sol explained, "we were on the right track. Eventually, we substituted physical properties that turned out to be adequate."

"I'm not sure how accurate my reading of your formula is," Douglas broke in, "but what I'm holding in my hand is a lightweight material that combines the tensile strength and resilience of rubber. You've had a real brainstorm, Sol."

"The cost of production is the big stumbling block. I've talked to quite a few private investors like yourself," Sol lied, "but it's not a game for pikers."

"What about Dunlop or Goodyear . . . have you gone there?"

"I won't go near 'em. At worst, they'll show me the door and steal the idea; at best, buy me out for a song. I'm not giving this away cheap."

A dream began to take shape in Douglas's mind. "You don't have to give it away at all. With me as your partner you can do it on your own. The field's wide open. Let the big boys spend their time collecting drops of latex from trees in Ceylon—we'll turn out a viable substitute right here in America. The Germans and the Soviets are way ahead of us, and that's no good."

Years of fishing in stagnant waters without a nibble on his line—

and now the biggest catch in town jumps right into his boat! Sol could hardly believe his luck.

"Fill me in on what's required—facilities, production costs and whatnot," Douglas said, "and we'll see where we go from there."

While Sol talked about emulsion processes and the use of catalysts and stabilizers, Douglas made rapid calculations in his head. Before Sol left his office, Douglas made a verbal commitment to finance a joint venture. In his ingenuous way, he said, "You've got the brains to do this on your own, Sol. What you don't have is a money man . . . that's where I fit in."

That evening, after Margaret Mary had gone to bed, Emily and Douglas sat on the terrace overlooking Lake Ontario in the soft spring twilight, and he told her about Sol Levant's invention and his own promise to back him.

"This isn't the sort of thing you usually get involved in, dear," she said. "Why would you go so far afield?"

"Rubber's a commodity, cutie," he replied. "And nobody knows how the commodity market operates like I do. The auto industry is entirely dependent on natural rubber. Don't you see where this could lead? The possibilities are endless—ladies' undergarments, for one thing." In his enthusiasm, he missed the reproving glance that Emily shot him. "And if that so-and-so Roosevelt gets us into a war with Mr. Hitler—and it's coming, you mark my words—well, the stuff could be a bonanza in wartime. Right now there's a huge demand in the agriculture field—tractor tires and so on. . . ."

Emily compressed her lips. "This Levant fellow sounds like a four-flusher to me . . . the type that's out to make a quick dollar any way he can."

"You're wrong about that, Em. There's a lot more to him than meets the eye. I've got a sixth sense about these things." He patted her reassuringly. "Come on now, cutie. I've never done anything yet to make you regret marrying me, have I?"

"Never. And I don't want some foreigner coming in here and spoiling things," she said, putting her hand to her heart. Emily did not even want to think about how close she had come, some years earlier, to missing the felicity and security of being Douglas's wife.

In 1929 Emily Kelly was a secretary at the Crowley Insurance Agency in downtown Rochester. One Friday afternoon in January, she plucked her purse and a pair of woolen gloves her mother had knitted for her from the desk drawer, flicked a piece of lint from one; then, careful not to chip the red polish on her long fingernails, closed the drawer, covered the typewriter, and snapped her purse shut. Her actions were mechanical, her mind on the fact that in less than a month, Douglas Winterhaus was going away for Lord knew how long.

"See you tomorrow, Mr. Crowley," she called as she passed her employer's office, where he sat hunched over a sheaf of papers on his rolltop desk.

Sam Crowley looked up, smiled, and returned her wave. He liked Emily. He liked her vibrant coloring and her quick tongue and her sense of humor. "Emily Kelly's in her prime—fine-looking and smart as a whip . . . she's something mighty special," he had once remarked. Watching her take her coat from the rack, he muttered to himself, "Best thing that could happen to Doug Winterhaus—if he can get up the gumption to leave his mother."

The elevator doors creaked open at the sixth floor. Emily pulled her wool coat close around her. How she wished it were fur, better protection against the cold gusts of wind that blew off the Genesee River and whipped through Rochester's streets. "See you tomorrow" echoed in her mind. How many tomorrows would she be seeing Sam Crowley's gray head bent over insurance forms? Another birthday had recently passed, her thirty-first. And in February Douglas was going to Palm Beach. It would be an ideal place for a honeymoon— if only she could get him to propose! Her pulse quickened nervously at the thought of leaving home, but one thought comforted her: no kinder man than Douglas Winterhaus existed. True, there was that German stubbornness, but underneath, his heart was pure gold. As she walked through the lobby, Emily practiced her posture by imagining a thread running from the top of her head to the ceiling. "Douglas is a peach," her mother often said, and Rosalie Kelly was a shrewd judge of character. It reassured Emily that in all the months they'd been going around together, he'd never pressed her beyond hand-holding and a peck on the cheek—unlike Kevin McMahon, who was brash and forward and had once had the nerve to put his tongue out when he was kissing her good night. A lifetime of such shenanigans—"Lordy!" she muttered under her breath.

But one must be practical. Lately, Emily, maid-of-honor at her two younger sisters' weddings and three of her best friends', had, in spite of her popularity with young men, been spoken of as a possible spinster. It was unthinkable. On Clinton Avenue it was dark and bitterly cold. As she passed the Mayflower Coffee Shoppe, Emily read the little motto that hung in the window:

As you ramble on through life, brother,
Whatever be your goal,
Keep your eye upon the donut
And not upon the hole.

"That mother of his is the main stumbling block," she'd told Rosalie, who had replied in her sweet way, "Some men need a little push, darling." There was no question that Douglas loved Emily, but timid as he was, he could end up alone. Emily made up her mind: Douglas Winterhaus was not leaving town without her. The invisible string held her head high as she walked to the streetcar. On her way, she stopped at Holy Name Cathedral to say a prayer before the statue of St. Joseph, patron of husbands.

In another part of town, on a quiet, tree-lined street, Douglas Winterhaus was taking a nap on the sofa in his mother's parlor. Since turning forty, he'd found that getting up for six-thirty Mass, watching the stock market until three, and then teaching calculus at the Rochester Institute of Technology made an hour's sleep in the evening a necessity. "Hi, Mother, how'd your day go? I'm bushed," was his habitual greeting at day's end.

Usually a rhythmic snorer, today his snorts exploded in erratic bursts, by-products of a vivid dream about Emily Kelly. She was sitting at her desk at the Crowley Insurance Agency, typing a letter. The letter was to him, and it said she had decided to marry Kevin McMahon.

Douglas forced his eyes open. The weight of the dream lay on him, but with the realization that Emily's betrothal was not a reality, his spirits rose. It was dusk; along Hamilton Street the streetlamps came on, silvering the pavement and falling through lace curtains onto an afghan his mother had thrown over him while he slept. He could hear her moving about in the kitchen; he rose and took the stairs two at a time to dress for the evening.

Thoughts of Emily filled his head. I'd better be on my toes for that young lady, he told himself, humming "You're the cream in my coffee," as he splashed water on his face and lathered it with shaving cream. A vision of her chattering away with her glossy hair coiled made him smile; he manipulated the razor gingerly around his upper lip so as not to graze his neat mustache. I could buy and sell that insurance outfit she works for ten times over, he speculated while flicking soapy residue into the sink.

It had been a blustery March day when he first saw her standing outside Holy Name Cathedral after Sunday Mass. Fur-trimmed ankle boots showed off her shapely legs, she wore a red cloche, and she was laughing, her head thrown back—Douglas thought he had never seen anyone so vital. He'd gotten Bishop Connors to introduce them and he hadn't taken out another girl since. Not that there had been much competition before, not with his schedule.

In the twenty years since Douglas had left the University of Wisconsin, there had been only nine months he could call his own. At the age of thirty-one, he had informed his mother that he wanted to be at the heart of the stock exchange and, to her dismay, taken the sleeper to New York and found himself a cheap room in Greenwich Village. He'd walked to Wall Street each day, and almost every evening took a streetcar to Broadway; of the forty plays he saw that season, *Irene* was his favorite. In June, he'd come home. The fuss his mother had made over the telephone about how much they all missed him was an excuse, but in reality he had been lonely in New York.

Living at home hadn't bothered him until he met Emily almost a year ago. His mother was a sweetheart, and Stephanie, his half sister, was a good kid. But it was high time he had his own family. Sure, the thought of marriage had occurred to him—why not? He combed his damp hair straight down over his forehead and traced a part on the side. "Face it," he said to himself in the mirror. "I couldn't get married if I wanted to. I've got too many responsibilities." Fine as his mother was, she wouldn't sit still for his leaving, and even Steffie, who never said a mean word about anyone, wasn't too wild about Emily. "Women," he muttered, "Good night, nurse." For the life of him, he couldn't understand why they didn't get along better. His whiskers swirled down the drain. Forty-one in August, he brooded. A good Catholic fellow should have a wife and children to care for.

Taking care of people was second nature to Douglas. A child when his father died, he'd been running the show ever since. His

mother, Geraldine, had also outlived her second husband, a French-
man named Henri Louvain with whom she'd had three children before pneumonia struck him down. Henri was long on charm and
short on cash flow, Douglas had once remarked. A mental count of
his current dependents included Steffie, who made a little money as
an art teacher; his half sister Lucille, to whose husband he'd given
ten thousand to get started in business; and Gerard, his half brother,
a husband and father long before he was on his own two feet. Added
to some ten people now sharing his income, Douglas suspected, would
be several of Emily's relatives if he married her.

Downstairs, Geraldine was making a cheerful racket in the
kitchen pounding dough to be cut into noodles for Sunday's soup.
The effort turned her face pink and added to an impression of
heartiness. At sixty-three, she was still handsome, tall and strapping,
her soft white hair set in waves beneath a fine net. She swept the
dough into a mound, smoothed it with the rolling pin, then flipped
it over and stretched it thin as waxed paper.

"That looks good as ever, Mother," Douglas said from the
doorway.

Geraldine looked up. "My, don't we look snappy tonight! Going
out on the town?"

"I won't be late."

"Lunch is at one on Sunday, dear. Don't forget."

"Have I ever forgotten? You don't think I'd miss that noodle
soup, do you? Say, Mother, how would it be if I asked Emily to
lunch? Give you girls a chance to know each other better."

Geraldine wiped her brow with the corner of her apron. "Why
would I want to do that?"

"For my sake."

There was a pause. "All right," she sighed. "If it makes you
happy." The prospect of Douglas getting married filled Geraldine
with dread: two husbands in the ground and Gerard lost to that domineering woman from Batavia—it was enough; she had no intention
of giving up her firstborn—above all, as she'd remarked to Steffie,
"not to that hussy with the painted fingernails!" "When are you
leaving for Palm Beach, dear?"

"On the fifteenth."

"I saw a lovely wallpaper at Sibley's the other day—great big
red roses. I thought I might redo your room while you're away."

"You shouldn't take on anything extra, Mother."

"I do hope you get a good long rest, Doug. Your sister and I depend on you so."

"Don't you worry about me. Don't you worry about a thing. Looks like I'll have to get out the snow shovel," he said as he pulled on his storm coat and went whistling out the back door.

Douglas had never seen Emily cry. Not in all the time he'd known her had anything brought a tear to her eye—neither a sad movie, nor a cut on her knee at the skating rink, nor her younger sister Loretta's wedding when all the other girls had wept. But now tears trickled down her cheeks in a fit of unhappiness caused by, of all things, *him*! They sat in his Packard outside her house. The porch light was on, casting a yellow path across the icy walkway. He'd just been saying what a swell evening it had been—going to the George Eastman House to see the very first color motion picture, then on to the Sagamore, where Emily had been so charming that Fred and Margaret Odenbach, the hotel's owners, had joined them for a soda. These tears had come out of nowhere.

"I never would have expected . . . you of all people . . . leading me on . . . ," she choked.

He pressed a handkerchief into her hand and watched helplessly as she wrung it into a wet knot. "Aw, come on now, Em."

"What will people say?" she sniffled. "We've gone around together a whole year, and now you're just going to up and leave without so much as a fare-thee-well?"

"I don't get it. Who's been saying anything like that?"

"You *are* going away, aren't you?" she scolded. "And you don't know when you're coming back? It's no secret Kevin McMahon's been after me to marry him, so I guess you don't care a hoot about me. Otherwise you'd never take a chance like that."

Douglas stared at the snowflakes melting on the windshield. "I wouldn't say that, Em. I wouldn't say that at all."

"Well then, what *would* you say? Getting you to say anything at all is quite a feat. All I know is, for a good Catholic man, this is pretty irresponsible behavior."

"This isn't like you, Em."

"I'm going in," she said.

"Hold your horses, will you? Let me think a minute." They both stared straight ahead. To her intense irritation, he started to hum. Then he asked, "Will you come to lunch on Sunday? It's just family." He cleared his throat. "Mother asked for you."

A light went on upstairs in the darkened house where Emily lived with her mother and father and a brother who had been blinded in the war. It's now or never, they'd warned her. She took a deep breath. "I think not, Douglas. It's better if we don't see each other anymore. Obviously you've been wasting my time."

Douglas dropped his head. For the first time, he considered the possibility that Emily might walk out of his life. Where would he ever find a girl as fine as she was, as gay and as much fun? Hell, he loved her! "What do you want me to do, Em?"

"The usual outcome of two people going out together as much as we have . . . who . . . care for each other . . . is marriage."

"Phew! I don't know. This might not be a good time. Mother is—"

"Fine," Emily interrupted. "Good night then. I have one more thing to say. If I don't go on that trip to Palm Beach as Mrs. Douglas Winterhaus, then don't you ever bother phoning me up again. I'd like to go in now." She remained with her hands folded in her lap, waiting for him to get out and open her door. He did so, then followed her slowly up the porch stairs, managing to mumble "I'll call you tomorrow," before the door was closed in his face.

When Douglas told his mother that he was going to marry Emily Kelly, Geraldine locked herself in her bathroom for three days. From the hallway, he reasoned with her and tried to calm her. When at last he gave up and went downstairs to the parlor, he and Steffie could still hear her sobbing. But her tears were of no avail. Douglas had proposed to Emily, and he was not a man to go back on his word. Moreover, he was in love. In the end, it was Stephanie who prevailed, coaxing Geraldine out for a truce in the face of the inevitable.

For years afterward, people said that the Winterhaus-Kelly wedding was the most beautiful Rochester had ever seen. That night the bride and groom took a sleeper to Florida. Emily sat stiffly on the edge of the lower berth and cried for over an hour, calling her mother's name.

Although it came as no surprise to him that his bride was innocent, Douglas had not expected a woman of thirty-one to be so desperate about leaving home. He patted her back, soothing her until she fell asleep. It took many nights for the marriage to be consummated. As Emily had feared, she did not find the sex business much to her liking; however, it was her conjugal duty, and Douglas made up for it in many other ways.

It was February of 1929. Douglas Winterhaus's net worth was three million dollars. Delighted to spend it on his bride, he took the honeymoon suite at the Breakers Hotel in Palm Beach. America was on a binge, at the height of its opulence and glamour, unknowingly at the brink of disaster. For Emily, dining a table away from J. P. Morgan under glittering chandeliers, playing shuffleboard on the same deck as Gertrude Vanderbilt, dancing at her first nightclub, sailing on a chartered yacht to Havana, wearing the latest flapper styles and the ermine cape, diamond ring, and emerald bracelet Douglas had given her, it was a dazzling, scandalous, frightening new world. Her new husband revealed a different side—more relaxed, almost carefree. And with a Panama hat pulled low on his forehead, he was positively debonair. While Doug was in his element, the fever and glamour, the climate of staggering wealth intimidated Emily. Money madness infected the country. One evening, waiting for him outside the jewelry shop in the lobby, she was approached by a distinguished-looking gentleman who announced that he'd made an outrageous coup in the market that day, and wished to celebrate by buying her whichever jewel she fancied. Naturally she refused. Douglas told and retold the story. "Those were great times in this country," he reminisced after the Crash.

Despite the Depression, the next few years were good ones for the Winterhauses. Douglas took his own losses with equanimity. "I had one sleepless night in '29," he would say later. "I can't say I predicted the full extent of the bull's ferociousness, but at least I saw far enough ahead to avoid taking a total bath. As J. P. Morgan said, when your shoeshine boy starts giving you tips on the market, it's time to get out."

Douglas's distress over the election of Franklin Delano Roosevelt as President of the United States was mitigated by Emily's giving birth to a daughter, Margaret Mary. The following winter he took them to the Pancoast Hotel in Miami Beach, a more appropriate place for a family than the Breakers; for the next few years he brought along Emily's sisters and their children as well. It made her happy to do things for them, and if Em was happy, so was he.

Professionally, Douglas had the soul of a gambler. With personal fulfillment came a renewed urge to widen his horizons; to be, as he explained to his wife, more than a big fish in a little pond. As the years passed, he began to make tentative overtures about moving to New York City. Then came the momentous announcement that he planned to go into business with an out-of-town inventor named Sol Levant. Emily put up strong resistance. By nature she feared change, newness, risk. Her ambitions did not go beyond Rochester. There she was secure; they belonged to all the right clubs (with the exception of the Genesee Valley Club, whose membership was almost exclusively Protestant), her friends and family were devoted to her, Margaret Mary was in kindergarten at the Sacred Heart Convent, and most important, Emily was close to her mother. The notion of a foreigner as her husband's partner was a threat—and a Jewish man at that!

But Douglas remained firm. "Don't go throwing a monkey wrench into this deal, Em," he told her. "You mark my words: Sol Levant and Doug Winterhaus will make a great team."

And so they did. With his financial expertise, his even, unflappable temperament, and impeccable reputation, Douglas was a perfect foil for Sol's whiz kid ways—all garrulousness and flash. Once Sol moved to Rochester and things got going, royalties began pouring in.

"What we should do is form a company," Douglas advised presently. "Taxes will kill us if we don't get established in a more favorable climate—Delaware, say, or Vermont. We should take a drive up there and look around for a factory site."

"Now you're talking, friend," Sol agreed. "I myself would vote for Delaware. But I'm not taking a step without you."

"For some time now, I've been considering a move to New York City. It's not easy operating so far from Wall Street. I just have to convince Em. What say you give it some thought yourself?"

They shook on it. Sol did not like what he'd seen of Rochester—the small-town mentality and the interminable winters—and he was eager to move on. Shortly after marrying a sweet Gentile girl named Virginia Brady, he announced that they were relocating in New York City.

The transition was not so simple for Douglas.

"I don't know a soul in New York," Emily protested.

"You know Sol and Ginny," he reminded her.

"Well, yes. And I recognize Sol has some good qualities . . . I've admitted that. But I still don't trust him. Anyway, how can we leave Mama? She's not at all well."

"Now, Em. She's got your dad, don't forget. You'll only be a few hours away. Just give it a try for the winter. We'll never give up Rock Beach, no matter what. It'll be all right . . . you'll see. Don't you worry. I'll take care of everything."

They called the new company Plastech. Its headquarters were in Dover, Delaware; Sol Levant was its president, Douglas Winterhaus its treasurer. The Winterhauses lived at 1021 Park Avenue where two maids assisted Emily with the housekeeping; little Margaret Mary went into first grade at the Ninety-first Street convent.

In New York, Douglas was a changed man. His family would always come first, but he was newly energized by the rhythm and activity of Wall Street. "These boys speak my language the way no one in Rochester does," he told Emily.

"Dudley Bell is no slouch," she replied defensively, referring to a broker at Taylor-Ridley. "He and Florence just bought the Keating house on Sandringham Road. I've always loved that house . . . the beautiful Georgian staircase in the entrance hall . . ."

"Dud's all right, but he's not a very sophisticated investor, Em. And he always had it in for me. Here, I'm shown a lot of respect."

The figures would eventually speak for themselves, Douglas decided with characteristic sanguineness; in time, Emily would adapt to living life on a higher, more exciting plane. Toward Virginia Levant she displayed an almost sisterly affection; it was beyond her how someone so ladylike could put up with Sol.

One evening in May, during dinner in the cathedral-ceilinged dining room, Margaret Mary, seven years old and unusually tall for her age, burst into tears when her father informed her that she was enrolled in second grade at Ninety-first Street. "I hate it here!" she cried. "That gloomy old convent . . . you have to curtsy to everybody! Then I have to play in the dumb park!"

"Why, honey, I thought you loved this apartment," Douglas said.

Margaret Mary twirled a brown corkscrew curl ferociously on her finger. "When that elevator door bangs shut, I feel like I'm locked in here. I miss the lake. I want a house and a yard . . . and a baby sister! I don't like being an only child!"

Douglas cleared his throat. "Well . . . that's a pretty tall order."

Into the strained silence Emily tinkled a little silver bell to summon the maid.

"It's only a few more weeks till summer vacation, Princess," Douglas reminded his daughter. Her face brightened when he added, "You'll be back in your room at Rock Beach before you know it."

This much he could assure her; of the rest he was uncertain. Conjugal relations were an iffy proposition with Emily. He had become a master of subjugated libido, offering up his frustration for the souls in purgatory and hardly ever, even to himself, admitting his need for human comfort and the physical expression of his feelings. While the maid scraped crumbs from the table onto a little silver tray, he summoned the old, habitual fondness and smiled at his wife. Perhaps when they were home again, back in their lovely blue bedroom with the balcony overlooking Lake Ontario, she would feel relaxed, more affectionate.

In June the three Winterhauses boarded a sleeper for Rochester, two of them hopeful that it would be for good. As the New York Central chugged through the night, bypassing the whistlestops upstate, Emily, sleepless in the compartment's lower berth, twisted her rosary around her fingers and listened to the steady grinding of the wheels. No matter how much money Douglas made, she thought resentfully, they'd always be nobodies in New York. She'd tried to explain it to him a hundred times: "To come here *cold,* and expect to break into social circles . . . well, it's just not possible. Especially with a Jewish man as your partner."

His response had been a resigned sigh. In Rochester, it was the Sibleys and the Gannetts and the Van Veldts; in New York, the McDonnells and the Astors—in Emily's mind there would always be someone who had it better. Even when he took her to a basketball game, she complained that the McCurdys had a better season parking place. Only in the deepest recesses of his heart did he harbor a thought that she held him back. Intractable, certain that he knew what was best for his family, he went about providing for them, averring that they were his reason for amassing wealth, never admitting that he reveled in it for its own sake. But the fact was, next to his two "girls," there was nothing that gave Winterhaus a bigger thrill than watching the numbers grow. Part of his religious conviction was that prosperity was a divine reward for goodness; to this end, he enlisted God's help with prayer and sacrifice.

Several times a week during that summer, Emily drove into town to be with her mother, who was still ailing, while Margaret Mary played happily on the beach with one or another of her cousins under the governess's attentive eye. On Douglas's fiftieth birthday, as he had hoped, he and Emily made love. The act was a source of great comfort to him; he only wished that his wife did not seem merely to be putting up with it. Arguments about returning to New York in the fall were finally settled by Emily's mother. "There's no better man on earth than Doug," she reminded Emily. "Do what he wants for now and let him come around gradually to your way."

Kicking and screaming, Margaret Mary was deposited in the second grade at Ninety-first Street. An interior decorator spent long days with Emily at Stair & Co., choosing furniture. One evening in October, Douglas brought home a sample of a new Plastech product.

"It's a maternity girdle," he told Emily. "You see, this panel stretches as the woman grows. We're going to mass produce the thing—sell it in supermarkets and drugstores as well as department stores. That way we can cut the cost down to a fraction of any previous model. Try it on and let me know what you think of it, will you, cutie? Who knows?" he added with a playful smile. "You may be needing one yourself!"

"Douglas, please!" Emily remonstrated. "I'm way past that stage. I wouldn't be caught dead wearing that contraption. Imagine if I got into a traffic accident while I had it on!" She grasped the girdle and tested its elasticity, pulling it between her hands like taffy. "That doesn't mean it won't sell," she commented, to his delight.

"What say we call Sol and Ginny and celebrate? What're you in the mood for, Em—LaRue? The Pilgrim Club?" he asked, reaching for the phone.

Emily's dark eyes flashed. "The Pilgrim—with Sol Levant? What can you be thinking of?"

"You'd be surprised. Things are changing in that area. One of the brokers at Goodbody told me today that Oscar Bache got into Piping Rock."

"You're fooling me!" she exclaimed. "Even so, I don't want to be the one to break new ground at the Pilgrim."

"Right you are. If the Levants are free, I'll give Pavillon a ring."

"That's fine. One thing about Jewish people, they know where the food is good."

Sol Levant's high energy level had brought him success; success brought him a taste for comfort and certain things he prized: fine art, Cuban cigars, French wine, a pretty woman. That evening, when the lights were lowered at Pavillon as the waiter bore a flaming baked Alaska to their table, Sol raised his glass and bid Douglas join him in a toast to the beauty of their wives. Douglas reached under the table and squeezed Emily's hand. "Having fun, Mommy?"

"Yes, I am," she replied gaily, flushed and a little tipsy on champagne.

"I think Em would make the ideal model for our latest product, don't you, Doug?" Sol teased, adding with a nudge in his wife's ribs, "Skinny Ginny here don't have much use for a girdle, right, doll?"

Virginia's cheeks reddened, but she pressed her thigh against his. In a festive mood, the four went on to El Morocco and danced until two.

Afterward, suffused with champagne and affection for his wife, Douglas joined Emily in her twin bed. "You're an old sweetheart," she murmured. Tenderly, almost gingerly, he began to make love to her. "You do see why we have to be in New York, don't you, dear?" he asked, stroking her back.

"For now," she whispered.

Things were falling into place, he thought happily, making a vow to protect his precious wife and daughter until the day he died and, God and the stock market willing, long afterward.

At that moment of physical union, had anyone asked, Douglas would have said that he'd never been happier in his life.

Eight months later, in the New York Lying-In Hospital, Emily gave birth to the baby she had, to her amazement, conceived on Douglas's birthday. They christened her Katherine Ann, after a favorite martyr and Jesus' grandmother. The pregnancy had taken everyone by surprise; even the doctor had diagnosed Emily's early nausea as appendicitis. No one, least of all Emily, had anticipated her middle-age fertility. The childbearing months were an ordeal, the delivery traumatic. Joyful as the occasion was, it was not something they could risk happening again. As for Margaret Mary, she learned early in life the truism: Be careful what you pray for; you may get it.

By the hour Douglas hung over the crib, marveling at the strength of the tiny fingers gripping his blunt thumb. Often he stole into the nursery at dawn to play with the baby before the governess was awake. To anyone who would listen, he bragged about his new daughter's sunny disposition. "Katie's the belle of Park Avenue, all right!" he would say. "The doormen love her, the policemen know her by name. She's everybody's favorite." Barred from the marital bed, he doted on her, anesthetizing his sexuality, gradually sealing off that part of him that yearned for physical love.

Archbishop Spellman baptized Katherine at St. Ignatius Loyola on Park Avenue; her Best & Co. dresses were hand-smocked; her perambulator came from England, her governess from France; nothing, in short, was too good for this child of the Winterhauses' later years, and nothing, if Douglas had anything to say about it, would be allowed to mar the perfection of her character. Or even her bite. To avoid thumb-sucking, he attached to the crib a metal contraption, not unlike handcuffs, that restrained her wrists at night. But time and again she outsmarted him. "The little minx!" he crowed. "I can't figure out how in Sam Hill she does it, but no matter how securely I fasten the darn thing, she wriggles out of it and gets her thumb in her mouth."

For Katherine's first birthday, Sol and Virginia Levant sent an engraved silver cup. It was their last joint act before announcing plans to divorce. Throughout this crisis, Emily naturally sided with Virginia; now, she commented, it was a proven fact that Sol's character was as low in his personal life as she'd always suspected it was in business.

"How you can allow this so-and-so to have any control over our money is beyond me, Douglas," she said one evening over coffee in the drawing room.

Douglas tapped his mouth with two fingers as he blew out a long breath.

"You don't know what he's going to do from one minute to the next," she ranted. "He's the majority stockholder, not you. He's got you locked in—and me too, I might add."

"I've done all right so far."

"You've certainly done all right by Sol. Without you, he'd still be selling cigars."

"He's the first one to admit that."

"Oh, is he?" Emily set down her gold-rimmed Sèvres cup. "Is that why he's so secretive about the accounts? You can't trust those people as far as you can throw them. I can't understand your obsession with this company anyway. We're not even earning dividends on our money." Agitatedly, she rubbed a spot of cream from the coffee table.

Frustration lined Douglas's forehead. With the funds he'd deposited in Emily's account, she was worth more than he was; it was a mystery to him why she continued to doubt him. "Dividends are small potatoes compared to Plastech's growth potential."

"But why have so much tied up in a private company," she persisted, "run by a man like Sol Levant? I'd be much happier if I were in something solid, a known quantity like Eastman Kodak. You should read what Westbrook Pegler had to say today about the socialist influence on the Jewish people . . ."

Douglas's eyes turned glassy. Emily knew that the conservative columnist was Sol's pet peeve; she would drag Pegler in from left field to discredit Sol. While he finished his coffee he tuned her out; then, rising, he said politely, "Guess I better get to my charts, dear."

As he left the room, he heard his wife pick up the telephone and give the operator her mother's number in Rochester.

Meanwhile, Sol was having a struggle with himself, a battle between looking past and forward. His loyalty to Doug was interfering with his future, and that could not continue. Emily's frosty tone when she answered his call the next day weighted the scales. "Your wife hates my guts," he said abruptly when his partner picked up the phone. "But I guess I'm not telling you anything you don't already know."

"Where's this coming from?" Douglas asked.

"It's nothing new. I've just been keeping my mouth shut."

In a placating tone, Doug said, "You know women. Em's just being loyal to Ginny."

"If I thought that was it, there'd be no one more understanding. But it's got more to do with my religion than my ex-wife. I'd lay my jugular vein on it."

"Bosh! Em's just not feeling up to par. Her mother's been ill and she's worried about her. Let's not bring religion into it."

"You're a gentleman, Doug. Nobody could've treated me better, if you'd been a Jew yourself. But I guess the Catholic Church wouldn't have made you a Grand Knight of the Holy Sepulchre if you weren't a superior person. I made no mistake about you. Be that as it may," Sol went on quickly, "right now I've got a proposition for you. I'd be willing to buy you out . . . even though it breaks my heart to think about it."

"What in Sam Hill are you talking about, Sol? It's out of the question. My understanding is that we're in this together for the whole ride."

"Things change. Given your diversified portfolio, the Plastech business is superfluous. Whereas in my case . . . a small private company I can run my own way—"

"Now wait a minute. We may well decide to go public at some point down the line."

"You know my philosophy on that: never, never, *never* go public! People get greedy, things get out of hand. You leave yourself wide open. Plastech won't be thrown to the wolves," Sol said adamantly.

Douglas demurred. "We'll discuss that at a later date, Sol. By the by, I thought I'd take a run down to Dover the first of the week. Last time I was there, one of the books was out of the office. I want to go over it with the accountant."

"Ahhh . . . I don't know, Doug," Sol said quickly. "This week is bad—the man's mother just had an operation. Put it off for a week or two. Everything's running smooth."

Like a grain of sand lodged in an oyster shell, suspicion nagged at Douglas's brain, but he said only, "Righto. Now let's drop the subject of my selling my interest in Plastech."

"Whatever you say, old friend. The offer's open."

"Thanks but no thanks."

Saturday's mail brought Douglas a communication from his and Sol's mutual friend in Rochester, Ray Harris, congratulating them on Plastech's venture into the lucrative field of prophylactics. Standing in the foyer, turning pale, Douglas read silently: "The confidential report is exciting as hell. As an investor, I fully endorse the idea. My personal judgment is that 'Toro' is a catchier name, certainly a more positive notion than 'Nocon.' " "Good night, nurse!" he exclaimed, dropping the letter onto the hall table as if it were contaminated.

"What is it, dear?" asked Emily, on her way in to the foyer.

"Nothing, nothing for you to worry about," he muttered, but she was already scanning the letter through her bifocals.

In a low, furious voice, she said, "I've always said that Sol is a vulgar, low-class man, but this is beyond the beyond!"

For once Douglas had to agree. "What concerns me is the Church's position. We'll see about this."

At eight-thirty on Monday morning, he burst into Sol's office, demanding, "What the hell's going on around here?"

Sol was facing the window. Turning slowly, he inquired, "What's your beef, Doug?"

"Since when are we manufacturing junk like prophylactics, I'd like to know?"

"It's a logical use of the material," Sol replied calmly. "We're going to make a fortune."

"How long has this been in the works?"

"Things take time, you know that, what with research . . . six, nine months maybe."

"And why wasn't I consulted? What's the story around here?"

"Look Doug, you got a lot of irons in the fire. I didn't want to bother you until we were further along. Anyway, would you have approved?"

"What do *you* think?"

Sol's raised shoulders said, "There you are! I didn't want you to have guilt, my friend, that's all. Sometimes lack of full disclosure can be a favor. What you don't know don't hurt you, am I right?"

"I don't like it, Sol. Not one bit." Douglas sat heavily on the couch against the wall.

"So you got nothing to do with it. Forget about it. It's on my conscience."

"I can't go along with that. My position is squarely against proceeding—"

"You expect Plastech to forgo sales of this magnitude because of your personal morality? The whole world isn't Catholic, you know. I respect your religious beliefs, Doug, but don't impose 'em on me. I don't call that fair. And I can't let it stand in the way of the company's progress."

"It's not even good business, Sol. It cheapens the company. You want to tell your grandchildren you were in the contraceptive field?"

Sol turned a pencil around and around between his fingers. He and his partner had one thing in common—neither of them could stand to admit he'd made a mistake. But Doug had a point. Sol stood up, came around the desk, and put out his hand. "When you talk, I listen, Doug. You're a brilliant guy—nobody knows that better than me. I'll give this condom business some more thought."

They shook hands. At the door, Douglas said without turning around, "You owe it to me to give in on this point, Sol."

From the dining room window, Douglas could see across Park Avenue to St. Ignatius Church. Emily was fatigued after a day of shopping for a spring wardrobe and had had the governess feed the children early and put them to bed. Throughout her account of a salesgirl's rudeness at De Pinna, he only half listened, staring out at the stained-glass window. The ormolu clock in the hall chimed nine. The telephone rang. A moment later, the maid appeared at the pantry door.

"It's Mr. Levant, sir, calling from Delaware. Shall I say you're at supper?"

"No, no, I'll take it." Douglas tossed his napkin aside and went into the library.

Sol's voice came crackling over the wire. "Regarding our conversation, Doug, I hate the thought of bad blood coming between us. It's the law of diminishing returns. Maybe the time has come for a parting of the ways. Have you thought any more about it?"

"What does he want?" Emily asked, coming quickly into the room.

"I'll handle it," Douglas said over his shoulder.

"What's he saying?"

Douglas put his hand over the receiver. "He wants to buy me out."

"Don't let him jew you down," Emily whispered.

"Please stay out of it," he hissed, and told Sol, "No dice."

Emily left the room in silent fury.

For nearly a week, she spoke to no one but the children and the servants. Finally, alone with her husband at supper on Sunday, she exploded. "I can't believe . . . I simply cannot get it through my head that you could countenance this"—she lowered her voice—"this contraceptive business."

"Sol knows my position on that," Douglas replied. "We'll work it out. You can't make these decisions overnight. He'll come around. We've been too close for him to not see the light."

"And what about me?" she demanded. "Don't my wishes count for anything? I want you to sell out! The whole thing makes me sick and miserable! You said he made a fair offer. Just sell the stock, let him keep his money."

Her words were still thrumming in Douglas's head when Sol called him for breakfast on Monday. They met at a coffee shop on Broad Street. In the midst of a rampage against "that libelous son-ofabitch, Westbrook Pegler," Sol broke off to comment, "You look down in the dumps, my friend."

Douglas sighed his great, beleaguered sigh and confided, "It's hell at home."

A concerned look spread across Sol's face. He reached into his breast pocket and withdrew a checkbook. "Tell you what," he said, uncapping his fountain pen. "I'm going to do something no businessman would believe, but this is how much faith I've got in you." He flipped open the checkbook and pushed it across the table. "Just take this and fill it in for whatever you think is your share of the company. And no hard feelings, so help me God."

That was how Sol told the story to anyone who asked. His ex-wife, Virginia, questioned his methods to his face, accusing him of manipulating the situation. "You can't be fairer than giving a man a blank check, can you?" he responded. The fact that Doug Winterhaus, that most honorable and respected of men, wrote in an amount that made Sol feel as if he'd just exchanged the island of Manhattan for a string of beads, well, that was hardly his fault, was it? Could anyone doubt that he, Sol, wouldn't have made it anyhow, without Winterhaus's help? But he would always give credit where it was due. Doug had believed in him before anyone else. It was just too bad that wife of his was an anti-Semite. No one should get the idea that he, Sol, was dancing on anybody's grave. Why, as they'd left the coffee shop, he'd said to his mentor, "Doug, when I get to the office I'm going to burst into tears. But it's for the best. There's one thing I'd bet my jugular vein on: you and I will be friends for life." And on that they had shaken hands.

It was not long before a relieved Emily pointed out that there was no real reason for them to stay in New York any longer, so far from their family and friends. "You know how Margaret Mary hates the elevator," she reminded Douglas.

"Whatever makes you happy, Mommy," he said, patting her hand absently.

The brokers at Taylor-Ridley welcomed Douglas back, expressing no surprise that he'd given up the rat race in New York. "It's a jungle down there, isn't it, Doug?" Dudley Bell inquired, but got only a grunt in reply. Three weeks after he was reestablished in the firm's lone private office, Douglas opened *The Wall Street Journal* and read that Plastech, "a small company with headquarters in Dover, Delaware," was being traded on the open market. According to the president and chief operating officer, Sol Levant, the move was based on the recent acquisition of a large block of stock. Due to discreet management policies, the *Journal* reported, the company's stock had long been undervalued. (The missing book, Douglas thought bitterly.) When queried about a rumor that Plastech had a contraceptive in the works, Mr. Levant, known to insiders as something of a wag, denied it vehemently. "I wouldn't want to tell my grandchildren I was in the rubber business," he was quoted as saying.

Over the next few years, it came as no surprise to Douglas that the stock of what became Amalgamated Plastech, Inc., skyrocketed. His resentment at his wife's interference surfaced in an occasional morose mood or a fleeting outburst of frustration, to which she responded by reiterating her conviction that they had been duped by a swindler, a dishonest manipulator—in a word, a Shylock. Their mutual friend Ray Harris let Doug know when Sol married again, and when he divorced a second time and married a young Danish girl, with whom he moved to a large estate in Lower Merion outside Philadelphia. No one needed to tell Douglas how the company—*his* company—was doing; it was impossible to pick up *Fortune, Barron's,* or *The Wall Street Journal* without being assaulted by every sickening detail of its meteoric rise.

The topic was avoided at home. Whatever bitter memories plagued Douglas were dealt with in his usual silent, reclusive way: his face an impassive mask of concentration, he would sit by the hour on the living room couch, a Victorian mirror reflecting the thinning gray and blond hair at the top of his head, his shoulders hunched in a rumpled jacket while he methodically laid out a deck of cards, then thumbed three, discarded them, thumbed three, discarded them, as intent as if the stakes were real, playing Solitaire until either he dozed off or Emily erupted in a fit of exasperation.

Meanwhile, Sol Levant became one of the richest men in America. He received numerous citations and awards; two administrations honored him for selfless devotion to his country. When people asked him how he could have lost touch with his ex-partner, he was said to have replied, "I just got too big for him."

Douglas Winterhaus went back to being a private investor, trading heavily in commodities. A large network of relatives continued to rely on him for financial support, a responsibility he assumed naturally, as if it were his destiny, only occasionally grousing about the "pack of ingrates." He retreated more and more into the tight circle of his home, becoming known as a prophet of doom, a sober Sam who would be a recluse were it not for his wife Emily's charm and gregarious nature.

"You mark my words," he said more than once at family gatherings, "the day will come in this country when gold will sell for more than one hundred dollars an ounce." The men laughed, Emily frowned, and her sister's husband muttered, "There he goes with the gloom and doom stuff."

In the mid-forties, Douglas cornered the mustard market and found himself courted by R. T. French & Co. A book came out about Rochester called *A Northern Plantation*, in which Douglas Winterhaus was dubbed "the cast-iron pipe king." "Small potatoes," he commented, gazing into the distance, his blue eyes clouded with gathering years and lost dreams.

CHAPTER 4

One Man's Family

With the exception of the stock market, whose fluctuations Douglas continued to predict with stunning accuracy, things seemed to go their own way willy-nilly in the fifties, regardless of his careful charting. A rash of deaths depleted his and Emily's circle of friends— a sure, depressing harbinger of old age, although he enjoyed robust health and looked fifteen years younger than his age. Solely to please his wife and elder daughter, he'd bought the house on Windsor Court Road, but Emily continued to look wistfully at Georgian houses, and Margaret Mary, he realized with a heavy heart, was one of those children who goes away to school and never really comes home again. One week after graduating from Briarcliff Junior College, she turned up in Rochester with a taciturn midwesterner named Tyler Duncan, Jr. whom, she announced, she intended to marry. Emily took an instant dislike to him. A Presbyterian. Worse, an out-of-towner. He was given a set of fresh towels and relegated to a maid's room in the attic. While Margot locked horns with Emily, Katie sided with her sister, and Douglas despaired that he'd lost control over that last sphere of patriarchal influence, the family. His proud Teutonic spirit— a legacy from Bavarians back to Albert the Swabian—suffered intensely.

"Our Lady wouldn't do this to me," he asserted, conferring with his wife in whispers at the foot of the back stairs on Tyler's last evening in town. After he left, Douglas pleaded with Margot, threatened, cajoled, called her fiancé everything from a nonentity to a fortune hunter, even sent a private detective to Amherst to investigate his college record; he and Emily broke their hearts on it, but in the end, Margot got her way: at the tender age of twenty-one she became Mrs. Tyler Duncan, Jr. and, in a shower of rice and family tears, moved to St. Louis. They'd lost her. Douglas mourned; then, like a mariner turning his face to the sea, he contemplated his younger daughter. "Fourteen and on her way to becoming a beauty," he told "the Girls" at Taylor-Ridley, "once she fills out a bit." In this one area of his life, he vowed, nothing would go wrong. Katherine Ann would make up for all the mistakes they'd made with Margaret Mary.

"Acting's no profession for a high-class girl," he told her, proud as he was of her starring roles in school and community productions. "What you are, Katie, is a writer. I don't know what the nuns think you're going to do with all that French and Latin. You should be picking up skills you can use in life—cooking, typing."

"I will not learn to type for one simple reason, Daddy," Katie replied in her maddeningly logical fashion. "If I don't know how to type, I can't be a secretary. And I *know* I am *never* going to want to be a secretary."

"I'll tell you one thing, young lady," he sighed. "You'd better marry a very rich man."

"Oh, Daddy! Money isn't everything," she remonstrated.

Contentiousness was one thing, serious rebellion quite another; Katie's, when it came at sixteen, caught him off-guard with its vehemence. Never had a girl been so culturally and intellectually deprived she maintained. As for socially . . . *socially*! In scathing tones, she denounced the local Catholic milieu as a mixture of bowling parties at Oak Hill Country Club and sodality dances with St. Thomas Aquinas boys. She doused her hair with Light and Bright; she declared that it was intolerable to go on being suffocated in Rochester. Her intense theatricality lent force to the scenes; moreover, her restlessness seemed to rouse something long dormant in her father. He began to speak to Emily of spending the winter in New York. Katie could finish high school at the Greenwich convent as a five-day boarder ("That'll keep her out of trouble!"); then, when she went on to Manhattanville, which was his plan for her, they'd be nearby. Emily, who'd been dreading losing her baby to college, was swayed by this argument. Although she reacted to Douglas and Katie's complicity with the customary "You Winterhauses always stick together," she acceded. Douglas flew to New York, enrolled Katie at Greenwich for Fourth Academic, and signed a five-year lease on an apartment at the Carlyle, an elegant hotel in the East Seventies with a number of permanent residents.

On a dazzling morning in September, he drove Katie to the Rochester airport, assuring her that he and her mother would follow by the end of the month. She hugged him at the gate and expressed her gratitude. "Don't mention it, Skeezix," he said huskily. "You deserve nothing but the best."

Seated next to her on the plane was a business acquaintance of her father's, a man she had met a few times at Taylor-Ridley. Approaching sixty, Ray Harris was tall, distinguished-looking, and possessed of enormous charm; they chatted throughout the flight. As the plane circled Manhattan, he said, "I've got an idea. Why don't you come with me this morning? My car can take you out to Greenwich later. I'm driving over to Philadelphia to have lunch with an old friend of your dad's, Sol Levant."

The back of Katie's neck prickled.

"He's just married again—number three," Harris continued. "This one's a gorgeous Danish gal in her twenties. Good old Sol— he's over fifty. God! What a kick he'd get out of seeing Doug Winterhaus's beautiful grown-up kid. You were only a baby, you know, when—"

"I know . . . I know!" she interrupted. "Thanks, Mr. Harris, but I just couldn't. I mean, it's impossible."

The plane dipped into an air pocket over Idlewild, but the queasiness in her stomach had nothing to do with the flight pattern. Even talking about the man made her feel disloyal. See Sol Levant? *Talk* to him? Never! She might as well sup with the Devil in hell. It was out of the question to meet her father's worst enemy.

But at the back of her mind, an old idea took shape: there was another reason she dared not meet Sol Levant. He was Jewish, and if he were anything like Eddie Frankel, she wouldn't be able to hate him anymore.

CHAPTER 5

Incense Makes the Heart Grow Fonder

The ride from New York City in the Carey Cadillac took thirty minutes on the Merritt Parkway. Katie sat on the jump seat, staring sullenly out the window while behind her Douglas conversed with Margot, who had come east to visit her family, and attempted to ignore his younger daughter's ill humor. "Anyone seeing you," Emily had said when she'd kissed her good-bye at the apartment, "would think you were going to a funeral."

The suit Katie had chosen to wear was black, purchased at Bergdorf Goodman over Emily's objection that it was too sophisticated for a young girl just out of boarding school; her once dishwater-blond hair had been lightened to burnished gold and fell unconventionally below the braided satin collar. Thank God Mother didn't come, she thought. We'd have fought the whole way.

The chauffeur turned off at Purchase; they passed a riding field and a walled estate, then drove for a quarter of a mile along a stone fence overrun with ivy until they came to the twin-pillared gate with its carved legend: Manhattanville College of the Sacred Heart. "You're going to have the time of your life here, cutie," Douglas said.

"Sure I am," Katie said miserably. "After being shut up at Greenwich for a year, I can look forward to four more years of the nuns and nothing but Catholic girls."

65

"Maybe a few nice Catholic boys now and then," he said, smiling.

Katie shut her eyes. "I *loathe* Catholic boys."

"You don't mean that. Does she, Margaret Mary?"

"Please don't call me that," said Margot, running a comb through her short dark hair. "It seems to me that thirteen years of the convent should be enough punishment for anyone. At least you can go home to New York on the weekends, Kate."

With a sigh, Douglas folded *The Wall Street Journal* on his lap and stuffed it into a side pocket already bulging with financial papers. "I'm not making that mistake again . . . letting one of you girls run off to a non-Catholic college."

"What you don't realize, Daddy," said Katie, "is that at this point, I'd be a stronger Catholic in a place where I had to *defend* my religion, instead of here where everyone thinks alike. It's the way I am. You don't know me at all!"

"And you don't know the world, young lady." The set of his jaw softened as he looked at his daughter's profile. "You're a lot prettier when you smile, did you know it?"

"Really, Kate. You remind me of Patches in one of her snits," Margot scolded.

Katie glared at her father's reflection in the glass partition. He has absolutely no compunction about forcing me to come to this prison, she thought. About ruining my life.

The limousine rounded the circular drive and halted in a muted crunch of gravel at the entrance to a crenellated stone dormitory. Farther up the road at the top of a rise, a Norman mansion loomed like a battlement. Once the opulent country estate of a publishing magnate, "the Castle" now served as cloister for the Madames of the Sacred Heart; its stone walls cast a shadow that reached back into Katie's life as far as she could see. And behind those walls, about to welcome the incoming class, was none other than her old nemesis, Mother Veronica Graves, listed in the catalogue as Freshman Warden. A warden no less! College in a *convent*! Gone were her ambitions for Radcliffe, Bryn Mawr, or Stanford, dashed by her father's obdurate refusal to subsidize any but a Catholic institution. And not because her *faith* was in jeopardy, she thought angrily. Unlike Margot, she'd swallowed the catechism whole and had no thought of defection. It was too much!

Katie yanked open the door and stepped down from the car.

Behind her, Margot laughed. "Four hundred virgins—it's like a Greek myth! Why you let Mother and Daddy railroad you into this, I'll never understand."

Six upperclassmen were piling out of a White Plains taxi, each one checking to see who had arrived via limousine and chauffeur and would require cutting down to size during hazing. Under her breath, Katie vowed, "If I'm not married by the time I'm their age, I'll kill myself!"

As she mounted the steps to the dormitory, her hostility took on a theatrical note; she saw herself as a character in a drama, costumed in elegant, inappropriate black, compelled to follow the script while her father played Père Goriot to her sulking Delphine.

"I need some money, Daddy," she heard herself say aloud and watched, aghast, as he pulled out a roll of bills and peeled off several twenties in front of the two scholarship students assigned to carry luggage. They exchanged a glance. Katie blushed; it was a bad start, she knew, but went on acting the brat at full tilt, as if bent on making a bad impression. She found Manhattanville as sterile and alien as the moon; stripped of *goûter, congés, Prîmes,* and May processions ("O Mary, we crown thee with blossoms today! Queen of the angels, Queen of the May!"), it lacked the mystique of the convent and had replaced it with no particular character of its own. Only the statue of the Sacred Heart and the nuns gliding across campus as if they wore roller skates beneath their habits made her feel at home.

A stocky girl with muscular legs identified herself as a member of student government and directed them to the bulletin board where room assignments were posted. Her breath suspended, Katie's eyes flicked down the list of names: Quinlan, Reichenbach, Tagliaferro, Walsh (Please God! Don't let it be a total nerd!) and stopped at "Winterhaus, Katherine: #301, Single." Not even on the freshman floor, she thought bleakly, but with the overflow upstairs, surrounded by juniors.

"But that's a catastrophe!" Margot said behind her. "You've got to have a roommate. The worst thing you can do is to seem *different.* Let's see if we can get it changed."

"No," said Katie, her mouth set in the obstinate paternal line. "Never mind. It's fine. As a matter of fact, I prefer to be alone."

Nothing could have been further from the truth, but as this last trump card was stacked against her, something hardened in Katie; the seed of rebellion in her soul took root and she told herself she *was* different, much as she had once said "I have a heart murmur," secretly proud of the romantic affliction that excused her from obligatory convent activities like field hockey or marching in the St. Patrick's Day parade.

"You'll get more work done this way, Skeezix," said her father as they waited for the elevator.

"Right," she replied tersely, staring straight ahead.

A special assembly was held in the auditorium. Rita Maloney, a slender brunette Torquemada elected to lead the tribal rite of hazing, read the roll of freshmen, along with a humiliating task assigned to each. One was directed to wash the cars in the parking lot, another to make a large sign reading STUPID, SPURIOUS, SLOVENLY and wear it for the week; several were told to make a hundred braids in their hair.

At last Rita came to the W's. Her eyes narrowed dangerously as she announced Katie's name in the megaphone, followed by, "A thousand-word essay entitled 'Why I Should Not Be So Arrogant,' to be read aloud in the dining room tonight." The student body gasped as one.

A blatantly uneven apportionment of degrading assignments called attention to the fact that if a freshman stood out in any way—looks, brains, money—she was dead. Exceptions were two New Yorkers from prominent families who were virtually passed over; the Hazing Committee, many of whom lived in the city, were wary of alienating anyone with social clout who might retaliate in a predictable future of committees and private clubs. The schoolgirl meanness, at which Catholics are particularly adept, at Prince Street and Greenwich had been petty and amateurish; this was the Big League, Katie realized. That same afternoon, a clique consisting of five graduates of the Ninety-first Street convent congregated at a round table in the snack bar, where they eviscerated with a scathing glance or an audible cutting remark whichever hapless victim wandered into their line of fire. As well as the nastiest, they were the *neat*est girls Katie had ever seen; not a hair strayed from their pageboys or feather cuts; the button-down collars of their monogrammed shirts were speared with identical gold circle pins from Tiffany's; their skirts, Shetland sweaters, and Brooks Brothers raincoats were impeccable as they handed out assignments to freshmen to smear their hair with indelible ink or crawl the corridors like dogs or accost male visitors in the lounge.

The religious community stayed out of it, citing student autonomy, yet school rules were stringent: lights out at ten, and an automatic campus for anyone venturing past her doorsill afterward. Shortly after ten on the first night of hazing week, Katie heard someone tapping on the baseboard in the next room. Crouching, she acknowledged the signal and put her ear to the heat register. The voice of her neighbor, a junior named M. J. Taylor, apprised her that the New York clique had singled her out for rough treatment. Like prisoners in *Notes from the Underground* they communicated; words were garbled, lost, then a sentence burned itself into Katie's brain: "The word is they plan to cut your hair." Her hand shot to the nape of her neck. "Can they *do* that?" "Whatever you do," M. J. advised, "don't antagonize Rita."

A night of fearful dreams and little sleep followed. When Katie returned to her room the next evening at nine-fifty, the Hazing Committee was there in full force, two lounging on the bed, one sprawled in a chair, another rummaging through her closet, still another glancing through a *Vogue* she'd left on the nightstand. And perched on the window ledge was Rita, a power-mad glint in her eye. They took turns grilling Katie about her clothes, her allowance, her father's occupation, her plans for the debutante season. It was galling . . . degrading . . . beneath *contempt* to smile politely and make oblique replies to the interrogation, but the sound of a scissors shearing off her golden hair resounded in Katie's ears, and hating herself for it, she held on to her temper. The shrill peal of the lights-out gong spared her further humiliation. The six slunk out the door, their vampirish thirst temporarily slaked. M. J. Taylor proved to be right; having encountered little defiance from Katie, the committee turned its attention to a green-eyed beauty from Buffalo named Maggie Fraser who, when they appeared at her door, slammed it in their faces; as a result she was so hounded that she left the campus, permanently branded a rebel, until hazing was over.

The complicity of the Sacred Heart nuns in this organized cruelty tarnished Katie's view of the order. Cynicism poisoned her first year at Manhattanville. For days at a time she kept to her room, reading, sleeping, receiving her friends, emerging only for a late evening appearance in the snack bar. Classes bored her to the point of somnolence; term papers she tossed off an hour before they were due. During exam week, while freshmen filled the study room with anxiety and cigarette smoke, she went to the movies in White Plains, earning mediocre grades and a reputation as a facile, lazy brain. Except for the Drama Club, she scorned extra-curricular activities. Attendance at the first fall mixer, manned with recruits from Iona and Holy Cross, was required; thereafter she eschewed college social events, spending every weekend at the New York apartment. In a fit of social excess during the Christmas holidays, Katie was presented to society at four debutante cotillions—three in New York and one in Rochester—that brought her in contact with the cream of those cities' most eligible, usually intoxicated young men. Spring brought a double tragedy: her Grandmother Louvain died, and Todd Babcock, the object of her earliest romantic fantasies, was reported lost in a boating accident on Lake Ontario. A rich convent diet of Communist atrocity stories, served up by visiting missionaries, inspired her hopeful fantasy that Todd was not drowned but kidnapped by a Soviet vessel; when his body washed up on the Canadian shore a month later, she progressed from depression to despair. Only onstage, immersed in another character, did she feel truly alive. With an eye to a future in the theater, she dropped the girlish nickname of Katie and referred to herself from then on as Katherine.

June: her first summer of freedom! Freedom, in this case, meant being one of eight girls from eastern Catholic colleges on an organized but unchaperoned tour of Europe—seven weeks, nine countries. Previous vacations had been spent with her parents at their favorite resorts: the gracious, antebellum Homestead in Virginia and New Hampshire's sprawling Victorian summer hotel, the Wentworth-by-the-Sea. What these Old World establishments had in common—apart from invitational tennis tournaments, emerald putting greens, stables, tea dances, and guest appearances by the Princeton Glee Club—was that their clientele was restricted, a word that she'd long ago learned was a euphemism for No Jews Allowed.

"Why would they even try to get in? They have their own places," Emily always said, although no Christian seriously doubted that if the ban were lifted, the Catskills would empty overnight.

The first evening aboard the *Ile de France*, Katherine was chatting outside the cocktail lounge with Wilder Framingham from Rosemont College, who was her cabin mate and easily the most beautiful girl on the ship, when out of the corner of her eye, she noticed a dark-haired young man ogling them from the quarter deck. By their clothes ye shall know them: in his Ivy League duds, he was the only acceptable male on the horizon. The faded blue button-down shirt he had on with his blazer and khakis deepened his suntan to bronze. He approached, and Wilder's dimples came out like binaries. Katherine directed her gaze hopelessly at the girl's wide-set delphinium eyes, retroussé nose, and the only complexion she'd ever seen that could accurately be described as peaches and cream. Being Wilder's friend had taught her one of life's bitter lessons: men will choose looks over intellect every time. But in more ways than one, Neil Kolodny, who introduced himself as a Harvard junior from Fort Lee, New Jersey, proved to be an exception. "I came over at first because she's so gorgeous," he admitted to Katherine later, "but once you started to talk, I was hooked."

And talk they did throughout the crossing. They roamed the decks by the hour, laughing, lost in literature, discussing Balzac and Strindberg and Thomas Mann, sharing their passion for Russian novelists, debating the meaning of "The Grand Inquisitor." Katherine could hardly believe her luck—a boy who talked about books!

"He doesn't drink too much, he doesn't care about football or sailing—he's not like anyone I've ever *known* before," she confided to Wilder.

The O'Connor girls told her the Awful Truth.

Vivacious sisters from South Orange, Sheila and Carol Ann came upon her sitting on deck one gray and chilly morning, wrapped in a blanket and addressing postcards.

"Who're you writing to?" asked Sheila, the athletic one, her figure as flat and angular as the hockey stick with which she regularly led the Trinity team to victory.

"My parents."

"I hope you didn't mention Neil's last name."

"Why?" Katherine asked curiously.

Chubby Carol Ann tugged at a button that hung by a thread on her raincoat and said, "Because. Then they'll know he's Jewish."

The ship pitched, or so it seemed to Katherine's stomach. She squinted up at their faces, featureless blobs against the sky's steely glare. "What makes you think he's Jewish?"

The sisters exchanged a look. "He's got an *acc*ent," Carol Ann informed her gently.

"Don't you hear it?" asked Sheila. "He says 'hang-ger,' for God's sake."

"And 'dent-uhl,' " Carol Ann mimicked.

"I thought that was a New Jersey accent," Katherine said.

"Believe me, if you lived there, you'd know the difference," Carol Ann assured her, pocketing the button. "Feel like a game of shuffleboard?"

Katherine shook her head. "Is Kolodny a Jewish name?"

"Suh-lightly!" Sheila hooted. "Don't they have Jews in Rochester or what?"

"I think it's crummy of him not to have told you," Carol Ann said sympathetically, and raking the dampness through her curls, followed her sister to the shuffleboard court.

The sea sprayed the deck with a cold mist; Katherine gathered up her books and headed below. Her head buzzed. A Jew. The word rolled around in her brain, mysterious, foreign; they might as well have said he was a Lithuanian. As she was going up the wide staircase to the lounge, Wilder was coming down. "The O'Connors just told me that Neil's Jewish," Katherine confided. "Do you think it's true?"

Wilder, who had spent her formative years on horseback in Gladwyn, Pennsylvania, opened her eyes even wider and whispered, "I don't know."

They sat down on the stairs to consider it. And from that moment, the fact of Neil Kolodny's Jewishness never completely left Katherine's mind. You don't get eighteen years of anti-Semitism drummed into your head for nothing.

For the duration of the voyage, Katherine avoided the subject of religion with Neil and nourished a theory that the O'Connor sisters were mistaken. On a storm-tossed evening, when all but the hardiest passengers had sought refuge in their cabins and the orchestra had left the lounge, Neil sat down at the piano to play; as she watched his long, tanned fingers on the keys and listened to the music that seemed to emanate from a secret well of sadness, saw the way his shoulders moved and his eyes glowed when he was deep in Gershwin, she felt her feelings swerve from fondness to sexual attraction. But later, when they stood on deck in a gale, waves churning, wind blowing through their hair, the unspoken held them back. With a mixture of relief and disappointment, she wondered why he'd never even tried to kiss her. The next day, the *Ile* docked at Le Havre.

Gradually, the group of girls had come to look upon Neil as a sort of mascot. He went with them on the boat train to London; he booked a room in their hotel, delaying his departure for Paris till morning to accompany them to the theater. At midnight, after everyone had retired, he called Katherine and asked her to come to his room to say good-bye. In an apprehensive frame of mind, she made her way along the corridor. His door was ajar; she pushed it open and found him reclining on the bed, wearing black trousers and an undershirt, reading the Gideon Bible. It was as if she were seeing him for the first time; he appeared before her unmasked, unalterably Jewish. His nose grew longer as she stared at it; a wiry stubble sprouted high on his cheeks; thick black eyebrows met in the middle of his forehead. She rattled on about nothing while he rose and made his way to her at the door. When she paused for a breath, he said ponderously, "I've been reading the Psalms." "Oh," she said, thinking, He's about to tell me.

They looked at each other; then his lips grazed her forehead in a stilted farewell. She fled, scurrying up the back stairs to tell Wilder that it was too complicated and he too moody . . . all in all, just as well that they were going their separate ways for the summer. Perhaps forever.

Neil had a blue cable-knit sweater he wore the first time he came to see Katherine at Manhattanville. She caught sight of him through her window, striding up the cinder path under the elm trees, his chin thrust into a plaid scarf, his scowl challenging anyone who dared on this sylvan Catholic campus to make something of his presence. They went into the city on Saturday evening; there, far from the normal collegiate round of athletics and alcohol, they ate escargots at a bistro in Turtle Bay and listened to Mabel Mercer sing of lost love in her smoky contralto at the Blue Angel.

At two o'clock in the morning, Neil pulled his car over to the curb on a dark street near the East River and began to recount the story of his life. As if to make up for his discretion aboard the *Ile*, now he bombarded Katherine with descriptions of growing up Jewish in Jersey City.

"When I was six," he related between drags on a cigarette, "I used to have to walk to school through the ghetto. There were always gangs hanging out in the streets—micks, wops—and they'd throw rocks at me and yell, 'Dirty kike!' " He made a little hissing sound as he inhaled. "Later, when my old man started making some money, he moved the family to Fort Lee. I went to Dwight, this tony private school, where I played basketball. Two guys would get on either side of me—huge blond jocks—and they would take turns shoving. One would ask the other, 'Did you push him?' and he'd say, 'No, didJEW?' " He stubbed out the butt in the ashtray with little jabs, old angers and bitterness burning afresh in his eyes, giving off sparks that worked wonders when he drew Katherine toward him for their first feverish kiss.

On subsequent nights in Cambridge and New York, thrashing about in his car, nearly impaled upon the gearshift, she had a sense of making up to him for the slights and cruelties inflicted by her fellow Christians. Necking with Neil was not only fun, it was a mission.

To preserve her virginity that autumn took all the backbone and moral fiber forged over fourteen years of convent training. Guilt is a powerful aphrodisiac, as all Catholic girls know, but no matter how frenzied they became, at the crucial moment she held him back with wrists of steel. For one thing, the price (i.e., Hell, with whose topography, thanks to Dante, she was as familiar as the network of streets in the Barnard tract) was high; for another, giving in spelled the death of romance—Stendhal and Tolstoy and Proust all said so; hence, where was the advantage for an incurable romantic? Far from imagining herself in love with Neil, Katherine focused on his intellect, his wit, his musical talent, and the undeniable thrill of the forbidden.

Meanwhile, back at Manhattanville, where Christian charity was supposed to flourish, Mother Graves said, "I have nothing against Neil personally, but I do wish you could meet a boy with rosary beads jingling in his pocket."

Katherine's suite mates, Mary Agnes and Charlene and Sally, asked, "What do you *see* in him?" Wilder wrote from Rosemont to ask: "What is there to *do* at Harvard if he can't get into a decent club?"

The need to defend Neil to the nuns and her friends made Katherine like him more. Having put off introducing him to her parents, she tried to prepare him for an inevitable encounter as Thanksgiving approached.

"Mother and Daddy aren't really anti-Semitic, they're just provincial," she explained during one of their lengthy phone calls. "I mean, Mother has a thing about a lot of people . . . Italians, for instance, Polish people—"

"Does she know many Polacks?" Neil inquired dryly.

"No, but there's a large contingent in Buffalo, and that's close enough to make her nervous. It's not only nationalities but professions—psychiatrists are out, writers, any kind of intellectual, scientists—"

"*Scien*tists?"

"My whole family thinks they're atheists by definition. When I think about it, my mother has narrowed the world down to about twelve people living in a ten-mile radius of Rochester. You mustn't take it personally if she's a bit cool."

Though Emily nearly fainted at the swarthy sight of Neil Kolodny on her doorstep Saturday evening, she was reflexively cordial as she conducted him into the spacious living room overlooking most of Manhattan. Katherine was nowhere in sight. Later he described the scene: Emily offered him a drink, indicated the chair opposite hers, and asked how he spelled his name. Neil hesitated. Why wasn't he more like his brother, who would've waltzed in wearing a yarmulka? He prayed Emily wouldn't ask *his* name—*Seymour*, for God's sake! Tradesmen, biblical figures Jews are named after, not buildings like the goyim. He thought of the men in Winthrop House—Chauncey Ludington, Eliot Wilmerding, Dilsworth Hall—and for a wild moment considered saying she'd heard him wrong, he was called one of these. She could probably win a spelling bee with those guys' names.

"N-e-i-l," he told her.

"No, I meant Kolodny," she said, leaning forward to accept a light. "What nationality is that?"

"Kolodny?" he repeated, holding a match very still at her cigarette. It didn't sound right. Was that his name? "Hungarian," he said as beads of perspiration formed on his nose, a physical manifestation that never failed to betray his nervousness. "Of course, we're third generation," he said, wishing he had his birth certificate with him. The match burned his finger, and he dropped it into an ashtray on the coffee table.

"What business is your father in, young man?" said a voice from the other end of the room.

There's someone else *here*! Neil thought, his eyes flitting to the fireplace where, he now saw, *The Wall Street Journal* hovered over a large upholstered chair. The paper was lowered, and familiar bright blue eyes peered at him from behind rimless glasses. Rifling through suitable titles for Herb Kolodny's chain of service stations, he came up with "Transportation, sir."

"In New Jersey?"

"Yes, Mr. Winterhaus." He cackled. "We have transportation in New Jersey."

The joke fell flat.

Emily drew on her cigarette. "Katherine tells us you play the piano," she said dubiously, as if her daughter were not always truthful. "Do you study music at Harvard?"

"Not really. I play by ear. My main interest is philosophy." At last he was on safe ground, confident of holding his own in a spirited discussion of Spinoza, or Buber, or even Aquinas. "I've read Plato in the original," he boasted.

Emily looked puzzled. "What do you intend to do with *that* after you graduate?"

"He's going to open a little philosophy shop, Mother," Katherine interjected, appearing in the archway in a blue taffeta dress. The look on Neil's face was that of one struggling in quicksand.

"Don't be fresh, Katherine," said Emily, uncrossing her still sensational legs and stubbing out her cigarette.

Douglas's newspaper crinkled. "I don't like your taking that tone with your mother, young lady."

"You're both so condescending about anything intellectual, Daddy. If it doesn't make money—"

"Hah! You're a fine one to scoff at money, Toots." Out of the blue he threw Neil a beleaguered smile. "You've got your hands full, son." *The Wall Street Journal* went up again. "Have fun, kids. Don't be too late."

Emily followed them to the door, where she reached out and pushed Katherine's long hair away from her face. "That's a beautiful ring, Mrs. Winterhaus," Neil commented, his eye caught by her large, emerald-cut diamond.

"Thank you, Neil. My husband has excellent taste."

"Never buy stones retail," advised Douglas from his sanctum. "I always buy them loose . . . otherwise, you don't know what you're getting. No point in squandering money on settings. I've had the same diamond man for twenty-seven years—Sam Goldblatt. Fine fellow."

"It was very nice to meet you, Neil," said Emily courteously but with a hint of finality.

" 'Night, Mother. 'Night, Daddy," Katherine said as she turned to go. Neil put out his hand. "Good night, Mrs. Winterhaus . . . Sir," he added to the newspaper.

"What's that? Oh!" Douglas peered around the paper. "So long . . . uh . . . Neil. Glad you came by. We like having young people around, don't we, Mother?"

Emily's reply was lost as she closed the door. Katherine rang for the elevator and Neil glowered at the moving dial on the wall. "He can get it for me wholesale. From Sam Goldblatt. What's he trying to do, relate? Your mother's so . . . *Irish*."

The elevator door opened; they rode down in silence.

Thick Persian carpets muffled the sound of their footsteps as they crossed the lobby with its carved marble fireplace, Aubusson tapestry, and gesso mirrors. Following her into the revolving door, Neil asked with a crack in his voice, "Could we arrange to meet at Berchtesgaden next time?"

Emily and Douglas opened the house on Windsor Court Road for the Christmas holidays. Margot flew in from St. Louis a few days before Tyler, who was proving to be a devoted husband and a banker with a future despite her parents' dire premonitions of philandering and penury. The evening before his arrival, Emily's sister and brother-in-law, Loretta and Fred Stokes, joined the Winterhauses for a celebration. Seated next to Katherine at the dinner table, Uncle Fred grinned mischievously. "Shouldn't there be an eight-branch candelabra on the table this year, folks? In honor of Katie's new heart-throb. What do they call 'em, honey? Normas? Nimrods?"

"I'm not sure what they're called, Uncle Freddie." Her face was crimson, although she should have been used to his teasing; he'd been doing it her whole life.

"Come on! You must speak the language by now. How long you been dating this fellow?" Above a polka-dotted bow tie, his Adam's apple bobbled with glee. "He doesn't take you to the synagogue? Vy not, may I ask?"

"Very funny." With a nervous glance in her mother's direction, Katherine pleaded with him under her breath, "Could you give it a rest, please? You'll ruin her Christmas."

Fred winked across the table at his wife, Loretta, a pretty woman with inky blue hair.

"Easy, Frederick," she chastised him gently.

But making waves at the Winterhauses was great sport for Fred Stokes. He owed his house and his job to his brother-in-law; once, Katherine had overheard him saying to Aunt Loretta, "It's a pain in the butt having to be grateful all the time . . . no harm razzing 'em once in a while." Now he looked at Emily with a wicked glint in his eye. "Have you done your Molly Goldberg imitation for the prospective in-laws, Em? It's a peach!"

"I voulden tink of it, Mr. Nussbaum," Emily laughed. Abruptly she suggested they take their coffee in the living room; as Douglas pulled out her chair, she said with forced good humor, "Freddy's giving us the business again, dear. But I'm not going to let anyone spoil Christmas with unpleasant thoughts. Katie doesn't need advice. She's eighteen. She knows *every*thing."

The family trooped into the living room. Emily picked up her needlepoint from the library table and went to sit with Loretta on the twin loveseats at the far end of the room, while Douglas retreated to the wing chair in the bay window. Margot sat on the couch, her feet on the coffee table, *Harper's Bazaar* propped against her knees. Katherine straddled the piano bench, as Uncle Fred picked out a shaky "Havah Nagilah" on the keys. In vain Emily attempted to concentrate on her needlepoint.

"Has it occurred to you, Katherine," she blurted, "that if you marry this boy, you won't be allowed in Oak Hill Country Club?"

Mock horror transformed Katherine's face. "No more bowling? No more creamed spinach? Until you said that, Mother, I hadn't even been *tempted* to marry him."

Margot turned a page. Without looking up, she said, "I've been meaning to tell you, Kate. Remember Inge Nordeman—that big blonde in my class at Briarcliff? Well, she married a Jewish doctor and they moved to St. Louis. They live fairly near Tyler and me. Within a year she came down with a case of terminal acne. Her skin's a mess."

"What's that supposed to be, a plague visited on her for marrying a Jew?" Katherine snapped.

"Well, not directly. But the stress . . . you know. Her family . . . his family. None of our friends invite them. She says their entire social life revolves around gastroenterologists and their wives. You'd better think twice about Hammacher Schlemmer."

Katherine laughed. She got up and went to the tree in the bay window, where she tightened two flickering bulbs with angry twists. A hair tonic stain fanned out like an aureole on the brocade behind Douglas's head. "You said you thought Neil was very bright, Daddy. Besides that, he's the *kindest* boy I know."

"That's not the point, dear," said Emily, inadvertently jabbing herself through the canvas with her needle. She stanched the wound with a lace-edged handkerchief. "He did strike me as a perfectly nice person the one time I met him. And I'm sure you wouldn't like anyone who wasn't kind. But can you imagine—Katherine Kol*od*ny? It's so ordinary."

"You can really be an insufferable snob, Mother," Katherine declared.

"Hear, hear, none of that! Watch how you talk to your mother, young lady!" Douglas chided, adding consolingly, "Don't worry, Em. Katie's not going to throw herself away on just anyone. She thinks too well of herself for that."

"I don't know who you're *ever* going to think is good enough for me, Daddy." Katherine swept her arm in an arc over the crèche at the bottom of the tree. "You do remember that all these people, including the Infant, were Jews?"

"Don't be sacrilegious, young lady. You know perfectly well that mixed marriage is a mortal sin."

"It is *not*!" A silver ball slid through the branches and crashed on the floor. "Where do you *get* those ideas? They're a holdover from the Albigensian *her*esy or something! I mean, Daddy, you walked out of *Inn of the Sixth Happiness* because Ingrid Bergman marries a Eu*ras*ian in it!"

"Still accusing Mr. Roosevelt of being Jewish, Doug?" asked Fred merrily.

"No question about it," Douglas stated.

"Why would you want to cast a slur on such a fine President?" Loretta interjected.

"Hmph," Douglas muttered. "Sold the country right down the river."

"Why do you say it's a slur, anyway, Aunt Lory?" asked Katherine, on her knees picking up shards of the ornament.

"Don't be saucy, Katherine. You've gotten very fresh lately. I don't know who's influencing you," Emily said pointedly, "but you're certainly not the bright, happy child you used to be."

"Oh, God! I haven't been a bright, happy child since I was six!" Tears of frustration scalded the backs of Katherine's eyes. "Do you know any warm, funny, brilliant Catholics who play the piano and will like *me*? No . . . because they don't exist!"

Fred exchanged another look with his wife, this one eloquently expressing their gratitude that five of their six sons were safely married to Catholic girls (except for Tony's wife, Mimi, who came from Corning and was a convert, which, as Loretta always said, wasn't quite the same).

Harper's Bazaar landed on the coffee table. "You're so sensitive, Kate," Margot said through a bored yawn.

Humming tunelessly, Douglas closed his eyes and rested his head against the back of the chair.

Emily drew a strand of yellow thread through the canvas; as she left the room, Katherine heard her say to Aunt Loretta, "I don't know what Douglas and I have done to deserve such a perverse child."

Early on a wintry evening two months later, Katherine stood beside Neil on the doorstep of his parents' house in Fort Lee, New Jersey. Another couple was with them, Neil's roommate, Sam McGreevy, and his date, one of those long-haired, moody intellectuals who flourished at Radcliffe in the late fifties. Anyone with any sense would have reshuffled the deck: Sam was a bright, uncomplicated Catholic on his way to Harvard Business School, a tailor-made son-in-law for Emily and Douglas Winterhaus; while Judith Filerman was perfect for Neil: a dark lady of the sonnets, slight and *triste,* her pre-Raphaelite eyes probing relentlessly for hidden meanings in the most ordinary conversation, a copy of Baudelaire's *Les Fleurs du Mal* open on her lap in the car all the way from New York.

While Neil dug in his pocket for his keys and a veil of snowflakes collected on her pale hair, Katherine examined a small bronze box, about one inch by three, attached to the doorjamb, and inquired what it was. A condescending smile flitted across Judith's face. "It's a mezuzah," Neil explained. "You might say it's our version of a crucifix. There's a passage from the Torah in it." Katherine did not comment. All that was alien, forbidden about Neil was exemplified at that moment by the religious symbol. It bespoke cabalistic rituals and dredged up ancient convent lore—dormitory spook stories passed from one pubescent boarder to another about Jews who drank the blood of Christian babies. And beyond it was a family buffet and two people who, according to Neil, would disown him if he married a shiksa.

But unlike Emily, Rose Kolodny was a shrewd student of psychology. Her face glowed with pleasure as she greeted them in the foyer. "Neil, darling! You've brought Katherine . . . how wonderful!" She kissed her son and turned to Katherine with a warm smile. "You're even prettier than he said. A little thin maybe, but gorgeous!"

Not a trace of malice could Katherine discern in this attractive, matronly woman whom her son had called "the termagant of Jersey City." Her large brown eyes sparkled with the light of humor and a benign intelligence; her manner was straightforward. When Neil left them alone for a moment, she linked her arm through Katherine's and steered her toward the dining room, introducing her to friends and relatives along the way as if she considered this tall blond Catholic a prize rather than a Fate Worse Than Death; if she heard a neighbor say, after they'd passed, "Rose's son is going with a shiksa . . . it's a *shande un a charpe* [a shame]," she gave no indication, but only patted Katherine affectionately before going off to greet a new arrival.

Empty plate in hand, Katherine scanned the buffet. The smile slid off her face; there was hardly any food there that she recognized. Was this what kosher meant? Here a spongy mousse sat in a welter of quivering gelatin; there a fluted mold held a mysterious beige paste. A sort of fruitcake in the center oozed honey, and to the right, she surmised, was marinated herring, repulsive enough when her father ordered it as an appetizer, here a *hillock* of herring squishing on the platter. Against all culinary logic, slices of salmon were arranged with globs of cream cheese. The texture of everything was soft; only the rolls were hard, and they were like rocks— round with doughnut holes. Spying a tray of cold cuts, she looked around for white bread to make a sandwich, but there was none, only dark brown and yellow.

"Here, darling, let me serve you some whitefish," offered an elderly man with a beard, plunging his fork into a shriveled, crisp-skinned creature with head and tail intact, which bore no resemblance to her knowledge of the species, the one that swam in Lake Ontario and was filleted and broiled to golden perfection by a succession of family cooks. The man, who introduced himself as Uncle Zev, nodded when she told him she was with Neil.

"A party with old people—you need this, right? Neil's my favorite nephew—but flighty. He should make up his mind what he wants to do in life. Law school would be good."

"It seems a shame not to go on with his music. He's so talented," she replied. "I'm convinced he could do anything—be a composer or play in a symphony."

Uncle Zev glanced across the room at Neil over the top of his glasses. "What you got there, girlie, is an unfinished symphony."

Katherine laughed, enchanted with him, and graciously accepted the quartered tomato he extricated for her from a bed of oily onions; but when he moved on and she looked in vain for something else to eat, she was forced to conclude that she was her parents' daughter after all: a provincial little girl with no flair for adventure or exploration, no taste for the wider gastronomic world beyond that of prime ribs of beef, medium-rare steak, lean loin lamb chops (nothing less than a clambake could lure the Winterhauses from animal flesh on any night but Friday). Backing away from the table, she felt herself hemmed in by short, dark people jostling each other to get at the food. "Dig in, Kate," said Neil in her ear, giving her a start. "Mom will be crushed if you don't have two helpings of everything."

Two hours later, imprisoned by his arm around her shoulder, Katherine swung back and forth on the glider in the sunporch while Judith, the Cliffie, monopolized Neil with a disquisition on Martin Buber. An understanding Sam whispered in passing, "Don't take it personally, Kate. Judy thinks Christian girls are just for practice."

Herb Kolodny never appeared ("Probably upstairs changing his will," Neil cracked), Seymour had stayed at Brandeis, and Marcy, their sister, had left early with friends. But Rose won Katherine's heart, darting from room to room, spreading cheer, charging the atmosphere with gaiety and life. "If this is a Jewish mother, I want one," Katherine whispered to Neil. When it was time to leave, Rose came to the door to say good-bye. She kissed Neil, then squeezed Katherine's arm. "Now I know how you keep that gorgeous figure. You eat like a bird!"

* * *

Winter waned. Dispirited, ever paler, Emily moped around the apartment. On a windy Saturday in March, Douglas asked Katherine to meet him for lunch at the King Cole Bar. Seated across from her at a small table against the wall, he put down his fork after a few bites of deviled crabmeat. "Your mother's not well," he began. "You must have noticed how thin she is, how pale—" He looked down, his chin quivering.

Fear struck at Katherine's heart. "What do you think it is?"

"I fear the worst," he said in a broken voice.

She exhaled the forbidden word. "Cancer?"

He nodded, and when he raised his head, his milky blue eyes skewered her with their suffering. She reached out a hand to him, hardly able to breathe. His tone turned cold. "And it's your going around with this Jewish boy that's doing it."

There was a dramatic pause. "Aha," Katherine said, withdrawing her hand.

At her husband's insistence, Emily had a thorough physical examination. "Fewer sweets," the doctor advised. "Otherwise, you're fit as a fiddle." Not long afterward, Emily entered Katherine's room early on a Saturday morning. The windows were open and a soft, sooty breeze drew the glass curtains out so they flapped like flags. Ordinarily Emily would have closed the windows, but now she leaned listlessly against the dressing table, watching her daughter brush her hair at the bureau a few feet away. When she spoke, her voice was a pathetic bleat.

"How long is this going to go on?"

Katherine met her gaze in the mirror. "What do you mean?"

"This . . . this Neil business," Emily said with distaste.

"I don't know, Mother," Katherine said impatiently. "He's a *friend*—I like him, that's all. Now, do you mind if I eat my breakfast?"

Unmollified, Emily pursued her down the hall to the dining room, where she stood over her, gripping the edge of the table. Her silk wrapper hung open carelessly, and Emily was anything but a careless woman. "Do you realize what you'd be doing to your father and me if you marry this boy?"

Katherine looked at her with genuine curiosity. "What?"

Emily's voice dropped. "You'd be giving us Jewish grandchildren."

With a cry of exasperation, Katherine threw down her napkin and stormed back to her room.

As in most romances with an impediment, real or imagined, the impediment had become more important than the romance. While Katherine had lost interest in Neil as anything more than a friend, peer and parental pressure radicalized her, binding her to him with ties of moral and sociological outrage. Easter vacation would be a logical time to put distance between them, she thought, but then her parents whisked her off to the Colony Hotel in Palm Beach, where she languished by the pool, her new awareness making the restricted surroundings repellent. Neil wrote every day—anguished, sometimes rhymed expressions of frustration:

> *Fear no red-cloaked hand of repression!*
> *Neither Church nor family nor state*
> *Shall keep us separate!*

Sunday was the feast of St. Joseph, whose statue stood in a niche outside Katherine's room in the sophomore corridor. When she got back to Manhattanville that evening, she saw that a spray of flowers had fallen from his pedestal; she replaced them, looking up at his painted face. St. Caspar of Milquetoast, a convent cynic had dubbed him—the silent, long-suffering Jewish family man to whom students were exhorted to pray for a good, Catholic husband. And then it struck her: the Church was *crammed* with Jewish heroes. Throughout her childhood the nuns had paraded them: Moses the Masculine; David the Underdog; Sampson the Strong, yet vulnerable to a woman's love; John the Baptist, the Precursor of Christ Himself, whose pain was permanently, romantically depicted by a scantily clad figure on the cross, before which they would stand by the hour, their faces transfigured with love. And *then* they have the nerve to say you shouldn't marry a Jew! she thought as she stomped into her room. The mirror over the bureau showed a wild-eyed creature, a harridan she addressed with inward ire: And who's their feminine ideal? *Mater Admirabilis*, that's who! The Mother of God, a Jewess, whose portrait hangs in every Sacred Heart convent the world over, depicted as a delicate, blue-eyed Botticelli blonde!

The bathroom door opened and her suite mate stuck her head through. "Hey, Ophelia," she said. "You got a phone call earlier. There's a message on the bulletin board."

It was from Neil, inviting Katherine to spring weekend at Harvard. Presented with a permission slip, Douglas refused to sign; a clash ensued that left her emotionally drained but determined not to be bullied.

The sky was a radiant blue over the Charles, where sculls skimmed the surface of the water and the golden youth of the fifties strolled along the riverbank. But there was little joy in the weekend. Katherine was in a melancholy mood. There was a new, rough edge to her necking with Neil. At last she admitted sadly, "I love you, but I'm not *in* love with you." On Sunday morning, he insisted on accompanying her to Mass. Feeling his skeptical glance on her as she genuflected, she regretted the experiment; mutual unease settled around them like a cloud of incense in the pew. He sat stolidly while she rose, knelt, sat, and rose again with the congregation; she felt his presence as an intrusion. At one point, he leaned his head close to hers, his eyes on the statue of St. Joseph, and said in a strained voice, "I just got the feeling that he looked back and saw me and said, 'You're one of *our* boys—what're you doing in here?' "

Her response was a frazzled smile. She felt like an overloaded circuit; she wanted it to end. All afternoon, she avoided his eyes and sat far from him while he played the piano in the Dunster House lounge, his face drawn above the blue cable-knit collar. In the middle of "Every time we say good-bye, I cry a little," she saw his tears spilling onto the keyboard.

Two weeks later, Katherine told her parents that Neil was going to ROTC camp for the summer and she wouldn't be dating him anymore.

"Thanks be to God!" Emily murmured, folding her needlepoint and holding out her arms for a hug, a gesture Katherine ignored.

Douglas glanced up from his charts at the desk. "That's all to the good, cutie," he said. "Wish him luck for me, will you? I always said he was a fine fellow . . . just all wrong for you." A light came into his eyes as he looked at Katherine. "You deserve nothing but the best, Skeezix. But you'd better learn to be more practical. You can get into a lot of hot water if you stray too far from your own kind."

CHAPTER 6

The Choice

"Bless me, Father, for I have sinned. It's been four months since my last confession. I've been separated from my husband for a week."

"I don't want to be married anymore, Katie," Christopher had said simply. Behind him, the Christmas tree shimmered in the corner of the room, the only jarring note in his carefully realized minimalist environment. As a newlywed in New Haven, Katherine had learned how sacrosanct to architecture students were their purist concepts: form follows function and everything in the apartment must be white. "I have a feeling I'm going to wake up in the middle of the night and find you standing over me with a can of white paint," she'd teased him. Those were the days when they were kindred spirits, talking by the hour, laughing until they were weak, clinging to each other in the night: happiness marred by Katherine's growing suspicion that her young husband had a tragic view of himself which no amount of love could cure.

Now, with the kitchen light falling in slats through the bamboo shade onto the round white Formica dining table, she waited for him to continue. A Joan Baez record was playing, her voice reed-thin and very high. Christopher stood within arm's reach of the bourbon on the bookcase, his tall frame in the banker's gray suit listing toward the twinkling lights, beige hair already thinning, aristocratic features blurred a bit with the years of abuse. He set his glass on the shelf and uncapped the bottle. "I feel as if I have all the disadvantages of an artist and none of the advantages," he said.

In the dining alcove, antiseptic as an operating room, Katherine sat quite still with her fingers splayed across the Formica. No hysterics for once; too late for tears. This was not negotiation but notice. Worst Fears Realized.

The frayed edges of shock bled into panic as she thought of the child with buttercup hair asleep in her high-side bed the night before her third Christmas. A little girl named for her father. She heard her own voice, thin as parchment: "But . . . what about Chryssie?"

Christopher squared his shoulders. "I am not an emotional hostage to Christabel," he declared.

Katherine's soul screamed. A madwoman, she raged within the prison of a frozen body, phantom fists beating against the wall of her breast to get at him. You cold WASP bastard . . . monster . . . son of a bitch! What does that mean? What kind of line is that to use about your daughter?

But no sound or gesture surfaced. The remains of two fat white candles guttered in their Lucite holders on the table. Christopher drained his glass, watching her open and close her mouth like a fish tossed by a vandal wave onto the sand. The record ended. Into the silence, he hiccuped. A sentimental look came over him as he began to back out of the room. "I always knew it would be hard to leave you and Chryssie," he said in a sad voice.

Always? she thought, her eyes wild on his face. *Always?* We've only been married three years! Barely a year ago, during the Cuban missile crisis, he'd talked about building a bomb shelter so they wouldn't be separated in *death*! This past Thanksgiving they'd wept together over Kennedy's assassination. And only last Friday he'd stayed home from work to spend the day in bed with her! He must have been planning it then, as they made love. Her blood chilled as she recalled the words he'd spoken afterward: "Fantastic! It was as if you were my girlfriend instead of my wife."

Another Baez record fell with a plop onto the pile, and the pure, wistful voice began again. He's been playing that same music over and over for days, she realized. I should have known something was coming. She was still sitting at the table when he left. He closed the door carefully behind him, as if not to disturb her, nor Christabel's slumber, nor the festive array of holly and candlelight and pungent pine needles that filled the apartment.

As slowly as if she were moving through water, Katherine went to the phonograph and lifted the needle. It was years before she could bear to listen to Joan Baez again.

The priest was stern. "Do you have permission to be separated?" he demanded from behind the narrow screen.

Kneeling in the dark, Katherine's body was as taut as a violin string. This is it, she thought, manic laughter building from her toes. If I let go, I may never be able to stop, I might just collapse in a pool of hysteria. "Permission from whom?" she inquired.

"The bishop," he replied.

Oh. The bishop. Of course. "My husband just *left*, Father," she explained, as to a child. "There really wasn't any time."

"Is he a Catholic?"

"No, Father. Episcopalian."

"Oh . . . well. You see?" His tone shifted the blame to her, while in the background, an entire church choir harmonized "I told you so," under the baton of Douglas Winterhaus.

Christopher Lindley Kellogg had impeccable social credentials and a profile that belonged on a Greek coin. His bearing was regal, his manner patrician; once, when he was climbing the steps of the Yale Bowl, another Yalie was heard to inquire, "Who's *that* sonofabitch?"

After flatly refusing to return to Manhattanville for junior year, Katherine had been accepted as an acting major at the Yale School of Drama. Ambition fueled her in those days; the discovery that with a look, a gesture, or the timing of a line she could provoke tears and laughter from an audience filled her with a sense of excitement and power that seemed more like happiness than anything she'd ever known. In her melodramatic way she told herself that once Todd Babcock drowned, love was no longer important; the next best thing was applause.

But then one day in My Brother's Place, where she had gone for a mid-afternoon cheeseburger, a tall young man in a camel's hair coat seated in the booth next to her looked up from his copy of C. Wright Mills's *The Power Elite*, brushed his blond hair out of his eyes, and introduced himself. Groton, Princeton, and the Yale Architecture School had produced this Aryan prince. His looks and intelligence undid her: as if life were a Philip Barry play, she became infatuated with worn-at-the-elbows tweeds that fairly shrieked Old Money and a mid-Atlantic accent that conjured up squash courts and summers in Watch Hill.

After three months of midnight suppers and occasional wrestling matches on the sofa in his Spartan apartment on Chapel Street, he presented her with an ultimatum: "Either have an affair with me or let's get married."

"You don't care which?" she asked him, astonished.

He thought it over. "Not really," he said equably.

She thought it over. She wanted to be normal. She wanted children. She wanted, despite the rebellious streak, to make her parents happy. How pleased they would be, after years of criticizing her ethnic preferences, that she'd come up with a WASP from a Good Family. When she called to tell them she was engaged, to her amazement, they were not pleased. No matter *who* Christopher was, her father said, he was still in school and she was an extravagant young lady.

"I'm making a reasonable compromise, Daddy," said Katherine. "At least he's the *son* of a very rich man."

Douglas pointed out that Christopher would not enjoy the fruits of his birthright until several people still in excellent health died.

Emily pointed out that she knew of his mother's people—the Lindleys were a prominent New York family and had a history of divorce.

And of course, both parents pointed out that he was a non-Catholic.

But they had impaled themselves on Margot's resentment of their interference; Katie was even more headstrong, Douglas warned his wife. What if she were to elope? "Dear God!" Emily gasped. "What would people say?"

During spring break, Christopher took the train to Rochester to meet them. As long as she lived, Katherine thought, she would remember the way he looked when she went to pick him up at the dingy downtown railroad station, sitting on a bench in his British custom-tailored suit among the derelicts, like Prince Philip touring a depressed area. The provincial city appalled him; her parents' use of euphemisms offended his sensibilities (when Douglas mentioned a cousin who'd "passed away," he winced; when Emily said her sister was "stopping by to visit with them," he squinted at her as if she'd lapsed into Chinese); and living under the watchful eye of

Jesus Christ drove him up the wall ("I went in to take a *leak* and He was looking down at me!" he complained to Katherine). But love prevailed. He promised to abide by the rules and conditions of the Catholic Church, and assured Douglas that his father would continue his generous allowance until he started to make money as an architect. Not to be outdone, Douglas pledged to continue Katherine's allowance until Christopher graduated. A wedding date was set for midsummer, and a European honeymoon planned.

A week before the wedding, Douglas took Katherine for a drive in the Cadillac, the best place he could think of to hold a completely private conversation. The day was humid and he'd unconsciously followed an old shortcut, he said, realizing they'd come as far as Irondequoit only when he felt the breeze from Lake Ontario, damp and sharply cooler against his face. The lake house had gotten to be too much for Emily, and when they took the apartment at the Carlyle it had been sold; he hadn't wanted to come down here after that. The familiar scent of pine trees and new-mown grass along Rock Beach Road filled Katherine's nostrils and prodded memories so poignant that a lump rose in her throat. There was the Van Veldt house, its gray siding battered by a nor'easter, and the Bradley estate, its lovely English garden sprouting weeds.

"The old places don't look the same since Fred Spencer passed on, do they, Snooks?" he said.

"Nope. They seemed much bigger when I was little."

"Everything always does."

"I guess so. Like the circus. But I'll never love another house the way I loved the lake house."

"That makes two of us, cutie."

He slowed as they came to the end of the road, coasting to a stop at the mailbox across the street from a white house with green striped awnings and sunporches all around. Masses of ivy hid the stone wall, and the gate on which Katie used to swing was missing a hinge. A breeze rippled through the blossoming trees, carrying their fragrance across the lawn.

"Remember how I used to eat so many cherries that I'd get sick to my stomach?" Katherine asked.

"You never listened. That tree's a beauty, isn't it? It's almost as old as I am—over a hundred! Ho, ho, ho."

They stared at the house. She looked away first; it depressed her to see it looking so run down. Douglas's hand lay between them on the seat. The familiar sight of his blunted thumb and little finger pierced her with a stab of love and regret. A passage in T. S. Eliot came back to her:

> *. . . the evening that brings together*
> *For casual talk before the fire,*
> *Two people who know they do not understand each other,*
> *Breeding children whom they do not understand*
> *And who will never understand them.*

No one I chose to marry would have been good enough for Daddy, she told herself, partly to lessen the sting of his obvious disappointment.

"I want to talk to you about something," he said gravely, his eyes on the wheel. "I hope you realize how serious this is—this marriage business. Are you sure Christopher intends to live up to his promise to raise the children Catholic?"

"Of course, Daddy."

"It's no joke marrying a Protestant. Divorce doesn't mean the same thing to them." He turned to face her. "Think about it. What if he should leave you? What would people say?"

"Why do you let Mother put words in your mouth?" she snapped.

Unshed tears collected in his eyes. "Mother is very concerned about these things. You can understand . . . Rochester is a small town." His shoulders sagged. "All I care about is that the four of us get to heaven."

Katherine laughed, then wished she could take it back, realizing that in the end it *was* all he cared about. It was part of his integrity. She ran her finger over the vein in his hand. "Don't worry, Daddy. We're all going to ride in hanging on to your shirttail."

They sat quietly for another minute, then he turned the key in the ignition. With a last look at the old house, he said as they drove away, "Always remember, Katie, the only thing that matters in the end is family."

Katherine and Christopher wed that summer, no more mindlessly than most of their generation. At the reception, the best man toasted the bride and groom as an eminently well-suited couple: both Yalies, both tall and intelligent, almost like siblings in their blond good looks; one could easily visualize the four children they planned to produce. A daughter was born the following spring in New Haven;

they named her Christabel, after Christopher and a poem by Coleridge that Katherine loved. Confident of her ability to juggle art and maternity, she tried out for the fall major production at Yale; but the baby developed a dangerous cough and Christopher wanted company while building his architectural models in the evenings, so as soon as the run of the play was over, she dropped out of school to devote herself to them.

Randolph Kellogg, who had retired at thirty-five from the family textile business, chose the occasion of Christopher's graduation from the architecture school to announce that, in order to foster self-reliance (a quality he had heretofore suppressed in his son), he was terminating his allowance. Fair's fair, Douglas said, and followed suit with Katherine. In this manner were the young couple catapulted to that not uncommon juncture in the lives of offspring of the rich: sudden, abject poverty. Forced to subsist for the time being on a small legacy from a maiden aunt, Christopher suggested that for the first couple of years, they go far from the temptations of New York and reminders of their premarital fortunes. One of his visiting professors was a prominent architect in Los Angeles, he told Katherine hopefully. "Maybe he'll hire me, being an old Blue and all."

"I'm sure he will! I *love* Los Angeles. I spent one Christmas vacation there with Alison Sinclair, my Greenwich roommate. Her parents have the most wonderful house in Malibu."

A bemused look came into his eyes. "Do you see me in a belted polo coat at the Polo Lounge, like Fitzgerald?"

"Oh, *divine!*" Katherine cried, throwing her arms around him. "And I'll wear a big straw hat and the Pertegaz suit I got in Spain on our honeymoon."

In their own way, in their own time, people adjust to a change in fortunes. For these *nouveaux pauvres*, the wardrobe died the hardest.

After bidding farewell to two sets of disapproving parents, they tucked Chryssie into a car bed in the back seat of Katherine's Ford convertible, packed the trunk with luggage and one of the two Wassily chairs that Jane and Randolph Kellogg had given them for a wedding present ("Early electrocution," Katherine dubbed Breuer's tubular steel and leather slats, to Christopher's despair), and set off, abandoning, like so many others, tradition and roots for the sun and anonymity of Southern California. From Seattle, they drove down the coast. Eastern to the core, Christopher fell in love with the sight of Coit Tower rising out of the mist, and the Golden Gate Bridge, gleaming redly in the gray light. After a week in Los Angeles (where the prominent architect was cutting back due to a building slump), he said, "I prefer to live in San Francisco."

"It's Boston with fog," Katherine protested. "There's no *there* there." But for these children of the fifties, it went without saying that the Man would make the final decision. They lived in Bohemian poverty in a two-room apartment in Pacific Heights. Almost like artists, as he pointed out when he left her, but not enough.

In San Francisco, a sentiment prevailed that it was sufficient good fortune to inhabit that beautiful city by the bay; decent wages were for lesser places. The prestigious architecture firm that hired Christopher as a draftsman paid him seventy-five dollars a week, thirty of which, by Katherine's reckoning, went for the bar bill at the Princeton Club, a necessity to assuage the rigors of his impecunious existence. Otherwise, they kept to a strict regime: dining out was limited to once a week at a local pizza parlor; the *New Yorker* subscription was canceled; in a master stroke of frugality, Christopher negotiated with the landlord for fifteen dollars off the rent in exchange for managing their small apartment building. Twice a week from then on, Katherine vacuumed the halls and scrubbed the parquet floor in the foyer. God's little joke, she mused. She had turned down a vocation and ended up on her hands and knees like Sister O'Rourke, anyway. Humor was her link to sanity; Christopher and she could still laugh together, and, appearing frequently on a daytime television talk show, a nebbishy little comic broke her up with his routines about the drudgery of marriage. His name was Woody Allen, and nobody since the young Jerry Lewis had struck her so funny.

Symbol of her husband's restlessness was their third-floor apartment on Jackson Street—cramped, bourgeois, unacceptable even in its pristine whiteness. "I'm sick of these middle-class apartments on middle-class streets," he complained. "I want to live in a building with more than five floors. I want a view."

Christopher's fantasy of a richer, more meaningful life in a high-rise was a short fuse to which Fate put a flame: Sandra Lombard, an alluring interior designer in his office with a history of causing marital trouble.

Meanwhile, Katherine went about her menial chores, disposing of her conservative political notions along with the garbage from five apartments and acquiring, to Christopher's consternation, the leftist leanings of a rich-kid convert. "It's hard to be a Republican on your hands and knees," she told him.

"But what about our heroes?" he asked. "What about John Foster Dulles? What about William F. Buckley?"

"Everyone should be required to be poor for a year," she replied. "It changes the perceptions."

One day a cousin from Rochester dropped in unannounced and found her kneeling in a sea of soapsuds in the foyer. His eyes popped. "You've got it all wrong!" he told her. "The princess isn't supposed to turn back into Cinderella."

Reminded of the spoiled, silly girl she had been, she replied vehemently, "It's good for me."

In October Christopher got a raise, and they moved to a larger apartment. A domestic melody thrummed in Katherine's brain: she cooked elaborate dinners, dusted the Wassily chair, and rented a sewing machine to stitch new curtains. In the evenings, to the gentle whir of the Singer, Christopher often got drunk. Sex dwindled. She began to watch the second hand on the clock as they made love; it went around on an average of four times. On Sunday mornings they would drive across the Golden Gate Bridge (scene of countless suicides totted up regularly by the *Chronicle*) to Sausalito and stroll along the docks.

"Let's go to Europe by boat next time," she suggested once. "Before the ocean liners are defunct."

"We'll never be able to afford to go to Europe again," he declared flatly.

"Fast man with a wet blanket. I wish you wouldn't do that."

"Do what?"

"Say we'll *never* be able to do something."

Chryssie, at two and a half no stranger to tension, dropped her mother's hand and skipped on ahead, pulling a toy wooden dog behind her on a string. Katherine's eyes followed her progress. "Maybe we won't," she said. "And maybe it'll be all right if we don't. But I'm twenty-three years old! Don't take all hope away from me!"

A seagull swooped down and landed on a piling; Christopher blinked, shying away from it. "Anything's feasible if we don't have four children—or even three," he stated.

"But we agreed on four children! Nothing's more important than a family. We've talked about that a hundred times! You always said—"

"I don't give a damn what I always said. That was before I knew how much money I'd be making. Anyway, there's statistical evidence that only children are more successful."

"Oh, Chris! I can't believe you've changed that much," Katherine cried, and heard her accusatory, wifely tone echoing down the ages.

A few yards ahead of them, Chryssie tottered along, chattering to her wooden dog. A motor boat chugged past; in its wake, the sailboats rocked in their moorings. Christopher sat on the dock and rolled up his khakis. He wore an air of depression the way he'd expected to wear the belted polo coat: elegantly, romantically, Katherine thought.

Leaning back against a piling, he said, "My father always said he had no doubts about my ability to make money, but what it comes down to is this: a man chooses between the work he loves and doing something he hates in order to make enough money to have a good life. I chose the former."

"You're paraphrasing Yeats. Have you ever read *The Choice?*" she asked.

He shook his head, a spark igniting in his eye. Katherine's literacy was one of the things that had first attracted him to her; not long ago he'd remarked that she was using television like a club to bludgeon it to death. With long graceful fingers, he swept his hair back from his forehead and watched her as she recited:

"The intellect of man is forced to choose
Perfection of the life, or of the work . . .

Da da, da da . . . something . . .

That old perplexity an empty purse,
Or the day's vanity, the night's remorse."

"Fantastic! That's it exactly. It's the male dilemma," he said.

Turning her gaze to Paradise Island across the bay, she narrowed her eyes at the picnickers dotting the dense shrubbery. "I can't wait to hear your version of the female dilemma—the day's diapers, the night's dishwater?"

"Caustic Kate. Nobody forced you to stop being an actress." She glanced down at him in surprise. He had made no comment when she left the drama school; at the time it had seemed inevitable. He crossed his ankles and stared at his Topsiders. "I can't handle being responsible for someone else's life," he said.

Stung, she no longer saw the birds or the blueness of sky or the oil-slick water lapping against the boats, but only an image looming before her: a golden idol that symbolized the sacrifice of her acting career, turned to lead by the alchemist at her feet. "We agreed we wanted a family," she repeated doggedly.

"Catholics don't have families. They have teams."

Despite herself, she laughed. Encouraged by the sound, Chryssie clambered up on the rail and waved at them from the end of the dock. Every independent move she made terrified Christopher. He yelled at her to get down. "You're always talking about how lonely you were as a child," Katherine said. "How can you wish the same thing on her?"

He got to his feet with an aggrieved air. "All I know is, when I'm forty years old, I don't want to have to choose between a Jaguar and a baby. I want the Jag."

With that, their eyes met in a cold, hostile glance, and the coin of love flipped to show its opposite face.

Not long afterward, Katherine's Greenwich roommate, Alison Sinclair, called from Los Angeles to say that her father was flying up to San Francisco in his private plane on a Thursday, and would love to bring them back with him to their house in Malibu for a long weekend. Christopher had to work but urged Katherine to take Chryssie; she agreed, and as Bart Sinclair's Cessna carried them out of the fog, she had a euphoric sense of escape.

But after two days, she missed her husband as one feels twinges in a phantom limb. They were a family, she thought; nothing mattered but that. Nothing. At Battaglia in Beverly Hills she splurged on an extra Christmas present for him—a pair of the Egyptian cotton boxer shorts he'd complained he could no longer afford. As they were being gift-wrapped, a warning voice said in her ear: He could take these off to go to bed with another woman.

She and Chryssie flew home on Sunday. In the crowd of strangers at the airport, Christopher stood out, handsome, haggard, looking as if he'd missed them, too. While Katherine was cleaning the apartment on Monday, from an upended wastebasket, torn fragments of a note fluttered out. It was his handwriting; he must've written it to her, she thought, and with a rush of tenderness, knelt on the floor to piece it together. "I want you" was written on one scrap; on another, "more than any woman I've ever"; a third said, "If only you could love me"; the fourth was a salutation. Her heart stopped. The name was not hers but that of the office Lorelei, Sandra Lombard.

Confronted with the evidence, Christopher was non-communicative. Gradually Katherine gathered that the enchantress had given him little hope, thus turning his infatuation into obsession. "I have more in common with her than I do with you," he said once.

"Like what?" she managed to choke out.

"For instance," he said, "she's interested in silkscreen prints."

Unlike his wife's, Christopher's politics survived those dreary days. The marriage did not. For Christmas he gave himself a subscription to *The National Review* and a separate apartment, one with a sliver-sized view of the bay.

"Is there any chance he'll change his mind?" asked the priest from the shadows.

The old panic returned. "I don't know," Katherine said, adding in a rash desire to implicate the Church, "he says he can't be married to someone who won't practice birth control."

"Now you know that's a mortal sin. You mustn't endanger your immortal soul by going back to this man and using contraceptives."

"It's a mortal sin to get divorced, too, isn't it? Either way I go to hell."

The priest clicked his tongue against his teeth in irritation. How men hate it when women are logical, she thought. Christopher was always accusing her of being a Jesuit.

"It's not a mortal sin to get divorced. Only to remarry."

"Oh." That makes sense, she thought bitterly.

"You can live a good Christian life without being married."

"Without sex, you mean?"

"There are other kinds of love than having a bed partner."

The lump in her throat was jamming her vocal chords. "I'm twenty-three years old, Father," she managed to choke out. "Are you telling me that my sex life is over because I made one mistake?"

The question settled upon him like ash after a fire. In a muffled voice, he replied: "This is why the Church counsels against marrying a non-Catholic. Pray that God will enlighten him. We can do nothing without God. I will pray for you. Now, is there anything else?"

"No, Father," she whispered.

"For your penance, say three Our Fathers and five Hail Marys and make a good Act of Contrition."

"OmyGodIammostheartilysorry . . ."

The panel fell into place like the blade of a guillotine. Numbly, Katherine pulled aside the velvet curtain and stepped into the aisle. Since it was the Christmas season, there was a longer line than usual outside the confessional. She passed it with her head lowered, hiding her ravaged face, mouthing a childhood petition: "Lord, let me hide my pains and sufferings so that I may be the only one to suffer from them." What a singularly Catholic virtue was pain, she reflected; how it was embraced, even coveted in the convent as the royal way to salvation. Year after year, a fresh crop of green-jumpered girls punished their knees on chapel benches, chirping, "Hail, holy Queen, Mother of mercy, our Life, our Sweetness and our Hope. To thee do we come, to thee do we cry, poor, banished children of Eve." How poetic she had once found it to be an exiled daughter of Eve.

Now, after days of weeping, she felt only empty, drained of any emotion but hopelessness as she stood before a flickering field of votive candles that banked Our Lady's altar, looking up at the Virgin's face, a mask of sorrow contemplating three souls in purgatory who clutched at the hem of her chipped blue cloak. Katherine bowed her head like a prisoner in the dock. Sentence had been passed by Martin Rochambeau, assistant pastor, seventyish. Christopher's departure would rob her not only of a husband and a father for Christabel, but the state of sanctifying grace. Without the protection of the sacrament of matrimony, how was she to resist temptation for the next thirty or forty years? Something beyond the radiant personal warmth of John the Twenty-third had made her stop the car and weep openly when the news of his death came over the radio; it was a sense of doom for the Church. When would they allow his like to reign again? Her mother had already dismissed the reforms of the Vatican Council with a disdainful "That's all those foreign bishops."

Searching for a way like a lost traveler at a crossroad, Katherine found every path marked Damnation: divorce, going back to Christopher on his terms, remarriage. She shut her eyes, trying to think of a way out, but like a rusty wheel her mind clanked back to the sixth commandment: Thou shalt not commit adultery. At the mere thought of it, the flames of hell leapt close enough to scorch her soul. A voice came out of the past: Mother MacDowell, quoting Scripture: "Enter ye in at the strait gate: for wide is the gate and broad the way that leadeth to destruction, and many there be which go in thereat. Because strait is the gate, and narrow is the way which leadeth into life, and few there be that find it." Would "Foul" MacDowell approve of her at last, Katherine wondered, thrust by her husband's actions to the straightest, most dreaded gate of all, single blessedness?

The irony, she reflected, was that her marriage to Christopher had been an attempt to Do the Right Thing. At least to find someone who wouldn't fall under her mother's heading of "foreigners," a word delivered with opprobrium whether she was referring to the Italian clergy, the French boy Katherine had dated, or Neil Kolodny.

"It's as if a wicked fairy showed up at your baptism," Emily had said once, "to offset your God-given intelligence and goodness with one curse: bad judgment."

Unacceptable to her parents though Neil had been, Katherine doubted he would have abandoned her as cruelly as the socially desirable Chris Kellogg had done. How proud her bridegroom had been of his uncircumcised penis, she thought bitterly. "So much more aesthetic, don't you think?" he'd inquired, fondling the foreskin; whereupon she, a virgin bride who'd never seen another in the flesh, had demonstrated with that peculiar blend of pent-up passion and innocence common to convent girls how enthusiastically she agreed.

Something about being in church invariably turned her mind to sex, Katherine thought. She knelt to recite her penance, made the ritual promise to amend her life—out of her hands though that seemed to be—and emerged from the cathedral onto a wide sweep of granite steps leading to Van Ness Avenue, that boulevard of junk food stands and automobile showrooms. A sharp, moist wind that swept in from the bay blew her raincoat open. Without the energy to button it, she started down the steps, flinching at the steely light and jangling traffic noises.

A parking ticket fluttered beneath the windshield wiper of her blue convertible, the car her father had given her in drama school— could it be only three years ago? She didn't have the heart to tell him that his direst prediction had materialized. The last time she'd spoken to her parents on the phone, she'd pretended everything was normal. She got in and stared bleakly at the dashboard clock. Thank God Daddy's paying for kindergarten, she thought. Chryssie stayed till noon at the convent on California Street; that meant another hour to drive aimlessly up and down these damned hills, brooding about the rotten luck and (thanks, Mother) plain bad judgment that had gotten her into this fix.

Louise Asher came to Katherine's rescue. The two women had struck up a friendship in Los Angeles two years before; since then, they'd seen each other whenever Louise came to San Francisco to visit her widowed father. Her waist-length auburn hair was coiled into a bun at the nape of her neck; her flashing eyes darted into life's corners to ferret out absurdity and mock it; and though her profession was the rather mundane one of script girl at MGM, the richly colored caftans and native jewelry she wore gave her an exotic air, like that of a gypsy or an Italian diva.

At first, her visits had sustained Katherine through the isolation of a strange city and unremitting domesticity. Once Christopher jumped ship, her presence became an oasis in the desert of Katherine's empty days and nights: lonely weekends spent wandering through Tiburon; two sleeping pills at bedtime and when she awoke, two more to sleep again; Chryssie sent to the baby-sitter to avoid her being tainted by the pain; curtains drawn against the sunshine.

Though Louise had a large and generous heart, her acerbic wit tread a razor's edge of viciousness, making Katherine in her hypersensitive state sometimes wonder if she were there to commiserate or herald her downfall. At twenty-nine, Louise was unmarried. Like many people, she had considered Christopher Kellogg an ideal husband, an enviable catch in those days when a woman's worth was seen as a reflection in the eyes of the man who had married her. Now that he'd removed the mirror, Katherine's image was gone.

"Face it, Chris is a hard act to follow," Louise pointed out one sunny Sunday as they sauntered along the Sausalito wharf with Chryssie between them. "Especially in this town." She looked across the street at the No-Holds Bar, where stockbrokers came out of the closet to jostle drag queens, and the stale sweat-socks odor of amyl nitrate mingled with Canoe. "What are your choices? You can't sit around moping forever, praying he's going to come to his senses. You've got to *do* something, Kate. You've got to get a job."

"I know," Katherine groaned. "But after two years at Manhattanville, and two at Yale, guess what the employment agencies tell me."

"What?"

"I'm overqualified. Then they ask if I can run a PBX, whatever the hell that is, and when I say no, they say I'm *under*qualified. My education has equipped me to be an actress or a theology teacher."

The memory of her first foray into the world of the work force made Katherine cringe. Lacking training or contacts, she had consulted the Alice Ames Employment Agency, where a brisk but not unsympathetic interviewer had faced her across a Naugahyde-topped desk, working a wad of chewing gum as Katherine suggested, "I've had so many elocution lessons, I thought maybe I could be a receptionist."

"You're looking for a glamour job, honey," the woman had replied. "We give those to the eighteen-year-olds right out of school. How old is your child?"

"Two and a half."

"Who's going to take care of her?"

"In the afternoons, I'll get a sitter—"

"It wouldn't pay you for the salary you could get. You won't break even."

I know that, Katherine thought. But how else am I going to Meet People? *Tall* people, older than three. So far, her resources had been limited to the park.

The interviewer frowned and cracked her Juicy Fruit. "Why don't you try modeling? You're pretty and you're thin enough."

I'm thin enough for a March of Dimes poster after two months of being unable to swallow, Katherine thought. "I'm too old. I'm twenty-three."

There was an awkward pause.

"Listen, hon, I don't mean to butt in, but this isn't for you. Why don't you go back to your husband?"

"He doesn't want me back," Katherine told her in a tight voice. "But thank you very much for your help."

On her way down a flight of stairs that led to the grayness of Market Street, she heard the woman call from the top: "Don't say you're twenty-three—you look younger!" Turning, unable to trust herself to speak without tears starting, Katherine could muster only a shaky smile. Humiliation and hopelessness vied for the upper hand. She who in New Haven had been Juliet . . . Desdemona . . . Ophelia . . . had just been informed that in San Francisco, being a receptionist was considered glamorous!

Her alternatives had narrowed decidedly. Now that Christopher's key no longer turned in the lock each evening at six-thirty, she could not continue her marital pattern: mornings at Pacific Heights Park, children clambering over the jungle gym and digging in sandboxes as industriously as if they were getting paid for it (mothers, all older than Katherine, watching from wooden benches, *not* getting paid for it); afternoons while Chryssie napped and the jaws of her four-room, neo-Bauhaus trap closed around her, succumbing to a bad habit. It had started innocently enough—watching a friend from the drama school who had a television role. Insidiously, in the weekday void, it had become an addiction. Guilty, ashamed, while her body mechanically performed the housework, she had let her mind slide into the quicksand of soap opera: *As the World Turns, The Secret Storm, Search for Tomorrow*.

Once, when a lurid plot line had infiltrated her dinner table conversation, Christopher had snapped, "For Christ's sake, how can you watch that crap?"

"If I have to make the bed and do the dishes anyway, what difference does it make if the television is on?"

He'd enunciated slowly, as to an idiot; "Because, Katherine, your brain will atrophy."

"I don't see how it affects you," she'd snapped.

But Christopher was right. Certain arbitrary rules must be set. Some people will not drink before noon; from the day he left her, she would not turn on the television before the six o'clock evening news. Daytime viewing, unless it was a Senate investigation, represented a toboggan ride to suicide.

So she nodded sagely and said, "I know," when Louise Asher told her she had to "do" something; a job was not yet the panacea it was to become a decade later, but a logical prescription for an abandoned wife. Louise had had a head start. Without a legal male tie in whose reflected glory she could bask or cower, she had the motivation to pursue a career: survival. And as a plain high school girl in San Francisco, drilled by a critical father in the twin possibilities of poverty and spinsterhood, she had acquired a skill that Katherine, from her lofty plateau of privilege, had disdained. Louise typed.

For weeks Katherine twisted in fitful sleep, alone in the king-sized bed, waking to the foghorn's lugubrious alarm. She grew to loathe San Francisco: the perpetual mist, the perpendicular hills, Herb Caen's column. The women she knew, those older, complacent mothers in the park, were solicitous at first, then avoided her as if she had a communicable disease. It was a few years before divorce struck America like a medieval plague, but Katherine's case was a portent. Already she'd heard bits of information in ladies' rooms, snatches of conversations on a streetcar. California was the worst, they said. One in four.

Even Christopher, who had always deplored the idea of becoming a statistic, invoked *The Kinsey Report* in response to her suspicion that he'd betrayed her even before they separated. It was February, the hour late enough that Katherine had turned on the lights in the living room of the apartment to which he came as a frequent visitor (once free of the marital bonds, he'd rediscovered what a great "pal" she was, he told her); reflexively, he went around after her, turning them off to cut down on the electric bill. While she was preparing dinner, he came to the kitchen door and acknowledged, "I'm one of fifty percent of American men who've been unfaithful." It seemed that Sandra Lombard's commonality of interests had not, unfortunately, included *him*, and to console himself while his wife and daughter had been in Los Angeles, he'd taken up with a trio encountered in a Sausalito bookshop. "A couple about our age and her aunt, who was visiting from Sweden—recently divorced . . . bright and very simpatico, and apparently high up in government circles in Stockholm." The list of attributes prefaced his admission that he'd brought her home to their bed. "She's forty. It was strictly a one-night stand," he concluded dismissively.

Holding a wife's soggy bouquet of radishes and carrots, Katherine turned from the sink and saw him opening a fresh quart of vodka. Water ran up the sleeves of her yellow cashmere sweater and collected in puddles at the elbows. "Christopher, why don't you say it? Do you want a divorce?"

As if it were a chess pawn, he placed the bottle cap on a square of white tile. "I'm doing what I'm doing," he said after a moment. "It's up to you to react accordingly."

She stuffed the vegetables in the crisper. The refrigerator door closed. She leaned against it, a sense of ebbing energy rubberizing her bones. Married people fall into patterns, she reflected, and theirs was set: Christopher acted; she was acted upon. Between her weight loss and her vanishing spirit, she would soon be invisible.

So she did something rash. While he was in the bathroom, she went through his address book and found the unfamiliar Scandinavian name: G. Bergsson, with an address and phone number scribbled underneath. The next morning she dialed it. A woman answered. Katherine hung up and was there in ten minutes, pacing across from the house (a Charles Addams creation, she noted, one of the gabled Victorian jobs of which Christopher was so fond), undoing and doing up the brass buttons on her navy blue coat, nerving herself for the encounter. It was one of those mock-spring California days when one has to rack one's brain to remember what month it is; the sun was hot on her face but the trees were still in hibernation, their branches a black scrawl against the cerulean sky. The house was on the corner at the top of a steep incline. A random gust of wind carried her, as weightless as the flurry of leaves scuttling at her feet, into the crossing, and it occurred to her that San Francisco is an ideal city for alcoholics—drunk or sober, people walk at an angle. She took a deep breath and jabbed her finger against the bell.

A pretty, flaxen-haired woman of thirty or so came to the door. She had a round face and porcelain blue eyes that blinked when Katherine identified herself—a flicker of recognition, followed by something else: the pained, slightly embarrassed look of a witness to an accident, sympathetic but relieved it was not *her* blood on the pavement. Wordlessly, she conducted Katherine into a bright, incongruously modern living room and called out the name Gunilla. At the back of the house, a door swung open and another, older woman appeared, flicking back hair that was as pale and dry as hay. There was in her manner that curious blend of arrogance and reticence seen in certain Europeans traveling in America, as if they feel at once culturally superior and materially insecure. "How do you do?" she addressed Katherine pleasantly.

"This is Christopher's wife," said the younger woman, and Gunilla's welcoming smile faded.

For a long awkward moment, no one spoke. In vain Katherine searched Gunilla's face for some sign of recognition, or a scintilla of sex appeal. Had she come to the wrong house? Perhaps, in some grotesque comedy of errors, blundered in on someone *else's* husband's mistress? Her bewildered eyes sought out the younger woman's sympathetic gaze. "You do . . . know Christopher Kellogg?" she asked uncertainly.

"Oh, yes," came the firm reply, and as she left the room, she cast her aunt a look that was unmistakable. It said: See what you've done?

Gunilla Bergsson regarded the intruder with more resignation than alarm, like a practical nurse accustomed to dealing with hysterics. They sat opposite each other on straight-backed Danish chairs beside a bank of windows that looked onto the park where Chryssie played each day. Lines from a poem went through Katherine's head:

> *Pain has an element of blank;*
> *You cannot recollect when it began,*
> *Or if there were a day when it was not.*

But she knew she would remember that room forever: the flimsy russet furniture, daisies in a pottery jug on the coffee table, Marimekko pillows stacked on the bleached wooden floor, a child's hobby horse in the corner. A perfect stage set, but as in an actor's nightmare, she couldn't remember her lines or identify the play; was it Ibsen or Strindberg, and who was this aging actress with Ingrid Bergman's voice playing the Other Woman? It's not possible that Christopher went to bed with her, Katherine thought dazedly. She's not even a well-pre*serv*ed forty!

Gunilla was one of those fair-haired women who appear vanquished by life early on. In the unforgiving winter glare, her facial lines were deeply engraved, the skin on her neck the texture of dried apricots. Katherine's young eyes were fixed in fascinated horror to that neck as her mind played and replayed a film of Christopher and Gunilla in *her* bed. She tried to form a cogent explanation for her presence. Limping to a conclusion, she said, "Christopher hasn't told me what's wrong—or even if he wants a divorce. I thought he might have said something to you when you were . . . with him . . . something that would help me to understand . . ."

Her voice died like a gull's cry on the wind. She had counted on the complicity of women; now, with Gunilla's eyes blank upon her, she halted, her cheeks hot with humiliation. And in the ensuing silence, a sudden revelation sent residual nuggets of jealousy tumbling down a chute of horror: Gunilla bore a startling resemblance to Christopher's mother! The sensual Lindley mouth, the high-bridged nose, the morning glory eyes—she was a dead ringer for Jane Kellogg! Oh my God, Katherine said to herself, he's sicker than I thought.

As if they'd been discussing the weather, Gunilla made a gracious, noncommittal speech about how she understood why Katherine had come, but there was nothing she could recall that would shed any light on her situation. She turned her hands over on her lap in a gesture of helplessness. For an excruciating moment they stared at each other. Then Gunilla shrugged and said defensively, "He told me he was divorced."

A stone is hurled into a pond, ripples fan out: so Katherine's shock and hurt spread in ever widening circles. "Didn't you see the crib?" she asked.

Gunilla's eyes glazed over. She shook her head and rose, terminating the interview. As she ushered Katherine to the door, she said grimly, "Don't concern yourself that I'll tell Christopher we've spoken. I won't be talking to him again."

That evening, after Chryssie had fallen asleep, Katherine lingered in the nursery, sitting on the wide windowsill with her back to the courtyard, hugging her knees. The silence in the apartment was deafening. The man-in-the-moon mobile drifted over the crib and turned into Gunilla's broad-planed face. When the telephone rang, she snatched at it gratefully.

"Are you watching my apartment or what?" Christopher demanded without preamble.

"Watching your apartment?" she echoed dumbly, before the facts clicked into place: (1) Gunilla had told him; (2) they presumed Katherine had found her by staking out his apartment; (3) he had been sleeping with her all along . . . was still sleeping with her.

"She wanted to know how old you are," he said evenly. "When I told her, she asked how it was possible for anyone to have reached the age of twenty-three and know so little about the way life is."

"It's not the way life is!" The intolerable pressure on her heart burst and she began to sob convulsively. Christopher hung up.

The next day, a woman in the park told her about a Jesuit at the University of San Francisco. "He's a sociologist," she explained, "And his specialty is getting difficult annulments put through."

An annulment. A light at the end of the tunnel. Katherine made an appointment for the end of the week.

* * *

Terence Hartigan, S.J., Ph.D., leaned back in his chair and crossed his feet on the battered oak desk. Despite the meager setting—a large, sparsely furnished room with two curtainless windows—his office had an air of coziness. Katherine's gaze moved from the wall of books to the rugged masculine face studying hers. He resembled no other priest she had ever seen. Thick brown hair curled past his Roman collar almost to his burly shoulders; his nose, which appeared to have been broken more than once, streaked like a lightning bolt across his face; and his voice was low and guttural. None of the patina of piety common to parish priests clung to him; his speech was direct, forthright, the language of the streets. But in his dark eyes burned the fire of Divine love. Father Hartigan was a man with a passion for God; it motivated his life and at times gave him the air of a romantic poet. Among the intellectual religious, she had known only one other like him, Mother Manning at Prince Street, who had once paraphrased a line from an introduction to Blake's poems: "Those with true vocations are lovers under another name."

Harrowing as the events of the last weeks had been, Katherine found herself relating them dispassionately, like a journalist more concerned with accuracy than emotion. In the brief silence that followed her recapitulation, Father Hartigan gave a curious smile. "It's odd," he said, "You tell it as if it happened to someone else. We'll have to find out who you are under all that."

His words took her by surprise. She looked at him and, under his penetrating gaze, felt the wall of ice she'd constructed around herself begin to melt. It was painful, frightening, but at least her blood was flowing again.

In the weeks that followed, like a shaman Father Hartigan wielded the power of a gifted healer, serving as Katherine's psychiatrist, counselor, confidant, and friend. Once he told her, "Christopher is right to hate the kind of Catholic you are. You're all laws and no love." As time went on, he expressed his frustration with a moribund Church, "an institution of old men in skirts," and confided his problems with the establishment. On a windy evening in March, when he was escorting her through the darkened campus to the parking lot, he told her with a degree of pride that he had been banned in Oakland.

"After my last sermon there, the archbishop forbade me to come into his diocese."

"What did you say to warrant that?" she asked.

"Something subversive," he said with a glint in his eye, "like, 'God is love.' "

Christopher, an admirer of the writings of Hans Küng, the liberal German theologian, expressed a desire to meet Katherine's rebel priest.

They had two long sessions together.

"He seems perceptive," Christopher acknowledged afterward.

Encouraged, Katherine asked Father Hartigan if he thought there was a chance of salvaging the marriage.

"For a marriage to succeed, both people have to try," he replied. "Christopher doesn't seem to want to try."

Agonized over Chryssie's love for him, terrified of the future, Katherine stubbornly allowed herself to be buffeted by the shifting winds of her estranged husband's behavior: evenings when he dropped in to sleep with her; others when he borrowed the car, returning it in the morning with its ashtray clogged with lipstick-stained cigarette butts. In a last-ditch attempt to restore herself to the girl he had fallen in love with, she went to work for the Committee to Elect Henry Cabot Lodge President. Then her father sent her a check for Easter. She cashed it and took Chryssie to Los Angeles for a week at the Sinclairs' beach house.

Alison's parents had known Katherine since she was seventeen. Staying with them in their sprawling Malibu villa, not unlike the lake house, made the intervening years drop away. Alison, whose dusky beauty, sweet nature, and placid temperament attracted men in droves, divided her time between a carefree round of party-going and dating and one of those glamour jobs—girl Friday to a movie star. It was hard to believe they were the same age, Katherine thought one evening as she sat on Alison's bed, listening to her chatter about her hectic social life. Why had she gotten married? How could she have thrown away her youth? Katherine asked herself. Moments later, Chryssie passed the door, looked in and said, "Hi, sweetie darling Mommy," and the questions evaporated.

The beach held a special allure for Katherine at that time of year, deserted by all but the surfers in their coves. One morning, as she and Chryssie tramped across the sand to the water's edge, she paused to gaze at the northern coastline jutting into the sea. The sky was cloudless and radiant. Breathing in the salty air, she suddenly felt her heart expand as if an iron band around it had loosened, releasing a torrent of pent-up pain. The waves swelled and subsided as always; there was something reassuring about their permanence. For the first time in months, she saw beyond the narrow vision of her own suffering and perceived, in the breadth of the horizon, some eternal plan. It occurred to her suddenly: The worst is over; from this time on the healing begins. Chryssie reached up; Katherine grasped her hands and spun her around until they fell in a giddy heap on the sand.

The day they returned to San Francisco, spring had come with its febrile promise of new beginnings. Katherine's personal renewal was not lost on Christopher, but his next attempt to induct her into his harem without resuming their conjugal state failed.

Father Hartigan advised them to break off all communication for six months. "No phone calls, letters, nothing. It's a desperate measure," he told Katherine, "but sometimes it works."

It was all she needed. She called her parents to tell them about the separation, consoled her mother as best she could, and gratefully accepted Douglas's offer to reinstate her allowance. In June, when Chryssie's kindergarten was over and the lease on the apartment had expired, Katherine bequeathed the Breuer electric chair and the homemade curtains to Christopher, packed her daughter, their clothes, and the AM/FM radio he had given her for her twenty-fourth birthday into the Ford, and fled to her friends in the south. Five miles outside of San José, she stopped the car at the side of the freeway, got out, and tore the Lodge for President sticker off the bumper.

CHAPTER 7

Worldly Vanities

All along, Katherine told herself that she'd go back to Christopher if he pulled himself together. It was her duty—to God, to Chryssie, and to Rochester. Father Hartigan had correctly surmised the effect Katherine's absence would have upon her husband; after a few weeks Christopher wrote to suggest a reconciliation. As she read the letter, she wondered what sociological principle the priest had applied. Was it necessary for a man to lose a woman in order to realize that he loved her? Was it human nature to be profligate about what one possesses and lust after the unattainable? In any case it no longer mattered—the Jesuit's plan fell through because of something none of them had foreseen: her own change of heart.

Driving down Wilshire Boulevard three years before, seeing it through Christopher's eyes, she had recoiled at the ugliness of the flat landscape littered with packing boxes masquerading as offices and banks. She'd thought, A person's soul must shrivel up and die in this place. But all in all, she was happy there. After twenty years among rigid easterners, years enduring bleak winter twilights when church bells tolled reminders of boarding at the convent, she welcomed the glaring white light, the hot sirocco-like winds, and the insouciant rootlessness of Southern Californians. So she stalled, writing Christopher that she needed more time to heal. Too soon to face the windy slopes of San Francisco, the unresolved problems, the mornings waking beside a spouse whose parting words had been: "I love you, Katie, but I don't think you can be *in* love with someone who carries in the groceries with you." Once she shepherded Chryssie through the difficult days of adjustment, she felt a rush of exhilaration, a shot of pure joy that she'd experienced before in Los Angeles and attributed to the city's matchless climate, but was now, in fact, an awareness of being young and pretty enough to turn heads in the street, and a sense—such as had overtaken her only as a student in Paris—of being completely free. She embraced it after the numbing months of pain in San Francisco.

Staying in a motel on Wilshire Boulevard lent a holiday aspect to the first weeks of that hot bright summer of Katherine's release. Chryssie was lonesome for her father, but since divorce was not an issue—the word was never mentioned—she adapted quickly to her mother's cheerful mood and spent hours splashing happily in the swimming pool. A privileged background gives one a taste for a vagabond existence; to support theirs, bit by bit Katherine divested herself of the stock certificates that Douglas had given her for a rainy day; she could not conceive of a wetter one. Through Alison and Louise she made friends, was invited to parties, and discovered to her amazement that "Foul" MacDowell was on to something—single blessedness was not such a sorry state after all. On the Fourth of July they moved into a furnished apartment in the flats of Beverly Hills, and shortly thereafter, as a further sign of independence, Katherine gave a cocktail party. In the fall she filled in for a vacationing assistant at an art gallery and put Chryssie in nursery school. Each step took them further from their former life.

Six months passed. Christopher wrote again, asking Katherine to return. Toward him she felt no more rancor, nor was there anything left of remorse or regret, only an occasional pang when Chryssie parroted a phrase of his or mirrored his smile. Toward their daughter, she felt overwhelming love and responsibility. If Chryssie said yes . . . Katherine took a breath and read bits from the letter at supper one evening, then asked how she felt about returning to San Francisco. "I don't know, Mommy," the little girl replied, her eyes grave and terribly practical. "We'll go back, and Daddy won't come, and you're going to be so crazy in your life." Katherine laughed. "Thanks very much, Cassandra. What is that—the curse of the cat people?"

One art gallery led to another. Katherine took a permanent job and told Christopher she wasn't prepared to make any decisions. Emotionally she drifted. In time the gloss of Los Angeles faded. After another six months she felt like Violante, the heroine of Proust's story "Worldly Vanities," which tells of a country girl who goes out of curiosity to the Austrian court with the firm intention of returning to her beloved Styria, but in the end, although without illusion about the emptiness and superficiality of Viennese society, she stays on, held by "a force which, if nourished from the first by vanity, will overcome disgust, contempt and even boredom: and that is habit."

On a cool December morning, with high clouds scudding across the sun, Katherine walked the few blocks from her apartment to the Le Fèvre Gallery on little Santa Monica Boulevard, trying not to notice the gaudy ribbons festooning the lampposts or the Disney reindeer bridging the traffic lights or the Christmas tree lot on the corner, whose Scotch pines were sprayed pink and dusted with Styrofoam snow. The parade of Rolls-Royces and foreign sports cars was commencing early on Rodeo Drive. Christmas is a time of reckoning for the film community: backs are scratched; palms greased; obeisance paid to those currently, if precariously, in power; acknowledgment made by grateful directors to mistresses and grips; wives assuaged; debts paid off. People who have everything outdo themselves for those who have more.

While Katherine's sensibilities were offended by the excess, at the same time they were becoming hardened by her environment, a rarefied one in which awareness of another kind of life gradually eroded. In Southern California, realities of the human condition are blurred in the aeonian glare of the sun, the surf, the white-hot sand, the thwacking of tennis balls across a thousand courts, the prodigious prosperity, the notion that this is Paradise, and if you're clever enough to have found it, you must deserve it. In the tumultuous sixties, the city's one major family-owned newspaper frequently consigned unpleasant world events to back pages. Mention racial strife to some, and they thought of their problems getting a green card for the cleaning woman. White Angelenos were nothing so much as baffled by the Watts riots; from the freeway, the ghetto in the nether region of peaceful Pasadena seemed a pleasant, well-kept place, better than most. Why, they've got white fences around their houses, people were heard to say in puzzled tones after the conflagration. The seeds of Katherine's budding social conscience fell on hard ground in Beverly Hills, where girls who had failed math at Beverly High knew the exact footage of their new houses and their husbands' incomes to the last decimal; where Bel Air matrons dropped into the

Le Fèvre Gallery in search of a Van Dongen, say, to go with Valerian Rybar's walls, or an Utrillo with just the right dominant color to match the Scalamandré draperies (which they called drapes); where young wives of aging movie moguls picked out Renoirs and Chagalls for their boudoirs. Such random aggrandizement suited the gallery's owner, a rakish middle-aged bachelor emigré from Lyon named Didier Le Fèvre, with a mane of chestnut-colored hair and a Maurice Chevalier accent—the sort that grows thicker with every year in America. Like more than one canny art dealer, he publicly pandered to his film world clientele while maligning them behind their backs. "Why did Moses lead his people into the desert?" he had typically asked Katherine once, then cackled, "Because he was ashamed to bring them to the city!" Every afternoon Didier played golf at the Los Angeles Country Club, whose white wrought-iron gates barred many of his clients by virtue of their profession or religion. Didier would go to any length to sell a picture, but drew the line at playing golf at Hillcrest, a club he called Grossing-garish West.

When Katherine arrived, her employer was descending the spiral staircase from his office in anticipation of the arrival of Sandy Cohen, the bride of entrepreneur and collector Abel C. Cohen, who had recently acquired a Vuillard. Moments later a burgundy Bentley drew up to the curb, the chauffeur opened the door, and out stepped a particularly Hollywood Cinderella.

A shy salesgirl at Robinson's until Cohen secured a divorce from his wife of thirty years to marry her, the young strawberry blonde now dripped with jewelry and chattered incessantly as Didier ushered her inside. Her breasts, once flat as a boy's, were cantilevered over her slender frame. Clouds of mink billowed around her ankles as she leaned over, squinting at the framed painting that Didier propped against the wall. *"Voilà!"* he exclaimed. *"Un vrai chef d'oeuvre.* You are to be congratulated on your choice, Madame Cohen."

"It sure is little," Sandy whined, "but it's goin' in Abe's bathroom and he loves it, so what the hell." When Didier whisked the painting upstairs to secure the wire, she slipped her fur off her shoulders and gave Katherine a cursory glance at her desk. "Jeeze, it's hot in here," she said. "Am I ever glad I don't have to do this shit anymore."

Her voice was reminiscent of Judy Holliday's in *Born Yesterday*, Katherine thought, smiling at her pleasantly.

Didier returned and guided his client to the door, saying, *"Peut-*

être Monsieur Cohen is aware that Vuillard is one of the Nabis—this is actually a Hebrew word meaning 'prophet.' "

"Ya don't say," Sandy replied as she went out.

On his way back through the gallery, Didier remarked to Katherine, "She probably thinks I mean p-r-o-f-i-t. That's the only language that group understands." Promptly and without a trace of irony, he asked to see the invoice, exulting over the price fetched by the Vuillard, and pointing out, "It was not one of his better periods."

Her lunch hour could not come soon enough.

Shortly before noon, she left to meet Louise Asher at the Cañon Drive Nutrition Center. A taste for health food was one of the habits Katherine had acquired that she ascribed directly to the move to the West Coast three years earlier. ("We're doing all the California things," she'd told Christopher once. "Playing tennis on Christmas, eating macrobiotic food, and getting a divorce.") Since she was a few minutes early, she decided to run into Tiffany's to see Eve Pratt, a friend who was working there for the holidays. The store was small, no more than the size of a living room in many of its customers' opulent houses; at the noon hour it was bedlam, filled with strident voices demanding attention. Eve's moon face, flushed under its cap of ginger hair, floated into view across the room. Katherine waved, then browsed through the tray of silver trinkets until Eve broke away from her customer and came over to say hello. She appeared more harassed than usual; that morning a fledgling actress had loudly chewed her out for a faulty monogram on stationery intended for her agent.

"I was tempted to quit on the spot . . . *any*thing rather than be humiliated by one of those transients whose careers have all the brilliance and life span of a firefly. God! You should see the loot she bought," Eve said disgustedly.

"Did she get many of these?" Katherine laughed, holding up a sterling silver toothpaste-tube squeezer suitable for engraving. "Los Angeles is unreal. Nowhere in America is money so recently acquired, so unstable, so corrupting and"—she added, thinking of Sandy Cohen—"so ingenuous. You would not bel*ieve* what goes on at Le Fèvre's."

"Speaking of the gallery, how's your divine boss?"

"Divine?" Katherine snorted. "He's a lecherous old goat."

"He's not a day over fifty. Listen," Eve said, her eyes sparkling with the light of matchmaking, "I have a friend I want you to meet. I've known him for years. You two might really hit it off. Not for a romance necessarily—he's reclusive, and you don't dig older men. But you'll have an interesting evening. He's very, very funny, and he has the most beautiful house in Los Angeles."

"What's his name?"

"Jed Bernard."

"That sounds vaguely familiar."

"He's a writer," Eve explained, looking nervously over her shoulder as the store manager approached. "So is it all right if I give him your number? You won't be sorry," she promised as she rushed off.

Louise Asher straddled a stool at the counter of the Nutrition Center, eyeing a carrot balefully. A wool caftan flowed around her ample figure. When Katherine slid onto the stool next to her, Louise gave her an appraising look with her dark eyes, which were outlined with kohl, and remarked, "You're looking even more quintessentially California than usual today. All that blond hair and white teeth—you'd think you didn't have a brain in your head. Don't men find it terribly confusing?"

Katherine laughed. "What it does is attract the wrong kind." She ordered a vegetable salad and a carob shake.

They talked about work and a married director who was pursuing Louise; then, between munches of a stalk of celery, Louise said, "Remember when you first came down here? You swore that in six months you were either going back to Christopher or moving to New York. What happened to that plan?"

"Things change," Katherine replied vaguely. "One sort of . . . gets a life. Chryssie's school . . . friends . . . a job. Right now I don't feel I can take Chryssie that far away from her father. Depending on what happens, we'll go back East someday. You know how I feel about Los Angeles—it's a great place to live, but I wouldn't want to die here."

"Christmas is the dregs in L.A., isn't it? Not a good time of the year to be single."

"I always feel like the Little Match Girl at Christmastime anyway, with my nose pressed against the glass to watch tableaux of happy families. Have you ever noticed how all the cars on the road turn into station wagons with fathers at the wheel?"

"Is Christopher coming down?" Louise asked.

"It's not definite. I'm making contingency plans. Nothing elaborate—just a week at Disneyland and buying a controlling interest in F.A.O. Schwarz."

"The trouble is, you'll never replace him. Not in this zoo of transplanted midwesterners and show biz types. You'll never meet anyone with Chris's class."

Katherine gave a wry smile. "Listen. Let me tell you what I've learned about class. Half of those golden graduates of St. Grottlesex are drunks. They've been inbreeding ever since they came over on the Mayflower, and all some of them have left are high foreheads and weak characters."

Louise examined the gold ankh that hung from a chain around her neck, turning it to and fro as she said, "I always thought being Mrs. Christopher Lindley Kellogg was part of the attraction."

"Don't rub it in. I paid for my youthful snobbery with four years of Thanksgiving dinners spent talking about great-great-great-grandfather Governor Bradford and the first turkey in Plymouth!"

The waiter removed Katherine's plate and poured tea into Louise's cup. When he'd moved off, Louise asked pointedly, "Then why don't you get a divorce?"

"God, I hate that word!" Katherine said with a shudder. "It's the worst one in the English language."

"Have you even *talked* to a lawyer?"

"There's a Spanish curse: 'May your life be filled with lawyers.' If it comes to that, I hope to get an annulment."

"What?" Louise's yelp startled a pale young man on a neighboring stool. Heedless, she shrieked, "You've got a four-year-old child! On what possible grounds?"

Dropping her voice, Katherine explained, "Canon lawyers are admitting a new form of evidence, according to Father Hartigan—similar to when civil courts introduced psychological evidence. His opinion is that Chris was incapable of making a commitment to a Catholic marriage, or even understanding what that means." Above the rim of her cup, Louise's expression was bemused. "It's complicated," Katherine said dismissively.

"What intelligent person is concerned with anything as irrelevant as religion in this day and age?" Louise inquired.

"There are a few of us left," Katherine laughed. "Graham Greene, Maritain, Camus, Teilhard de Chardin. I admit that Chryssie already has a better attitude about it than I do."

"You're not bringing her up Catholic, are you? After all the trouble it's caused you?"

"Yes, I am. But without the hysteria. I mean, I don't snatch the meat out of her hands on Ember Days the way my father did." Katherine looked at her watch and signaled for the check. "What can I tell you, Lou? They got me. They got me early, and I bought the whole thing—objective right and wrong, the Immaculate Conception, the Holy Ghost, transubstantiation—all of it. There's just no way to explain faith. It's a gift and a curse. Right now, I sort of think of myself as being on sabbatical."

Louise leaned over to see the check, and with her head close to Katherine's, inquired, "Is that because you're sleeping with Andrew Byrne?" Color flooded Katherine's face at the reference to the young photographer with whom she was having what she hoped was a secret affair. "If you believe all the Catholic bullshit, how do you justify *that?* Isn't it considered a mortal sin?" Louise persisted.

Reaching for her wallet, Katherine gave a significant sigh. "I'm in such trouble anyway, I suppose I figure I might as well be hung for a sheep as a lamb," she said, and plunked down a five-dollar bill.

As Katherine walked back to the art gallery in the sulphurous sunshine, Louise's questions rankled; their roots took hold in her mind, forcing her to face a moral issue that she tried always to keep at bay, reminding her how she had felt upon opening that particular Pandora's box.

Calvin Hollingshead the Third. Ironic that this cold clinical preppie should have been the man with whom she had committed her first adulterous act. It must have been because he was so aggressive, she told herself, for she had refused more likable candidates, and now, more than a year later, it was the only thing she remembered about him. That and the fact that he was from out of town (which made the whole thing so much easier), a Canadian who was in Los Angeles for the week of his Dartmouth roommate's wedding.

For the first three months in Los Angeles, Katherine had been staunchly celibate. Her fall from grace came at the end of August, when tropical days that sapped ambition and cauterized serious thoughts were followed by starry nights that made one yearn for romance. Louise might well ask how Catholics justify having sex outside marriage, she thought now. The truth is, they *don't* justify it. They just do it. Perhaps because their concept of original sin gives them an understanding of human frailty, they sin, knowing it is wrong, and hope for forgiveness.

In Katherine's case, as usually happens when one is young and impetuous and passion bubbles below the surface like a natural spring, matter had prevailed over mind. Her spirit had willed the months of chastity, but at last she could no longer resist the pull of strong male arms . . . an attractive young man whispering flattering things in her ear . . . her own body straining toward his. When she finally succumbed, she murmured, "The decline and fall of Katherine Kellogg," as he pulled her into her bedroom.

An hour or so later, when the fumbling act was finished and the stranger (who, Katherine decided, must have learned sexual technique from his nation's Royal Mounted Police: "Hold it . . . slow down . . . faster . . . move to the right . . . ," etc.) had crept into the night, she'd felt an urge to check for a scarlet letter under her bangs. What had seemed Ernest Hemingway before the fact was pure C. S. Lewis after; she understood the awful frustration described in *The Screwtape Letters* at being damned for something that wasn't even fun. As she'd pulled on a robe, a fragment from "The Waste Land." had buzzed in her head:

> *When lovely woman stoops to folly and*
> *Paces about her room again, alone,*
> *She smoothes her hair with automatic hand,*
> *And puts a record on the gramophone.*

"Bless me, Father, for I have sinned. It's been six months since my last confession. I committed adultery once."

It being the Church of the Good Shepherd in Beverly Hills, scene of Elizabeth Taylor's first wedding and countless funerals of movie stars, there was hardly a flap, only the automatic "For your penance, say five Our Fathers and make a good Act of Contrition."

"OmyGodIammostheartilysorry. . . ."

"Live day by day," Father Hartigan had said. "Don't think in terms of twenty years."

Absolved, she would begin again.

Five months later she met Andrew Byrne. Their first physical encounter caught fire, and when the pattern of their passionate nights became consistent, she could no longer sincerely promise to amend her life; confessions were made only in the event of a plane trip; furthermore, in this state of mortal sin, what was the point of going to Mass? The fact that Andy was a Catholic, lapsed or not, only increased her culpability: two souls damned on her account.

Andy was twenty-seven, cast in the mold of strong, silent, blond movie stars like Alan Ladd, much in demand professionally as a freelance photographer, and socially as that rara avis, an urban heterosexual bachelor. Although Katherine objected openly to the sardonic facade with which he camouflaged an endearing vulnerability, even more undermining were her secret, superficial reservations: with his water-combed hair, his Southern California accent (not unlike that indigenous to upstate New York), his narrow collars, ties and lapels, his parochial school background, Andy was redolent of Rochester. At times she felt almost incestuous with him, so similar was he to her male cousins from St. Thomas Aquinas High School. Underlying all this was a sense that this man of like upbringing, this Irish Catholic who'd been an altar boy and traveled in her set, *knew* and might *tell* what she was really like. The thought sent a hot flush to her face.

For a time she had experimented with being "bad" for its own sake. Rereading St. Augustine, she'd searched through his *Confessions* for examples of voluptuousness that paralleled her own. But intense pleasure with Andrew was always followed by such harrowing guilt that the next day she'd find herself shaking with tremors as she sat at her desk at the art gallery. Her inability to excuse their sins of the flesh baffled him.

"Aside from everything else," she'd explained once, "I'm still married."

His smile had turned cynical. "That's why it's called adultery, Katherine. It's for adults."

She'd found excuses: It's based on love . . . it's the sin God most easily forgives . . . I'm not hurting anyone—nobody's wife, nobody's children—certainly not Christabel, whom she took great pains to shield. The only one who was being hurt was . . .

And at that point, more and more adept at blocking out what she wished to avoid, she would mentally change the subject. So the thought had lain, like a sleeping monster at the back of her mind, until Louise Asher prodded it awake. The real damage was to herself.

***

By the beginning of December, Katherine's affair with Andrew had begun to unravel under the strain of her guilt and a sense of incompleteness. Recently, in the aftermath of passion, he'd told her, "I'm torn between losing you and losing my freedom." The bachelor's anthem, she'd thought; since she was not even divorced, she was hardly a threat to his freedom. Was it his uncertainty that was making her so restless? she asked herself on the way back to the gallery after lunch with Louise.

That evening, driving with Andy to one of the promotional restaurant openings that he was frequently assigned to cover, he said something that revived Katherine's theory that God was a practical joker, up there moving people around like pawns on a chessboard, laughing Himself silly. The conversation had drifted into one of Andy's lengthy movie critiques, which always made her mind wander; only half listening, she could tell from his expression that it was another case of more joy in Hollywood over one failure than a dozen successes.

". . . without a doubt the worst piece of crap I've had to sit through this year!" he was saying. "How they got three major stars to do it is a mystery. You have to wonder if they even read the script."

He paused as if expecting a response, so she asked distractedly, "Who wrote it?"

"An old Hollywood hack named Jed Bernard," he replied, flicking his cigarette out the window.

Katherine sat up very straight. "Really?"

"Yeah. Why?"

"It's the second time I've heard his name today. What do you know about him?"

"Oh, you remember—*Time* called him the boy wonder in the forties."

"What else has he done?"

"Those old radio shows—*Pasquale's World* and *Living with Tessie.*"

"*Living with Tessie?*" Katherine cried. "I loved that program! Eve Pratt knows him. She says he's the funniest man in Hollywood."

A stricken look passed across Andy's face; immediately he covered the reaction with a sardonic smile. "She trying to set you up with him? He's a bit long in the tooth for you, old girl."

Beams of white light strafed the sky over La Cienega Boulevard. Andy turned into a brick courtyard in front of the restaurant, where a gray Greek chorus of photographers clustered at the entrance scanning the arriving guests hopefully. When the sequined, tangerine-tressed starlet Georgia Jerome flounced from her Mercedes convertible followed a few respectful paces behind, like a caricature of queen and consort, by the gossip columnists' favorite dentist to the stars, Dr. Melvin Sprague, the paparazzi went berserk. Blinking against the glare of flashbulbs, Katherine thought how refreshing it would be to go to a party that wasn't held in a restaurant or a store, a party without klieg lights. The place was a Nathanael West nightmare, a silver Quonset hut shaped like a whale, the front door painted iridescent blue, the threshold studded with jagged plastic teeth. An image came into her mind of Dr. Sprague running amok and attacking with a pneumatic drill. At the entrance, Andy said hello and good-bye to the *Times* food critic, a plump woman named Siri, who was already on her way out. "I mean, what can you say to people who serve a chopped chicken liver swan?" she hissed. "Take me to your Leda?" Katherine suggested, drawing a guffaw from Andy.

It was eleven-thirty before Andy felt he had enough rolls of film to satisfy his picture editor. "Definitely a C group," he commented as they drove away, turning onto the dark and ghostly stillness of Wilshire Boulevard. "Want to get a drink somewhere?"

"I'm exhausted. Do you mind just taking me home?"

After a moment's silence, he asked, "Are you going to go out with this Bernard guy?"

The jealous note in his voice was unwelcome; Katherine had forgotten about Jed Bernard. "It was only to meet him, not a date."

"Interesting distinction," he said testily.

"This is hardly an assignation, Andy. You said yourself he's old. What must he be—forty? Forty-five, even?"

"But he's a *celebrity*, Katie. That gives you a chance to be a star-fucker like all the other tootsies in this town."

Katherine narrowed her eyes at him.

Oblivious, Andy continued, "Well, he's not really a star anymore, but he was married to one. You look a lot like her, as a matter of fact—Laura Loder."

"Mmmm . . . so I've been told."

"So"—he gave a harsh laugh—"that'll make it at least star-fucker fucking."

After a shocked silence, she said, "I have your permission, then?"

He shrugged. "Go ahead. It'll give you some new material." A moment later, he stopped outside her apartment building. In one swift, angry movement she yanked open the car door and got out.

"What the hell's the matter with you?" Andrew demanded, struggling to catch up with her as she crossed the grass divider to the sidewalk.

"What's the matter is your damned attitude!" she said without turning. "I don't monitor what *you* do, so where do you get off trying to control my life?" Her anger was out of proportion; even though she recognized it as fallout from a larger issue, she felt unable to change course, like a child hurtling down a slide.

"Calm down," Andrew said, the worst possible response. "I was kidding."

She whirled around. "How *dare* you call me a star-fucker?" she flashed at him, then stalked into her building, leaving him dumbfounded in the street.

Once the baby-sitter was paid and the door bolted behind her, depression seeped in at the edges of Katherine's anger. A parade of voices trooped out of the past: her father ("You'd better learn to control that temper of yours, young lady"), "Foul" MacDowell ("Woe betide you if you fail to correct this character flaw"), Neil Kolodny ("How do you expect to stay married if you won't take shit from a guy once in a while?")

Her hand on the wall switch, she glanced around the living room—no more than a hotel room really, with its monochromatic dove gray furnishings and vulgar gold-leaf trimmings—tasteless and more than she could afford, but for the time being it suited her. Everything about it said Temporary.

A little sighing sound came from the alcove off the dining area, where Chryssie slept on a pullout couch; she was lying on her back, one arm flung out, the other cradling a stuffed kitten. Katherine went to her, brushed back her yellow bangs, and dropped a kiss above the line of her eyebrows. Pulling up the quilt, she realized the little girl's conversation had been peppered lately with references to her father, now that there was a chance of seeing him soon. Katherine could hardly recall a Christmas that had not been fraught with pain; she vowed this one would not be so for her daughter, even though calamity seemed to cling to it like a tick. She sifted through the current opinions on sharing one's bed with a child. Psychiatrists and Dr. Spock advised against it. The pediatrician, Dr. Erwin Marcus, had responded to Katherine's query with a shrug. "What can I tell you? In the ghetto we were too poor for Dr. Spock. Five of us slept in one bed. My brother's a *faygeleh* and I'm perfectly normal."

"Four wives to you is perfectly normal?" she'd laughed.

Another, bigger shrug. "I didn't say I was perfect."

Dr. Marcus makes more sense than any shrink, Katherine thought, scooping up Chryssie and the kitten and carrying them in to her bed. But sleep was slow to come. She got up and went to the bookcase where, from a row of novels, she extracted *A Burnt-Out Case*, the latest from Graham Greene, her literary mentor in preoccupation with sin and guilt. It was a restless night; early-morning dreams merged with traffic noises to produce a recurring childhood nightmare of Nazi soldiers scouring the neighborhood while she, attempting to flee, found herself rooted to the spot.

"I hear you look like Grace Kelly and you have a daughter named Christabel."

The voice on the telephone was low and rasping, and Katherine knew immediately who it was. Her room was dark now, at six o'clock; after another day of stultifying boredom at the art gallery, she had left Chryssie playing cards in the living room with Abby, the little girl who lived down the hall, and collapsed on the bed.

"Well," she said, sitting up on the edge, lighting the bedside lamp, "I do have a daughter named Christabel."

"You don't look like Grace Kelly? I'm hanging up."

She started to laugh, revived by his bantering tone. "Who is this?"

"My name is Jed Bernard, madam. Possibly you've heard of me from Eve Pratt?"

"Oh, yes, of course. Hello. How are you?"

"If I knew how I was, I wouldn't be in analysis. Did she tell you that I myself have a daughter named Christabel?"

"No! Really? That's amazing—"

"Seemed odd to me," he said.

"It's such an uncommon name." Fate? she wondered. No, unlikely. There was not a trace of youth in his voice. "Uhh . . . Who do *you* look like?"

"I'll send you a shot of me as a young man. You'll cry like a baby—I do. Now tell me, did you name your kid after Christabel Rivers, too? Only women I should have married, by the way."

"No, Chryssie is named after her father, Christopher."

"Of course. Chris Kellogg—little short Jewish fella, right? My governess used to tell me about such people in the Winter Palace. We had *heard* there were Jews in the village, but no one ever saw them." He went on talking with a kind of manic volubility that stimulated Katherine even as it put her at ease. The fact that they were strangers had almost slipped her mind when he said, "I must insist that you describe yourself to me, madam. This is an expensive call and I have three others to make."

"There are days when I look like Imogene Coca," she said cheerfully.

"It's lawsuit time. I'm suing Eve for my dime!" he yelled.

"Other times"—she hesitated—"well, maybe I should warn you, I've been told I look like Laura Loder."

There was a silence. Then: "Hello, operator, what number is this? I think you've given me the wrong number."

Katherine laughed again, though she sensed a streak of bitterness beneath the joke.

"Perhaps we should meet anyway," he said. "Would you like to come up to my house for a drink? This isn't a proposition, mind you. But I don't . . . *date*." His tone reduced that activity to the lowest form of human endeavor. "My house is a special kind of place. I'd like you to see it."

She hesitated.

"You checking your dance card for the cotillion, kid?"

"Did you mean this evening?" she inquired.

"No, I mean a month from now. Of course this evening—you think I plan these things ahead of time? Which is it, yes or no?" he barked.

"I just got home. I'd have to change and—"

"Forget it. You're out."

"No . . . no, I'd like to, really. Would seven be all right?"

"Fine. You'll be out by eight. On the other hand, you may never leave the hill." He gave her the address, adding, "I'd pick you up, but my car won't go in a cheap neighborhood." Indignation rendered her momentarily speechless; then she realized he had no idea where she lived. His jocular tone turned to honey. "Forgive me this one time, will you? I promise I'll make it up to you."

She hung up, thinking ominously, Famous last words.

The first time Katherine saw Jed Bernard, he was standing at the top of a flight of stone steps leading to his garden, smoking a meerschaum pipe. A white floodlight from the roof of the house shone on her face as she ascended the stairs—a theatrical ploy, she decided, to put one at a disadvantage. His voice came out of the shadows, growling a greeting, and she thought again how old he sounded. But then he came into focus and she caught her breath. Tall, with jet black hair, he wore a dark green cashmere turtleneck sweater under a tweed jacket with a Continental cut. His face was suntanned, his nose proud and fiercely aquiline, his eyes an unusual shade of light brown—the eyes of a Slavic poet, their kindliness belied by the cruel line of his mouth and the deep, sensual cleft in his chin. Max De Winter at the gates of Manderley, she thought . . . Heathcliff on the moors. No, said an inner voice. Philip Roth perfected. Every girl's dream of the Jewish writer.

"Welcome to Mayerling," he said, puffing on his pipe, his eyes never leaving Katherine's face as she took the first steps of a journey whose course had been plotted long, long before.

CHAPTER 8

Mayerling

"You managed to find the house without any trouble?" Jed's voice sounded rough, like the cinder path where he stood.

"Yes . . . I mean no. No trouble at all. I can't believe this exists . . . this beautiful country road in the middle of Beverly Hills."

"Holmby Hills," he corrected her.

"I feel as if I'm in Connecticut."

"Do you, my dear? And you're Karen Keller, I presume?"

She laughed breathlessly, as if she'd scaled a height instead of a short flight of garden stairs. "You're close. It's Katherine Kellogg." On the next to last step she paused, unable to go farther because he still stood there, peering at her in the dusk.

"Are those your teeth?" he asked.

"Only in Los Angeles do people ask questions like that! Of course they're mine . . . I swear."

"Why would you swear in a high-class neighborhood, madam?" He turned away, asking politely, "Would you care to go inside?" and before she could reply, hunched his back and beckoned to her with a crooked index finger. "We can go in the main quarters. I usually stay out in the back over the garage, but the master's away."

Then she looked beyond him and saw the house. Set on the crown of the hill, nearly invisible from below, its rough-hewn planes were spread low and dark against the evening sky. Like a slumbering cat, it curved into the land as if it were part of it. Ivy grew around leaded casement windows and up a faded brick chimney, from which a thread of smoke rose above the trees; here and there along vine-covered eaves small white spotlights glowed. From Quasimodo to matinee idol in a flash: Jed stood tall and erect near the oak door, an overhead light scooping dark crescents beneath his eyes. As Katherine followed him into the house, her attention was caught by a silver mezuzah tacked to the doorframe, and for a fleeting moment she was eighteen again, standing on a snow-covered front step in Fort Lee with Neil Kolodny, their differences magnified by the unfamiliar religious symbol. Here it provoked only faint surprise: it was not something she would have expected to find in the house of a man as sophisticated as Jed Bernard.

The foyer was paved with cool green flagstones. Across from the door, diffused light spilled over a pre-Columbian figure that hung on a rough driftwood wall above a well of bleached pebbles, creating the effect of a pagan grotto. A door to the left was closed; the one on the right opened onto a small, cozy study. Gypsy music poured from two giant speakers flanking a wall of books just inside the arched entrance to the living room. A few framed photographs were arranged on one of the speakers: the former President and First Lady, inscribed to Jed in her round, boarding school scrawl; the musical comedy star, Bertie Hayes; an Airedale; and glowering behind a grizzled beard, a rabbi. Jed saw Katherine's curious glance. "My grandfather," he said. "One of the great men."

"Oh," she responded brightly and raised her eyes to the bookcase; on the topmost shelf was a tarnished bronze menorah. Into her mind flashed an image of her mother, gliding gracefully into a dead faint.

Jed stood before a glass wall that ran the length of the house, silhouetted against an aquamarine island of light from a swimming pool, eyes narrowed as he lighted his pipe, studying Katherine through the smoke. Halfway in to the living room, she paused, struck by its magic and something else: a sense of déjà vu. Individual details were unfamiliar—the tall ceramic table lamps, the leather donkey straddling the huge open hearth, a sharp-edged Braque oil on the brick wall above it—but a deeper instinct told her she had been here before, if only in a dream. It was as familiar as the lake house. Like sea spray, the impression evaporated before she could catch hold of it, but it grazed her subconscious that here—three thousand miles from home in a place that bore no real resemblance to anything she had ever known, standing before a man, a Jew, old enough to be her father—she had come after a lifetime of displacement to rest where she belonged.

Jed walked over and stood close enough for her to see her own image in his eyes; their translucent shade made her think of brandy in a decanter when the light shines through. Raising his hand over one side of her head, he announced solemnly, "This entire growth must go."

She flushed and moved away with a nervous laugh, though she hadn't a clue what he meant by the vaguely insulting comment. The living room, she saw, flowed into what had obviously been intended as the dining room, but was now taken up by a pool table, its green baize lighted by a jewel-like Tiffany lamp. Pocket doors opened onto a swimming pool that curved gracefully against the lawn, bounded by rose bushes at one end, and at the other by an olive tree. In the distance, on another, cruder planet it seemed, the lights of Beverly Hills glittered.

"Eve was right," she said, gazing outside.

"Speak up, madam," said Jed.

She turned. He stood with his back to the blazing fire. "Eve Pratt said you have the most beautiful house in Los Angeles. It's true."

"Lovely girl, Eve—I've always said so. *Grrreat* taste, a brilliant mind."

"She said you've lived here twenty years."

"What would she know, that *meshugginah?*" he said without skipping a beat. "No more than fifteen—seventeen at most. My God, hard to believe. I've lived here man and boy. Ever since *Living with Tessie*. That was a show I wrote that ran for eight years. And it still stands up."

"Oh, yes, I know!" Katherine exclaimed. "It was my favorite program when I was little. I wasn't allowed to be up that late, so I used to sneak the radio under the covers."

"Marvelous," Jed said dryly. "I suppose it's a shock to you to discover I'm still alive. Now, little girl, what can I get you to drink? A glass of Ovaltine?"

"Very funny."

"That's my *bus*iness, kid," he muttered as he went to the bar, which bridged the living room and the kitchen. A shadow darted across the lawn; moments later an Airedale nosed open the glass door and came up to Katherine with his tail wagging. She bent to pat his shaggy head.

"That's Simon," Jed told her. "I owned his grandfather, too. A long time ago I kept cocker spaniels. They're pretty, but they're too frigging neurotic. No matter how beautiful something is, if it bites your hand when you go to pet it, you gotta get rid of it."

Simon ambled off to the fireplace, where he sat erect, a model for the cover of *Country Life*. Katherine perched on a leather barstool. "Your house reminds me of a hunting lodge," she told Jed.

"Mayerling . . . MAYERLING!" he cried. "Women come up here, they never leave the hill." In the light from a small hanging lamp, he studied her face. "You're quite pretty, if you like overbites. What are you, about twenty-three?"

"I'll never see it again," she laughed.

"*Oy, gottenyu! Alteh bubbes* they're sending me—do you believe that? You're not an actress, are you?"

"I was. But I gave it up when my daughter was born."

"Good move. We must be grateful for small things. California girl?"

"No. I'm from the East."

"I'll be the judge of that. I need some more ice back here. Since you're not an actress, there's a possibility you can function on some level. Do you think you could get me some from the fridge? It's my housekeeper's day off."

While she went off to investigate the kitchen, he kept up a steady stream of patter. "I once gave a party up here when I was married—Laura, Shirley MacLaine, Eva Gabor—would you believe that among them those pishers couldn't put a meal together? I went out and put marks down on the floor—fucking *tape* like on a movie set so they could find their way around. Only way I could get a matzoh sandwich."

When Katherine returned with a tray of ice, he held out the bucket and said, "I'll tell you something about Hollywood. There but for the grace of show business go carhops, elevator operators, and waitresses."

The telephone rang. Picking up the receiver, Jed crooned, "House of love," then abruptly sobered and turned his back to her. "Sammy, where you been, cripple? You don't answer my calls for two days? The picture wasn't that bad." He listened briefly. "The picture *was* that bad. Fine. Anything with Frank is *gornisht*, you know that. He puts you away. I told him to change one thing, I found myself on a plane with my daughter to Hawaii. All right, my friend, I've got the greatest idea you ever heard in your fucking life . . . people fall down when they hear it. It's a comedy western—perfect for Duke. I want a decent step deal on this one, you follow me? I'm not writing on spec so some putz can flasloe me around later with *bobkes*." A short pause. "Not a nickel under a hundred grand. Okay, kid, get back to me." He hung up and caught Katherine watching him. "On the other hand," he said meekly, "I'll take fifty."

"What language are you speaking?" she asked. "Is that show biz talk?"

"A little show biz, a little Yiddish, a little Jed Bernard," he replied, handing her a drink.

She followed him to the study off the foyer, where a fire burned in a raised grate and casement windows gave onto the courtyard. Katherine went to sit in the armchair close to the fire, Simon at her heels. "HALT!" Jed cried, and they both froze in their tracks. "You *dare* to sit in my chair, madam? he said, so she made a U-turn to the couch across the room. When Jed sat, Simon collapsed at his feet, resting his muzzle on one black Gucci loafer. The idea of dialogue abandoned, Katherine sipped her drink and reflected on the fact that what Jed Bernard required was an audience.

After one swallow, he set his glass aside and picked up a book from the table at his elbow, holding it up so she could see the title: *Survival in Auschwitz.* "Great fucking writer, Primo Levi. Have you read this?"

"I couldn't get through it. Too depressing."

"De*press*ing? You bet your ass it's depressing." He turned to an imaginary audience. "You all know Rebecca of Sunnybrook Farm? Goes through life just asingin' and adancin'. God forbid a little thing like a pogrom should ruin her day." Brandishing the book, he told her, "Three times I've read this. I have the finest collection of Nazi books in the world. As a wise man once said, 'We must never forget the camps.' "

The Nazi books were elsewhere, Katherine surmised, since the bookshelves she could see were filled with leatherbound scripts and scrapbooks with gold-embossed titles such as *Living with Tessie, Pasquale's World, Minneapolis 1930–'34*, and *Hollywood 1945–'50*. A collection of silver cups on a top shelf appeared to be tennis trophies. "Whose are those?" she inquired.

"Mine. I was Downstate singles champion at fifteen. But I don't play anymore."

"Why not?"

"Can't stand losing. The worst thing in later life, my dear, is to be in competition with yourself. But you were telling me the story of your life, cripple." His eyes fastened on his wristwatch, he motioned for her to speed it up.

By now Katherine's sense of insecurity, which was at best a skittish horse at the starting gate, threatened to bolt. "Why do you call me 'cripple'?"

"I call everybody cripple," he said matter-of-factly.

"Why?"

"Because everybody *is* one . . . either mental or physical. Think about it."

To consider this sardonic view of the human race, she directed her gaze at the fireplace. Propped against the hearth was a poster-sized color photograph: the head of a young girl, eight or nine, caught in a moment of surprise so that her head whirled about and her straight, wheat-colored hair flew around her defiant jaw. Huge green eyes stared out with the startled look of a deer caught by headlights on a country road. There was a wistful, tomboyish quality, and an air of seductiveness unsettling in one so young. "That's a wonderful picture. Is it your daughter?" Katherine asked.

A light came into Jed's eyes and his expression softened. "Winston Roddenberry took that shot last year for *Life*. The man is one of the great photographers," he said.

"How old is she?"

"I never ask. She has her life, I have mine."

"Does she live with her mother?"

"I have custody. She sees her mother on the weekends."

After a brief pause, Katherine asked, "How does that happen?"

"Simple. I took Laura to court and won. Three years ago."

An alarm went off in Katherine's head. She said carefully, "I thought a woman had to be practically on the streets before she could lose custody."

"Not at all."

Then, obliquely, he told her about the fight: how he'd never said Laura was unfit; how the court had finally decided to leave it up to Chris, who'd said she wanted to live with her father. "And I did *not* fix the judge, if that's what you're thinking," he said harshly.

"Could you have *done* that?" she asked in a horrified voice.

He shrugged. "It's possible." After taking a long drink, he set the glass down, and said in a tone that indicated the subject was closed, "Laura's domestic arrangements were not in the child's best interest."

Katherine did not pry further. The record ended. A log fell in the fireplace, sending up a shower of sparks. Impaled upon a memory of Christopher's one rash threat to take Chryssie away from her, she looked across the room at Jed Bernard and saw him all at once as the Enemy. Which, she gathered, finally gave them something in common.

Abruptly, he rose and held out his hand. "Come . . . let's take a little walk."

Simon followed them into the cool evening, where a dry wind rustled the palm trees and the air was perfumed with jasmine. High above the dirt road a row of poplars was feathered against the darkening sky. Jed pointed to the hillside, which was thick with bougainvillea and red berry bushes, the ivy brown and curled at the edges.

"We're in the middle of a fucking drought, you know that? It hasn't rained for three years. The last time it did, the whole hill caved in. Slid right down to Rosewood. I came out and stood here in the rain, yelling: It's God's punishment! Jews should not own land!"

Jed's self-deprecation and the image of him inveighing against the heavens had the desired effect: the somber mood dispelled, he kept her laughing as they strolled along the road, bending once to pick up a stick and toss it for Simon, who went loping after it. All of a sudden, a loud braying shattered the silence. "What's that?" she whispered.

"That's Rowdy. What's the matter, you never saw a donkey before?"

Her mouth went slack with astonishment. "A *donkey?* Who keeps a donkey a block from Sunset Boulevard?"

"It's for the kid."

They reached a bend in the road. There, tethered to a tree behind a split-rail fence, a small gray burro nibbled at sprouts of tall grass. His appetite seemed previously to have defoliated the hillside behind him. Jed produced a carrot from his jacket pocket, passed it to Katherine, and suggested she make friends with Rowdy. She hesitated, not being intimately acquainted with the species, but he pressed the carrot upon her, growling, "Don't be a knibbler. I cannot *stand* knibblers." To illustrate the word's meaning, he blinked and rubbed his eye, pantomiming a nervous, timid soul. Then he reached over the fence and patted the animal's neck. "Good evening, sir. How are you this evening? This is Mrs. Keller. If you play your cards right, she might give you something to eat. Here, kid," he said, taking Katherine's hand. "Feel his nose. You will never in your life feel anything softer than Rowdy's nose."

Determined not to act like the knibbler she suspected she was, she fed the carrot to the donkey and stroked his nose, which was indeed soft as velvet, while Jed turned up his collar and dug his hands in his pockets. "It's frigging cold," he said finally. "Let's go up."

A footpath zigzagged uphill through the ivy. She climbed ahead of him to the top, where a narrow wooden gate opened onto the swimming pool; steam rose from the water like a scrim over clumps of starry, white-headed flowers blooming against the house. The dog tore across the lawn and rolled on the grass near a battered wooden swing that hung on ropes from the olive tree.

"Will that hold me?" she asked.

Jed gave her a look. "I should think so. What do you weigh—ninety?"

Moments later she was sailing into the sky. Jed stood with one foot on the diving board, his face upturned to follow her trajectory. The thin curve of the rising moon, poised like a scimitar behind the olive tree, made her aware of the time. Reluctantly, she skidded backward to a halt, twirled on the swing, and found herself looking through glass doors at a vast bed, swathed in fur, fit for a czar. "I'm sorry . . . I forgot . . . you said you were going out. I should say good night," she stammered, jumping off the swing, nearly stumbling over Simon in her haste.

Jed glanced at his watch. "I have to go to a screening at the Beverly Hills Hotel at eight. Just some studio people. It's Brando's new film. Perhaps you'd like to come?"

A door opened in Katherine's mind, and through it she saw glimpses of a glittering world filled with fascinating people—a world she'd once had every intention of inhabiting. Then at breakfast on the morning of her wedding, Hulda, the German woman who had kept house for the Winterhauses for eighteen years, had said as she bustled about the kitchen, "Margaret Mary I could understand getting married so young. But you, I always thought you were made for a life of glamour, Katie." A last chance warning. But Katherine had only glanced up with a rueful smile and said, "You and me both, Hulda." The routine of marriage, the boredom, for which nothing— not her parents' experience nor her extensive reading of Russian novels and romantic poets—could have prepared her, had not diminished the dream; hunger for excitement and a fatal attraction to glamour still ran like a river through her nature. A private screening . . . the studio. It was too much to resist. Jed was looking at her, waiting for a response.

"Make up your mind, my dear. I don't ask twice."

"That would be very nice. Thank you," she said with a brilliant smile.

He took a step forward so that his face was inches from hers. "Crazed little blue eyes," he said softly.

CHAPTER 9

The Screening

Jed Bernard at the wheel of an open black Ferrari was a menace: tweed collar upturned, hair streaking back from his forehead, eyes nearly golden in the half-light, clearly enjoying the image of a young blonde beside him, he careened along Sunset Boulevard straddling the center divider. With one hand Katherine gripped the dashboard; with the other she subdued her flying hair while attempting to maintain the illusion of nonchalance. Deciphering his conversation took concentration: along with the Yiddish words (many of which, he explained, had a midwestern flavor) that peppered his speech, there were the malapropisms—a comical mangling of multisyllable words, especially those with consonants—and others (like "knibbler" and "flasloe") whose definitions were available in no dictionary, but which, once pronounced in his rasping voice, were unforgettable. The traffic signal at Whittier Drive flashed red, and he jammed his foot on the brake.

Waiting for the light to change, he glanced over, as people are wont to do in Beverly Hills, to check out who was in the car next to him. "Arly! How are you, *boychik?*" he called to the driver of an Alfa Romeo convertible.

In the yellowish light from a streetlamp, Katherine recognized the familiar quirky grin of Arlen Stone, a handsome young actor known as much for a series of romances with co-stars as for his considerable dramatic ability.

"Hangin' in there, Jed," he replied.

Jed took the pipe from his mouth. "I've got a great idea—

perfect for you. It's about a guy who only likes old broads."

Stone laughed.

"*Alteh givorns*—grandmothers!" Jed went on, warming to the subject. "He's got a great-looking fiancée, but when he checks into a hotel, he goes after the old *zhlub* cleaning the loo. Just can't help himself."

"I love it, Jed!" The light turned green. Over the roar of the motor, Stone yelled, "I'd like to hear more!" and pulled away, making the standard Hollywood gesture of hand to ear that pantomimes a future phone call.

"I myself would like to hear more," Jed muttered, shifting gears. "If I had any more I wouldn't need that putz."

Katherine looked at him astonished. "You mean it isn't written?"

"Not exactly. No point wasting a chance meeting. I thought it up now—when I saw him." He raised his eyes to the mirror and smoothed his hair. "It's not a bad idea. I like it. It could be comeback time. Do you like the title, 'The Old Ones'?" he inquired, glancing over at Katherine just as her teeth began to chatter. "Possibly there'll be a part in it for you, my dear, at the rate you're going."

"It's a great title," she laughed. "D'you always drive with the top down in December?"

"Yes, I do," he replied in a tone that brooked no contradiction. Even the traffic seemed to bend to his will as he ran the light at Camden, cut around the center island, and made a one-handed turn up the palm-shaded driveway of the sprawling pink palazzo that is the Beverly Hills Hotel. A young parking attendant raced to open his door under the striped marquee.

"Hey, Mr. Bernard! How ya' doin'?"

"Okay, crip," Jed grunted, unfolding his long legs from the sports car. "How's your mom?"

"She's good. Taking it easy. Says she's not coming out of retirement for anyone but you."

"Glad to hear it. One scratch on the Ferrari and you'll never work in this town again."

"But I can listen to your tapes, right?"

"Arrgghh!" Jed clutched the boy's throat playfully. "Again with the tapes! Don't *hok* me, Joey. I'll tell you what—we'll negotiate. You leave me up front, you can play the tapes. But if anything's busted, I'll have your job." Then he added, "One more picture like the last one and I'll *need* your job," and the kid laughed. On the way up the red-carpeted entrance, Jed explained their connection to Katherine. "Joey's mother was sixteen when she first came to work for me. Everyone told her I'd ruin her life. I made her quit smoking, told her to marry the schmuck her mother said wasn't good enough for her—they're still married, by the way—and gave her the down payment for their house. Now tell me how I ruined her life."

There was something vulnerable about Jed that touched Katherine; despite the braggadocio, the showmanship, the jaded facade, she had a strong sense of the child inside him that had never been squelched. It was there in the disarming honesty about his failures and in his hurt at being judged unfairly, and it made up, she suspected, for a plentitude of bullshit.

"Peter Finch . . . call for Peter Finch!" cried the famous Beverly Hills Hotel bellhop, his high-pitched voice ringing through the lobby as they entered. He stopped short at the sight of Jed, his wrinkled child's face splitting in a grin. "Hullo, Mr. Bernard. Long time no see. Been out of town?"

"Haven't you heard, Johnny? I passed away last month. This is a tape. Have you seen Mr. Fender?"

"He came in a little while ago—maybe ten minutes."

"Thanks. Let's go, kid," Jed said and went toward the stairs to the lower level just as the extravagantly beautiful Rumanian actress, Magda Lupu, strolled past the jewelry shop on her way to the Lanai. She had gone blond for a recent movie role and looked like an overblown yellow rose in saffron silk and canary diamonds. Her throaty voice carried across the lobby. "Jed, dahling! Vy haven't you called me, you naughty boy? You missed my vedding!"

"I was out of town, Maggie. I'll come to the next one."

"Oh, zis vun is forever, dahling! Vot are you doing viz zat young girl?"

"Go to your room, Mag," called Jed and hurried down the stairs, muttering, "The woman's mind is gone—she must be taken away."

"She's very beautiful . . . much more so than in pictures," Katherine observed.

"You should have seen her when she was with Aly Khan. There was no one with her glamour. But she's a narcissisis—" At her bemused smile, he translated, "Never stops looking in the mirror. I wrote a pilot for her once, called it *The Girl Next Door*. I'll run it for you someday. The experience gave me an entire coronary."

At the door to the screening room, which was hidden behind a curving staircase, Jed paused. His "You okay, kid?" was almost protective, she thought, but then he preceded her rudely into the room.

Six people were present: a television actress currently starring in a series, a young male writer, three producers, and the writer's companion, a curvaceous blonde in a revealing blouse and skin tight jeans. Each was engrossed in conversation with one or two of the others; ignoring this, Jed announced, "You're all here for the reading of the will, I presume," so that six heads turned to him and six people stopped talking to laugh. Satisfied that he had their full attention, he singled out the nearest three. "Roger Norman . . . Sammy Fender . . . Felix May . . . and that's the late Mrs. Norman in the last row, I believe," he said, pointing to an empty chair and drawing a smirk from the writer. "This is Mrs. Keeler."

"It's Katherine . . . Kellogg," she amended.

Felix May, tall and slick-looking in a cream-colored jacket, took her hand and held on to it. "Think nothing of it," he said smoothly. "I've known him for ten years and he still calls me Francis."

"Hello, Jed. How's your daughter?" asked Sammy Fender, a black telephone receiver to his ear.

"Fine, fine," Jed replied. "Studying nuclear fission. Going to be a scientist, like her mother. Laura's doing wonderful work, you know. With Schweitzer."

Everyone laughed, especially the brunette actress, who'd had a long run simulating a sinuous panther in a Revlon commercial, and was touted by her agent as a beauty with brains. Tilting her head back against the wall, she fastened her seductive gaze on Jed. "I'm Janine Harte."

"I'm sure you are, my dear," he said brusquely. His display of indifference to her obvious charms whetted her appetite.

"I hear you're the funniest man in Hollywood," she purred.

"I can't wait to meet myself," he replied, winking at Katherine.

Sammy Fender put the phone down. A ceiling pinlight glanced off his bald head, which gleamed above a teal blue shirt open to the fourth button. "Can we get started, please? I want to see what Brando spent the eight million on."

An unseen technician doused the lights. Roger Norman sat in the back row with his date, while the others scattered among three middle rows of plush seats, and Jed pulled Katherine to the front row. The title *One-Eyed Jacks* appeared on the screen. Just as she began to relax, he reached over and took her hand. She wondered uneasily if anyone could see—what would they think of her, holding hands with a man so much older than she? When she withdrew hers on the pretext of unbuttoning her jacket, Jed gave her a curious glance. In a town where sex is the coin of the realm, she supposed, women do not ordinarily react to physical advances with reticence. Out of the corner of her eye, she saw Felix glide his hand over Janine's thigh; on his third finger a gold wedding band flashed.

The credits rolled interminably. After the last one, Jed feigned waking up. "I would have done it differently," he announced. Everyone laughed as if the remark were hilarious; in public, Katherine noted, Jed was apparently expected always to be "on," to entertain—she wondered if it sometimes made him feel like a musician who's been invited to the party to play. *One-Eyed Jacks* was a long, soporific western. When it was over, Sammy Fender gathered everyone around him and solicited opinions.

Janine said, "I thought the aesthetic values were marvelous . . . it's a deeply felt personal statement," though she had been sound asleep when the lights came up.

A producer said, "He could cut half an hour easy."

Another said, "I don't give you a quarter for the story."

Roger Norman made a few pretentious comments in praise of the film's profundity, to which Jed responded, "It's got no legs—they won't give a shit in Kansas."

"I'd like to give Katy Jurado a little *hok*," Felix remarked.

"You'd like to give your grandmother a little *hok*, Felix," Jed replied.

"I've got to be up early. Thanks Phil," Fender called to the invisible projectionist.

"Good night all," Jed announced, then he bowed to the writer's silent companion. "I've loved everything you've said, my dear."

It was a mean remark, and antagonism flickered in her eyes. There's one person, thought Katherine, who doesn't think he's the funniest man in Hollywood. On the way upstairs, she said to Jed, "I can't say I found it easy to talk in that group, either."

"That's different," he said. "You know when to keep your mouth shut. What bothers me about her is that she's here with Roger Norman while his wife's with the kids in Malibu. Please. Don't get me started on these pishers."

In the nearly deserted lobby, perpetual gas flames furled in the corner fireplace like a memorial to the hotel's fabled dead clientele. The clock over the desk read ten-thirty. And everyone's going home to bed, Katherine thought. So much for glamorous private screenings. When Joey brought the car around, she noted with relief that he had put the top up.

Felix May followed them down the driveway in a Mercedes sedan, Janine at his side. As he pulled abreast of them at the stoplight, Jed called to him, "I had a car like that once, Felix. You push a button on the dashboard, it turns into a tank and invades Belgium." Then he gunned the motor, swallowing up Janine's laughter and leaving them behind in a trail of exhaust.

"Are *they* married?" Katherine asked.

In answer, Jed rolled his eyes.

"He's wearing a wedding ring. Is he divorced?"

"Not at all. Felix is married to Sol Seligmann's daughter, Alice, sole heiress to the Seligmann mining fortune, who left yesterday for St. Moritz. Felix is a putz. Alice finds out, he could lose the South African rights based on this evening alone."

"Doesn't he love her?"

"Sure he does. But Felix has a little problem. He's a psoriasis."

"A what?"

"If he takes a cab in from the airport and the driver's a woman, Felix has got to fuck her."

"You mean a satyr?"

"Same thing." Suddenly he bellowed, "PISHERS! Why do they go with married guys?"

"It really disturbs you?"

"I *hate* that! What's the point of being married then?" He drew up to his electric gate and pressed the remote control. "Laura and I went to St. Moritz on our honeymoon. You ever been there, kid?"

"Yes, one wonderful Christmas when I was nineteen. I've managed to go to a great many ski resorts without ever skiing once. Are you a good skier?"

He gave her a look. "My dear girl, no Jew stands at the top of a mountain on two pieces of wood, looks down, and says 'This is the best way to get to the bottom.' I do not ski."

She was still laughing when he braked the car a few feet from hers at the end of the dirt road. He leaned over to kiss her cheek. "You won't come up? No, of course not. I've had a fair time. May I call you again?"

His low voice mocked her, making her revert to the schoolgirl formality. "Yes, of course. Thank you for a lovely evening . . ."

"Good night, my dear."

" . . . I enjoyed it very much," she said as she got out quickly.

Before she could get her car door open, he gunned the Ferrari up the driveway and into his garage, and while she turned the key in the ignition, he snapped off the lights, leaving her plunged in darkness. Driving through the wooden gate, she thought of Andy for the first time that evening. He was right about one thing: meeting Jed Bernard had certainly given her some new material.

CHAPTER 10

The Two Christabels

Andrew Byrne, who was an adherent of the philosophy of absolute freedom, had little to say about Katherine's date with Jed when he saw her on Saturday evening. But he waxed eloquent on the subject of aging predators of young women, whom he considered the rightful province of young men. It wasn't until later, in the predawn hours when he was leaving, that he admitted jealousy had aroused his most atavistic urges: he who had never displayed the slightest interest in having children had fantasized impregnating her. Their lovemaking seemed to have reassured him. "Everything that's brittle about you disappears when we're in bed," he told her, strapping on his watch. "Women don't give themselves with such abandon if it's only sex—they aren't made that way." The theory had a familiar ring: Katherine recalled it was Christopher's rationale for the double standard. Like him, like most men, who got their information from Freud, textbooks, other men, and dishonest women, Andy fancied himself an expert on the workings of the female psyche.

And Katherine, whose information was filtered through the Catholic Church, felt an altogether different kind of guilt Sunday morning when she went down the hall to pick up Chryssie, who had stayed overnight with her friend Abby. It seemed to her that she had betrayed someone. But whom?

"Shun lewd conduct! Every other sin a man commits is outside his body, but the fornicator sins against his own body . . . God is

145

within . . . You are not your own . . . ," the pastor of Good Shepherd read from an epistle at the noon Mass.

Seated in a rear pew, Katherine stared straight ahead, guilty as charged. At her side Chryssie traced with a red crayon the outline of Christ's profile on the cover of the Catholic Register. When Mass was over, they went to the Pony Park. Around and around the ring Chryssie trotted on a miniature pinto named Apache, her small fingers entwined in its blond mane. Watching from the gate, a smile plastered on her face, Katherine thought, Sunday, bloody Sunday. Visitation Day. Divorced fathers converged on the park, standing around in clumps, smoking, trading jokes, kicking at the dirt, herding their progeny into one of four lanes: walk, trot, canter, or gallop. She wondered grimly if the parents of those lined up to gallop had been divorced the longest. The Pony Park was always clogged with kids; Chryssie loved it so they were regular customers, but Katherine considered it one of the circles of hell reserved for those who had rashly married the Wrong Person.

The Sound of Music was playing in Beverly Hills; they'd seen it twice, but went again Sunday evening, getting home after ten. Katherine had tucked Chryssie into bed, read her a story, and was on her way into the bedroom when the phone rang. As she picked up the receiver, she realized that she'd been wondering all weekend if she'd hear from Jed Bernard.

"Hi," said Christopher. "It's me. How are you?"

"Oh, hi! Fine. Hold on . . . I'll get Chryssie . . . she's not aslee—"

"No!" he said quickly, a reaction that struck her dumb. In a tone she remembered, a tone whose weakness made her cordiality curdle, he explained, "It's very painful for me to speak to her on the telephone."

Painful for you! What about *her*—she's *four!* she wanted to shout at him, but checked the retort because in the next breath he said, "I'll see her soon anyway. I thought I'd come down there for Christmas, if that's all right with you." Chuckling derisively, he drawled, "El Ay."

The dig went past her. She was thinking: a semblance of a family for Chryssie, if only for the holidays. "It's great with me. Chryssie will be thrilled!" she responded, and sank back against the pillow to talk to him, lingering memories of Jed Bernard rendered irrelevant.

But in the Monday morning solitude of the art gallery, as she stacked paintings in the storage room, Jed's image rose up before her, standing outside the house he had built on the land that was so much a part of him—the hillside where it was wild and where it was tamed into a flowering terrace; the garden where his precious olive tree grew, its quicksilver leaves whispering of some distant Levantine past; the long dirt road that wound to the top where the house stood, raw and rugged and as essential to his identity as the Slavic eyes or the deep cleft in his chin. The aging heartthrob on the hill, she thought, living with a little girl and the ghosts from a dozen scrapbooks.

Her employer had come upstairs quietly; lost in thought, Katherine was unaware of him until he was upon her at the file cabinet, imprisoning her with his arms, pressing himself into her back, asking in a jocular tone, "Shall I show you 'ow ze Greeks do eet?" Although she laughed good-naturedly as she slipped out of his grasp, a sinking feeling overtook her once she was back at her desk. Didier's conversation often had a suggestive flavor, but she had considered him harmless; this was his first overt pass. No matter how diplomatically she'd handled the incident, it made working for him in such close quarters uncomfortable and would probably, inevitably, lead her back to the unemployment line. While she was brooding about this, Eve called to ask if she'd like to meet for lunch.

When she got to Tiffany's at one, Eve was in the stock room; in the clock department, a Henry Higgins hat pulled low on his forehead, was Jed Bernard. Instinctively she started toward him, then realized he was flirting with—or, more accurately, performing for— a toothsome young salesgirl, so she veered in the other direction, surprised at the intensity of her irritation, depressed by the incorrigibility of men. It doesn't matter how old they get, she told herself disgustedly. From the jewelry counter she noted with a degree of satisfaction that the girl looked more mystified than amused. At that instant, Jed put a match to his pipe, looked over, and saw Katherine watching them. She lowered her eyes, intent on examining a heavy, diamond-studded gold chain that she wouldn't have been caught dead in.

Moments later she was exchanging loud Christmas greetings with Eloise Pondfair, an attractive middle-aged client of Didier's who was slightly hard-of-hearing, when she heard Jed say behind her, "Lower your voice, cripple."

Worried that the ultradignified Mrs. Pondfair would think he was addressing *her*, Katherine hastened to introduce them, but the woman cried gaily, "Jed! Where have you been keeping yourself? Do you still have that extraordinary house?" and leaned forward to kiss him.

"Don't touch my body, Elly," Jed said. "How are you, kid? What're you doing out in the world without Edgar?" Hopefully, wriggling his eyebrows, he asked, "Trouble in the marriage?"

Eloise laughed uproariously. Then she turned serious. "Are you feeling better, Jed? You weren't well the last time I saw you."

"Mezzo-mezzo," he replied, twisting his wrist. "You know how it is, Elly. It's lonely at the top. Of course, it's also lonely at the bottom."

Eloise laughed again, louder, revealing a so far unseen, almost raucous quality.

A salesman appeared with two enormous shopping bags overflowing with gift-wrapped packages and offered to put them in the trunk of the Rolls for Mrs. Pondfair, who flung herself on Jed to say good-bye, enveloping him in blue fox and Jungle Gardenia. Then, remembering Katherine, she drew herself up to her imposing six feet, said good afternoon and swept to the door.

"*Feh!*" Jed muttered. "Would you believe the *choleria* put her tongue in my ear?"

Katherine was still looking after her in amazement. "Incredible! Her entire manner changed—even her accent! You just reduced Mrs. Pondfair to a chorus girl!"

"Putz!" he said. "She *was* a chorus girl . . . in Vegas. Did you ever look at her legs?"

"What? It's not possible—"

"My hand to God. Edgar'd been *hoking* her for years when his wife died. But don't get me wrong, I like Elly. She's no dumbbell. And she doesn't pull that social bullshit on me." He took a step closer; a masculine scent of tobacco mingled with lime aftershave clung to him. "I'll explain you something," he said. "There's a Mafia expression—it's called 'declaring yourself.' In other words, if you're straight with me, I'll give you a fair deal. But if you pretend to be something you're not, I'll put you away. That's why the boys never let me lose big in Vegas."

Tilting his tweed hat, he cleared his throat loudly of catarrh.

"I'll give you dinner tonight if you want, crip. Be at my house at eight. No later—my kid's home."

And he was out the door before she could reply.

At seven-thirty that evening, her hair still wet from the shower, Katherine removed a TV dinner from the oven, to her daughter's noisy approval. Like many children of estranged parents, Chryssie's motivating force was the desire to please. "I wish I could have TV dinners every single night of my life," she said as the tray was placed in front of her on the dining table.

"Don't overdo it, Spider Eyes. Twice a week is the limit."

Chryssie was dressed in yellow velour pants, a pink-and-yellow-striped sweater, and yellow ballet slippers. The guilt of a single mother had swollen her wardrobe, and at four she was something of a fashion plate. Her dark blue, thickly lashed eyes had their imploring look. "Couldn't I eat with you while you get dressed, Mommy? Just till the sitter gets here?"

With a fleeting thought to a more gracious life-style, Katherine picked up the tray and carried it into the bathroom, where she set it on the clothes hamper. "Is this any way to bring up a kid?" she asked the air.

"Sure . . . it's fun," came Chryssie's bright, reassuring reply.

"Just be sure you drink every drop of your milk."

"Yuck," Chryssie commented, dragging her musical chair in from the bedroom. "Where are you going?"

"To someone's house for dinner. A man Eve introduced me to. He's got"—Katherine had been about to say "a daughter named Christabel, too," but stopped short; how to explain that she was leaving her with one of the endless supply of Proxy Mothers to dine with someone else's Christabel?—"a very funny sense of humor," she finished lamely. In the mirror she caught sight of Chryssie squirting mashed potatoes through the space where her front tooth had come out. "Christabel, stop that! Your table manners are terrible!"

Chryssie giggled. "This isn't a *table*, Mommy."

"I know, but you've got to learn. Otherwise you'll pick up bad habits." Katherine trailed off in despair, thinking, Where do I get this stuff—Universal Mothers' School? In a world without fathers or family dinners, God forbid we should neglect eternal verities like table manners. She turned on the hair dryer and let the warm stream of air ripple through her long hair. Through the window she saw a police car cruise past in the alley behind the apartment, and said over the blower's noise, "I bet there are more cops per person in Beverly Hills than any other city in America."

"You're screaming, Mommy."

"Oh, sorry."

The doorbell rang. Chryssie jumped up and ran outside, endlessly curious about what the grab bag of Proxy Mothers would yield. In her absence, Katherine swiftly ejected a tiny pink pill from its disk and gulped it down with water. Birth control was one of her more pragmatic sins, she figured, the Enovid as much a symbol of her fractured family life as the TV dinner. Toward both she felt a mixture of antipathy and gratitude.

"It's a different one from last time. She's old," Chryssie hissed from the doorway.

"Old can be good . . . like Grandmommy." To be fair, Katherine added, "And Grandmother Jane."

"That's true. She seems cheery anyhow."

The woman in the living room turned out to be a rarity among Proxy Mothers—one who seemed actually to prefer the company of children. When Katherine came out, she was seated on the couch in a flowered dress and black oxfords, withdrawing an array of doll clothes from a commodious purse. "Hello, dear. I'm Mrs. Johnston with a 't'," she introduced herself. The sight of the clothes sent Chryssie tearing off to get her Barbie Doll kit, while Katherine jotted down Jed's number. "Bye—I love you," she said as the little girl skidded past.

"I love you *more!*" Chryssie called, and Katherine ran down the hall, fifteen minutes late and wondering why she was going at all.

The door to Jed's house stood open. Simon bounded through it, barking wildly, and leaped at Katherine's car as she turned into the courtyard. From somewhere inside, Jed's voice yelled, "Simon, you putz, get down!" Prancing ahead of her, the dog led the way through the living room to Jed's bedroom. The bamboo curtain was raised, the pool flung out like a bolt of turquoise silk on the lawn. And propped against a bank of pillows in the middle of the enormous bed was the child in the photograph, stroking a tiger-striped cat. She appeared a few years older, her face more angular, her hair a shade darker, but beneath stringy bangs were the same haunting green eyes, the eyes of Laura Loder.

Katherine flashed her a warm smile. "Hi. You must be Christabel."

"Chris," the child corrected firmly. "I hate it when people call me that name."

"You hate your name? But it's a beautiful name! Did you ever read the poem?"

"I never read."

"Not even at school?"

"We've been learning the Mayan alphabet all year."

"What kind of school is that?"

"Pergessive. Tell me about the poem."

"It goes:

*The lovely lady Christabel
Whom her father loves so well . . .*"

At this Chris grinned widely.

*"What keeps her in the wood so late,
A furlong from the castle gate?"*

"I'll give you a furlong," Jed called from the bathroom.

"That's neato," Chris commented, studying her father's new friend with interest. "D'you want a drink? My dad's still getting dressed but I could get you one . . ."

"That's very sweet, but no thanks, I'll wait."

"Good. Could you do some more of that poem?"

The cat arched up from the pillow beside Chris's head and stared at Katherine as she recited:

*"It was a lovely sight to see
The lady Christabel when she
Was praying at the old oak tree . . .*

That's all I remember." The cat stalked through fur toward Katherine's outstretched hand. Scratching behind his ears so that he purred loudly, she asked Chris, "How come you're in bed? Are you sick?"

"I thought you didn't like that, Kitty," the child addressed the cat, giving him a dirty look. "Kitty usually only lets me pet him."

"What's his name?"

"That's it. Kitty. My dad names all our cats Kitty." Sentences tumbled out of her mouth in breathless succession. "I've got the flu. It's the second time this month I've had it and my dad's had it 'round 'leven times."

"Do you think I could catch it?" Katherine asked hopefully, sitting closer to her. "Then I could stay home from work and watch TV."

Christabel's lips parted in a smile, revealing perfect, even white teeth set in a wide jaw. Extraordinary beauty eluded her only because of her nose, an artistic ski jump that gave her face a slightly comic touch. Her expression was candid. "I saw you before in the art gallery. My dad took me down to look at you."

Katherine's eyebrows peaked. "Really?"

"Is that what you do all the time?"

"I've done it for a year or so, but I certainly don't consider it a career."

"Are you an actress?"

"I used to be, but I'm not now."

"I figured. My dad won't take 'em out anymore. He says they're all nuts. He says they'll leave on their wedding night if someone offers 'em a part." Chris wiped her hands on her T-shirt. Her fingernails were bitten and stained with paint. "I'm gonna quit school after junior high and be an artist and train horses. D'you wanna see my horse collection?" she asked, throwing back the covers.

"Halt!" Jed commanded, emerging from the bathroom, his damp hair combed straight back from his forehead, black as his turtleneck sweater. "Don't make a move out of that bed, chukkabukker. Have you and Mrs. Keller been chatting?"

"Yeah, Dad."

"Good evening, my dear." He bowed slightly in Katherine's direction, then popped two pills into his mouth and drank from a silver goblet.

"Are you sick, too?" she asked.

"I'm not a well man."

"What's wrong?"

"You got time for the list?" Placing one hand over Chris's forehead, he asked, "How are you feeling, dollface? Any better?"

She flopped further down in the bed. "I'm not eating that soup Adelaide made, Dad. It's gross,"

"You've met my charming daughter?" Jed asked Katherine.

"She's been working a lot with Emily Post lately . . . made tre-mend*ous* strides, haven't you, baby?"

"Da . . . aa . . . aad!" Chris protested.

Jed walked out of the room, followed by Simon. "I'll get you a drink, kid," he told Katherine over his shoulder. "Vodka and tonic?"

"Please . . . thank you."

"You're welcome," he said, a smirk in his voice.

"Do you ride?" Chris asked abruptly, heaving herself up against the pillows.

"I haven't for years. I've been thinking about putting my daughter in a beginner's class at Will Rogers Polo Field. Have you ever ridden there?"

Chris's expression suddenly turned sour. Dismissively, she said, "The people are mostly snobs," and stared intently at her finger-nails. "You got a kid? My dad didn't tell me that. How old is she?"

"Four. And guess what? She's got the same name as you."

"No kidding?" Chris said in a flat voice.

"Trouble on the docks," Jed muttered, overhearing them as he came back with Katherine's drink. "I want you to go to bed early tonight, Chris."

"You must want to get back to school a little bit," Katherine said.

"Oh, she's *crazy* about it," said Jed. "Adelaide chains her to the car every morning to get her there."

"Who's Adelaide?"

"My housekeeper."

"We used to have Inga, this really neato Swedish girl," Chris interjected, "but she fell in love with my dad so he hadda get rid of her."

"I'll keep that in mind," Katherine said.

Chris grinned. "I guess I'll eat with you guys after all," she said, bouncing out of bed.

It followed that for the first time since they had met, Katherine witnessed Jed Bernard relinquish center stage. Throughout the meal, Chris monopolized the conversation in her rapid speech pattern, words tripping over one another, malapropisms ajumble, at times almost unintelligible. Jed was rapt throughout. Only when the house-keeper, a broad, unsmiling woman in a white uniform, crept in on the rubber soles of her white oxfords, did his mood change.

"That was very good, Adelaide," he would say with unusual deference, and "Would you bring some more matzoh, if you please, Adelaide?" and "Thank you, Adelaide," when she removed his plate.

"You're welcome, Mr. Bernard," Adelaide whispered.

"The reason I'm so much taller than everyone in my class at Gateway is 'cuz I'm only half-Jewish," Chris rattled on. "All the other kids are all-Jewish and real smart, but I don't care cuz I'm the only one who's any good at sports."

It certainly sounds wrong for her, Katherine thought, to say nothing of the housekeeper. She turned to Jed. "What made you choose Gateway?"

"The head of the psychiatric department at UCLA recommended it for Chris," said Jed.

"Oh. Really?"

"You wanna hear part of the Mayan alphabet?" Chris asked.

Jed chuckled. "They're not big on reading or arithmetic up there, but all schools are bullshit anyway."

Again Adelaide materialized, this time with soggy rice pudding; again Jed heaped praise on the meal. As soon as she was out of earshot, he muttered, *"Ferbissina* broad," compressing his lips, drawing them down to demonstrate the word's meaning: truculent, sour.

Chris leaned close to Katherine. "Guess how old my dad is," she said.

He cast her a warning look. "Come on now!"

"Guess!" she insisted, a diabolical gleam in her eye.

Age, that great tormentor, had Jed writhing in his seat. Katherine thought to flatter him by saying forty, though he must be forty-three or four, but Chris was signaling wildly, blowing out a noisy 'Ffff . . .!" so she ventured, "Forty . . . two?"

"Fifty!" the child crowed, sitting back triumphantly to survey the damage.

Stricken by the number, Katherine glanced at him, saying weakly, "Really? I would have said much younger." *Fifty!* she thought.

Chris settled back in her seat, a wicked smile on her face.

His eyes on the bowl of fruit in the center of the table, Jed muttered, "Strawberries in winter—my, my . . ."

Into the silence that followed, Katherine began to babble. "California's amazing, isn't it? The supermarkets are like no place else on earth. I mean, the fruit and everything—"

"Think the rain'll hurt the rhubarb?" Jed asked her caustically.

The Statler Brothers were singing *Flowers on the Wall* on the stereo. He got up and went over to it, keeping time with his hips as he leaned down to turn it up. Meanwhile, Chris appeared to be wrestling with a private demon. She played with her glass, tipping it precariously, and shuffled her silverware around, all the time watching her father out of the corner of her eye. As he came back to the table, he said peremptorily, "Go to bed, Chris, before you give me an entire coronary."

"Piss off," she snarled.

Jed flushed and took a step toward her, but she flew from her chair and into the living room, dancing around behind the couch, making faces and taunting him. He lunged for her; a ceramic lamp teetered on the edge of a side table. Swearing, he righted it just in time and grabbed her sleeve, but liquid as mercury, she wriggled out of the robe, raced to the front door, and ran barefoot into the night, her long, grimy T-shirt flapping about her coltish legs.

"Goddam sonofabitch!" Jed yelled on her heels. Like a referee, Simon watched noncommittally from the hearth; once satisfied that nothing out of the ordinary was occurring, he lowered his head between his paws again.

Adelaide padded in to clear the table, giving Katherine a look of complicity, like one white hunter to another in the presence of savages. On her way back to the kitchen with the tray, she was nearly torpedoed by Chris, who darted out past the pool table and cut through the living room. Just then Jed came back in the front door. A banshee, Chris went shrieking around him down the hall to her room. He followed. Her door banged shut.

Silence.

Katherine weighed her alternatives: remaining at the table, moving to the living room, leaving. At Adelaide's reappearance, she crossed to the couch, reluctant to be aligned with the *ferbissina* side. Five minutes passed. She contemplated slipping away; then Jed leaned his head around the archway, inquiring cheerfully, "What're you doing in here all alone, kid? Chris wants to show you some of her drawings." Speechless, she watched him disappear again. Surely Simon was a more rational creature who would confirm that this was unusual behavior, she thought, but the dog's eyes were squeezed shut. She rose and followed Jed down the hall to Chris's bedroom.

Here the scene appeared to her as if through the wrong end of a telescope: far, far away was the perfect child in a perfect room sheathed in a warm, inviting glow. The lamps shed an orangy light; circus posters decorated the walls, a blue aquarium bubbled on a night table, a canary chirped in a golden cage, a black-and-white television flickered at the foot of the bed. She looked from Chris's face to Jed's. Placid. Unruffled. The fight was over. Only she, like wreckage after a storm, felt splintered. And where was her own child? she asked herself. Asleep in a pullout couch, watched over by the aged Mrs. Johnston with a "t." A far cry from the sun-filled nursery in New Haven, where Christopher hung a Calder mobile over the antique crib and danced around with his baby on his shoulder. She crossed to the daybed and sat down, peering disconsolately into the aquarium, wondering if she should buy Chryssie a goldfish.

"Sit over here, Katherine, I want to show you my stuff," Chris said sweetly, moving over to make room on her bed. While Jed fiddled with the television, they turned the pages of a sketch pad crammed with deftly drawn animals—except for the last page, upon which was a watercolor that Katherine imagined might have been assigned by the shrink. Three figures stood in front of a lopsided house: a tall dark-haired man, a tiny blond woman, and between them a normal-sized, towheaded child. Overhead, jutting from the moon's pale sphere, a dagger dripped blood. Chris's version of the nuclear family, after the explosion of divorce, Katherine thought. "These are very good, Chris. I've loved seeing them," she said and rose. "I really have to go home now."

"You'll do no such thing!" Jed reached over and turned off Chris's bedside lamp. "Go to sleep, dollface."

"Leave the TV on, okay, Dad?"

"Anything, anything," he muttered as he left the room.

Chris beamed up at Katherine. "I'll draw something just for you next time, okay?"

"That'd be great. Sweet dreams." She closed the door quietly, her nerves jangled by the child's tyranny.

When she came into the study, Jed was sitting in his chair, gazing into the fire. Without looking up, he said sadly, "Sometimes I feel so sorry for her."

Katherine's mouth fell open. "*Sorry* for her? But she's got everything up here. Christabel—I mean, *my* Christabel—would—"

"Why would they have the same *names*, O Lord?" A brief smile faded. "Chris has problems. She's lonely."

"Somehow a daughter alone with her father doesn't seem as

lonely to me as one with her mother. I think Chris is very lucky—"

"You don't understand," he interrupted. "Your knibbler has an intelligent mother. It's a whole other ball game. She doesn't have to spend every weekend the 'The Juke Family,' undermining whatever you do for her." With his pipe, he made an imperious gesture. "Sit down, kid. You make me nervous hovering."

'I'm sorry. I really do have to go. Thank you for dinner," she said, backing toward the door.

"Very well." Jed sighed and got to his feet. "You've exhausted me, my dear."

"*I've* exhausted you?" Katherine repeated incredulously.

"That's right," he said, going past her to the foyer.

She grabbed her purse from the pebble-strewn shelf. The man was *impossible*; what had *she* to do with the evening's misadventure?

The night air was soft, alive with the rustle of palm trees. Behind Chris's shutters, all was silent. Katherine bid Jed a cool good night and got into her car; as she started the motor, he tapped on her window and she rolled it down a few inches.

"Friday's Chanukah," he said. "We're having a little celebration up here before Chris goes off to Manhattan Beach for Christmas. Why don't you come up"—the excuse she had begun to formulate died on her lips as he continued—"and bring your little one. She might enjoy it. My stepson, Ricky, will be here, possibly Alvin, my nephew. It's nothing special. Just family."

Family. The word reverberated in the night.

"That sounds great. We'd love it."

Through the dark, deserted streets of Beverly Hills, Katherine drove home with Douglas's words echoing in her ears: "The only thing that counts in the end is family." She turned onto El Camino. It seemed that behind every lighted window there was a family. In every house but hers.

CHAPTER 11

Happy Families
Are Not All Alike

When she was four, Christabel Kellogg was in the vanguard of a generation whose concept of family would be based largely on situation comedy. Often while Katherine was getting dressed to go out, Chryssie would be sitting cross-legged like a small Buddha two feet from the television set, absorbing information about married life and interpersonal relations from Ozzie and Harriet, Robert Young, or Danny Thomas. Even The Munsters gave Katherine guilt. Callow bachelors of her acquaintance bore scant resemblance to the family men served up nightly by Hollywood, in this instance remorseless as the Church. The all-American video dad of the mid-sixties was successful, fun-loving, good-natured, a trifle bumbling, and almost always *home*—not so very different from her own father.

Whatever Douglas Winterhaus's faults—stubbornness sprang to mind, narrow-mindedness, lack of compassion for human failings, a complete inability to admit that he was wrong about anything—his love had been the great stabilizing factor in Katherine's life. Although she shrank from commitment, the most casual dates were graded on their potential as father figures for Christabel. Andrew Byrne got a D in that department—in all the months she'd known him, he'd exhibited no surrogate inclination; the hours he chose to spend in Katherine's apartment were when her daughter was asleep.

"Stop worrying about it," Louise had advised her. "*Time* recently did a study on the subject. Psychologists say that as long as the parent is happy, the child will be."

"That's bullshit!" Katherine had retorted. "It's one of the myths that an increasingly selfish society is perpetuating in order to sanctify divorce. The truth is that the two things are often diametrically opposed. Chryssie hates it when I work; moreover, men who are right for me are invariably wrong for her, and vice versa." With a dejected sigh, she added, "At least I don't seem to be able to put the two things together."

It rained the Friday of Chanukah and the air turned sharply cooler. At six-thirty, Katherine took from Chryssie's closet a blue-and-white-checked wool skirt and jacket purchased for the occasion, handed her an undershirt and, wielding a hairbrush, admonished her to hold still.

"Wait!" said Chryssie, hopping from one foot to the other as she hiked her white leotards higher on her legs. "D'you think Mr. Bernard will have a Christmas tree, Mommy?"

"Probably not, because he's Jewish," Katherine replied, making a futile pass at the wispy yellow hair with the brush.

"I wish I was Jewish," Chryssie muttered.

"Why's that?"

"Because." Chryssie tilted her face back and stuck out her dimpled chin to be zipped up, but when Katherine set a navy blue peaked cap on her head, she objected through gritted teeth: "Do I *have* to wear that?"

"It looks adorable. Because why?"

"Because why what?"

They giggled together. "Why do you say you want to be Jewish?" Katherine asked, brushing the hair that fell beneath the cap.

"Oh . . . because Judy and Cathy are Jewish, and they're my best friends. Also, Judy says they give their kids presents *every day* for *eight days* at Chanukah!"

"That," said Katherine as she flicked off the light and pushed her daughter out the door, "is not a good reason to change your religion."

"It's a jockey!" Jed exclaimed when he saw Chryssie standing on his doorstep. "Chris!" he called out. "Come and see—Katherine's brought a jockey with her!"

Chryssie gaped up at the tall, dashing figure in a gray turtle-neck and tweed jacket.

"This is Mr. Bernard, honey."

In her fascination and awe, Chryssie reverted to a convent kindergarten habit and dropped a quick curtsy.

"*Gottenyu!* The poor little kid's got polio or what? You didn't tell me," Jed cried, pulling Chryssie inside. "Glad you could make it, knibbler. Amazing you can race horses with an infirmity like that."

Whinnying and wielding a riding crop, Chris Bernard cantered down the hall, shod in white cowboy boots with the same paint-stained, oversized T-shirt hanging from her bony shoulders. A lumpen-faced child with brown springy curls dogged her heels like a faithful retainer. Her name was Julie, and she had freckles, a too-eager smile, and a servile manner that gave the impression she was ready to kill should Chris demand it. Fringed leather chaps were tied over her dungarees. Chryssie snatched the cap from her head and stashed it behind a pre-Columbian vase. The two Gullivers scooped up their Lilliputian and ran off down the hall. One anxious, over-the-shoulder glance was the last thing Katherine saw before Chryssie disappeared into Chris's bedroom.

Jed's house was a festival: candles burned in the menorah; the lights of the Christmas tree were reflected in the glass wall, dancing over the pool; mistletoe hung from the lintel and flowers were everywhere—jumbled pink and yellow roses on the coffee table, tall vases filled with berry branches against the wall.

"What a beautiful tree!" Katherine exclaimed.

"It's for the kid. I'm not depriving Chris for some Jewish *bubbe montses.*"

"Jewish what?"

"Grandmothers' tales. Would you believe I decorated the son-ofabitch myself? There's a girl in there"—he hooked his thumb toward Chris's bedroom—"who was supposed to do it. She's been asleep ever since she got here. Cripples!" he bellowed. "I hired her two days ago to take care of Chris—sort of a companion, so Adelaide can do other things, you follow me? I thought it'd be nice. Chris and I met her in Carmel last fall. She was kind of a flower child. The pisher took to her bed immediately—no help whatsoever. I'm sending her back first thing in the morning."

His predicament made Katherine think of a little boy she'd seen in the playground, alone on a seesaw and looking desperately for someone to balance the other end. "Maybe she'll recover tomorrow," she said.

"*Ver veys?* When will I learn, O Lord? You don't hire Jewish girls. Knibblers, every one of them." He sifted animosity through his teeth. "This one's called Stacey—I always love a good biblical name like Stacey. She takes one look at the tree and says she's allergic—starts to *varf* herself sneezing. They're all allergic to something. When my sister Sonia comes to visit, we have to get rid of the cat. Sinusitis, female troubles, back problems, headaches." He began to pace. "Saul Bellow calls it the passionate hypochondria of Jewish women."

"Saul Bellow's a misogynist. Jewish men are never sick, I suppose?"

"I'll give you a misogynist," said Jed, winding up a fist. Then he laughed. "I myself have never had a well day. But enough of my troubles, my dear." He settled into the armchair by the fire and crossed his feet on the ottoman. "Make me a vodka and tonic, will you, dollface? I want to have a chat with you about Cardinal Spellman's war."

Halfway to the bar, she turned to gape at him. "Cardinal Spellman? You blame *Cardinal Spell*man for Vietnam?"

"Ho, ho, *HO!*" Jed's cry was jubilant. "Diem was Spellman's boy! You're a smart girl—figure it out. Kennedy was a Catholic, Spellman had his ear . . . why else do you think America backed that mandarin putz?"

First of all, Spellman was for Nixon," Katherine stated. "He was an archconservative, as are most of the Irish clergy in New York . . . *and* Boston. Secondly, Kennedy wasn't all that Catholic—"

Ignoring her, Jed continued, "The Ngo family built up this big issue of getting the Catholics out of the north. Save them from Communism, you follow me? Eight hundred thousand of them streamed into South Vietnam, and Diem was the big hero. Under the banner of anti-Communism, and of course with America's help, he turned himself into a dictator. Raped his own country. The Saigon government is so corrupt it makes Ho Chi Minh look like Thomas Jefferson. 'Turn Catholic in order to get rice,' was the word in the south. Have you read Graham Greene?"

"Memorized him," Katherine laughed.

"Read what he says about Diem—'separated from his people by cardinals, going to weekly confession, believing God is always on the Catholic side.' You think it's a coincidence, I suppose, that Diem's brother is the archbishop and Madame Nhu has Buddhist barbecues? You think they didn't have a hot line to the Vatican and a lobby going in Washington?" A deep line formed between Jed's eyebrows as he sucked on his pipe. "Why do we always back the wrong man? Americans have no understanding of Southeast Asia. We've got no business there."

As he spoke, Katherine poured tonic over ice, put the cap on the vodka, and stirred the drinks with some agitation. This interpretation of recent history, loaded though it might have been, came as a revelation. She had accepted the war as a fact of life; everyone she knew was in favor of America's involvement in Vietnam. Communism was the enemy. That truism was mother's milk at the convent, where missionaries brought eyewitness reports of children tortured, peasants' fingers lopped off, nuns raped by Communist devils. Photographs of protesters had begun to appear in the Western edition of *The New York Times*, but demonstrations were considered the business of draft-age kids who were, understandably, reluctant to be killed. "I'll admit," she conceded as she brought Jed his drink, "if I had a son, I wouldn't want him to go. I'd probably *take* him to Canada. But—"

"But nothing." He took a sip, grimaced, and set the glass down. "We should get out."

"But we're committed there. We can't just leave. How could we?"

"I'll tell you how," said Jed, leaning forward, his eyes narrowed with intensity. "The same way we got there. Just get on the fucking boats and *leave!* Hup, two, three, four, up the gangplank and *go home!*"

The argument dissolved in Katherine's laughter. Outrageous as it seemed, Jed's theory made perfect sense to her.

"My idea of a dream debate would be you and William F. Buckley," she said.

"I'd put him away!" Jed cried, his eyes glittering.

"I think you might."

With a wry smile, he said, "Not really. He's a whole other ball game . . . fucking brilliant." He pulled at his drink. "Politics was my first love. I always wanted to go into the foreign service."

"Why didn't you?"

"I tried. I applied to Georgetown, where a very nice man told me I'd never get anywhere because I was a Jew."

"No!"

"My hand to God."

As Katherine considered this, memories of Rochester arose to give him credence, and her curiosity about the young Jed Bernard was piqued. "How did you get from politics to show business?" she asked.

Endlessly restless, Jed got up and roamed around the room as he recounted a history of acting successes in college; a Broadway debut that made him an overnight sensation, without patience for the repetitiveness of theater; the creation of *Tessie* and *Pasquale*; beating Madison Avenue at its own game by getting the network to put them on sustaining. In nineteen forty-one, the boy wonder of radio went to Hollywood.

His gaze lingered on the photograph of Bertie Hayes. Well into her fifties when it was taken, the legendary Ziegfeld star was descending a marble staircase in a tunic and trousers, a cigarette holder in her hand and a faintly mocking smile on her carmine lips, still sporting the raving red hair and (judging from the inscription) wise-cracking mouth that had captivated Broadway before Jacob Bernard Bronstein was born. In response to Katherine's query about their relationship, Jed painted a self-portrait of a brash, talented twenty-six-year-old making fourteen thousand dollars a week in an era when a man could keep most of it, or spend it, as he had, on black butlers and black custom-made suits and black Cadillac convertibles to squire a string of actresses to Mocambo and LaRue. Before he blew it all, Bertie took charge. " 'Listen to me, kid,' " he quoted, imitating her snappy delivery, " 'land is basic. There's not one of these broads that's ever going to mean a fuck to you. Build yourself a house and hang on to it, 'cause the day will come when you'll need it. It'll be all you got.' "

Others said Bertie had seen better days, that the once-blazing Ziegfeld star was on the wane, but not Jed; to him, she was still the funniest, classiest dame alive. And long after the husbands and lovers were gone, the man in her life was Jed Bernard. He made her laugh. This character fashioned out of Damon Runyon in a turtleneck sweater and oversized trenchcoat broke her up. Once she said, "Jacob, if I were fifteen years younger, I'd give you a little *hok*," and he growled, "*Feh*! Don't talk dirty, Bert." Yet his love for her surpassed any he could muster for a mere mistress. She was his mother, his mentor, his best friend. Bertie taught him taste. She furnished the house for him, saved him from one or two disastrous marriages, and showed him how to hold his own in a town full of killers.

Bertie's salon, into which she brought Jed, consisted of the writers and comedians who formed an elite Hollywood group in the forties. Night after night, while some forgotten starlet cooled her heels, Jed sat with Bertie kibitzing or playing gin rummy. One midnight, after he'd spent the evening coaxing a girl into his bed, Bertie called to ask him to come to her house because she couldn't sleep. He told her no, absolutely not; but after he hung up, he took another look at the girl (who'd made him lock Simon the First out because she was afraid of dogs), decided he hated her by then, drove her home, and went directly to Bertie's. Gathered at her house on any given evening would be Ben Hecht, Oscar Levant, Eddie Cantor, Al Jolson, and Fanny Brice, who'd dubbed Jed "the kid." They became his family, an emotional and intellectual haven in the midst of what he called the *mishegoss*: grinding out jokes for the great comedians like Benny and Hope and Danny Thomas, creating shows for the dumb blondes and crazed comedians who peopled his world, eventually running FBC network on the Coast. As he described it to Katherine, Hollywood in its heyday came to life in the room in all its wit and glamour and eccentricity.

"Before I built the house," he recalled, "one time I bet Bertie a hundred dollars she couldn't make me laugh. The next day when I came home to my apartment, she was sitting in the living room, playing cards with Bea Lillie. They had hats on . . . fucking *hats*! Otherwise they were stark naked! 'You know Lady Peale,' Bertie said, very nonchalant. I didn't crack a smile . . . didn't bat an *eye*! I made myself a drink and sat down to read the paper. Then the kitchen door opened and Eddie Cantor sailed in on *roller skates* . . . also stark naked! I fell *away*—choked on my frigging drink!" Radiating energy, laughing, he concluded, "I told them it was worth a C note to catch old Banjo Eyes with his cock out!"

In her spellbound state, Katherine had lost track of time, the children in the next room, everything but him; now as he crossed the room and sat heavily in his chair, she saw that his face had fallen into the tired, sad expression of earlier in the evening. It was as if a shadow had passed over him. He said quietly, "They carried me off the field when that woman died."

A shriek resounded from the children's quarters. Jed and Katherine looked at each other in alarm. A second later, Chris galloped out followed by Julie; they rounded the corner toward Jed's bedroom as Chryssie ran into the foyer, wearing a sheet over her head. The two older girls doubled back and confronted her. Chryssie leaped into the air and yelled, *"Boo!"* making everyone laugh.

"Marvelous," Jed remarked as they ran off. "They've turned your kid into a Klan member already."

Simon lifted his head from the hearth, a growl starting; the iron knocker clanked against the front door. Jed went over, and as he opened it, raised his hand like a claw, croaking, "Quoth the raven, nevermore!"

A boy of about sixteen entered; he had shoulder-length brown hair, finely drawn features, and a slight frame that was swamped by a bulky red reindeer sweater.

"Ricky, my boy! Good to see you." Jed cradled the lad's head under his arm and rapped it gently with his knuckles. "Straighten yourself *out*!"

When Ricky looked up at Jed, his expression took Katherine by surprise. A stepchild of Jed's, particularly Laura's son, might be expected to have ambivalent feelings about him, but what shone from Ricky's eyes was pure, uncomplicated love. There was none of the compulsiveness or neurotic tincture that colored the emotion between Jed and his daughter. As different as a man and boy could be, each appeared beguiled in the presence of his opposite.

"Hey, Jed!" Ricky cried in a voice that hovered on the brink of manhood. "I'm glad to be here. The house looks terrific. How're you doing? How's Chris?"

"Up to her ears in community work, I expect. We're worried that she's going to be too repressed. Katherine, this is my son, Ricky. A *farkrimte* kid if ever there was one."

On cue, Ricky dropped one of his packages as he put out his hand to say hello.

"Put the presents down, Rick," Jed commanded. "Just put them under the tree before you break something. You never were anything with props. This kid," he told Katherine, "broke every vase in the house when he lived up here. The ones he missed, his mother got later." He rumpled Ricky's hair fondly. "He was four years old the first time Laura brought him up the hill. Just like your knibbler. The scaredest little boy I'd ever seen."

"When Jed yelled at me, I used to run outside and hide under a cottonwood tree."

"You spent four years under that tree, Rick."

"You said you were going to furnish it."

"Speaking of knibblers"—Jed started for Chris's room—"I better see if the jockey's still alive. Who knows what those *chayehs* might do to her?"

Katherine turned to Ricky. "What are *chayehs*?"

"Wild animals," he replied with a grin.

They exchanged idle conversation until he noticed a large photo album stashed on the lower shelf of the coffee table. "I haven't looked at these for years. Would you like to see pictures of when I lived up here?" he asked shyly.

"I'd love to."

Seated on the couch, with the album on their knees, Ricky turned the pages. There was Jed, ten years younger, devastatingly handsome in a dark suit with a sprig of orange blossoms in his lapel, one arm around Ricky, who appeared to be about six, a grave little boy wearing what must have been his first suit. His light eyes stared at the camera with the bewildered, powerless expression often seen in children attending a parent's wedding.

And there, too, was a solitary picture of Laura Loder, in her twenties, a highball in her hand, a familiar pout on her face as she stood under the olive tree. Her shoulder-length, then dark blond hair and spectacular figure were set off by a clinging black dress that made Katherine recall a newspaper account of Barbara Hutton's fourth wedding: "The bride wore black and carried a Scotch and soda." The remaining pages were filled with snapshots of Chris, doted upon by Jed at every stage of development.

"Scary how much she looks like Laura," Ricky remarked.

"Dinner is served," murmured Adelaide behind them.

At the table, Jed put himself between Chris and Ricky, with Katherine on the other side of Chris, who had changed into a green corduroy skirt and vest and brushed her hair. Bowing his head, he pronounced a garbled Jewish blessing. Then he reached across Chris for a plate of matzoh, one eye on Julie, who was eagerly helping herself. "Let me ask you something," he said. "Have you considered brain surgery? The way you're dismembering that chicken, you'd be one of the greats." He looked around the table. "Can you believe this? On Chanukah, I'm the only Jew in the place."

"I'm Jewish," said Chris.

Jed twisted his hand back and forth. "Half."

"Me too!" Chryssie piped up, causing everyone to look at her and laugh.

"Where does she get that, the *petzel?*" Jed inquired of Katherine.

"Wishful thinking," she replied.

"What's a *petzel?*" Julie asked.

"Little putz. You're a *petzel,* I'm a putz, especially that we should be eating the chicken together on this of all days—one of our more cheerful holidays, when we celebrate only five thousand dead."

For the rest of the meal, Jed held court, telling stories, reminiscing with Ricky, explaining to Chris why she was not getting a horse for Chanukah. At one point he looked across the table at Chryssie. "Tell us about your life, knibbler. Are you in school yet?" Everyone turned to look at her. Unaccustomed to dinner table competition, the little girl took her time with a reply.

"Well . . . first there was kindergarten . . . at the convent in San Francisco, and when we came down here . . . I went to The Little French Schoolhouse. Now I go to Buckley."

Jed's mouth quivered. "Where does that put you, kid? Do you graduate this year?"

"I'm in Reading Readiness," she replied.

His jaw fell open. "You I don't believe altogether. Listen to how good she talks, Chris!" With a mischievous gleam in his eye, he said, "Let me ask you something, Univac—you don't mind if I call you Univac, do you?"

Chryssie shook her head, her eyes riveted on Jed's face.

"D'you think the economy's in trouble? Got any tips on the market? I never heard a kid talk as good as you in my fucking life!"

Jed's language and rough style left Chryssie unperturbed, to Katherine's surprise, but as a result of being the cynosure of five pairs of eyes, she emitted a small belch, at which Jed cried, "*Greptsing?*" reached across Ricky, and pulled her toward him by the ears. "Univac, what are we to *do* with you?" Her answering giggle brimmed with pleasure and the excitement of one unfamiliar with male attention.

After supper, Jed sat next to the fire with his feet up, and instructed Chris to distribute the presents. The children clustered around the tree while Katherine sat on an ottoman against the glass wall. There was a scarf for Ricky, a watercolor of a horse from Chris to her father (which prompted a teasing, "You're too direct, kid. Why don't you hint around a little?"), a pencil box for Julie, and a game for Chryssie. Chagrined at having come empty-handed, Katherine kept Jed's present to her unopened on her lap.

"Open it," he urged finally.

Everyone looked at her. She untied the ribbon, removed the tissue paper, and turned over a little blue book to read the title.

"Show them," said Jed.

Blushing, she held it up so they could see the bold white letters: *How to Be A Jewish Mother.*

CHAPTER 12

The Second Coming

On the morning of Christmas Eve, Chryssie sat at the breakfast table pushing Cheerios around in a bowl of milk and chattering about what they would do after her father arrived. Across the room, Katherine was putting the last of the ornaments on a small fir tree in the window.

"How many days exactly is Daddy staying?"

"I'm not positive, honey—two, I think," Katherine replied, holding a crystal snowflake up to the light, then hooking it onto an upper branch. "Go see what time it is, will you please?"

Chryssie wriggled off her chair and went to the kitchen door. "The big hand's on two and the little hand's on nine."

"Oh, no! I'm going to be late again! Hurry up, Noodle, get your stuff and I'll take you to Abby's."

On the way down the corridor to Apartment 1C, where Abby lived with her mother, Chryssie asked for the tenth time, "What time are you getting here to pick me up for the airport?"

"Twelve-fifteen. I know, I know, I'll be on time, I promise."

"You'd better," Chryssie warned, on her tiptoes to ring the bell.

After a moment, Abby came to the door rubbing sleep from her eyes. "Hi," she croaked, slung an arm across Chryssie's shoulders, and made a U-turn to her room. "Don't make any noise 'cuz Mom's still asleep."

"Your mom sleeps late," Chryssie commented as they crept past Nina's door.

"So?" Abby said, hands on her hips.

Chryssie looked startled. "So nothing," she replied.

"O-*kay*," Abby said.

Katherine closed the door, thinking what an unlikely pair they were, a weed and a hothouse flower growing side by side. Abby, who looked like one of those sentimental renderings of French orphans with her scrawny legs, huge dark eyes, and pixie haircut, was three years older and canny as a street kid, though the only ghetto she had ever known was Beverly Hills; while Chryssie, reduced to sleeping on a pullout couch in a furnished apartment, bore the aristocratic stamp of the Kelloggs on her features and displayed manners instilled by the Sacred Heart nuns. It was one of those improbable childhood friendships based on propinquity, which, when their different worlds had pulled them apart, they would remember with a poignance reserved for lost loves.

Abby's mother, Nina, had kinky red hair and the longest legs in town. She'd saved enough money from a ten-year stint as a cocktail waitress to retire to full-time motherhood. No mementos of her former profession were in evidence, and she said things like, "I wouldn't fill my gas tank in Vegas," in a bitter voice that made Katherine wonder what sorts of indignities she'd suffered there. A measure of reserve existed between them as women, but as mothers their complicity was complete. Once Nina had declared, "I've been bounced around by some rough trade in my time, but I'd do any goddamned thing to protect Abby. She's my only true love."

The morning at the art gallery was quiet. A few minutes after noon, Katherine went upstairs to Didier's office to tell him she was leaving for the airport and would be back by two as arranged, then she sprinted the five blocks home. Nina answered the door, her eyes puffy from too much sleep. "I'm on the phone, hon," she greeted Katherine. "The kids are in Abby's room."

The door was open. The two little girls sat tailor fashion on the floor between the twin beds playing jacks. As usual, Abby was way ahead, bouncing the little red ball and snatching up one jack after another with the precision of a Swiss watchmaker.

"How tall is your dad?" Chryssie asked her, a tiny line between her brows as she watched Abby's moves intently.

"Fourteen . . . fifteen . . . ," Abby said under her breath.

"Do you know?"

Abby swore. "You made me miss," she said, handing over the ball. "Which dad d'ya mean?"

"The last one—Sam."

"Five-ten."

"Mine's six-two. He's really handsome—wait'll you see."

"I already know that. You showed me the pictures. Your turn."

With that, Katherine stepped into the room. Abby said hi and Chryssie scrambled to her feet, hurtling out the door with a cry of farewell.

As they tooled along the freeway, Chryssie pointed to the western horizon, where a strip of sea glittered like a silver streamer. "Christmas is always fun, no matter what," she said, bouncing with excitement in the passenger seat.

No matter what, Katherine's mind echoed, her right hand on Chryssie's knee. How much did she remember of another Christmas, the one when she was three? In an album Chryssie kept beside her bed, there was a snapshot to remind her of it: Christopher holding her on his lap in the Wassily chair next to the tree; presents were strewn all around—a tricycle, the stuffed kitten, a small camel's hair coat spilling out of its tissue paper—and "The Night Before Christmas" was propped up in front of them, but his eyes were too bleary to focus. A few days later, he went away without telling her he was not coming back.

Abby was an old hand at such matters. Once when they were playing Fish in the living room, Katherine had overheard her educating Chryssie: "Fathers never tell you why they're leavin'. They're too chicken. They let the mothers do it."

Not to be undone, Chryssie had related: "Daddy moved to this gray house on Union Street. We always used to go down Union Street on the way to school, but one time I pointed to the house and said, 'There's his office!' and Mommy's face got all funny like it does when she's trying not to cry."

"Yeah, my mom gets that look."

"After that she always took another way to school."

"Who do they think they're kiddin'?" Abby had asked rhetorically.

"This is going to be the best Christmas of my life!" Chryssie predicted now as Katherine pulled out to pass a Rolls-Royce. Twisting around, Chryssie cried, "The wheel's on the wrong side—and lookit who's driving!"

Katherine chuckled. "Santa Claus in a Rolls. Only in Los Angeles."

"Abby says it's crap about Santa."

"Christabel! What kind of language is that?"

"Abby's."

"That's true. But what are you, a sponge? Daddy'll croak if he hears you using words like that."

"Are we almost there?"

"Yep. Are you excited?"

"Uh-*huh*!"

Wedged between a limousine and an airport bus, the blue car crawled around the airport in the holiday traffic jam. At the PSA terminal, a loudspeaker was announcing the arrival of Flight 8 from San Francisco; Katherine grabbed Chryssie's hand and took off at a gallop down the brightly lit tunnel.

Just as they reached the gate, the doors opened, letting out a stream of passengers. In the first wave were three black men of uncommon height wearing yellow satin jackets with purple numbers. Hoisted in her mother's arms, Chryssie scanned the crowd. A tall blond man in a business suit bobbed in and out at the rear. Katherine felt Chryssie's heart thumping beneath the sailor dress, heard her sigh when she saw that the man was a stranger.

All around, people were hugging and kissing and saying "Merry Christmas," and "Happy holidays!" A woman with pink rollers in her hair embraced a fat man in a Hawaiian sport shirt. A group of Mexicans waved to an elderly woman and sobbed with joy. Hand in hand, a pretty young stewardess and a little boy with a tag around his neck got off. How long before Chryssie would be in his shoes? Katherine thought. Soon they'll have a special class for them on airlines. Baby refugees . . . kid commuters . . . the detritus of divorce. Oh God. Where *was* he? The line had thinned to a trickle. "Is everybody off the plane?" she asked the stewardess.

"I believe so," she said and hurried on with her charge.

Behind her, a pilot wearing aviator sunglasses smiled at Katherine. "Can I help you?"

"My husband—he was supposed to be on this flight."

"Sorry, miss. That's it."

"Perhaps you could have him paged at the airport," said another pretty young stewardess—they were all pretty and young—looking past Katherine to Chryssie, whose eyes were filling with tears.

"He probably missed it . . . there's such a crush out there. How awful—on Christmas."

At the phone booth, Katherine dialed Christopher's number. The ringing drilled in her ear: seven . . . eight . . . Forcing a casual tone as she replaced the receiver, she said, "Daddy's not home, honey, so he must be on his way. The next flight's in an hour. We'll just get something to read and wait. Come on, I'll buy you some comic books."

Chryssie read *Archie, Wonder Woman*, and *Richie Rich* before it was time to peruse another batch of deplaning passengers. Once again the crowd dispersed without yielding up its prize. Katherine felt as if she were in a scene from a war movie; Chryssie tearfully uncoiled her arms from her neck when the PSA official closed the door with a bang.

"It's the holiday," Katherine explained, leading her toward the escalator. "This kind of thing happens all the time. I'll take you back to Abby's and then I'll come meet the next one." She would have flown to San Francisco to get him in order to erase the bereft expression on her daughter's face.

"But you've got to go back to work!" Chryssie wailed.

"Big deal. I'll get fired sooner than I expected."

During the ride home, the motor hummed and the wheels turned and the freeway traffic made a whooshing noise, and Katherine imagined that to Chryssie they all said: He didn't come . . . he didn't come. The little girl was staring out her window, softly singing: "Supercalifragilisticexpialidocious."

Nina opened the door of her apartment wrapped in her rose-colored Japanese kimono with the green satin dragon on the back. Katherine explained quickly, then asked if Chryssie could stay till five. "Sure, hon. The kid's always welcome, you know that," Nina said and coughed.

"Thanks so much, Nina. You're a lifesaver." Katherine brushed a kiss across Chryssie's cheek. "I'll come get you the minute we get back from the airport, okay?"

"Okay," said Chryssie, nodding very fast.

Abby was in the living room eating a bowl of Froot Loops, her dark eyes glazed from watching *Let's Make a Deal*. She glanced over as Chryssie squatted beside her. "So? Where is he?"

"He's coming later." Chryssie stared hard at the small screen. A middle-aged woman dressed as an asparagus was jumping up and down in front of a washing machine. "Is that all she won?"

"Nope. She got a bedroom set." Abby sat up and shoved a pile of jacks over to her. "Guys never show up when they say they're going to, you know."

Chryssie raised her shoulders to her ears and dropped them in an elaborate shrug. "I *know*," she said and, blinking, picked up the red rubber ball and bounced it.

By the time Katherine got back to the gallery, Didier had left for his golf match, expecting her to reopen. Upstairs in his office, she gave the operator Christopher's number, picturing the telephone ringing in his empty apartment, the one where he had brought her late one night to make drunken, sordid love. During the frenetic maneuvers in his narrow bed, he'd knocked a glass half full of vodka off the night table; it shattered on the floor. Long after he had begun to snore thunderously at her side, she had lain awake, staring at his bird's-eye view of the bay, afraid to move lest she cut herself on the shards of broken glass lying all around. She remembered trudging up the hill in the early-morning light, her makeup smeared, her clothes disheveled as a prostitute's.

Didier's office was stuffy. Beads of perspiration formed on Katherine's forehead as she listened to Christopher's phone ringing. When, on the seventh ring, he answered, his voice a liquid slur in her ear, she closed her eyes in despair.

"Why weren't you on the plane?" she asked tensely.

"Jus' got home . . . lil' office party at the office . . . sorry about that," he said and burped.

Toward him she felt nothing, neither anger nor hatred nor love; all her emotions were subsumed in a frenzy to deliver him to their daughter. "Which flight are you planning to take?"

"Gotta reservation on the four clock, but I'm having trouble getting a taxi. Can't unnerstanit . . . they keep hanging up on me."

"Oh, God," she breathed, before her the vision of Chryssie at the airport, her face falling apart like a jigsaw puzzle under the stark fluorescent lights. Thinking fast, she checked her watch and said, "Are you sober enough to function if I can get a taxi to pick you up?"

"Cert'nly," he replied.

"Okay. Just be ready, please."

She hung up and dialed Information for the number of Yellow Cab in San Francisco. When the dispatcher answered, she used shameless feminine wiles to cajole him. "All I ask is that you get him out there by three-thirty . . . whatever shape he's in."

"Okay, lady," the man finally agreed. "What the hell, it's Christmas."

At three-thirty, there was no answer at Christopher's. Relieved, Katherine closed the gallery at four and sped back to the airport.

PSA's Flight 405 from San Francisco was twenty minutes late. When at last the doors opened and the passengers poured through, she studied each male face intently, as if there were a chance she might fail to recognize her estranged husband. Before half the planeload had disembarked, she knew with chilling certainty that Christopher was not on the flight.

The Yellow Cab dispatcher in San Francisco had a new, unpleasant edge to his voice. "We got him out there all right, lady, but he only had a dollar on him. The driver took him home to get money. He never came out."

"Oh, no! Look, what can I do? I'll triple the meter . . . I'll send you a check, I promise, only—"

"Sorry, lady, we don't take checks, especially from L.A.," he snapped and hung up.

Holiday travelers surged toward Katherine in the terminal tunnel, their faces jaundiced in the harsh yellow light. She felt like the creature in Munch's painting "The Scream." Blindly she passed the children's crayon drawings on the tiled walls, tears seeping beneath her sunglasses. A middle-aged man with a briefcase looked at her, then glanced away quickly, as startled as if she'd removed her dress. Two young women in the Information booth exchanged a look as she went by.

In the car she repaired her face with powder, but when Nina opened her apartment door, she took one look at Katherine and said, "That lousy bastard." Chryssie raced in from Abby's room and Nina knelt to give her a squeeze, drawling kindly, "Come over first thing in the morning, sweetie pie. We've got some stuff for you."

The little girl sought her mother's eyes. "Is he home?"

Wordlessly, Katherine shook her head.

All the old excuses were resurrected as they went down the hall to their own apartment: "Daddy's not feeling well . . . he said to tell you he's so sorry but . . ."

The telephone was ringing as she unlocked the door; she raced into the bedroom to pick it up, hearing the television spring to life in the living room. "How's it going?" Andy asked pleasantly, for once unconcerned about the presence of a man in Katherine's apartment. "Husbands don't count," he'd told her.

"He didn't come, Andy," she whispered into the phone. "I spent the whole damn day at the airport."

He made a sympathetic sound. "Bad luck, Kate."

"I feel so sorry for Christabel." Her voice cracked. Independence was Katherine's style, but the crisis impelled her to plead, "You couldn't possibly come over for a while tonight, could you?"

"Look, you know I promised Mom I'd be there for dinner. I'm really sorry, but—"

"Oh, right, I forgot. Never mind," she said briskly. "It'll be all right."

"Maybe he'll show up tomorrow. If not, I'll come by in the evening. I've got a present for Chryssie."

"That's nice. Thanks."

She replaced the receiver and sat with the phone on her knee, staring at it, too despondent to move. It rang again. She picked it up and heard a slow, familiar growl.

"Cripple? Is that you? Where have you been?"

"Oh, Jed, hi. I just got home."

"What is this with the little voice? You're speaking from the bottom of a well, I presume. *Tisha b'Ov* time?"

"No, no. I'm fine. How're you?"

"Ferpacht!" he exclaimed, which by now she knew meant "put away."

"What? Why's that?" she asked bleakly.

"I had to rise today."

"You had to . . . ? Oh, no—" In spite of everything, she began to laugh. "That's Easter. He rose on Easter."

"Really? What's today then?"

"His birthday."

"Oh, yeah. So, what're you doing for Christmas, you and the kid?"

"Oh . . . um . . . I'm not sure. Christopher never showed up. He had too much to drink at his office party and—"

"Stay where you are," Jed said without a moment's hesitation. "I've got to be somewhere at eleven, but I'll come over first."

"Oh, Jed. I'd be so grateful —"

"Why would you marry a *shikkerer*?" he growled, and hung up.

At eight-thirty the doorbell rang. Chryssie ran to open the door, and there stood Jed, elegantly turned out in a black velvet dinner jacket with an enormous package in his arms. "Do you believe this? he greeted them. "The Jewish Cary Grant playing Santa Claus to two Gentile people at the height of my career?" As he swept past them to the living room, he said under his breath to Katherine, "You tell anyone about this, you'll never work in this town again." He held the present out to Chryssie. "Merry Christmas, Univac."

She tore off the paper, squealing with delight as she uncovered the biggest doll anyone had ever seen—as tall as she was, wearing a ruffled pink nightie. "Where in the name of God," Katherine asked him sotto voce, "did you get that at this hour?"

"It's one of my ex-wives. I had to get rid of her—she was acting like a child. Get me a vodka tonic, would you, kid?"

He looked around for a place to sit. Rejecting the couch, he settled himself awkwardly in an upholstered chair at one end of the coffee table. The room seemed to shrink around him as he took out his pipe and searched in vain for a light. Katherine raced to the kitchen, where she made him a drink with one hand while rummaging through drawers for a match with the other. Seen through Jed's eyes, the apartment was embarrassingly tacky; never again would she complain about meeting at his house, she vowed to herself as she hurried out with his drink. In her rattled state she spilled it on the coffee table, mopped at it clumsily, and raced to get another.

More than an hour later, the second drink remained untouched and Chryssie's face looked as if the circus had come to town. Any doubts Katherine might have had about Jed's essential goodness vanished as she observed him pulling on his pipe and performing for her daughter, while elsewhere in Beverly Hills a glamorous party convened without him.

Ashes fluttered to the carpet. "Did I tell you I directed a home movie when I was seven?" he asked Katherine solemnly, knocking out his pipe in a small ashtray.

"No."

"It was *Beauty and the Beast*. I was in it, and Sherbie the dwarf."

"Which one were you?"

"Putz! There are two parts. I'm not playing the beast!"

"A real dwarf?" Chryssie asked.

"A dwarf!" he cried. "Billy Barty was a tall man compared to Sherbie. He used to look up to Billy Barty. His mother, Hazel, was four foot two! Later, he was married to a Mexican woman. I shot the whole thing in Mille Lacs Park."

"Excuse me," Katherine interjected, "but . . . uh . . . how did you happen to be talking to this dwarf?"

"He's my cousin! Aunt Hazel's boy!" Jed cried.

"What? How old was he?"

"Four."

Clutching her doll, Chryssie rolled around giggling.

"How could you tell he was a dwarf at four?" Katherine managed to choke out.

"Because"—Jed's face creased and his shoulders shook—"he was standing next to a grape, and he was shorter!" All three exploded. "He sat on a dime and his legs dangled!" Jed wheezed, his eyes streaming.

Highlights from *Fiddler on the Roof* followed, with Jed playing all the parts. Then he left the room and came back a high-stepping chorus boy, waving his arms, flirting with the audience; for an encore he was a white slave trader in a steamy climate, hitting a native servant and snapping, "Tonga, take a week off!" while their rollicking laughter spurred him on.

Finally, around eleven, curled up in her quilted robe with the doll slumped against her, Chryssie fell asleep. Only then did Jed glance at his watch. "From the knibbler to Dean Martin and those putzes. This I don't believe altogether."

At the door, Katherine kissed his cheek and said, "You are my idea of a good Samaritan."

"Again with the biblical talk! You're a *machamoves*, you know that?"

"A *what?*"

"*Malech-hamoves*, properly. It means 'angel of death.' " He made her repeat his version after him until she achieved the proper aspiration in her throat. "That's it. Pretty good, Malcolm. That was one of Benny's characters: Malcolm Movitz." Jed's reflection in the hall mirror was illumined from below by a Christmas candle. "Do I look sick to you?" he inquired, peering at himself.

"You look like a million dollars," she responded sincerely.

"That little, eh? Too bad you couldn't come with me, kid," he said in an offhand way, "but you probably wouldn't be interested, would you? Just a lot of boring movie stars sitting around. I'll be in bed by one," he assured her, broadly stifling a mock yawn. Then he picked up the burning candle, handed it to her with a stern "Go to your room," and bounded down the corridor.

The smell of his tobacco lingered in the living room. Katherine pulled out the tree lights and carried Chryssie in to the big bed. Her voice muffled against her mother's shoulder, the little girl murmured, "Mr. Bernard saved us, didn't he, Mommy?"

"The man is a regular messiah," Katherine said softly. "No question about it."

CHAPTER 13

Epiphany

"So, are you going back to your husband, cripple?"

Katherine shifted her eyes away from Jed's probing gaze. Through the casement windows, she could see the sycamore tree in the courtyard drooping under the weight of a recent rain; with Chris away, a feeling of seclusion hung over the house; a spell of coziness and unreality cast by Jed in his flamboyant orange sweater, a crackling fire, and the mournful strains of gypsy music on the stereo. The study resembled a lair; a shaggy Greek rug was spread like a sea of grass over the floor and the wide backless couch where Katherine was seated. It was as if the world below the hill was shuttered; for a while she could put aside reality: Christopher's belated, remorseful arrival on her doorstep at four on Christmas afternoon; their indecisiveness about the future; Chryssie's sobbing all the way home from the airport the next day, pleading with her to make the plane turn around. The last thing Katherine wanted to talk about was her marriage. She leaned back against the pillows, brushing flecks of lint from her black slacks.

Jed crossed his sneakered feet on the ottoman. "You shouldn't pour out all your feelings like that, Katherine. Hold back a little when someone asks you a personal question."

She laughed. "The answer is no . . . for now," she said lightly. "I feel . . . Christopher thinks we should avoid making any permanent decisions."

"The man's a monument of Jell-O," Jed remarked.

Katherine did not reply. After Christopher had left, after Andy had come over with a present for Chryssie and the three of them had aped a family for an awkward hour, her dreams had been dogged by a shadowy male figure who shifted identity from husband to lover, dissolving into a faceless composite of the two. Upon awakening, she had been stricken with a primeval longing for a strong man. It's a national treasure hunt, she'd reflected. Perhaps the species has gone the way of dinosaurs. Now, looking at Jed's roughly chiseled face in the fire glow, she felt a stab of regret—for his age, her youth, the tyranny of timing. At supper, when she'd asked about the antique gold medal he always wore, he'd told her it had been given to him by an Italian princess after an idyllic week in Venice while all Rome gossiped about her absence from the prince. What a romantic figure he must have been, she thought. But the interlude was long ago, before his marriage to Laura, before Chris's birth, before the romantic fatigue that had set in with middle age, before she, Katherine, was out of kindergarten. It was only nine-thirty now, but already dark circles were scored under his eyes and the idea of a movie abandoned once he'd settled into his chair with Simon at his feet. He clicked on the lamp beside him; in its soft glow she saw the hard line of his jaw, saw the droop of his mouth as he reached for the pipe rack, moving aside the dog-eared copy of *Survival in Auschwitz*.

"Actually, I was still thinking about the princess," she said. "Who's had a more glamorous life than yours?"

"I'll tell you something, kid," he replied, a faint smile on his lips. "It's always Jacob Bronstein watching Jed Bernard."

It was his most endearing quality, Katherine thought, the candor. On an impulse, she asked him how many times he'd been married.

Without blinking, he said, "Once—to Laura."

"Eve told me you were born in Russia. Is that right?"

"No . . . Minneapolis! You've seen the scrapbooks."

"Of course. I thought so but . . . there *is* something slightly foreign about your accent."

Patiently, in a child's singsong, he recited: "My name is Jacob Bernard Bronstein. My parents are Nathan and Ida Bronstein. I live at 1421½ Thirty-ninth Street. My *bubbe* and *zayde* come from Kiev-Gibernev." Leaning forward, he gave her the full benefit of his amber gaze. "That's where I get these eyes—the color is typical Kiev." He rose, saying wearily, "Don't believe all the stories about me, my dear. You'll hear many of them." From a group of photographs on a lower shelf of the bookcase, he chose a small sepia one, handed it to her, and stood over her while she studied it. An olive-skinned little boy of five or six sat astride a tricycle in a sailor suit, looking—no, glaring—at the lens with an expression at once fierce and vulnerable.

She glanced up at Jed, then back to the child, trying to see one in the other. "Is this you?"

"No, putz, it's Mickey Rooney. Of course it's me!"

"Well, how poor can you have been if you had a tricycle?"

"It was rented!" he yelped with comic outrage. "The outfit, too. I had to give them back after the picture was taken."

Katherine's eyes kindled with sympathy. Like other privileged children acquainted with poverty only through literature or folklore, she had endowed it with a romantic mystique.

A discreet tap was heard at the door. Adelaide peeped in; she wore somber street clothes and spoke in an apologetic tone. "Will that be all, Mr. Bernard? My niece is waiting for me at the bottom of the hill."

"What *is* it with you, Adelaide? Have her come up." Jed's hearty invitation won only a thin smile in response. "I won't be needing anything else, thank you," he said. "But you'll be back Sunday evening before Chris gets home, right? So you can give her a hot meal. She gets nothing but cold spaghetti in Manhattan Beach."

"Thank you for dinner, Adelaide," Katherine said. The housekeeper had surpassed herself, singeing a steak until it was dun-colored clear through, with no trace of animal blood lurking in its congealed mass.

"You're welcome, Mrs. Kellogg," Adelaide whispered and closed the door.

"It was delicious!" Jed called after her. He was quiet for a moment, his face still in the harsh outline it had assumed at the mention of Manhattan Beach. A fresh can of tobacco being opened broke the silence with a hiss. He dug into it with a huge pipe. "It must have taken guts for you to leave your husband," he said after a moment.

"No guts at all. He left me."

He gave her a surprised look. "Now why would anybody do that? What could he have found out? You squeeze the toothpaste from the bottom of the tube? You snore? What, O Lord?" She started to reply, but he held up his hand. "Wait . . . let me guess. It was

California that did it, right? If there's a grain of neurosis, this place will bring it out."

Katherine folded her arms. "There was a time when I believed if we'd stayed in New York—where we belonged, as my mother would say—we'd still be together. I thought I was going to die when he left me. Now, sometimes I thank God he did because, being Catholic, I would probably have stayed no matter what."

"Does he have money, the putz?" Jed inquired.

"Not now. It takes a long time for architects to make anything. Someday he'll inherit a fortune though."

Jed threw up his hands. "The entire East Coast is waiting for someone to die so they can start living! They must be taken away! How could he leave the kid? Did he explain that?"

"I remember when we were first married, he used to say, 'How can anyone do that? I could never do that.' Then, when he left, he said, 'I am not an emotional hostage to Christabel.' "

"Do you believe a line like that? Only the goyim talk that way," Jed said in disgust. He began to pace. "I myself was at the height of my career when I married Laura. Four years, and I'll spend the rest of my life paying for it. When you've got a kid, they've got you by the *baitsim*; otherwise, you walk away . . . that's how it was with Sally."

"Sally?" Katherine repeated, a slow smile forming. "I thought you were only married once."

Jed looked abashed. "I hate to say I was married twice—it sounds terrible. I was very young, you understand. She was a professional ice skater—Sally Leigh. Ever hear of her?"

Katherine shook her head.

"Her real name was Sarah Levy. She was a piss-cutter, the cutest thing on ice since Sonja Henie, with a little turned-up nose I was putz enough to believe wasn't fixed. When we got engaged, I took her home to Minneapolis. My grandfather took one look at her and said, 'Jacob, you will not finish half a loaf with this woman.' "

"What happened?"

"We got married. I used to manage her act at night and write *The Comedy Show* during the day. Then I got offered a big job in Hollywood. It was nice—we had a little house on Canyon View, we bought a cocker spaniel. But Sally was bored. She kept *hoking* me to throw a big Hollywood party. So I invited everybody I could think of. We sat there with the booze and the rented glasses and the fucking hors d'oeuvres until eleven o'clock, when it became obvious that no one was going to show up.''

"Do those things really happen?"

"Sure they happen. A few weeks later, she took her act to Vegas. I got a call from her one morning at two o'clock. She said she was in bed with her agent and wasn't coming home. I had a minor nervous breakdown; then I got rid of the cocker spaniel and the house on Canyon View, and moved into a bachelor flat on Dayton Way with the first in a long line of Airedales named Simon. Two years later I was making fourteen thousand dollars a week and going with Christabel Rivers.''

"Did you ever see Sally again?"

"Yeah. Once I ran into her at a party. She said, 'You know something, Jacob? All I ever wanted was to be Mrs. Jed Bernard.' ''

The fire had burned down; Jed got up to put on a fresh log. "Ten years later, I met Laura. I was thirty-eight, rich, successful— I needed *that*. It was a marriage made at Nate 'n' Al's.''

"You must have been happy in the beginning," Katherine said.

He turned from the fireplace. Drawing his lips back for emphasis, he said, "Not . . . one . . . good . . . *day!* On the wedding night, she called me a dirty Jew.''

"No!"

"My hand to God. Every Jew's greatest fear about marrying a shiksa. It's what your parents always tell you will happen, and it did. I should've known something was wrong when she showed up for the wedding in a black dress." He stood over Katherine, frowning at her. "Are you going to keep clutching that pillow, my dear? I assure you I'm not interested in an affair.''

Until then, she hadn't realized she'd been holding it against her like a shield; she released it self-consciously as Jed went back to his chair, saying, "And I'm not a fag. I have a long list of credits.''

The record ended. The only sound in the room was the crackle of the fire and a sputtering of rain in the chimney.

"If you had it all to do over again, is there anything you'd change?" Katherine asked softly.

Jed gazed into the fire. After a moment's consideration, he replied, "All the women. It was a waste—for them and for me. I was fifty my last birthday. I'm coming to the end of something. There's only one more thing I really want.''

"What's that?"

He looked at her across the room. "A serious relationship. I've got Chris, I wouldn't change the past. And I've got the house—not bad for a kid from the ghetto. But I would like to have stayed with one woman."

And with that, Katherine's heart—her tender, naïve heart, the heart that Emily always said would get her in trouble one day—went out to Jed Bernard, a little boy in a borrowed sailor suit astride a rented tricycle.

Some instinct made him seize the moment; he moved across the room, sat beside her and took her in his arms.

It was an awkward, passionless kiss. As their mouths strained for congruence, Katherine tried in vain to imagine what it would be like to make love with him. Did he do jokes? Did he keep a straight face? Could she? In a swift movement he pulled her up, then led her through the small guest bathroom into his bedroom. She went unprotesting, her normal instinct to resist evaporated, her loyalty to Andy forgotten, docile as never before, the double image of Jed as a child and Jed as a sympathetic aging man conquering her as no amount of persuasion could have done. The thought of sin did not enter her mind until he pushed her onto the huge bed. The luxurious softness of the fur blanket cushioned her fall. "Hermès," Jed muttered. "Lana gave it to me."

There was no question that along with compassion, Katherine's childhood devotion to movie magazines had aided his seduction, but visions of Lana and Rita and Laura faded once they had shed their clothes and he lay over her on the bed, his eyes half-closed—more, it seemed, in concentration than concupiscence. As was not uncommon for Katherine, but quite unexpected with this man so many years her senior, her maternal instincts were aroused; her arms encircled him, her hand stroked his hair in a protective, comforting manner, more like one ministering to a hurt child than a woman in the heat of desire. His body was a dark mass rising above her, his olive skin silken to the touch as she ran her fingers over his back. He fell upon her with incoherent mutterings.

Their hurried motions were altogether out of sync. After what she assumed was an introductory coupling, he rolled onto his back and cradled her head on his shoulder, his eyes on the ceiling. Passionate and eager she might be, but never aggressive: Katherine waited politely, even shyly, for a cue to resume. She lifted her eyes to his face—the face, she realized with a start, of a dark, mysterious stranger.

And what that illumination stirred in her she had felt with neither husband nor lover, but was familiar as a recurring dream: the thrill of the forbidden. All at once she thought, This is the first time I have ever made love with a Jew. And then laughed at herself for thinking it.

A barrage of barking from Simon at the gate across the lawn startled Jed into action. Though drastic measures hardly seemed necessary, he vaulted out of the bed uttering an oath, snatched up a gnarled walking stick from the fireplace, pulled on a Greek sailor's cap that was lying on a table, and charged into the night. Katherine hoisted herself up on her elbows to watch him hobble around the perimeter of the pool, stark naked and brandishing the shillelagh; the cap and a straight-legged gait gave him a nautical air—a bawdy Cap'n Andy. He disappeared through the small wooden gate. Time passed. He did not return. Feeling increasingly awkward in the bed, she wondered, Was that *it*? Was this Jed's not-too-subtle way of telling her to go home? Should she get up? Offer to help? Indecision paralyzed her. Just as she decided to flee, he trotted back. From the threshold, he inquired sternly, "Are you going to dress, madam? Simon is easily embarrassed."

That makes two of us, she thought, leaping out of bed and gathering up her clothes, grateful for the mask of night to hide her nakedness and her burning face.

When she had repaired her makeup and dressed, she emerged into the study to find Jed seated in his armchair, wearing khaki shorts and an orange cardigan, scribbling on a legal pad. He barely glanced up as she entered. Adjusting his half-moon glasses, he said, "Sit down, dollface. I just wrote the greatest fucking scene you ever heard. People will fall down laughing. Let me read it to you." He peered at her over the top of his glasses. "It won't bore you?"

Katherine stared at him, and slowly shook her head. For the next forty-five minutes, until her eyes were closing from the lateness of the hour and the warmth of the fire and the tedium of a complicated plot, Jed told her the story of *Way, Way West*, the perfect vehicle for Duke Wayne.

CHAPTER 14

*Consummation
of a Mismatch*

It had been an act of mercy, springing more from *Agape* than *Eros*. She had gone to bed with Jed Bernard because she felt sorry for him.

So Katherine explained her behavior to herself when she got home that evening, after she had paid the baby-sitter, tucked Chryssie in with the stuffed kitten, undressed for the second time, and put on a striped cotton pajama top she'd filched from Christopher. Christopher. He flitted through her mind like a phantom, Banquo's ghost accusing her with bloodshot eyes. She clicked off the bedside lamp, banishing his shadow with the light.

For a long while she lay awake in the dark, expecting—as was customary after sex—Archimedes' Principle to apply: in a mixture of emotions, the weight of the heavier would force the lighter one to float away; thus remorse inevitably displaced pleasure. But she felt fine—well, not fine exactly, but not guilty either. Technically she had committed a mortal sin, she reminded herself. Why wasn't she quaking? To excuse herself as some kind of sexual Florence Nightingale was faulty logic; in the sixth grade she'd learned that the end does not justify the means. Possibly she was operating under the popular Catholic impression that guilt occurs in direct proportion to enjoyment. Face it, she thought, the experience wasn't that great. But then why had the dreary encounter with Calvin the Third left her engulfed with guilt? Sleep came before the puzzle was solved. It did not occur to Katherine that in her lexicon of emotions, there was only one that mitigated guilt, and it had more to do with destiny than chemistry.

On the twenty-ninth of December, Andrew Byrne's sense of impending trouble was confirmed during an early supper at Lawry's Steak House. The remains of a half-eaten cheeseburger congealed on his plate. Katherine had been silent for a while, the waitress had been gone for what seemed an eternity. He reached into his shirt pocket for a Camel, lit one, and with a fatalistic, adumbrated air, like someone deciding that as long as he has a shovel in his hand he might as well dig a hole with it, he sought Katherine's eyes and said, "I have nothing in particular planned for New Year's Eve. Is there something you'd like to do?"

She snatched at the ambiguity. "There is, actually. I've been invited to a party. Do you mind terribly if we don't spend it together?"

Another night she might have gotten away with, but New Year's Eve carries a fateful significance. He had given her an out; gracelessly she took it and then had to look away, the hurt was so plain on his face. There followed a brief, bruising argument during which, like all lovers on the wane, as one retreated the other clutched. The pain she had suffered over Christopher had hardened her heart; better now than later, she thought. Andy was the one who had said it wasn't forever.

When he dropped her off at home, she called Jed to tell him that she would be able to accompany him to Jessica Kendall's New Year's Eve party after all.

Jessica Kendall was a handsome Englishwoman once married to the famous Shakespearean actor, Martin Kendall. After their divorce, she turned her scintillating wit to use as a social commentator for *West Coast* magazine, becoming queen of the British colony in Hollywood. Annually, on New Year's Eve, she gathered about her a dazzling array of living legends, current stars, and intimate friends, resulting in that rarity, a successful Hollywood party.

Most of Katherine's December wages from the gallery went for a strapless gown of coral crepe, draped in the fashion of Madame Grès; her sparkling eyes and a smile that refused to die foiled any attempt at sophistication as the parking attendant opened the car door and she stepped out at the foot of a flight of stone steps leading to Jessica's house. Jed held her back with a hand on her arm.

"Don't look so glum, kid. We don't have to stay."

Like a set for O'Neill's *Mourning Becomes Electra*, the colonnaded mansion loomed at the end of a cul-de-sac above the Bel Air Hotel. On this last night of the year, it gave off a special glow, its cavernous rooms alive with music, glittering lights, and the laughter of the world's most glamorous people—or so it seemed to Katherine as they entered the great marble foyer where Cary Grant and the Gregory Pecks were chatting with Jennifer Jones, who, Jed told her, came out of seclusion only for Jessica.

The hostess was in white silk, her generous curves billowing, her conversation too laced with candid observations to be called gracious. Charm and beauty she had, in the manner of a gorgeous asp. Strings of rubies flashed like warning signals at her throat and wrist as she came toward Jed, her arms outstretched. "I can't believe it, my sweet! Every ten years you turn up with a new version of the same blonde!"

"You know what I always say, Jess: keep the jokes and change the girls," Jed replied. "I see you're still here at Tara. I thought you were going to get rid of it."

"I discovered something, darling. All those years I was married to Martin, I thought I hated this house. But after our divorce, I realized it was *Martin* I hated!"

They went on bantering, an earthy Noel and Gertie, batting words fleet as shuttlecocks across an invisible net of one-upmanship that bound them in the game but came between them as man and woman. "She's wonderful! Why don't you marry *her*?" Katherine said when Jessica went off to greet Marlon Brando.

"Please!" Jed said. "The woman would eat me *alive*. Competition is not healthy for the cock, my dear. I love Jessica dearly, but I couldn't fuck her."

"Why not?"

"Old flesh," he said succinctly.

Katherine flinched, thinking, What fools men are. Separately a little sad, together Jed and Jessica would own the world. "Did it bother you that Christabel Rivers was older?" she asked.

"Ah, that was different."

"How so?"

"I was a very young man, and *she* was a *star*. Even then, once she'd taught me everything, I had to go. You never want to stay with someone who knew you when; you want to show off what you've learned. That's why it's okay for you to be with me now, kid. You'll have a whole other life after me."

They passed through a mirrored hall where white-coated waiters glided among the guests carrying trays of champagne in fluted glasses. Katherine took one and drank it quickly to take the edge off her nervousness. *"Shikkering?"* Jed inquired archly, apparently able to see from the back of his head, since he was glancing through the door to a game room, where a group of men were seated around a card table. An Egyptian actor who had recently gained international recognition in a desert epic wandered out, tucking a roll of bills into his dinner jacket. He clapped Jed on the back. "Perhaps it is you who brought me luck tonight, my friend!" he cried, and cast Katherine a melting look with his liquid brown eyes as he bent over her hand. Jed remarked to a passing waiter, "I knew him when he was a rug." Katherine and the actor laughed wildly.

"Did you make that up this minute?" she asked Jed when they moved on.

"No, kid," he said dryly. "I've been working on it for months."

"Were you just *born* funny?"

"I'll tell you who's funnier than me. Nate Bronstein. You meet him, you'll leave me like a shot. I'm a *road company* of my old man. He'd love you, too. My old lady was always yelling at him for giving credit to shiksas."

"Credit for what?"

"For *living*, putz! Credit . . . credit. He let 'em buy stuff without paying. It made him feel good to have them come in the store, he said. 'Shiksaleh,' he'd call you."

They stood at the top of three wide steps leading to the drawing room. French windows opened onto a large formal garden, where a waterfall tumbled from a rocky ledge into a swimming pool. Among the heady collection of film stars milling about the room, Katherine saw several whose glossy photographs had adorned her childhood scrapbook. Floating down the steps, she absorbed the party through a haze, a theatrical scrim threaded with enchantment. But as the evening wore on, she became vividly aware of how flat, how dull were the conversations of the most celebrated stars, the most successful film makers, the moguls, compared to Jed's. He was greeted affectionately by many, warily by some, and by others with a kind of grudging respect.

Three veteran funnymen trading jokes at the bar fell silent when he came into view, turning to him with a surprisingly deferential air, as if expecting the ultimate comedic statement. Nearby a dance floor had been cleared. As the group traded quips on the rim, a young romantic leading man shuffled by with a limpid blonde in his arms and waved to Jed. A moment later, catching Katherine's eye over the blonde's shoulder, he crooned suggestively, "Does your mother know you're out, *Ceceeelia*?"

Katherine blushed. "Having fun, dollface?" Jed inquired with an indulgent smile.

"Oh, yes! Aren't you?"

"I've done it for a long time, kid. But I like seeing you here. You're ten years old." She smiled happily. "I take that back," he said. "Nine."

A high-pitched male British voice carried across the room, hailing Jed. Katherine recognized the man instantly and braced herself for a rude encounter. Among actors with reputations for reducing female co-stars to tears, Laurence Traherne had no equal.

"Hello, *boychik*. Where've you been?" Jed greeted him.

"The provinces, dear boy. How d'you do?" he said courteously to Katherine. "I've been touring. Chekhov, mainly. And *The Overcoat*."

"What's that?" Jed inquired.

"Gogol," Katherine murmured.

Traherne gave her a surprised look. "A cultured woman in this desert? I congratulate you, Yacob. Did you ever notice how people in this town refer to everything as a project? It's grotesque. I told the president of Film Gems that I was doing *The Seagull* and he said, 'That's an interesting project.' The bloody Bible's a project to these Philistines. We must dine together soon, darlings."

"You'll come up to the house—we'll talk about the old country," Jed said.

"But he's a perfectly charming man," Katherine said when Traherne had gone. "It seems as if the ones with the reputations for being the meanest are the nicest."

"Always was that way, kid. Larry's just fucking brilliant, that's all. He doesn't suffer fools gladly. You're learning something about gossip: don't listen to it. Make up your own mind about people."

"What was that about the old country? Isn't he British?"

"Please! Larry's a Latvian Jew. Took me five minutes after I met him to figure that one out. He's one of the rare actors who's not in a lot of trouble without a script in his hand."

Seeing a vacant table and two chairs, he sank into one. "Bring me a little dinner, will you, dollface?"

Katherine filled a plate from the elaborate buffet. Jed picked at it without interest and was out of his chair at eleven-fifteen. "I promised the Rosens we'd be there before twelve. Let's go, kid. Do you mind?" he added absently, on his way to the door.

Katherine cast a wistful look over her shoulder, "I *had* sort of hoped to stay here for the rest of my life, but . . ."

On the balustraded veranda, Jed exchanged greetings with a producer who was arriving with his new wife, a young German actress. "That woman will put him away," he predicted as he descended the stairs. Still brooding about it when they drove down the winding driveway, he said between puffs of his pipe, "I had a German girlfriend once. It was a few years ago. I had a Mercedes then, too. We drove to La Jolla one weekend. I'm sitting at the Bath and Tennis and the news comes on the radio that Eichmann is about to be tried in Israel. She wasn't a bad girl, Helga, but at that time I took one look at her and thought to myself, What the fuck am I doing in La Jolla with a Nazi and a Mercedes parked outside the cabana? I left Helga, left the car, and flew to Israel the same day. Never went back to pick up either one of them."

"Not even the car?"

"Nope. Had no desire to see it again."

"Were you at the trial?"

"Sat in the first row through the entire thing. Close enough to look in that cocksucker's eyes. You don't go through something like that and come home to someone named Helga."

"What was he like?"

"Eichmann? Cold bastard. Icy. Basically, the man was a clerk."

"The banality of evil," Katherine murmured.

"Have you read Hannah Arendt's book?" Jed asked.

"Parts of it."

"*Again* with the skimming! Don't give me these phrases—banality of evil—unless you know what you're talking about." His eyes narrowing at the memory, he said, "You know how the young Israelis felt? They didn't *understand.* 'Where was the Jewish army?' they kept asking. I'm telling you, it's a whole new ball game in that country. But for the Jews who remembered—well, that's why they had to put him in a glass booth."

"I wonder if it's wise to dredge all that up in Israel. The emotions such a trial provokes must be terrible."

"They weren't good," Jed said grimly.

"I remember my father taking me to see *Judgment at Nuremberg* at the Roxy in New York. You could feel a rumble of rage building in the audience. I sank down in my seat, terrified somebody would find out that our name was Winterhaus," Katherine said.

Jed turned his head to look at her. "It's a joy to be with you, Mrs. Himmler. *Machamoves!* What would you like to talk about after the Holocaust, Malcolm?"

"You could tell me where we're going. Who are the Rosens?"

"Old friends of mine," Jed said. "Julia's one of the great women. With Saul I broke a cardinal rule once—collaborated with him on a script. People don't work with me, they work *for* me. I had to throw him out of the house. We didn't speak for five years, but we made up."

Moments later, he turned onto a suburban street and stopped in front of a two-story clapboard house half hidden behind fruit trees. A small, gruff-looking man in a Shetland sweater and cords opened the door, took in Katherine and Jed in their evening clothes, the Ferrari at the curb, and called out, "Julia! Scott and Zelda are here!"

Of the ten people gathered around the fire in the cozy living room, one was a physicist from Los Alamos, two were UCLA professors, two writers, one a rabbi, and another that indispensable guest at a serious Los Angeles evening, a psychoanalyst. Julia and a professor's wife were the only women present.

The rush to arrive by midnight remained a mystery. The New Year came and went without acknowledgment as the group exchanged impassioned opinions on subjects as varied as Vietnam, Spinoza, writers' block, nuclear energy, and Zionism. Meanwhile Julia, a friendly, attractive woman in her forties, brought Jed food, laughed at his jokes, saw to his every need as if his arrival were the return of the Prodigal Son. Her husband's bantering with Jed contained equal elements of admiration and envy. From a rocking chair, the psychoanalyst, who had written a scholarly monograph on the black humor of Jews, observed Jed intently. "Personally," the physicist remarked at one point, "I don't feel a great wave of anti-Semitism in Beverly Hills. I'm happy to give a little something to the UJA, but don't ask me to migrate, I beg of you."

"Oh, really, my friend?" Jed responded. "You think it can't happen here?" Everyone turned to listen as he quoted Ben-Gurion's warnings about a perilous future for the Diaspora. A fresh argument ensued.

The intense, fractious interchange was a severe contrast to the gaiety of Jessica's party, but what struck Katherine even more was how different it was from the artificial repartee she was accustomed to hearing among Gentiles on similar occasions. Zionism was not a subject she was familiar with or held strong opinions about, but she envied the openness, the passionate conviction, the freedom of expression, and felt herself cast once again in the role of an orphan, looking wistfully through a window into a warm, inviting room.

While Jed was still engrossed in the debate, Saul sat beside her on the faded corduroy couch and repeated the story of their rift. "I was so goddamned mad when he threw me out, I swore it'd be the last time I'd ever talk to him. But—"

"But . . .?" she prompted.

Saul raised his shoulders in a philosophical shrug. "In a world of dullards," he said, "you don't turn your back on Jed Bernard."

It was after two when Jed brought Katherine to the top of his hill. This time there were no tactics, no hesitation, no coyness about her staying with him. The alchemy of champagne and festivity had freed them from strategies or inhibition. And now, when he took her to bed, she held back none of the tenderness or fervor that had seemed to put him off the first time. Brimming with emotion, she took his face between her hands and covered his forehead, eyes, and cheeks with kisses. In the impenetrable crust that had grown over his feelings, a fissure appeared—feeble, slight, but wide enough to admit a ray of light. Although his lips were against her cheek, she heard his voice as if from a great distance, saying hoarsely, "I haven't felt this way for ten years."

Ten years, she thought. The magic number. Laura. Afterward, she would remember that he kissed her once deeply on the mouth. She remembered because it was a long, long time before he did it again.

CHAPTER 15

Making Up
Her Own Mind

"He's a professional Jew!" Andrew Byrne exploded over a cup of tea.

It was the middle of January. Katherine had not seen him since shortly after the New Year, when she admitted that she had gone to bed with Jed Bernard. Hurt made Andy retreat for a while, but today, her day off, he'd called to invite her to tea. With the callousness of the newly infatuated, she had been quoting Jed ad nauseam since they'd arrived at Will Wright's Ice Cream Parlor twenty minutes before.

"How can you be taken in by that crap?" Andy demanded. "Hollywood's full of them—directors, writers, story editors. They all worship at the shrine of the shiksa goddess and then toss her aside like used Kleenex when it suits them . . . or they decide to get married to one of their own." Her attempt at a reply was lost as his voice rose an octave. "And the women will *never* accept you. You know what the last Jewish girlfriend I had said when she broke up with me? 'A Jew who dies on a Christian breast dies impaled.' "

"That's a line from Djuna Barnes."

"You read too much. It's made you completely unrealistic. And for someone who's supposed to be so smart, you're incredibly naïve," he said harshly. "You make him sound like a cross between Albert Schweitzer and Oscar Wilde. He's a *stereotype*, for God's sake!

It's all those self-deprecating jokes and saying 'fuck' every other word."

"The language bothered me at first, but I hardly hear it anymore. The way Jed does it, so casually, defuses it somehow."

"Christ!" Andy snarled, glaring at the hot fudge sundae melting in Katherine's dish. "Corliss Archer meets the Marquis de Sade."

His was not the only hostile reaction she had encountered. For a time after she met Jed, she had kept her references to him anonymous; jokes, anecdotes, radical political opinions had flowed from her lips vaguely attributed to "a man I know" or "someone I met recently" or "this person"; most of them had elicited blank stares or downright disapproval. At the Sinclairs' annual Ramos Gin Fizz brunch, Alison's father had been outraged at the suggestion that America should abandon its commitment in Southeast Asia. "You'd better not bring that pinko friend of yours around here, my girl!" he'd fulminated.

Meeting Jed Bernard had put Katherine in direct mortal combat with her background; she was prepared for a fight, but the gossip that swirled about her head whenever she mentioned his name frightened her. Unable to reconcile his reputation with the man she knew living quietly on the hill with his daughter, she nevertheless listened to every word, assaulted by half-truths, fiction, and innuendo. Now here came Andrew, fresh from a dirt session with a columnist from a local scandal sheet, to slander him with more rumors: tales of licentiousness, of ruthlessness in business. "When Tito Estar hired Jed as head of Titus Films, he said, 'I got me the toughest Jew in Hollywood to run my studio,' " Andy reported.

Katherine twirled a string of fudge around her spoon, trying to think of an appropriate response, avoiding his eyes.

He tilted his chair backward until it rested on two legs, fixing his gaze on a huge jar of multicolored jelly beans on a shelf behind her head. "I don't think hearing this makes any difference to you. I think it turns you on," he said miserably. Suddenly the chair came forward; he struck the table with the flat of his hand. "Do you know what you're *doing?*" he shouted, startling her with his vehemence into an awareness of how much she had hurt him.

"Andy," she said softly. "You know what a square I am. I hate these stories, but I know a lot them aren't true. Louise told me she heard he keeps whips behind his bed. He keeps licorice sticks behind his bed! I feel terrible about the pain I've caused you, but what can I do?" She hesitated. "I just . . . *like* Jed."

There was little left to say. They parted at the corner; when Katherine looked back to wave, Andy was striding down Beverly Drive without a backward glance. How could she explain to him that she had met the prototype of her childhood fantasies? How could he hope to understand that all the importunings of a decent, attractive, virile young man who was absolutely right for her would fall as on stone in the face of a mismatch between a middle-aged "professional Jew" and a militant blond Catholic?

A cold wind blew, scraping dry winter branches across the window of the apartment above as she went down the ramp to the garage. She got out the car and headed for Chryssie's school, brooding about what Andy had told her. He would have derived a measure of comfort from knowing how much confusion he'd provoked, she thought. At the top of Doheny Drive, a gaggle of little girls waited at the Buckley gate. They looked so vulnerable with their braids and freckles and open, trusting faces—when Chryssie broke away and jumped into the car, Katherine enveloped her in a fierce protective hug.

"Miss McDermott's engaged!" Chryssie cried, sitting back, her book bag at her feet. "And I'm invited to the wedding!"

Conversation about the teacher's impending nuptials took up several minutes; then, on an impulse, Katherine asked, "What do you really think of Mr. Bernard?"

The child's eyes danced. "He's neato!" she said, and with that simple phrase uprooted the seeds of doubt that Andrew had planted.

"You know what we're going to do this afternoon?"

"What?"

"We're going to look for a house to rent. It's time we had a real home again."

Furniture, possessions, a room of her own—it was the least she could do for her daughter, Katherine thought, now that they were launched on a flight over unchartered waters.

CHAPTER 16

The Education
of a Shiksa

"Break the matzoh in half . . . *carefully*, putz! Don't crumble it!"

"You're right. It's not as easy as it looks." Katherine discarded a botched attempt and tried again.

"That's it. Now slice the gefilte fish lengthwise," Jed said, as he took from the refrigerator a jar that looked as if it belonged in a medical laboratory. He hovered over her, his eyebrows knitted in concentration, his eyes trained on her every move.

Trying not to breathe lest some exotic odor emanating from the gelatinous contents turn her stomach, she extracted a spongy hunk with a fork, sliced four thin pieces and laid them on half the matzoh, slathered them with red horseradish from the jar he slapped into her hand as if they were in surgery, and covered the concoction with the remaining matzoh.

"Not bad," he commented. The accolade mitigated her queasiness. "Get me a cream soda, will you, dollface?"

There was a stash under the bar. She fished out a bottle of the vile stuff and put it with the sandwich on a tray which she carried into the bedroom while he trailed her, doing a monologue on the difficulties of getting a decent meal from a Gentile.

A weekend on the hill bore a resemblance to a two-day final examination, Katherine was discovering, thanks to Chryssie, whose excursion to Disneyland with Abby had left her free to stay with Jed. She had awakened Sunday morning to find him standing over her, holding his stomach, his face twisted with nausea. "Kitty got a mouse last night," he announced. "Left it on the front doorstep . . . could you deal with it, kid?" She thought it over and said no. The day before she had lugged a bucket of water down the dirt road to Rowdy, fed Simon and Kitty, and helped Jed rearrange his furniture in the study; in the evening she'd grilled the steak until it was gray all the way through as he insisted, only to have him push it away after two bites. Cleaning up mouse entrails was going too far. He hadn't insisted; but then it was only their first weekend together.

Now, seated in the armless chair beside the open glass doors, she watched with horrified fascination as, propped up in bed with the tray on his lap, he wolfed down his lunch, scattering crumbs like confetti over the fur blanket.

"Pretty good, kid," he conceded after the last bite. "Too bad you don't know how to make matzoh *brei*. My sister Sonia makes the great matzoh *brei* of all time." He gave her an appreciative smile as she removed the tray. "If only Sonia had looked like you, I'd never have left Minneapolis. On the other hand, I'd have died of starvation."

"I'm sure I could learn to make it," she said.

He shook his head. "I don't know . . . it's pretty complicated."

To please Jed, Katherine was willing to assay the most arcane Jewish dish—as long as she was not required to eat it. Winning his approval had become her aim. He had entered her life freely, with none of the reticence or vacillation or insecurity that she had observed in single men; her response was to place him, with Chryssie, at its center. First Andy was jettisoned, then her job. Like a high-wire artist, she lived on air for a while: she sold what remained of her stock and found part-time work reading scripts at Columbia studios for a pittance. After a few weeks of this fancy footwork, she lost her financial balance, tumbled, and was caught in the capacious, crowded safety net of Douglas Winterhaus. A girl with an allowance and no direction suited Jed perfectly.

Their meeting had been no accident, he finally admitted. The day she'd come into Tiffany's, he'd been there with Eve, and the sight of Katherine's blond hair, her crazed blue eyes, the quick spangled laughter he'd heard across the room had given him a sudden, unexpected tumescence. "As my old man used to say," he told her, " 'Jacob, *ven der putz shteht, ligt der seichel in drerd.*' When the cock goes up, reason goes out the window." Then Eve had told him that she was a Catholic, and he'd remarked through a stifled yawn, "It's hardly a challenge." Not all women found Jed irresistible, but with the ones he called "blond neuros," he never missed.

He vamped them with his wit and scintillating personality, his intense interest in their background, and an almost clairvoyant sense of their inner being ("I'm in your *brain!*" he would exclaim, hopping around gleefully when he divined Katherine's thoughts); at the same time he held himself aloof, beyond their reach, so that they were constantly off-balance, one minute warmed by the fire in his sensitive soul and softened by his tender heart, the next frozen out by his arctic moods and manic rages.

To the task of pleasing such a godlike figure, Katherine brought extensive training (fourteen years of convent education) and an awesome aptitude. The climate of love and suffering in which men like Jed Bernard thrive was as familiar as amniotic fluid to one who had spent her formative years at the foot of the cross, begging the Jewish Savior for forgiveness and promising to try to do better. That her goal was unclear (the childhood one of salvation could no longer be said to apply, given the sinful state of her soul) did not alter her response. The state of her soul was something that interested Jed greatly.

"I want to have a religious discussion with you," he announced after lunch, swinging his legs off the bed and lighting his pipe.

"A *religious* discussion?" she echoed.

"Listen," he said teasingly. "From other girls I can get looks, great sex, fantastic meals, but with you I get religious nuttiness. I was listening to the Crazy People this morning. . . ."

The Crazy People were Jed's Eumenides: a mechanical Greek chorus of religious fanatics and the lunatic fringe who telephoned in to the talk shows he listened to through the night, their Yiddish or Irish or domestic ravings keeping his personal furies at bay. Long after he fell asleep, the radio still crackled with their voices, insomniacs and night watchmen on the line from Fairfax Avenue and Long Beach and Orange County, venting their anger at Lyndon Johnson, the governor, Pope Paul, Golda Meir, and others of their ilk. Prime time was early Sunday morning; every nut case in Southern California called in to praise, challenge, or berate the moderator, Rabbi Birnbaum.

Puffing his pipe into life, Jed studied Katherine through the smoke. "Now what exactly do you mean, you're Catholic? Do you go to church?"

"Sometimes. I've slipped a little lately."

"Confession?"

"Every now and then."

He rose, hiked up his khaki shorts, and began to expostulate, pacing barefoot on the carpet, taking his glasses off, gesturing grandly with his pipe, his voice gathering strength, his face flushed with turbulent emotions rooted in what he called "the good old ghetto days." To climax his oration, he proclaimed, "More harm has been done in the name of organized religion throughout history than for any other reason."

"That's a preposterous statement," Katherine commented.

"Pre*poste*rous?" he mimicked. "I'll give you preposterous."

"Whenever you have a human institution, there are abuses—"

"You call a little thing like the Inquisition an *abuse?*"

"Mmm . . . the nuns skipped over the Inquisition at the convent."

"You bet your ass they did. Who do you think starts a pogrom? The *priest*, that's who! The hierarchy of the *Church*, who keep feeding every new generation propaganda about Christ-killers."

"But that doesn't negate the good things the Church does."

"Name three."

"Well, there are religious orders that dedicate their lives to caring for the poor, for orphans—"

"There are no Jewish orphanages, did you know that?"

"Why not?"

"Because there are no Jewish orphans, putz! Always there's an aunt, a cousin, something. What else?"

"Missionaries—"

"Halt!" Jed cried, holding up his hand. "*Mission*aries? You must be joking. Those cocksuckers are the worst! They cut off the natives' *hands* if they don't convert."

Katherine laughed. Into the eye of Jed's Jewish storm she sailed, holding fast to her defense of Jesus Christ, the Pope, and the honor of the Roman Catholic Church. He stood over her, lowering his face until it was a menacing inch from hers. "Explain to me how you can believe in the Immaculate Conception. You really think Jesus was born without Joseph humping Mary?"

"Yes, but that's not what the Immaculate Conception is."

He drew back in surprise. "Whaddya mean . . . whaddya mean? Certainly it is."

"No. That's the Virgin Birth. The Immaculate Conception means that Our Lady was the only person ever conceived without original sin."

"*Bubbe montses!*" he bellowed. "Are you sure about this?"

"Who else do you know who's had eight years of theology?"

"That's true," he said, smiling at her fondly.

Saturday had not been so rigorous. Early on a dazzling morning, Jed had wakened Katherine with a glass of orange juice; once she'd fed the animals, they holed up in the study and talked throughout the morning. Shorn of housekeeper and children, the house was a fortress, an oasis of lush foliage and cool water into which Jed plunged shortly after lunch. Moments later, he surfaced, raising his hand to inquire in a Yiddish accent, "Excuse me, is this a restricted pool?"

The joke made Katherine sad. Was there enough money or fame or love in the world, she wondered, to compensate for the rejections of childhood? The hours she had spent poring over his scrapbooks had yielded evidence that by the age of thirty he'd gained enough celebrity to land him on the cover of *Time,* but not enough to make him forget the ghetto; he'd lured enough movie queens into his bed to rival Valentino, but never enough to make him forget Mary Rose Keane and how she ran to confession after he'd had her. The mystique of Jed Bernard had taken hold of Katherine, an enveloping image that had begun with her first view of him at the top of the stairs and was embellished by his stories. The day before as they talked in the study, in his vivid, mesmerizing style he'd described what it was like to be Jacob Bronstein at fifteen, sitting in a borrowed jalopy on a subzero Minneapolis night with Mary Rose's eager virgin body jammed up against him, riding him like a pumping horse on a merry-go-round until his cock was ready to burst; he shoving it into her blindly, she moaning and shedding hot, remorseful tears, her guilt lending the sex a sweet excitement he had never quite recaptured.

Afterward, Mary Rose made him drive her to Our Lady of Perpetual Help so she could confess to Father Lubichek. Jacob waited outside, flexing his frozen fingers and wondering how she could be telling the priest about what they'd done. Was she giving *details*, for Chrissake?

"It's okay to do it with Catholics," his friend Murshie Shapiro had told him. "They get absolved afterwards. They go tell someone and it's wiped out. Italian Catholics are the best—they give you a hand job." Murshie had the lean, canny look of a ferret as he tore off a hunk of licorice. He and Jacob would go by the parochial school and chant at the girls coming out: "The holy pole is in your hole, so wiggle your ass to save your soul!" Waiting for her outside the church, Jacob thought, Everybody knows Catholic girls are crazed, but Mary Rose is something else!

When she came out they did it again.

But the true shiksa goddess was Cynthia Halley, who used to meet him on the corner outside the gates of her parents' huge white house on Hennepin Avenue, clear across town, almost an hour on the streetcar from 1421½ Thirty-ninth Street where the Bronsteins lived over a dry goods store in the heart of the Jewish ghetto around Plymouth Avenue. For the whole of his sixteenth year, Jacob rode the streetcar to take out Cynthia, the golden girl with lavender eyes and hair like streaming silk. She was rich; she never got sick; she had a narrow straight nose, her own horse (which might as well have been a unicorn to a Jewish boy from Plymouth Avenue), two long-haired cats (from which his mother and sister would have *varfed* themselves sneezing), and a large dog that romped with her on the Halleys' rolling terraces. Romping was a *goyishe* pursuit, Jacob told Murshie. Jews do not romp.

Finding someone like Cynthia Halley had been Jacob's fantasy since he was eleven, a skinny, ambitious kid with burning eyes, slamming tennis balls against a backboard in Loring Park, and across the court, swinging a racquet and bouncing in her tennis shoes, had come a thirteen-year-old, snub-nosed, Scandinavian wonder, the type of person who, his old man had later informed him, was good to *shtup* and bad to knock up—i.e., a shiksa. Tennis was Jacob's passport out of the ghetto. And when he won the Downstate Junior Tennis Championship, the shiksa goddess proved herself to be a *mentsch*.

Traditionally, awards were presented at the Tonawanda Country Club dance on Saturday night. Jacob had saved twelve dollars to rent a tuxedo. "Conservatively speaking," he told Katherine, "it was the high point of my life." Since when had a Jew played, let alone *won* a tournament? The day of the dance, he received a message from the committee that his trophy would be mailed to him; since club membership was restricted, he would not be welcome there. In the Northside ghetto and on Hennepin Avenue, Jacob had learned about hatred, and on Saturday evening, as music filtered through the elm trees on the lawn of the Tonawanda Country Club, he replayed the tournament with every ball a Gentile head.

His father, Nathan Bronstein, rolled his eyes at Jacob's anger and said, *"Gottenyu! Gornisht mit gornisht!"* Nothing from nothing. "They should all die!" Jacob growled, his hands clenched in tight, cold fists at his sides. Nathan raised his voice in song: *"Columbus! Tu di ich hob gornisht!"* (Columbus! To thee I owe nothing.) And his grandfather, the rabbi, said, "What is it, Jacob, what? You think you're missing something at that dance? Better you should spend your time learning something. Read Maimonides. Read Buber. Read the Torah. Have we survived two thousand years so you can run around hitting a little white ball like a *goyishe kop*?"

How could he explain it to them, these people who accepted insults and snubs as their heritage? They still talked about the czar. How could they know that he wouldn't rest until he got even with the Gentile cocksuckers?

Cynthia Halley got even for him. Cynthia's father ("that *shtarker*, Ambrose Halley") had forbidden her to go out with Jacob or any other Jew, which was why she had to meet him on the corner. That night she went to the dance with the heir to the Scripps paper-mill fortune; they were in the front row for the awards ceremony, which was climaxed by a drumroll, and the announcement: "The winner of the Downstate Junior Championship is"—the master of ceremonies moved the list to arm's length to check his vision, then said in an incredulous voice—"Jacob Bernard . . . *Bronstein*?" An embarrassed silence fell over Minneapolis's upper crust. Cynthia Halley rose, and with her head held high, made her way to the dais where she accepted the trophy on Mr. Bronstein's behalf.

In the autumn, Jacob packed his belongings into a cardboard box and left home. He was sixteen when he entered the University of Michigan on a tennis scholarship. He did not see Cynthia Halley again for fifteen years.

By the winter of 1947, Jacob had made a name for himself on Broadway and in Hollywood, but the name was no longer Bronstein. The wind was howling off frozen Lake Michigan on the day Jed

Bernard came to Chicago to accept the Chamber of Commerce Brotherhood Award for his popular radio series, *Pasquale's World*. He'd heard that Cynthia had gotten married to a fellow from Wauwatosa whose grandfather had a street named after him, so her call to his suite at the Drake came as a surprise. She was in the lobby, she said. "I saw the article in the *Trib* and thought it would be fun to have a drink, for old times' sake."

"Cynthia Halley," Jed replied. "My, my, my. You'll come up immediately."

She had on a mink coat and a blue silk dress, and Jed thought she was still the best-looking woman he'd ever seen. Later, in bed, he felt her tears on his face, but by then he was accustomed to making women cry. Nathan Bronstein got there as Cynthia was leaving. They shook hands in the foyer, and when she was gone, Nathan gave his son a look. "Pretty fancy fucking, Jacob," he said.

There had been fancier since, Katherine thought as she watched Jed paddle around his pool; but nothing that had made him forget Cynthia Halley and no one who was likely to.

Under a drooping azalea bush, Simon was having running dreams, yipping in his sleep; sounds of laughter and the rhythmic bounce of a tennis ball drifted across the ravine from a neighboring estate, but Jed was in a pensive mood, treading water, frowning at Katherine, who lay face down beside the pool, her head cradled on her arms.

"Do you know how many people there are you can talk to, chukkabukker?" he asked.

"In Los Angeles?"

"Say the world."

"How many?"

"Seven."

"That's a lot."

"I'm being generous." He gazed around at his garden. "I always think, I'll have people up here . . . share the place. But who will I ask? If Churchill were in town, that'd be nice. Or I'd like to have De Gaulle to dinner. But they're not, so . . ." He ducked and came up sputtering. ". . . I'd rather stay alone with you."

Katherine sat up and tied the string of her white bikini around her neck.

"What was that your old man used to give you for breakfast?" Jed asked.

"Spam sandwiches on Bond bread with ketchup. Not every day, of course."

"Yeechh! No wonder you're *farkrimte*. You expected to grow tits on a diet like that?"

She smiled happily. Why was it, she wondered, that Jewish insults seemed like love?

"In the army we ate better," he said.

"You were in the army?"

"Certainly."

"Which war? Korea?"

"What WAR?" he yelped. The water lapped at his chest. "The Second World War, putz! Were you alive yet?"

"Just. I remember blackouts at the lake house—having to keep the shades drawn. My father was a neighborhood air raid warden."

A choking sound came from Jed's throat. "In the neighborhood of Auschwitz he was a warden."

Katherine slipped into the pool and swam over to him. He put one hand on each of her shoulders.

"Did you enlist?"

"You had to. Fucking Hitler was taking over the world. That was one fight no Jew could stay out of."

"Were you scared?"

"Sure I was scared. You want to go on maneuvers with a bunch of rednecks? One slip and they're sending you home in a box with a note of apology from the government."

They had worked their way to the shallow end. Jed climbed out of the pool, wrapped a tiger-striped towel around his waist, and disappeared into the house. In a little while he was back carrying a telephone, which he plugged into an outlet in the patio. "Is there anything on earth that would keep you from answering that?" Katherine asked.

"Are you crazy? It could be a job."

At four o'clock, Jed lowered the bamboo curtain and lay with Katherine on the bed; there, as elsewhere, all her energies were directed toward pleasing him, a situation that he seemed to consider, in his own words, "perfectly normal." Her old crippling guilt was subsumed in an unresolved state of longing, yet once he fell asleep holding her fast in the circle of his arms, the feeling of security and peace that came over her was unlike any she had ever known.

***

On Saturday evening "the boys" arrived to shoot pool. A caravan of sportscars converged at the top of the hill, and since Jed was watching television, Katherine went to the door. Standing in a well of light, she heard a voice boom from the courtyard: "That's the best thing I've seen in this house in ten years!" A tall, craggily handsome man emerged from the shadows in blue jeans and a red crewneck sweater, his hand outstretched. "Wolf Adams, an aging Jew," he announced. ("Women go crazy for Wolf—*mad* for him," Jed had told her about his friend, who was a few years younger than he.) Behind Wolf came Kent Forgen, the straight man, she assumed. He had slick blond hair and wore a blazer with a yacht club insignia on the pocket, gray flannels, and spectator shoes, an outfit which made him look like a fugitive from a forties comedy. His precise diction was in sharp contrast to the minion beside him, Jimmy Lewis, who shoved pudgy hands in his pockets when Katherine said hello, replied, "Pleezed tuh meetcha," and never glanced her way again.

Jed ambled out of his bedroom looking like a deadly pool shark in an all-black outfit. He gave Jimmy a fast hello, greeted Kent warmly, and asked Wolf, "How are you, crip?"

Wolf emitted a piteous groan. "It's a *tsebrukhneh* man, Jed."

"*Grizhering?*" Jed asked in mock surprise. "That's not like you . . . you're usually such a happy-go-lucky fella."

General laughter followed the remark since Wolf invariably claimed to be "a broken man," and was considered by his peers to be the king of *grizher* (literally, to "grind one's guts"). He leaned his lanky frame against the bookcase. "A man from the State Department is touring Israel—" he began.

"Yes . . . yes?" Jed prompted, his eyes glittering with anticipation.

"They take him everywhere—the Wailing Wall, the Billy Rose Museum, the Frank Sinatra Home for Wayward Boys . . ."

Jed looked pointedly at his watch.

Wolf frowned but he picked up the tempo. ". . . at the Tomb of the Unknown Soldier, he sees a sign: 'Here lies Morris Ginsburg.' 'How can there be a name on the Tomb of the Unknown Soldier?' he asks. The guide says, 'Ah, as a soldier he was unknown, but as a *furrier. . . .* !' "

Jed cracked up completely. He rocked back and forth, wiping

tears of mirth away from his eyes while the others roared. Kent's contribution, which followed, drew a *klop* on the head and an affectionate "Never tell that joke again as long as you live, Kenteleh."

Jimmy grunted, "Let's shoot pool," and went to rack up the balls.

Jed led Katherine to a tall chair behind the pool table. "Sit there, dollface. Open your mouth and make me miss a shot, I'll kill you." As an afterthought, he added, "You don't mind?"

And she who had wrangled with father, husband, and lover about male oppression, said sincerely, "No, I like to watch men play games." Being there seemed absolutely right; there was nowhere else she'd rather be. Jed gave her a quick kiss on the cheek and announced happily, "This is the best girl I've had since Mary Rose Keane."

Wolf prowled around the table, hefting the cuestick, then striking a ball with a clean crack. "Go in, I beg of you!" Jed cried as the cue ball nestled behind his shot and hovered at the lip of the cup. "Scratch!" he crowed as it went in, clunking along the subterranean chute.

Competition gave a keen edge to their humor; Jed and Wolf bounced lines off each other, with Kent as the perfect foil and Jimmy an eager audience. The world seemed reduced to this smoke-filled room; Katherine felt as if she had a ringside seat at the greatest comedy act in the world.

That there was a dark side to these handsome Jewish comics, Jed and Wolf, was no mystery to her. It was evident in their history: four disastrous marriages between them, a string of ultimately unsatisfactory Gentile girlfriends, the *tsouris* with their children. What she didn't know was whether women like her, whom they referred to with rude affection as shiksas, were the problem or the cure. Whichever it was, the blend of Grand Opera and Grand Guignol they offered was irresistible to her.

CHAPTER 17

Louder, Faster, Funnier

The house Katherine found at the end of February was not a conventional one but a ski lodge: a small A-frame with a stone facade wedged against a hillside in a neighborhood that was a tolerable mix of bourgeoisie and Bohemia called Beverly Glen. One of the advantages, she told Jed, was that the Westlake School for Girls was five minutes away.

"Forget it," he advised. "Put the knibbler in public school."

"Why?"

"Always go against the grain, *buktsayna*. Univac's smart and she's got class coming out her *toches*. Send her to Warner Avenue. It's in the district, your father doesn't have to pay a nickel. Chris went there one year. Best school she was ever in, even if Laura did persist in calling it Warner Brothers."

A rock garden yielded pansies and marigolds alongside the house; there was a stone fireplace in the living room, a balcony off the master bedroom, a ceiling painted blue with puffs of white clouds in Chryssie's room, and a patio in the shadow of the hill—room for a dog and cat. On the misty winter morning they moved in, Jed pulled up to the curb in his Ferrari, arranged the furniture, put together Chryssie's new bunk beds, and left, vowing not to return until she was twenty-one. When Christopher flew to Los Angeles for Chryssie's fifth birthday, the evidence of permanence he saw dashed his hopes for a reconciliation; he had cut them loose, and they were drifting far out beyond his reach.

***

During the week, Jed's preoccupation with his daughter drove everything else from his life. Writing projects he'd begun on the weekend were abandoned upon her return from Manhattan Beach; except for a movie or an occasional dinner at Jessica Kendall's, he and Katherine rarely went out. According to Eve, there was a time in Hollywood when a party was made by Jed Bernard's presence. At the height of his success, handsome, savagely funny, usually with the most glamorous female star of the day on his arm, he had ineffable style. A socially hazardous habit brought him down: he said what others only dared to think. His rapier wit alienated as many as it fascinated. When he directed it toward himself, his audience howled; turned against them, it soured. His peers, although they acknowledged him as the master, finally tired of his commanding center stage as if by divine right; tired, in the greatest ego factory in the world, of taking a back seat to Jed Bernard. Eventually the avalanche of invitations had dwindled. He became a pariah of sorts, except to the few loyal hostesses of his own generation (some secretly in love with him) who still included him when they required an extra man. Unlike many of his contemporaries who were far less successful with women, Jed could be counted on not to foist a young girl on a middle-aged socialite's dinner table. There had been a parade of women in his life, but since Chris had come to live with him, he'd rarely been seen with one in public. When he'd turned fifty, he told Katherine, he'd vowed that he would hang it up before he'd make a fool of himself with young broads. The code he'd always had for the girls he called pishers—the starlets, the dummies, the ones with sex appeal but no distinction—was expanded to include those under thirty: as long as it was a professional arrangement or he didn't leave the house, his dignity would not be compromised (unless he was in Europe, where he did as he pleased).

Katherine's presence in Jed's life was greeted by his older female friends with a chilly, wary cordiality, followed by a total freeze. The sole exception was Jessica Kendall, who was unfailingly gracious and never lacked a suitor. In the early throes of romantic enthusiasm, Jed insisted, when he was invited by Blanche Kramer, an old friend who had married a well-known director and become an impassioned party giver, that Katherine accompany him to her soirees. It was like bringing a cocker spaniel puppy into a den of Dobermans. "She's just like Laura," Blanche remarked dryly to Jed. "Only she can talk."

After a while, divided loyalties made him play the extra man role when it was pressed upon him; then he'd dig out his black tie and be home in an hour, full of promises to make it up to Katherine, on one occasion bearing a purloined sack of chocolate truffles. Billy Wilder had caught him in the act, he said, and speculated that a blonde was waiting in bed for him.

Early in the spring he received an invitation from Sophie Mendel, widow of the legendary studio mogul, Irving Mendel, to a gala at her Coldwater Canyon estate. Although it was being held on a Thursday, one of Chris's sacrosanct school nights, it promised to be so festive that Jed agreed to take Katherine to it.

She wore a one-shouldered gown of seafoam green silk that she'd charged at Saks, and her grandmother's long emerald earrings, managing to turn heads even in the crowd of beautiful women filling Sophie's Palladian garden. The hostess, a renowned beauty in her early sixties, strolled under purple jacaranda trees among her guests like a bird of paradise trailing veils and cockatoo feathers. Jed waved to her across the garden and she blew him a kiss.

"Incredible," Katherine gasped. "She doesn't look a day over thirty."

Jed confided quietly, "That's not her head, you know. The entire thing is a transplant."

While dessert was being served in the tented garden, Katherine went to dance with her dinner partner, a dashing British screenwriter. When they returned, Jed was gone from the table. She waited for half an hour, then went searching for him through baronial rooms amid a blur of famous faces—stars, senators, governors—and found him at last in the service pantry, talking animatedly on the telephone to Chris. His face was in profile; its unguarded expression made her feel as jealous as if she'd caught him in a clinch with one of the world-class beauties outside. When he saw Katherine, he looked relieved. "I've had it, dollface," he told her as he hung up. "Let's go home."

Above his head, a wall clock said ten-thirty. Katherine gnashed her teeth and followed him out the door, calculating ruefully how many months it would take her to pay for the dress.

Jed put up a show of interest in other things—a new Nazi book, an idea for a script, women, shooting pool with the boys—but everything was secondary to Chris and everything would be sacrificed to her.

The presence of the two Christabels on many evenings during the week imposed a chastity that Katherine suspected Jed welcomed. About sex he was ambiguous: it was on his mind constantly (its various mathematical equations, permutations, and pleasures); on the other hand, the requirements of an actual affair with a living, breathing, and—worst of all—*eager* young woman like Katherine irritated him. "I've been with the great sex goddesses of my day, but you're hotter than all of 'em!" he complained. He tilled a rock garden of excuses: "I've got such pains, baby," or "This is a rough week, kid; you've just got to let me get through the next few days." Finally, when after some weeks she voiced her frustration, he expressed concern and made an appointment with his internist, who was practically a member of the family. The next day, Jed took her to lunch at the Bistro to tell her the results. Gleefully, he reported, "Sherman says a man my age needs a younger broad!"

Age was Jed's fallback position: upon the number fifty he bestowed the gravity appropriate to eighty. Fatigue visited him like a medieval plague, as did a panoply of illnesses, imaginary as Molière's. He took codeine as if it were a vitamin. Each morning upon rising, he examined himself for cancer or some other incurable disease that might have been visited upon him in the night. The appearance of a new mole or a bruise would provoke a suspicious "Ho, ho, *ho*! What have we *here*?" If he had a doctor's appointment, he would insist that Katherine drop whatever she was doing to accompany him, prompting her finally to wail, "You think the purpose of shiksas is to drive Jewish men to the proctologist!" During that intimate examination, Jed would sing, "Getting to know you . . ." to the specialist. When, for the third time in six weeks, he took to his bed with the flu, Katherine suggested darkly that he didn't need a nose and throat man, he needed a shrink. Turning his head on the pillow, he said philosophically, "It's too late for that, baby, I'm too far gone."

But the subject revived him; he got to his feet and launched into an impromptu sketch regarding the origin of psychoanalysis: "Freud wanted to be a surgeon you know . . . found out he couldn't stand the sight of blood. Fainted dead away in the operating room. 'I'll talk to them, that's what I'll do,' he said. 'Get a little office, let 'em lie down . . . it'll be nice,' " thereby dissolving Katherine's gloom, if not her frustration, into laughter.

Impotence was not the issue. Jed was neither too old, nor infirm, nor inept. He was a skinflint, the Silas Marner of sex doling out his favors. He veered from withholding himself to dancing around with snapping eyes: "It's comeback time! I feel so good I may even give you a little *hok*, *buktsayna*!" Kissing he eschewed almost entirely; the occasions when he relented were so rare that they were branded on Katherine's brain. Once, when she was sitting on his lap in the huge armchair beside the fire, her eyes reflected such moist, luminous longing that Jed's lips moved toward hers like a magnet. After a long, passionate kiss, he looked at her and said huskily, "What is *that?*" "Love," she breathed, her voice full of emotion. *"Feh!"* he cried, jumping up from the chair and depositing her on the floor.

Her perpetual state of yearning was intensified on the random Friday evenings when they went to the Daisy or the Factory, popular discotheques that appealed to Jed because they had pool tables in their front rooms. Half mobster, half movie star in his dashing getups, Jed would beat the pool sharks and hustling young actors in straight games and then go inside and dance with the devilish abandon of a randy kid in the ghetto. Women frugging nearby stared at him with frank lust in their eyes. Little do they know, Katherine thought, that after humping a woman (as he calls it), he sneezes so hard his head practically comes off. After the first such seizure in her presence, she had turned her face to the pillow to hide her amusement, thinking: Sexual guilt—one more thing Jews and Catholics have in common.

More than once he mentioned that it would be helpful if she "talked dirty" to him when he was "humping" her. Willing to try anything short of perversion, Katherine skipped through Henry Miller, Norman Mailer, and Philip Roth for inspiration. When the moment next arrived in Jed's bed, she took a deep breath and murmured a literary obscenity, her lips against his shoulder. He paused, started up again, then stopped, shaking his head. "Forget it, kid. It's coming out 'Uck me . . . 'uck me,' and if I start to laugh, we're out of business."

How love took root and grew in this arid sexual soil, Katherine could not explain. "Interlocking neuroses," Jed told her. "It's Sadie and Massie, honey. The oldest story in the world."

The paradox of Jed was his casual misogyny and the demon-

strable fact that women had always been at the center of his existence. No matter how he reviled them, or how selfishly he withheld
expressions of love, his intensity of emotion conveyed need, and to
Katherine, that was a gift.

He foraged for details of her background, and used them to
tease her: "You want to play with the baby altar, Skeezix?" and
"Camp *Madonna*? Baby, where you come from, it's a miracle you're
walking!" His alchemy turned tearful memories to laughter. Monogamy was an unnatural state, he asserted once. At her downcast
expression, he pouted, repeating " 'Didn't you see the crib?' How'd
you say that? Show me the little face." Her account of the untimely
drowning of her childhood crush, Todd Babcock, brought Jed out of
his chair, arms swinging like a creature from the deep, going, "Glug
. . . glug . . . glug! Poor Todd—the Commies got him!"

Monitoring her every word, he was on guard for the faintest
hint of anti-Semitism. On one Saturday evening, while serving him
supper in the study, she offhandedly referred to Judaism as a race.
His mouth turned down; he pushed the spaghetti away, castigating
her until she went home in tears. But when he called the next day,
she was there within minutes.

Summonses to his house were irresistible; soon enough, that
aerie retreat was the only place Katherine wanted to be. "Hee, hee,
hee!" Jed gloated. "Came up to give me a charity fuck and never
left the hill."

The other world she knew, bland and Gentile, unfolded at a
pace that seemed like slow motion compared to Jed's quick cuts. It
paled, faded, and slipped away unremarked. Friends complained they
rarely saw her. How to explain Jed's dictum: "You understand, my
dear, that you may never have anyone up here?"

"I can't see my *friends*?"

"Certainly you may. Go—*go* to Pasadena! I'll let you out every
once in a while because I know you'll come back on your hands
and knees."

But the social events she attended without him palled; by ten
o'clock she would leave the filet mignon at the Bistro or the chicken
à la king at the Beverly Hilton ballroom and drive to Rosewood to
fetch Jed a matzoh sandwich and a glass of tea. Then he would quiz
her about the events.

"Did they have balloons and give toasts?"

"Jews don't have balloons?"

"Nah. They're too busy blowing up each other's egos."

"They don't give toasts?"

"I'll give you a Jewish toast: 'May he live in thirty rooms with no maid. May he live in a mansion with the heat turned off.' That's a Jewish toast. These are nice people you're with, right? The men are putzes, but the girls are good-looking—blond, healthy skin. My Christabel's a dark caricature next to them."

From the moment Emily and Douglas Winterhaus had clapped her in handcuffs to her crib, like a bird hurtling itself against the bars of a golden cage, Katherine had struggled to be free of their world. Jed Bernard offered a dramatic alternative. And when she attempted to fly, he had only to twitch upon the string to bring her back. He knew no one she knew; the bastions of boredom like Oak Hill and the Chatterbox Club were shuttered to the likes of him. Yet the Semitic planes of his face, as familiar as those swashbucklers from the Bible so dear to the romantic hearts of the Sacred Heart nuns, made convent bells chime in her heart. In a matter of weeks, love worked its way into the marrow of her bones until she could no longer imagine life without him. She had only to close her eyes to see his hand lying next to her on the sheet, his father's ring and the Patek Philippe watch gleaming against his olive skin. She had only to think of his hand to be filled with love.

The paucity of sex had a twofold result: the suspension of her guilt and insane jealousy. The mere thought of him expending an ounce of his carefully conserved energy on anyone else drove her into a frenzy. Months after their affair began, the telephone still rang with calls from women; his lowered, insinuating voice turned her to stone.

One Sunday morning following his religious lecture, he told her: "You've got to understand, kid. Every guy cheats. If a young chick comes in with her tits flying, you're obliged to give her a *hok*— for mankind."

"I don't think all men feel that way," Katherine said tensely.

"Sure they do. Squares are the worst. They go to a convention, it's dig-a dig-a do time!"

"It's just not true!" Katherine cried. "Tell me I'm crazy, but you can't make me believe there aren't some decent men. Tell me I'm crazy, but—"

"Okay," he said equably. "You're crazy."

She started to cry. And if Jed loved Katherine's laughter, making her cry was his idea of a *really* good day. Tears were an aphrodisiac to Jed; no exotic potion would have aroused him to lead her into his fur-covered bed and take her roughly—leaving her drained and content while he hopped around sneezing—the way her weeping did. Fortunately for her, she was a cryer. Jed was forever drawing damp wads of Kleenex from behind cushions, saying, "I believe this belongs to you, my dear."

Such scenes were reserved for the weekends. From Sunday evening to Friday afternoon, Chris ruled the roost. Her needs, her whims, her mercurial moods hypnotized Jed. The slightest hint of her dissatisfaction plunged him into gloom. And having absolute power, she ruled with an iron hand. Most of the women who had passed through Jed's life since the child came to live with him had perceived this and either gotten out after a futile few weeks or campaigned for her favor; those who pointed out that she was spoiled had the briefest tenure. Some had loved Jed; all had been defeated by Chris.

In April, when the days were growing longer and the trees were in flower along Sunset Boulevard, Rivka Tamir arrived from Israel. She was a woman Jed had talked of often with great affection, citing her intelligence, her generosity, her emotional support over the ten years of their friendship.

Katherine first saw her sitting by the pool at sunset, the sky lighting her from behind so that she looked like a creature on fire. The hair that grazed her shoulder blades was golden red, her large eyes were hazel, her skin tawny. A rust-colored poncho was thrown across her shoulders, and with Jed standing over her, bare-chested, wrapped in a tiger-striped towel, Katherine was reminded of a painting of Judith and Holofernes that she had seen as a child.

Rivka's handshake was forged from steel. "I am very glad to meet you, my dear," she told Katherine in a husky, lightly accented voice.

Fighting a wave of jealousy, Katherine said, "It's wonderful that you're here, Rivka. Jed's been looking forward to your coming so much."

"Not at all," Jed growled.

Up close, Katherine saw that Rivka was older than she had first appeared—too old for Jed's Humbert Humbert tastes anyway. But when Rivka looked at Jed, there was no mistaking the emotion in her eyes: thwarted love. There were several such women to whom

Jed had a special attachment: over forty, Jewish, attractive, intelligent, in turn baffled and infuriated by his lack of sexual response to them. Because he kept them at a distance, he was enshrined in their hearts as the ultimate sex object. Katherine presumed that they eventually came to the conclusion that the mental stimulation he provided was worth the physical frustration.

"Don't get crazed and frighten her, Rivka," Jed said. "She's a nice Gentile girl."

"Gentile, shmentile," said Rivka. "Can she cook? You've lost weight, Jed. I make you my special blini tonight."

As an emissary to the United Nations, Rivka had come to America this time full of warnings about an Israeli-Arab conflict in the Middle East. For twenty years, she had been the sometime mistress and confidante of General Dov Aron, and his intelligence was that the Syrians and Egyptians were tabling their old feuds in order to attack the common enemy. Jed listened to her raptly, his eyes burning with interest as she talked of Tel Aviv and Jerusalem where, some years before, he had spent several weeks recovering from his divorce. It was then that Rivka had come to his rescue.

"Nobody better than you when a man's having a nervous breakdown," Jed remarked when she referred to that trip.

"He was a dying man," Rivka told Katherine. "That woman, Laura"—she spat out the name—"had broken his *kishkas*. You know what is *kishkas?*"

"Not exactly, but I get the idea," Katherine laughed.

"Please, Rivka, she speaks Yiddish better than anyone. What are you, kid? Tell her."

"A *machamoves*."

Rivka peered at her. "What? What's this? Oh, I see. A *malach-hamoves*—angel of death. Why do you call such a nice girl a name like this, Jed?"

"There's a lot of crying, a lot of biblical talk. I call her Malcolm," said Jed.

"Has anyone offered you a drink, Rivka?" Katherine asked.

"At last!" Rivka cried. "My throat is parched . . . *parched*!"

Katherine laughed. "It's like wandering in the desert to come up here—"

"See what I mean?" Jed broke in. "I'd like a vodka tonic, Malcolm, if you'd be so kind."

From the bar, Katherine could see them—Jed pacing barefoot

before the pool, puffing on his pipe, his towel flapping in the evening breeze, and Rivka, her blazing eyes fixed on his face, gesturing wildly as she spoke.

Suddenly the front door banged open and Chris charged into the house, tossed Katherine a greeting, and stomped outside in her white boots. A change came over Rivka: she greeted Chris with a kiss on the forehead, but the smile solidified and her expressive eyes were guarded. In a moment all three came inside.

"You have to come *now*, Dad," Chris was saying.

"I have guests, chukkabukker."

"Katherine's not a guest. *Now*, Dad . . . you've *got* to!"

"Talk to Rivka, will you, dollface?" Jed asked Katherine as he allowed himself to be pulled outside.

"What's that all about?" Katherine inquired.

Rivka shrugged. "The donkey . . . the bridle . . . some crisis or other. Who knows with that *chayeh*?" She strolled about the room, picking up the little Israeli figures—camels and donkeys and rabbis woven from straw and cloth—from the bookshelves. "I'll tell you the truth—she is the one who is breaking his *kishkas*. Jed is so blind. I fear it will all end in tragedy. You get along with her okay . . . or no?"

"Yes, I do. Except when she torments my daughter. And I do love her—the impossible behavior isn't really her fault. She's spoiled up here, and who knows what at her mother's. And they each tell her how terrible the other one is. I told Jed I wouldn't blame her if she had a nervous breakdown on the freeway halfway between here and Manhattan Beach, but he doesn't want to hear it."

"Huh—tell me about it. Last year I lived up here for two months trying to help. He makes it impossible."

Katherine said in a soft voice, "I don't think he's ever loved anyone the way he does Chris."

Rivka crossed and sat on the ottoman close to her chair, looking at her candidly. "That's because it is not so complicated to love a child. She makes plenty of demands on him, but . . . well, he can love her without the responsibilities of being a grown-up man."

From the back of the house came the sound of a door banging and loud, angry voices. The two women exchanged a grim look. With a sigh, Rivka rose and slung a leather pouch over her shoulder.

"I go to a hotel. On the weekend I come back. It's too much tumult for me. I'm remembering better now how it was." She extended her large, freckled hand to Katherine. "You tell him good-bye for me, okay? He won't even know I'm gone."

"Rivka, I know that's not true! Please wait . . . I'm sure that in a little while . . ."

"A little while, a little schmile. I'm too old for this." She took Katherine's face in her hands and kissed her soundly on both cheeks. "Jed is right—you're a good woman. No bullshit like so many of these American pishers. And you're his type . . . maybe things can work out for you. Let me give you some advice—don't give up your own life. *Not one day.* Jed is very demanding. It is easy to lose yourself with a man like him."

With that, she turned and marched out of the house.

When they were alone, Katherine and Chris Bernard got along well. They developed an affection for each other which was somehow separate from the jealousy each felt in Jed's presence. His arrival on the scene set off rival neurotic needs, a contest Katherine could only lose. During afternoon outings on which they insisted she accompany them, she found herself growing silent as the conversation revolved totally around Chris. The child's passion for horseback riding resulted in hours spent at the stables with Jed cheering her on. To Katherine he derided the sport as a "goyishe pursuit," but it was good for Chris, he'd add quickly with a light in his eye, enamored of her Gentile side. Rivka understood him well: all the shortcomings of his neurotic nature, all the reticence he felt at loving a woman were suspended when it came to his daughter. Into her he poured his hopes, his imagination, the passion of his youth, the fire that was in his soul. Reality was Katherine's preserve.

One afternoon she and Jed were standing outside the stall while Chris groomed her horse. Suddenly a massive gray gelding broke loose and galloped around a corner in their direction. Jed blanched. Under his breath he said to Katherine, "There's a fuckin' horse coming you don't believe." It was possibly the only sentence he addressed to her all afternoon, but it linked them as conspirators, and it made her laugh whenever she thought of it.

While Chris rode wild and free, Chryssie went with a beginners' group to Will Rogers Polo Field. Chris was fearless. She scorned helmets and went over fences like the wind; animals took to her as if she were St. Francis of Assisi. Chryssie, on the other hand, had to overcome innate terror to trot around the ring on an English saddle wearing a proper gabardine jacket with her chin strap firmly in place; before long she was competing in shows at the polo grounds. But caution guided all her sportive endeavors. No one ever needed to tell Christabel Kellogg to be careful.

"You're so Jewish, Univac," Jed would tell her, shaking his head. Impatient with her timidity, he announced one sunny afternoon, "I'm going to teach you to climb a tree if it's the last thing I do." And out he dragged her, skinny knees trembling, to the sycamore tree in the courtyard, where he commanded her to shinny up. "Why does she need to know how to do this?" Katherine demanded from the sidelines.

"Fine, Mrs. Nussbaum," Jed snapped. "You want a knibbler, that's your business."

"All right, all right. Give it a try, honey," Katherine coaxed, biting her lip as she watched Chryssie inch up the tree to the lowest branch. There, stubbornly, her iron will pitted against the blustering man who exhorted her to keep going, the child clung like a koala bear, refusing to budge any further; meanwhile Chris cantered up and down the driveway astride Rowdy, urging her on.

"She's not like Chris, you know," Katherine told Jed in an undertone. "Kids are different." But in her eagerness to provide a paternal figure, she was reluctant to criticize. The adventure ended in a draw.

Watching Jed dote on his daughter made the sporadic nature of Christopher's attention to Chryssie harder for Katherine to bear. Early in the summer, she had a crying spell about it.

"What is it you *want*, O Lord?" Jed asked.

"Well . . . I see all these children in the park with their fathers, and—"

"*Oy, gottenyu!* You're going to spend your life looking for someone to take that kid to the park. The park is *gornisht.*"

"She's the only one at camp who can't swim!" she blubbered.

"She's five! Okay, okay. I'll teach her how to swim this afternoon."

Thus came Christabel Kellogg's siege of terror in Jed's swimming pool. While Chris dove from the board, did handstands, and splashed about them like a porpoise, Jed took the trembling little girl by her arms and hoisted her over his head. "You ever heard of Esther Williams, knibbler?" he growled as Chryssie's eyes searched out her mother's across the patio, but Katherine ground her teeth and was silent. "People . . . *people, please!*" Chryssie entreated. "There are no people," Jed stated flatly, and in the next instant she was underwater. Katherine took a step forward; he glared at her to stay back. She dug her nails into her fists. The child surfaced sputtering, and made her way to the side of the pool, to wild applause from the three. The experience left her with no fear of Jed, to Katherine's surprise, and she recalled what Wolf had said about him. "With kids and dogs, there's no one like Jed. He's got a special talent."

It was Chris Bernard whom Chryssie feared. Chris, who locked her in closets, forced her up on Rowdy, and kicked sand in her eyes, hissing on Father's Day, "He's not your father and he never will be," was the one who made her life a hell and inclined her to spend more time with Abby or a school friend. Fortunately Katherine unearthed an ideal sitter: a Mexican woman who lived with her husband and a large, happy brood of children at Venice beach. The Mendozas' was the only unbroken home with which Chryssie was intimately acquainted, and she became their mascot. "They're the Spanish Addams Family," she told her mother, happily taking refuge there from time to time when Katherine was embroiled in the Bernards' domestic problems.

CHAPTER 18

The Cocktail Party

Female devotion was, in Jed's view, "perfectly normal." His response to Katherine's was to absorb her time, so that her attention to Chryssie and even the few hours she gave to writing critiques for Columbia irritated him. Total immersion was the way he related to a woman. If Katherine left the room, he'd demand to know where she was going; if she made a lunch date with a friend, he'd turn up at the restaurant to join them for coffee; if he left her alone at his house and returned to find her sitting on the floor of his study poring over his scrapbooks, ingesting details of his college days, tennis triumphs, the meteoric Broadway career, and celebrated love affairs, his attitude was: What better does she have to do?

When black moods were on him—and they came regularly, springing from sources as diverse as Chris's weekend's with the "Juke Family" (his name for Laura's collection of relatives in Manhattan Beach), stresses of work; remembrance of things past; fear of the future (e.g., cancer, losing his house, the ubiquitous Hollywood fear of never getting another job)—Katherine told herself the price was too high. Was she put on this earth to make up for two thousand years of Jewish suffering? It seemed Jed thought so. During these episodes, he insulted her, ignored her, and held over her head the greatest punishment of all: banishment from his life. Then she would retreat to her house in the Glen, bury herself in work, vow to put her life in order, and make plans with friends, only to drop them at his call. "You'll come up immediately," he'd say, and the cycle would begin again: Bliss, Torment, and Despair. "They're my attorneys, madam," Jed quipped.

Early in July, Katherine received an invitation to a cocktail party, an annual midsummer celebration given by a friend from the art world, Florence Bostwick, still another transplanted easterner, in this case descended from a long line of Connecticut Yankees. Jed had met only a few of Katherine's old friends; having shared his seclusion for months, and having traveled miles from the early, secret days of their affair, she accepted without a second thought and begged him to come.

Florence's rented guest house fronted an estate in the Old Guard neighborhood of Hancock Park. On that sultry summer evening, Jed got out of his Ferrari with a resigned sigh. "It's appropriate that you should bring me here on *Tisha b'Ov*," he told Katherine as they walked up the brick path.

"What's *Tisha b'Ov*?"

"It commemorates the time they rounded up all the Jews and killed only half of them. That's already a *good* day."

Katherine recognized the curator of the Pasadena Museum, Melissa Drake, and her stuffy fiancé a few steps ahead of them. She glanced at Jed. Getting him off his hill at all was a feat; his willingness to trek all the way to Hancock Park to meet her friends she chose to interpret as an expression of stubbornly inarticulated love. "I'll be out of here in fifteen minutes," he threatened her now. In his conservative attire—striped shirt, black knit tie, gray flannels, and navy blazer—he was a peacock in pigeon feathers.

"Be nice, Jed," she implored.

"What is that bullshit, 'Be nice'?" he growled. "You think I never went to a cocktail party with Gentile people before I met you?"

"These are a very specific breed of Gentile," she said with a weak smile. "They make Kent Forgen look like Bugsy Siegel."

"Listen, baby, what can it *be*? All you got to do is stand around and say, 'Hi, Fred. Hullo, Will. How's the sloop? Hear you got a new Smith and Wesson, Stan . . . bagged any Jews yet?' "

"Oh, God," she groaned.

He ran a pocket comb through his hair. "Hurry up, kid. I don't want to miss Skippy and Buff. I haven't felt like this since I was sixteen years old and Cynthia Halley took me to meet her folks on Hennepin Avenue."

Introducing Jed into such a gathering was like carting an atom bomb to a Fourth of July celebration, she realized presently. Florence's guests came supplied with dime-store fireworks: bons mots, Polish jokes, anecdotes from the world of finance, law, art, and journalism—ordinary sparklers that could be counted on, if not to dazzle, at least to entertain. A megaton explosion of humor and energy like Jed had a dampening effect at first, stealing their rickety thunder and scattering them into protective little enclosures, groups of three and four huddled around the bar or buffet table like clannish chimpanzees keeping the intruder out. After a few minutes, he loosened his tie and opened the top button of his shirt, pressed in on all sides by pretty women and perspiring young men throwing back drinks as if Prohibition had just been repealed.

Across the room, Katherine saw Andrew Byrne at the center of a group of female admirers, whom he'd been collecting lately like butterflies. He and Jed had met only once, briefly; now, when Katherine took him over to say hello, Andy affected a diffident air. Appraising Katherine's filmy white dress, he smirked. "I see you've come as Blanche DuBois. Last year at this party you were Gary Cooper."

Jed put his head close to Andy's. "The poor kid's failing . . . only got a few months to live. Don't speak of it or she'll start crying. Have you ever seen Katherine cry? Come up the hill anytime. You can catch her day or night—she leaves a trail of wadded Kleenex all over the house."

Andy's smile twisted and he turned away.

"Why are you skulking, young man? No one's after you. Straighten yourself out!" Jed cried, pulling Andy's head onto his shoulder.

Despite himself, Andy started to laugh. "You may be onto something, Jed. I do have a certain furtive quality."

"Furtive? You're a fuckin' *fugitive*!" Jed turned to the girls. "You all know the Catholic strangler?" They tittered appreciatively.

Behind her Katherine heard Louise's unmistakable raucous laugh and braced herself for Jed's reaction to her friend's effervescent personality, but as if he were playing a role he became suddenly courtly, injecting just the right amount of masculine teasing until Louise was batting her eyelashes at him, subdued and apparently smitten.

As they went from group to group, with growing respect Katherine observed Jed's talent for finding the precise note that struck a responsive chord in an individual. Outside of a KKK meeting, he couldn't have had a tougher crowd to play to, she thought. Yet he was winning them over.

At eight-thirty, a young woman arrived alone with a baby in her arms, apologizing to Florence that her sitter had failed to show up. A couple nearby rolled their eyes at one another; others glanced away; a few smiled sympathetically at the harassed mother. But Jed impetuously relieved her of her burden, taking the baby in his arms. "I want to have a serious discussion with you," he told him as he carried the infant through the mob to the French window, letting him play with his pipe. The baby lay back in Jed's arms and gazed up at him with trusting eyes. "I take the baby home with me," Jed muttered to Katherine, his handsome, arrogant features taking on a new dimension of empathy and tenderness in her eyes, a dimension unshared by any of the attractive, clean-cut, successful Mr. Rights in the room. The wave of love she felt for Jed at that moment was, in her mind, inextricably bound up in his Jewishness. And in this, she knew she was not alone.

All over Los Angeles, she'd begun to see them—the women who shared her fixation with Jewish men. They were not recognizable on sight; not all blue-eyed blondes were shiksas, in Katherine's specific definition of the term, and not all shiksas were blue-eyed blond Catholics. But most, she imagined, fitted Jed's description of "neuros." They gravitated to Jewish men, both instinctively and reactively, as a way out of the constricted world they knew; they were addicted to the famed Jewish warmth, humor, and intelligence, as well as to the black side, the side that once made her rail at Jed, "You don't have to be a masochist to love Jewish men, but it helps!" The room they were now in resembled the Los Angeles Country Club at cocktail hour. Shortly after they'd arrived, Jed had whispered in her ear, "Where are the Jews, Mommy?" and she'd laughed, amazed that her friends could be so blind as to what they were missing.

Two years in Los Angeles and she'd begun to wonder who was left in Brooklyn; at times it seemed that Flatbush Avenue had been transplanted to the heart of Beverly Hills. Into Martindale's bookstore came a steady stream of joke-cracking writers, directors, producers, and story editors from "Noo Yawk" who grew up on egg creams and stickball, and it seemed to be an Erasmus Hall High School reunion at Nate 'n' Al's Delicatessen, when the comic geniuses who turned their talents to cranking out scripts for Benny, Hope, Carson, and the sitcoms that are the daily fare of American humor, congregated to kibitz over their bagels. Some of them—many of them—were married to Jewish women and would have it no other way. But others—tortured, complaining, *grizhering*—relentlessly pursued their neurotic ideal of the shiksa goddess. One of their standard complaints was that Jewish women were inhibited sexually. It only amused Katherine, having often enough heard Andy's rhapsodies about the wildness of Jewish women, who were his erotic ideal. She imagined a split screen: on one side, Andy, saying, "They'll go down on you for hours!" and on the other, Wolf Adams, opining, "They never want to go down on you!" The narrator for this tragicomedy would be Jed, pulling on his pipe and philosophizing: "Forbidden fruit, my dear. That's what it's all about."

As soon as the grateful mother retrieved her baby, Jed expressed a desire to leave. Katherine went to say good-bye to Florence, but when she got back, he was leaning against the bookcase speaking with Eliot Gardiner, a newscaster for a local television station. Gardiner was a heavy-set, rather dandyish fellow never without a silk ascot, who managed, as some short men do, to give the impression of looking down even on people taller than he. The elongated vowels he was using indicated plainly that he was, as usual, drunk. In a declamatory tone, he told Jed, "It's time the Jews took the cross from their shoulders. Get on with it . . . know what I mean?"

Katherine turned pale and darted a glance in Jed's direction. His body was relaxed and his expression friendly enough, but there was a dangerous glint in his eye. "Really? You think so, old man?" he inquired evenly, his pipe clenched in his teeth.

"The Holocaust's been run into the ground," Eliot ranted. "I mean, nobody *cares* anymore. It's yesterday's news. Just because one madman committed an atrocious act twenty years ago, that's no excuse to keep it going. It's enough already." To underline this condescending imitation of Jewish argot, he gave Jed a playful punch on the arm.

Jed straightened, removed the pipe from his mouth, and set it on a table. "Six million is probably an exaggeration, wouldn't you say?" he baited the newsman.

"Of course!" Eliot agreed. "Plenty of other people died in that war. They don't go around feeling sorry for themselves and using it as an excuse for—" He paused to take a belt of Scotch. "A more accurate count would be"—savoring the last drop, he concluded— " 'round half that."

"On the other hand," said Jed, smiling a rictus smile, "three mil is not chopped liver."

A group standing nearby had stopped talking to listen. Frozen in horror, staring at Eliot's mouth as he framed a reply, Katherine prepared for Jed to take a swing at him. But at that moment a strange incident occurred, bringing about an unexpected conclusion to the discussion. Eliot swayed, lurched forward, and slid to the ground with a dull thud. Incredulous, Jed peered down at him; otherwise there was hardly a stir. No one could remember a cocktail party at which Eliot had not passed out. On this occasion, his timing was fortuitous.

Raising his eyebrows at Katherine, Jed jerked his head toward the door. She followed him quickly outside. On the sidewalk, he paused to knock out his pipe against the trunk of a plane tree.

"Don't let Eliot get to you," Katherine said. "He's a *shikkerer.*"

"*Shikkerer,* my ass. He's an anti-Semite," Jed retorted.

A streetlamp cast a chalky light on his face; it was drawn and tense and she saw etched there the scars of a thousand such hurts. The horror of it was that his suspicions were largely true. She had grown up among these people, the educated, provincial, Catholic well-to-do. Scratch the kindest-hearted of them and you'd find traces of anti-Semitism lurking there. Jed's shield was to attack before he was attacked, be the first to do the joke on himself, but it was flimsy armor that could be pierced by the random arrow of an ass like Eliot Gardiner. She could have wept.

To her surprise, Jed did not judge her guilty by association and send her home that night. And later, in bed, his long sigh of satisfaction, his arms pulling her up against him, were enough; she curved into him, feeling herself to be part of a man as she never had before. On that night of *Tisha b'Ov,* Katherine let go of any longing for the world she had known before Jed, and was drawn even deeper into the circle that enclosed them. To observers, she became more and more a hybrid. When she laced her conversation with *mame-loshn* or matched her tempo to Jed's, Gentiles looked at her blankly; his cronies accused him of creating a monster. "A shiksa who does jokes . . . what is *that?*" Wolf Adams demanded to know.

CHAPTER 19

Tsouris

In July, a series of events was set in motion that resulted in Katherine accompanying Jed as he descended, with all the artistry of his ancestors, into a realm of extreme human suffering.

Adelaide gave notice. "I've been out here ten years," she explained to Jed. "I feel an urge to go home to Wisconsin."

A week later, her black pillbox bobbing like a buoy atop her lacquered waves, she sailed down the driveway to her niece's car, into which she placed a valise containing all her worldly possessions.

"Suddenly it comes over her like a *goy tse peygern*," Jed grumbled as he watched her go from his office at the back of the house. (Katherine smiled to herself at the now familiar expression that equated great urgency with a Gentile's desire to die.) Long after the dust had settled on the dirt road, he stood at the window, plunged by the housekeeper's departure into a depression that baffled Katherine. Seated on the couch behind him, she recalled that only a few weeks before, when Chris had asked him what they'd do if Adelaide ever left, he'd said glibly, "Call the employment agency, honey." Help was replaceable but he was not, he'd wanted her to understand, yet now that the moment had arrived, all his fine bravado failed him. His forehead was creased with worry as he chewed on the stem of his pipe, working his thumb into the crook of his index finger.

The radio in Adelaide's room was playing dentist office music. "The temperature at the Civic Center is ninety-eight, and the air quality all over the southland is unacceptable," an announcer said. Jed turned away from the window. "Do you believe that? Three acres in Holmby Hills and that putz says I shouldn't breathe. Turn that thing off, would you, kid?"

Katherine went into the empty maid's room. The sliding closet door was open and two wire hangers lay crisscrossed over the jamb; all traces of Adelaide were gone. When she went back to the office, Jed was seated at his desk, doodling circles on a legal pad. The telephone sat at his elbow, a silent rebuke for his losing contact with the world. His professional life was a shambles—he hadn't worked in over a year—his bank debt was mounting and his energies sapped in the non-stop battle with the blond *chayeh* he'd spawned.

Without looking up, he asked, "How do you put an ad in the paper for someone to braid a kid's hair?"

"Please," Katherine scoffed, attempting to inject a note of reality. "I tried to braid her hair once. She nearly slugged me."

He sighed. "You know what I mean. In all the time she was up here, Adelaide never made one tender gesture toward Chris."

"It wasn't easy for her. She cared more about keeping the house for you. You can't have both. You need a different type of person."

On the desk was a Polaroid snapshot of the two of them standing in the courtyard with Chris between them, Katherine in her pale pink coat and Jed his Italian suit; Chryssie had taken it, she recalled, one Sunday evening as they were setting off for Ah Fong's. Jed's Jewish mania for Chinese food made it a weekly ritual; after dinner, he would always make Chris read everybody's fortune cookie aloud and then laugh until his eyes streamed at the way she garbled the words, her string of schools having failed in the basic task of teaching her to read. Now he fingered the photograph. "You don't look much older than Chris in this shot, kid," he said.

The obvious solution to his dilemma lay in a great unspoken void between them, neither one willing to address it. Katherine had made no move to get a divorce, and Jed was not asking. She wanted him to *want* to marry her, but whenever the subject arose, he'd mention "the girl on the boat," his fantasy of the perfect girl who was waiting for him in the future: blond, sporty, wearing a polo coat, running toward him on the deck of an ocean liner. "Imagine if I got married to someone else and met her afterward!" he'd said, and Katherine had teasingly called him "the reluctant debutante."

Now she glanced at her watch. "Jed, it's after five. I hate to leave you, but Chryssie's bus from camp is due. I promised to take Abby and her to a movie tonight, so—"

"That's all right, dear. Thanks for coming up," he answered distractedly.

At the top of the steps, she looked back and saw him through the window, his hands in his pockets, his head lowered, heading for Chris's room.

The next morning, Jed called and asked Katherine to come to the house. She found him in his office, making notations in the margin of a script in his chicken-scratch hand. When he glanced up at her, she thought she had never seen such a melancholy smile. He had a weary look, the flummoxed air of a man over his head in domestic waters.

"Hi, kid," he said quietly. "Sit down. I want to talk at you." Pausing, he leaned back in his chair. "I've decided to give Chris back to her mother."

And so it began.

The next day, Jed put in a call to Wylie Burke, the attorney of record in the custody case, although it was Jed who had masterminded the strategy, an important component of which was a nice, bland, Gentile lawyer. Coming out of Jed's bathroom, Katherine could hear Wylie's blast from the receiver.

"Are you out of your mind? After all you went through to get her? Is that what she *wants*?"

"I check with her all the time if she wants to live with her mom. She's always said she wants to keep it the way it is, but—"

"So?"

"So how does she know what she's missing? She's getting to an age when she needs her mother. It'd be one thing if Laura made it easy for me, but this way they treat her like an overnight guest down there. One time they told her she couldn't eat at the table with them as long as she lived up here. It's no good. We'll just switch the arrangement. I'll get her on weekends and Laura will have her during the week. I only want to know what are the legal ramifications?"

Katherine crossed the room. In the mirror she saw Jed making a pile from the coins scattered on his night table as he listened to Wylie. He said roughly, "Come on, Wylie, I'm giving the woman her child back. Voluntarily. For both their sakes. It's the right timing—schools out . . . Gateway's *gornisht* anyway. She can start public school in Manhattan Beach in September, you follow me?"

The lines around his mouth were dragging the flesh down, etching bitterness and loss permanently onto his face. He swung his legs onto the bed and leaned back against the pillows, saying into the phone: "I've given the last three years of my life to this, my friend. Exclusively. I don't have a lot to show for it except an unemployment card and a lot of *tsouris*." He shut his eyes to listen to Wylie, then snapped: "Warnings I'll get from a soothsayer, Wylie. From you I need legal advice."

As Wylie's reservations went unheeded, so did Katherine's. She was uncertain why she resisted the idea; why, after all the problems with Chris, she did not feel relief. But somewhere in her brain a red light was flashing, signaling that it was wrong to send her back—wrong for Chris, for Jed, and thus, inevitably, for her. Jed, however, was not to be swayed. There was no indication that Laura was exerting any more pressure than usual. It was wholly his decision; once he decided that it was wrong to keep their daughter from the psychological benefits of residing with her mother, he was going to go through with it if it killed him.

Katherine left the house before Chris came home from school; when she got there that evening, Laura and her young husband had already picked her up. Her room was unchanged—the aquarium still bubbled in the corner, the canary warbled in his cage, the circus posters adorned the walls—but the closet was stripped bare as Adelaide's. And the child's spirit was gone. A deadly quiet hung over the house. Katherine sat on the daybed, thinking that she had not even had the chance to see Chris or to ask her how she felt about going back to her mother.

In the first days after Chris's departure from the hill, Katherine nursed a hope that she would fill the empty space in Jed's heart. They went out more. His faithful coterie of friends asked him to cocktails and dinners, and he accepted everything now that there was no Chris to pick up after school, to take to the stables, to rush home to hug before she went to sleep in her orange and white-flowered room. The child's absence from the house was as palpable as her presence had been. In Jed's distracted state, Katherine saw portents of a future spent waiting for weekends.

The first Friday, Jed called Manhattan Beach to arrange to pick up Chris and was told by Laura that she had a cold and would be unable to come. Grumbling, he waited impatiently through the week. The following Friday, Laura informed him that Chris was spending the weekend at a friend's house. When he called to speak to her on Monday, Tuesday, and Wednesday, Laura or her husband told him Chris was out, or sick, or asleep. And Chris never called back.

Jed became like a wounded animal prowling his house, padding barefoot from room to room seeking some respite from the pain. He moved his desk into the study so as not to have to pass through Chris's room on the way to his office. To Katherine, he spoke of nothing else. Her drive up the winding dirt road took on a different character, filled now with trepidation that his mood would be morose or that Laura would have visited some new calamity upon him from her beach community.

The dead halt that Jed's absorption in his daughter had brought to his career panicked him suddenly. Like a doctor pumping a failing heart, he now attempted resuscitation through the instrument of Hollywood contact: the telephone.

"Leon Burman, please," Katherine would hear him say in a brisk, businesslike voice. A pause followed, during which she learned to hold her breath. Then: "Is he in for Jed Bernard?"

A longer wait would come, interminable seconds of silence. Then Jed's voice, elaborately casual. "Thank you, dear. Have him call me." At last he said to her with a new, chagrined expression, "Do you believe this? I can't even get my own agent on the phone."

Calls went out to other agents and producers. They all promised to call back. As far as Katherine knew, no one ever did.

"It's worse when you work at a studio," Jed told her. "They don't really fire you—they let you know slowly. One day they come in and take a chair out of your office. Then a lamp goes. It takes a lot of chutzpah to keep going to work after your desk has been removed."

For ten days in August, Jed closeted himself with Betty Hawkins, his loyal secretary of twenty years, a woman with a good heart and an admirably even temper, who appeared to be the only person to whom he had never addressed a harsh word. In that hot summer in his back office, they knocked out a story. Jed emerged with thirty neatly typed pages covered in blue, which he presented to Katherine, saying, "I don't believe this altogether. A man like me writing on spec? It's the greatest fucking treatment you ever read in your life. I won't accept a cent under a hundred grand. On the other hand, seventy-five would be good. Do you like 'Lily and Me' as a title?"

Now Jed circumvented the unresponsive agents and went directly to the head of FBC, who agreed to see him within the week.

"You'll come along, you'll wait in the car," Jed told Katherine, and so on the appointed day she sat dutifully in the parking lot reading while inside the studio that squatted like a barracks in the smoggy glare of the Valley, Jed pitched his story to the FBC executives. All her energies were focused on willing them to like it; she could not bear to contemplate his despair if he were rejected.

A scant hour later, she saw him threading his way through the cars, an enigmatic expression on his face. "Hi, kid," he said and slid in beside her.

"Well?" she asked eagerly.

He allowed himself a small, triumphant smile. "They bought it."

"Fantastic!" she cried. "Tell me . . . what did they say? Did they like the character of the old lady?"

He struck a match and put it to his pipe. "Not really. They preferred the uncles."

"What uncles? There aren't any uncles in 'Lily and Me.' "

"They turned down 'Lily and Me.' I made up another idea while I was in there. It's got a great premise." Starting the motor, he grinned. "Always good to have something in reserve, kid."

Fresh from this triumph, he suggested they drive to Manhattan Beach and take Chris out for an ice cream.

"Laura can't refuse to let her do that," he said as he fed coins into a roadside telephone.

But Laura did. And Jed returned to his house in deep despair and took to his bed.

Laura was tightening the screws. She took what Jed gave her and used the advantage to gain power over him, to avenge the custody trial, to turn their daughter against him, but primarily, if Jed's analysis were true, to create a drama in order to be once more in the spotlight.

One afternoon when Katherine came into Jed's house, she heard him talking on the phone. Though she couldn't make out at first what he was saying, from his desperate tone he could only be speaking to Laura; she had never heard him use it with anyone else.

"Can't you understand that I love her?" he said in a choked voice, and then began to cry openly, unashamed, beseeching his ex-wife to relent. Katherine left quietly, shaken by her private glimpse of the man nobody knew—no one but the once glamorous star of stage and screen who had the great Jed Bernard right where she wanted him: by the *baitsim*, as he would put it.

All laughter on the hill stopped when it became clear that Chris was not coming back. In public, Jed could still frame a comic line to suit the situation better than anyone, but at home with Katherine, long hours passed in maudlin discussions, rages against Laura, fury at the world. Now when they went out, he got into verbal fights with people over nothing; men and women alike felt the sting of wit turned to venom. During a dinner party at Jessica Kendall's, he lashed out so ferociously at a visiting Englishwoman that the hostess came over to steer the hapless victim away from him.

Hours were spent on the telephone communicating with lawyers.

"I want her back, Wylie," Jed barked, and Wylie had to explain that it wasn't that simple.

What seemed oddest to Katherine was that Chris was letting it happen. "They've brainwashed her, that's what," Jed said. " 'The Juke Family' . . . brainwashing's a way of life down there."

Chryssie's presence in his house exacerbated Jed's anguish. Sometimes she and Katherine slept in Chris's room and he allowed her to play with Chris's games, but he was often gruff with her that summer, as if by taking her in he was cheating his own daughter. With extraordinary sensitivity, Chryssie appeared to understand, her love for Jed apparently indestructible. Torn between them, Katherine rushed from one to another in a similar maternal role. There was little she could do to comfort Jed. She listened by the hour; she cringed as he cursed Laura; she stayed by his side until he fell into his customary sleep in the afternoons, then raced home to be there when Chryssie's bus arrived from Big Rock camp.

In the last blistering days of September, Jed drove to Manhattan Beach and waylaid Chris coming out of school. He returned to the hill a *tsebrukhneh* man, his shoulders hunched in a bright orange polo shirt.

"It's too hard for her," he told Katherine. "She says the going back and forth was too rough. Up here, she's got everything but friends. The contrast between my way of life and the 'Juke Family' was killing her. She likes her school down there—it's easier for her.

She says she needs some time." He passed a hand over his eyes. "It's sad, that's all . . . just sad."

They sat for a while in the redwood chairs beside the swimming pool. Kitty strolled across the lawn and stretched out under the wooden swing. Simon watched her from the doorway. "Is she going to come up on the weekends at least?" Katherine asked.

Jed's gaze followed a bluebird hopping from branch to branch in the olive tree. "If she wants," he said with a shrug. "I'm not going to push it. What'll be, will be."

His listlessness was worse to Katherine than the unbridled anger of the last weeks, his passivity more frightening. "D'you know what I think?" she blurted. He turned his head to look at her. "I think she never understood your giving her back. You'd fought so hard for her, and then, suddenly, after all the questions about did she want to live with Laura, to which she always answered no, you just sent her back. She must have been very angry."

Jed put his hand over hers on the arm of the chair. "You might be right, dollface. And those cocksuckers used her, turned her against me."

The language was the same, but the fight had gone out of him. The next day, his old girlfriend came over from the Valley to take Rowdy to the stables. By the end of the week, Jed had made plans to rent his house.

"I'm taking off, kid," he announced abruptly to Katherine on the telephone one morning. "Hollywood's finished for me. I feel a need for the theater. I'm going to spend the winter in New York . . . maybe write a play. Sally Dalton's going on the road with *Forum*; she's lending me her flat at the Osborne while she's away. I'm taking Simon to the vet on Friday."

Katherine held on to the phone, stunned, unable to absorb the suddenness of his decision, the callousness with which he was informing her. For days her pride would not allow her to react to Jed's remote attitude; finally, as they were getting into his car after a farewell lunch at Nate 'n' Al's, she burst into tears. His explanation was philosophical and utterly self-absorbed. "In my head I'm already gone, kid. I see myself in Sally's little pad . . . I can't think of it here. You've just got to let me get through the next few months."

On a bright autumn morning, he left.

Like a patient long on intravenous fluids, Katherine doubted her ability to live without the connection. She telephoned her sister in St. Louis, too embarrassed to reveal his abandonment to friends. "Jed's been my whole life for a year. It makes me feel there's no one I can trust," she confided. "There isn't," pragmatic Margot replied. "Not even yourself."

After five days that seemed like fifty, days through which Katherine wept, stared at walls, and lost weight, Jed called, full of funny stories about New York, eager for her to join him. "I just had to check it out before I asked you," he said. "Check out if there was anyone more interesting around, you mean," she replied. "Mmmm," he grumbled in response. "Well, there isn't. Nothing's any fun without you . . . I keep thinking how much you'd enjoy it."

His words fell on her ears with the resonance of a sonnet. Without a second thought, she made arrangements for Chryssie to stay with a friend from Warner Avenue School, took a two-week vacation from her job at Columbia Studios, and made a reservation on the next plane to New York.

CHAPTER 20

The Times They Are Achangin'

"I really missed you," Jed said. "Maybe we should consider getting married. What do you think, kid?"

There was a silence while Katherine absorbed the shock. They were in Sally's bedroom, a tiny room stuffed with actress paraphernalia—wig boxes, *Playbills*, mementos from Broadway shows stuck in the mirror of the dressing table where Katherine was seated. Behind her, Jed lay on the bed, watching her with a tender expression. Her glance grazed his in the mirror like that of one poker player sizing up another for a possible bluff. She went on brushing her hair. In the face of an actual proposal, all her arguments about marriage were revealed in their true existential light. Was she really ready to become Mrs. Jed Bernard?

"Why don't we just leave things the way they are?" she suggested with studied nonchalance.

"You think so?" Jed asked, the light in his eyes dimming.

"I'm not going anywhere, are you?"

He gave his Jewish shrug. "Where am I to go?"

On her way into the bathroom, one of Chryssie's camp mottoes flashed through Katherine's mind: "Trigger Bill says: 'The failure to choose may be the choice you have to live with.' " Splashing her face with cold water, she thought, Fuck Trigger Bill. But a moment later as she leaned forward to apply mascara, she stopped short, confronted by self-mocking eyes. Poker was not her game as much as checkers: if Jed retreated, she pursued; if he took a step toward her, she moved back. Was she hopelessly neurotic, or was it just that love is a seesaw?

"Cripple," she heard through the door. "How long you going to be in there?"

"One more minute."

"That's good, because I was a much younger man when you went in."

Hurriedly she brushed her teeth and joined him. She was young . . . with Jed again . . . the excitement of New York just beyond the door. The answers to psychological questions could wait.

In New York, Jed Bernard was a celebrity. Paparazzi snapped his picture at theater openings; the headwaiter at "21" was deferent, placing him at the third- or fourth-best table; Earl Wilson devoted an entire column to him. The sting of his longtime unemployment was removed. He was more relaxed than Katherine had ever seen him, and spontaneity sparked their sex life. They made love often; without benefit of marriage, the fortnight was an ideal honeymoon. Except to dispatch her to the Stage Delicatessen for a pastrami sandwich, Jed hardly let Katherine out of his sight. Her sister, Margot, breezed through town on a shopping trip; after an hour's exposure to Jed at the Oak Bar, she inquired of Katherine, "What kind of *relationship* is this? He even knows about Aunt Steffie! Tyler couldn't care less about that family stuff—I'm not sure he knows my middle name!" When she'd gone, Jed told Katherine, "Your sister's very attractive . . . and very German."

On the rare occasions that Katherine ventured out alone, she discovered that the sixties were in full swing. The Los Angeles she knew with Jed was stuck in the forties; her own friends there continued to replay the fifties; but in New York, a dragon had been loosed, a spangled beast that waved its tail and swept the old customs and worn-out habits away. Socialites and shopgirls walked the streets in skirts halfway up their thighs; people passed drugs around at parties as casually as canapés, lived openly together, and papered their walls with chocolate-brown enamel; and the town's hottest new psychedelic nightclub, the Cyclotron, was being run by Maggie Fraser, the beautiful redhead whose Manhattanville college career had been cut short by hazing.

Shortly before leaving Los Angeles, Katherine had received the

Manhattanville Newsletter, a yearly chronicle of high points in the lives of alumnae. According to the class notes, women were giving birth at an astonishing rate, their husbands were moving rapidly up various corporate ladders, and family members were occasionally falling ill or dying. Those few who had entered the convent wrote serene letters confirming the wisdom of their choice. Others who had not married had rewarding jobs or were engaged in eleemosynary activities. The rise in the national divorce rate was not reflected in the lives of Manhattanville girls by then; nor was the discovery of the Pill. Was she the only one, Katherine had wondered, whose husband had left her, whose marriage had failed, who did not have 4.5 children? When the class contact had called for news, she'd replied that she had none fit to print (she could just see the item: "Congrats are due Katherine (Katie) Winterhaus Kellogg for devoting her life to the care and feeding of an impoverished, middle-aged, twice-married Jewish writer in Hollywood"). But when she had lunch with Maggie Fraser one afternoon, she found out that she was not the only black sheep.

Maggie wore her straight red hair parted in the middle and hanging almost to her waist; over tightly wrapped cotton trousers, she had on a rumpled sari festooned with little bronze bells. At first glance, Katherine thought the girl sitting at the counter at Hamburger Heaven was a flower child, but then Maggie tilted her head and swept her hair over one shoulder, revealing the familiar Fraser profile: high forehead, perfect straight nose, pointed chin.

Rain pummeled the plate-glass window behind them and conversation went in circles as each tried unsuccessfully to comprehend the other's adult addictions. Katherine had been talking about her tempestuous affair with Jed for some time when Maggie suddenly interrupted her. "You know what I think you should do?"

Katherine leaned forward, riveted, since Maggie rarely gave advice. "What?"

"Take a trip."

"I'm *on* a trip."

Maggie smiled her Mona Lisa smile and adjusted the folds of her sari. "Ohhh. . . . ." Katherine said as Maggie's meaning dawned on her. "You mean a *trip*! LSD?" She began to laugh. "No . . . no, Maggie, drugs won't help me get over Jed. And even if they did, I'd probably just go out and find another Jewish man. I'm hooked."

Maggie's gray eyes were mystified. "I don't understand that. I don't think that Jewish men are very nice to women. I like"— she paused and her face took on a rosy glow—"Arabs!" she exclaimed.

"Now *there's* a group that knows how to treat women!" Katherine remarked.

Tea at the Plaza with Wilder would be a more conventional encounter, Katherine thought on her way to the hotel the following afternoon. Everyone had envied Wilder Framingham when she left Rosemont after sophomore year to marry her childhood sweetheart, Hugo Jergens, heir to the hand-lotion fortune. With their six-year-old son, Timmy, they lived outside Philadelphia, a few miles from where Wilder had grown up. Katherine was already seated at a small table near the chamber orchestra in the Palm Court when Wilder appeared, moving through the room in a lynx coat. She had always been a beauty, and a few extra pounds had given her a lush, Rubenesque quality, but Katherine observed a special radiance about her and wondered if her friend was pregnant. When the waiter brought a tray of tea sandwiches, Wilder took several and smiled at Katherine. "What makes you think that you're the only one who's divorced? Hugo and I split a year ago."

"Oh, Wilder, I'm sorry," Katherine said.

"Don't be," Wilder answered, waving her ringed hand in the air. "I'm thrilled to be out . . . especially of the country club set. During the day it's deadly and at night the favorite sport is wife-swapping. John O'Hara was just telling it like it is!"

A graphic description of sex in suburbia followed, causing a woman seated alone at the next table to part the palm frond in order to get a glimpse of Wilder as she spoke. By the time she was finished, the woman had turned quite pale beneath her chinchilla hat, and Katherine had a more positive view of Hollywood, where marriages seemed stable by comparison.

"Does *everybody* screw around?" she asked in a disillusioned voice.

"There's one group of Jewish couples who don't."

Katherine scanned her face for any sign of disparagement that might be likely to accompany such a remark from Wilder, but her friend continued innocently, "*And,* I have good news! After Hugo and I separated, I went back to school to get my degree. One evening there was a party at Penn—doctors, lawyers, you know, a professional group. One man kept looking at me with these piercing eyes—I mean, I can't *tell* you the intense vibes he sends out. We made a date to meet for coffee the next day. He's a money manager—teaches twice a week at Wharton. Anyway, I was in the Student Union and he was late. I turned as he came in and saw him through these double glass doors. There he was, this little Jewish boy from South Philadelphia—curly hair, round glasses, black jeans with embroidery—and I promise you, I saw a *golden arch* around him. A gold aura from floor to floor!" Wilder's eyes sparkled at the memory. "I knew he was married, so I wasn't really interested at first. But he just bombarded himself into my reality. You know how they are—it's like a philosophy of life: *I want this thing.* Nothing intimidates them; if their noses are too long or whatever—the things that might stop other men. As many times as I rejected him, he kept coming back."

"But he's married?"

"He's separated," Wilder amended. "His wife's just had an operation and he's paralyzed with guilt about divorcing her. I've almost lost him three times, but I'm hanging in there. I intend to become Mrs. Manny Schwartz no matter what!"

"Does Timmy like him?" Katherine asked, recalling that Timmy was a shy, studious little boy.

"You can't believe how Manny's brought Timmy out," Wilder said. "Hugo Jergens's paternal sense you could fit in a bottle of hand lotion. The company sends me a child support check, and even though the schmuck lives a block away, he sees Timmy once every two months. I never knew what love was until I met Manny. He *listens* to me . . . he actually cares how I *feel!*"

"Remember how you used to ask me what I saw in Neil Kolodny?"

"What did I know? There were no Jews in Gladwyn. I'll tell you when I first discovered Jewish men . . . it was when I was pregnant. Hugo and I lived in an apartment building in Philadelphia, and our neighbors were a Jewish couple. One day I was feeling completely depressed—you know, the way you get when you're pregnant—and I was sitting at my dressing table staring at myself, just feeling so unattractive and down. A few minutes later, the phone rang. It was this man's wife . . . she said he'd seen me from the terrace and thought I looked sad, so she should call and invite me over. Well, I'd been looking that way for days around Hugo, and he never even looked up from his newspaper!"

"It would appear," Katherine said with a smile, "that some shiksas are born and others are made."

"Manny's grandfather says the shiksa *is* the maid," Wilder giggled. "When I think back, I used to have sexual fantasies about Victor Mature—he's Jewish, isn't he?"

"Mine was Robert Alda. Italian, but the same idea."

"Actually, it was a love-hate thing, because in a way I despised Victor Mature," Wilder said.

"It's complicated," Katherine murmured, thinking, Who would have guessed when Wilder was queen of fraternity row that a secret desire burned beneath Hugo's Deke pin?

A week after Katherine returned to Los Angeles, Jed followed, fed up with the noise of New York, the tumult, the dirt, and living amongst Sally's wigs and hat boxes. During the Christmas holidays, while Katherine was in St. Louis with her family, from some remote corner of chance and last resorts he pulled a regular job. A corn-fed comic named Gilroy Cousins, particularly popular on college campuses because he was as stoned as his audience, hired Jed as head writer of his weekly variety show, *Kissin' Cousins*. The pressures of creating sketches with a youthful staff of writers on some lunar wavelength kept Jed at the studio for long, trying hours all winter. He came home exhausted late at night, frustrated and railing against the indignities of television. But there were flashes of the old Jed, his brain asizzle with ideas, once again the master for a group of fledgling comics. As usual, he was funnier in his living room than on paper; a new generation of writers made pilgrimages up the hill to sit at his feet and learn from him. But that spring, when *Kissin' Cousins* won an Emmy after, ironically, it had been canceled, eight of them clustered onstage and credited everything from divine inspiration to maternal support to the fried brain of Gilroy Cousins for their gold statuettes, but not one mentioned Jed Bernard, who was conveniently attending his father's funeral in Minneapolis. It was the Tonawanda Country Club all over again—they mailed his Emmy to him.

Unlike his vivid, voluble suffering over Christabel's betrayal, Jed's grief at the death of his father had a stoic quality. When he returned from the funeral in May, he spoke to Katherine less of feeling than of ritual. "I promised Mama I'd say Kaddish for Papa in Israel."

In the past, his references to Nathan Bronstein had been light-hearted—humorous, admiring anecdotes. More than once he'd assured Katherine that he was a road company of his old man. Now his only recollection was a bleak one: "The last time I saw him, he was sick and I tried to tell him I loved him and that I was sorry."

"For what?"

"*Ver veys?* For leaving home . . . not being a better son . . . the *tsouris* with Laura and Chris. I put my hand on his shoulder. He shrugged it off and said, 'It's too little, too late, Jacob.' " Then, with eyes that reflected unresolved pain, Jed turned the conversation to Chris, who had sent him no message about her grandfather's death, if indeed her mother had informed her of it.

Temporarily defeated by death, show business, and Laura Loder, that weekend Jed took to his bed. Wolf called on Saturday and was invited to shoot pool, but when he arrived at eight, Jed was too depressed to come out of his bedroom. Katherine made his apologies, confident that Wolf would empathize—the thing he related to most in the world was suffering. More than for any of Jed's other friends, she felt an affinity for Wolf, perceiving in him a keen intelligence and sense of emotional depth beneath the barrage of jokes. That evening for the first time, they spoke at length.

"Morty Glick introduced me to Jed fifteen years ago," Wolf told her as she poured him a brandy. "I thought he was wonderful . . . loved his originality. You know what Saul Rosen says about him: 'In a world of dullards—' "

" 'You don't turn your back on Jed Bernard,' " she finished.

"That's right." Wolf paused to light a cigarette. "The kid put him away. He went crazy—threw people out of the house for no reason. Once we didn't talk for six months, but—"

"But you always come back. The words don't seem to mean much. You and Jed will probably fight your whole lives, but on your deathbeds, you'll call for each other."

"Why would you bring up death, madam? Jed's right—you're a *machamoves!*" Wolf rotated the glass in the palm of his hand, looking at the swirling cognac. After a moment, he said, "I do think Jewish fellows give each other a bigger emotional commitment than Gentiles. I'll tell you something about Jed." Katherine leaned on the bar, her chin propped on her hands, her eyes on Wolf's face. "It was a few years ago and I'd just broken up with a woman, the greatest cocksucker I ever—oh, excuse me, dear. Anyway, I was a *tsebrukhneh* man. Finished in life. Like a dog I came up the hill. Jed moved out of his room and took care of me."

"Really?"

"I kid you not. Put me in there and let me stay for two weeks. Fed me chicken soup. In a crisis, he's the greatest. The man saved my life! Now Shelley . . . Shelley's another story."

The impish figure of Shelley Marcus came to Katherine's mind: unlike Jed and Wolf, he was never out of work in show business, due more to a talent for getting along with the producer than any great visual sense as a cinematographer. There had been a slew of blond actresses in Shelley's life who would have sworn that he was the funniest and most attractive of the group; while his four Gentile ex-wives would have said he was the most neurotic.

"There's no depth to Shelley. What you see is what you get," Wolf said. "The man can't keep a secret—even if you don't want to know, he tells you. What a neuro!"

"Where does all this neurosis come from? And please don't tell me your mothers. It can't be that simple."

"They don't help. Of my generation, there was no Jewish mother who didn't think we were going to walk on water. Most of our parents were immigrants, don't forget. This was the New World. Nothing could stop us; there was gold in the streets. We were constantly told we were the brightest, the best, the most dedicated—and to survive, we had to be. In order to succeed, Jews have to be smarter. Physically, we were never strong enough to be athletes. *Shvartzes* were athletes. So how do Jews get out of the ghetto? Jews could be comics! Humor is the essence of life—all ghetto people have it. But Jews are smarter—they refined it."

"How come you can say that but I can't?" Katherine demanded. "Once when I told a Jewish friend of mine in drama school that I thought Jews were smarter and funnier, he said, 'People who say that are the same ones who'll point us out in a pogrom.' "

Wolf nodded. "It's a controversial subject. My old biology professor at Yeshiva had a theory that's not too popular. I'm not saying I agree with him, but his contention was that the differences are cultural *and* genetic."

"How genetic?"

"For two thousand years, he used to say, tyrants have tried to create a master race. Like all tyrants, they had to have a scapegoat, and the Jews were usually it. So the smart ones got out, and the wealthy ones saw it coming and emigrated, making a rarefied, selected pool to breed. Obviously we're talking big generalizations here. Effectively, the tyrants—Hitler, the Cossacks—created a master race." He stubbed out his cigarette, adding it to the pile he'd collected in the ashtray. "Darwinian selection functions all day on a full-time basis. Any time there's an obstacle, there's an element of the fittest involved—whatever the nature of fitness is. If there's a helicopter crash, the tall guys get decapitated, the short ones walk away unscathed. You need look no further than the Middle East. The Arabs have been there for thousands of years, right?"

"Right."

"You'd think that would give them an advantage. But a bunch of rabbinical students from Poland came in and made the desert bloom. They've built a resort on the Red Sea that's something gorgeous. For two hundred dollars a day you can get the same waiter you get in the Catskills."

"So what are you saying—the strength is in the adversity?"

"Yes, and it produces a curious combination of qualities. There's the sense of warmth, certainly, the family thing. A kind of vibration of humanity that's out of place with the ruthlessness. How many times does a Jewish kid hear, 'You gotta do better than the next guy'? It makes our heads work differently no matter what we say sometimes. And every virtue has its corollary vice."

"For instance?"

"The aggressiveness—what we call *seichel*. *Seichel* is the flip side. A cunning, some might say sneaking, quality, depending from which side you look at it. We've learned resourcefulness, a knowledge of who the enemy is."

"And who is that?"

Clutching his side, Wolf groaned, "*Everybody!*"

Katherine laughed.

As he looked at her over the rim of his brandy glass, Wolf's eyes crinkled at the edges. "There's a certain type of Gentile girl," he said, "usually sweet, naïve, unsophisticated, who's a pushover for the wisecracking, street-smart Jew. I'll tell you a little story." He set down the glass and lighted another cigarette. "When I was in my twenties, I moved from one apartment to another in New York. I was going with a blond model from Alabama. She helped me move— carried furniture up three flights of stairs, painted the bathroom. In the middle of regrouting the tile, I said to her, 'Mary Lou, you gotta know. If there was any doubt you're a shiksa, this proves it.' "

"A Jewish girlfriend wouldn't do that for you?"

"*Never!*" Wolf cried.

"What exactly do you have against Jewish women, Wolf?"

"They want too much," he replied promptly. "They're too demanding."

"In terms of money?"

"In terms of everything. They're not serene. They're aggressive, like my mother."

Suddenly Jed's door opened. From the threshold they heard his voice say gratingly, "You're full of shit, Wolf. Get out of the house."

Wolf did, vowing never to return.

But this time their rift was short-lived. On the nineteenth of May, U Thant acceded to Nasser's demand for the withdrawal of the United Nations Emergency Force from Israel, and Jed put in a call to Wolf.

CHAPTER 21

L'chaim!

"The cocksuckers have blockaded the Gulf of Aqaba—it's an act of war!"

With this excited pronouncement to Wolf, Jed underwent a stunning recovery, launching a vigil over the hostilities that broke out in the Middle East during the early summer of 1967. As bulletins were broadcast with dramatic frequency—the massing of Arab armies around Israel's frontiers, the preemptive strike against the Egyptian air force, the Syrian bombing of oil refineries in Haifa Bay, the decimation of Kuneitra—Jed turned his bedroom into a command post, monitoring the radio by the hour, filling and refilling his pipe as he received calls from concerned friends, seizing on the crisis to lift him out of the grinding frustrations, worries, and failures of his personal life. Even his daughter's defection dwindled in the face of Arab threats of annihilation and renewed determination to push Israel into the sea.

One afternoon Katherine arrived at his house to find him arrayed in a Yemenite burnoose that banished any aspect of the Diaspora from his face and returned him to the desert of the nomads, from whence, of course, he had not sprung, but spent a week after the divorce from Laura.

For those six fateful days in June, the war consumed Jed. Passionate, atavistic loyalties were aroused in him no less than in Jews everywhere who left their homes and jobs in droves to fly to Israel and join the fight; only temporary insolvency held him back. With this motivation, he called his intrepid secretary, Betty Hawkins, and in two weeks produced a pilot script for *My Six Uncles* with crucial scenes set in London and Israel. Within a matter of days he had a firm commitment from the head of programming at FBC and a first-class ticket on British Airways.

"This is it, kid," he told Katherine as he pulled a suitcase from a storage closet and tossed it onto the bed. "After this project, show business is finished for me. I'm going to live in Israel." Though she had heard it all before, it did not diminish her fears that this time he meant it. With eyes hollow from weeping, she listened as he repeated his Zionist litany: "Ben-Gurion's right when he tells the Jews, 'Someday you may need a place to come to.' It could happen here!" Drawers were flung open, shirts and ties neatly packed, his bulky orange sweater folded into a corner of the bag, a photograph of his father tucked in a flap. Icy fingers closed around Katherine's heart. Having hardly slept since his abrupt announcement of his departure, she felt further ravaged by the impersonal nature of this harangue. " *'Columbus, tu di ich hob gornisht!'* " Jed sang in imitation of his father. "Jews are full of shit when they talk about assimilation. That *chochem* Blanche Kramer tells me, 'Don't talk to me about Israel. I have no interest in going there.' I wish her luck in any line of work. It may be the only place she *can* go someday!" The concept of the influential Mrs. Kramer fleeing Bel Air with her wardrobe of Balenciagas and Diors struck Katherine as highly unlikely, but Jed continued, "They kid themselves—Beverly Hills could be Berlin!" Taking his black Italian suit from its hanger, he pulled a long face and told Katherine, "You may never see the little fellow again." Then he closed the suitcase and hefted it off the bed. As he went past her, he snapped, "Are you just going to sit there?"

Somehow words found a route past her constricted throat. "Why are you being so cruel? Don't I mean *any*thing to you? Doesn't the last year and a half mean anything at all? You're just going to *leave* me like this, as if nothing about us mattered?"

Indifference filmed Jed's eyes. He endured an indictment of selfishness and terminal coldness, his only response the elaborate beckoning gesture that indicated he had heard all the abuse before. Uncontrollably wretched, her breath coming in spasms, Katherine reminded herself furiously that the motion signified his basic philosophy about being a Jew. Gentiles, especially shiksas, were prone to hurling invective; how could anything she was suffering compare with the Holocaust? The emotional ravings of a woman were small potatoes compared with two thousand years of persecution and gen-ocide. "Sure, kid, I know," he said, interrupting her tearful tirade. "You've given me the best year and a half of your life. So now what? You wanna tell me how to break up with you?" He raised his voice to a yell. "I WAS NOT BROUGHT INTO THIS WORLD TO WORRY ABOUT KATHERINE WEYERHAUSER!"

Birdie, the housekeeper, knocked something over in the living room. Jed's answering glare indicated that being overheard by her was the final indignity; he sought shelter in the study. Brought to the brink of hysteria by the eternal female fear of being abandoned, Katherine pursued him. His back was to her at the bookcase; a door closing told them Birdie had retreated. In a trembling voice, Kath-erine said, "It's not impossible that I'm pregnant, you know. Wouldn't you give a damn about that, either?"

When Jed turned, his expression reminded her too late of the company she'd put herself in. Hostility twisted his features; he drew his lips back from his teeth and color flooded his face.

"You want to fuck with me on that score, baby? You want me to hold your hand and tell you that I love you? Lemme tell you about love . . . I pissy on it! I pissy on Laura . . . I pissy on all you cunts!" In the grip of a murderous rage, he snarled, "You think you're pregnant? Lemme tell you how I'll handle it—I'll make one call and have you *rubbed out!*"

The words tore into her like lashes of a whip. Although their fiercest battles had never impelled him to strike her, at this she fled from him in terror, seeking an avenue of escape through Chris's room. Birdie was on the threshold, a distressed look on her face. When Katherine started to back away, Birdie held out her arms; she went into them like a child and burst into tears against her shoulder. Birdie patted her head, crooning, "Don't you listen to that . . . he don't mean a word . . . he never mean nothin' like that . . . no matter how he yells, he loves you, honey. When I worked up here before, he used to be lettin' 'em in the front door as I was shooin' 'em out the back. I ain't seen nobody but you this whole time. . . ." Through her misery, Katherine found this information immensely comforting. Suddenly Jed's presence loomed in the hallway behind them and she drew away from Birdie, reluctant to implicate her in the scene. "I'm going for a drive," Jed announced coldly. Moments later, they heard the Ferrari's engine revving.

Katherine retreated to the bathroom. She emerged to see Jed

coming back through Chris's room, his face ashen, his hands trembling. At the edge of the daybed, he collapsed, prostrated on his back with his hands covering his face, shuddering, emitting broken, incoherent phrases. Genuine alarm propelled her to his side, her own misery diminished in the face of his apparent emotional breakdown. She sat beside him, took his hand, murmured reassuring sounds, all the while trying to make sense out of his muffled words. Gradually it dawned on her that he was talking not about his psyche but his car. On the way down the driveway, he who routinely careened along Sunset Boulevard unscathed had driven into the stone wall. The calamity that had brought him to this state of shattered nerves was nothing more than a dent in his right fender. And who had been the cause of it? Guess! Anyone with the most tenuous connection to pop culture had to recognize this game; it was called: See what you made me do? But there it was—Jed had palpable physical damage to display. What could she do but acknowledge that his *tsouris* was, as always, greater than hers? Yet she was oddly cheered by his stroke of one-upmanship. To wrack up his precious Ferrari for her smacked of his unique brand of love. Magnanimously she offered to take the car into the shop for him and declared she would pay for the damages. The responding growl from beneath his hands, "I know . . . I know . . . you'll work your fingers to the bone," was the first sign of forgiveness. At that moment, Katherine thought, they were the quintessence of Jew and shiksa. Any self-respecting Jewish woman would have told him to shove it.

They said good-bye the following day at the top of the steps, where they had met a year and a half before. While a limousine waited in the background for Jed, Katherine asked in a determinedly lighthearted tone what he intended to do in Israel.

"Teach," he replied.

"Teach what?"

"Communications. Teddy Kollek's been after me for years to come to the University of Jerusalem."

"Oh. That'd be great," she said, stalling, making conversation to delay his departure. "Academic life's the best. You can travel and . . . there are all those long vacations. Summer . . . Christmas . . ." At his raised eyebrow, she broke off, stammering, "Oh, I . . . I guess not."

"Marvelous. That's really marvelous, kid. Christmas vacations.

It's easy to see what an asset you'd be in Israel." He chuckled and kissed the top of her head. "Don't forget to feed Simon tomorrow. The gardener's taking him to the vet on Friday."

She nodded mutely.

Jed got into the back seat and lowered the window. "Say good-bye to the knibbler for me again. So long, kid." He tapped on the glass; the limousine rolled down the driveway and around the bend in the road, disappearing in a brown cloud of dust.

Simon pushed his head against Katherine's knee. She crouched and pressed her face against his neck, wetting it with her tears as she used to do with Patches at the lake house when her parents left her behind. A single ray of hope sustained her: would Jed have dared ask her to feed Simon if he intended never to see her again?

For four days he allowed her to suffer in silence. Then he called from London, his voice full of the sound of missing her. "You've ruined everything for me," he complained. "I see girls with big beautiful eyes, I think they've got a goiter problem. Why don't you come over?"

"Because I can't afford it, and I couldn't let you pay for the ticket," she answered adamantly.

"I took care of that at the L.A. airport," he said. "I turned in my first class for two tourist tickets. You can pick up yours at the BEA desk. When does Chryssie go to her grandmother's in New Hampshire?"

"Next week."

"You'll have ten days. So come, asshole!"

Katherine smiled wanly. "How can I refuse a romantic invitation like that?"

"London's the greatest!" Jed said. "If you like, we could stop in Venice for a couple of days on the way to Israel." There was a capitulation to love in his tone, Katherine thought. Jed always traveled alone.

"Come on, Skeezix," he coaxed. "Wouldn't you like to see the Holy Land?"

CHAPTER 22

A House Divided

"You're not planning to take her to Mea She'arim, are you, Jed?" asked the young Israeli actor ominously. His fingers drummed a warning on the table as he looked from Jed to Katherine, who were seated side by side along the plush banquette. They were lunching at the White Elephant, a posh restaurant near the Dorchester, with Schlomo Sadan, Jed's dear friend, whose talent as a raconteur had kept them laughing for half an hour. But now his black eyes bored into Katherine. "Do not go alone."

"What's Mea She'arim?" she asked nervously.

Schlomo leaned forward in his chair. "It is a quarter of Ortho- dox Jews in Jerusalem. You could say that it is a ghetto in a land which has no comprehension of American ghettos or the mentality they produce."

A reflexive grumble came from Jed.

"The people are the most militant religious sect in Israel. They're quite crazed," Schlomo continued, his eyes dropping to Katherine's knees, which were exposed beneath a miniskirt. "Commonly they scream epithets at immodest Gentile girls and threaten to throw them into the *mikva*."

Her food forgotten, Katherine gazed at the magnetic actor. His physique was square and solid, rather like a tree trunk, and his brown hair was unruly. Among the effete Englishmen at the surrounding tables, he was as unlikely a sight as a lion in Mayfair. As they'd walked to the restaurant, only a few hours after her plane had landed at Heathrow under a drizzling sky, Jed had told her, "Schlomo's the greatest Shylock that's ever been! You can forget Carnovsky—when Schlomo cries, 'If you prick us, do we not bleed?' it's the frigging Red *Sea*! The man is the toast of London! The day the war broke out, he finished the evening's performance and then announced from the stage that he was leaving to join the Israeli army. They tore up the seats! Six days, they *ferpached* the Arabs; now he's back. I told him you were coming and that he should explain you a little about the war."

Her first glimpse of the swarthy character in cord trousers and a flowing tie, barreling toward them through the restaurant had forced a childhood convent doggerel from the depths of Katherine's unconscious:

> *Men with broken noses,*
> *Follow your leader Moses!*
> *Fight! Fight! Fight for Palestine!*

Which of course had caused her to turn bright red when Jed was introducing them, since the words—which up till then had meant as much to her as "Mairsie Doats"—would get her on the next flight back to Los Angeles, if these two could read her mind.

Katherine was very much on her best behavior. The sting left by Jed's cruel words before he'd left had been removed not long after she'd seen him waiting at the curb outside Customs, a chauffeured Bentley in the background. He'd hugged and kissed her, and as soon as they'd gotten in the back, gleefully pointed out the wads of Kleenex he'd stuffed into the cushions. "Just to make you feel at home, dollface," he'd chortled. Affectionate as he was, she had not been prepared for the embarrassing moment in the Dorchester lobby, when he'd presented her to three dignified men in morning coats at Reception as Mrs. Bernard.

"You don't know the *mishegoss* of my country," Schlomo was saying. "The army is completely schizophrenic. Every battalion had to have two lorries, two complete sets of dishes for meat and dairy. Moishe can defeat the Arabs but not his own rabbis. When are you going, you two?"

"The end of the week," Jed said.

"Really?" Schlomo's expression seemed to question the wisdom of this.

"It *is* safe to be there now, isn't it?" Katherine inquired anxiously.

"Absolutely," Schlomo replied. "It's more dangerous to walk around Piccadilly. But for you"—he knitted his heavy brows—"I'm not so sure. They will stamp a big C on your passport, you know."

She swallowed. "For Catholic?"

"Don't make it any worse. Christian is bad enough."

Jed, whose expression had been hidden behind a brandy snifter, exploded with laughter. "It's enough, Schlomo!"

Schlomo laughed, then turned serious again, addressing Jed. "Have you had your shots?"

"Shots? Do we need shots?" Katherine asked.

The actor's raised shoulders hinted at numerous possibilities, none good. "It *is* the Middle East after all. But you have no time now. Just be sure you don't drink the water."

Katherine intercepted his wink at Jed, but which of his warnings was in jest, she could not be certain. The conversation turned to the theater, and for another hour he regaled them with tales of tempestuous leading ladies and *faygeleh* actors; then, when he hurried away to make a matinee curtain, Jed and Katherine walked back to the Dorchester along Park Lane, which bloomed with black umbrellas.

"If we get married in Israel," Jed said in a half-teasing tone, "you'll have to go in the *mikva*."

"What's that?" she asked casually, pretending to study a seventeenth-century desk in the window of an antique shop.

"The bath . . . purification, putz!"

"Oh, great. You told me the rabbi diddles the girls in there."

"Nooo!" he cried. "Well, maybe a little feel now and then."

She looked at the pavement as they walked along. "You wouldn't seriously want me to convert, would you? You don't really believe in it, you say you wouldn't marry another Jewish woman, so—"

"It's for the children. It's better to have one religion."

She raised her eyes. "Well, would you become Catholic?"

"You must be joking!" he exclaimed, looking at her askance.

Jed was in a holiday mood. He'd been working hard on the script, he said. Now that Katherine was in London, he was knocking off. They motored to Sussex, where they spent the afternoon with Jed's friends, a painter and his wife, who lived in a manor house in the woods and gobbled up his every utterance; they lunched at Drone's, where women named Daphne and Felicity and Lady

Somebody-or-Other greeted him with languorous familiarity; they dined with a titled magistrate and her husband; they went with Jed's playboy cronies, a rather dissolute lot who found him hilarious, to Annabelle's, where a spectacular-looking young woman, black and imperious as a Masai, halted in the middle of the undulating crowd on the dance floor as they passed, and shot Jed a look of reproach. He nodded to her, but she tossed her head and stalked away. "That's Ivy," he told Katherine. "She's Dior's top mannequin this season. She was a little put out when I told her you were coming."

"Working hard on the script, eh?" she muttered between her teeth.

"Ba . . . by!" he protested, one hand over his heart. "You've got to get over this paranoia. What would I want with a six-foot-two *schvar* with great tits who loves a good *partouse* when I can be with the Rochester flash?"

Torture went with the territory, Katherine reminded herself, not altogether sorry that they were leaving the following morning for Venice. There, in that enchanted city of dreams, she thought, surely Jed would make love to her at last.

Clouds moved across the late afternoon sun above San Marco, spinning a golden web over the Campanile. The murky water of the lagoon glittered like mercury as the vaporetto putted along from the Venice railway station and coughed to a halt at the foot of moss-covered steps leading to the Gritti Palace. Italian room clerks were likely to be even less cavalier than the British about their unmarried status, Katherine fretted, so she skulked behind a marble pillar in the lobby while Jed registered. Across the domed salon, she heard the scathing tones of the concierge: "May we have the passport of the *other person, per favore?*"

Their room had a cathedral ceiling, a cool marble floor, a landscape from the school of Tintoretto on the damask-covered wall, and mosquito netting over the bed. A balcony reminiscent of Juliet's looked onto the Grand Canal. That night they drank Bellinis at the Lido, where Jed had once spent a summer with Christabel Rivers; her glamorous ghost haunted the moonlit beach. As a gondolier rowed them back to Venice through brackish waters, Katherine got the hiccups. Jed put his head in his hands, groaning, "I've gotta get a girl." But when they were in bed, with the sound of water lapping against the stone below, he drew her to him beneath the feather quilt and they made love with a fervor she had thought was lost. Her rapturous cries echoed in the enormous room. "Why must everything be a religious experience with you?" Jed growled, but he held her throughout the night.

The next day flew. They lunched at Harry's Bar and roamed through back streets and over bridges, emerging at San Marco to dodge a battalion of pigeons that swooped upward in a great batting of wings. An orchestra was playing Monteverdi beneath an awning at the foot of the cathedral. Jed took Katherine's hand as they walked across the piazza, and said in a dazed voice, "I can't remember ever having been with anyone but you." Her heart spiraled over the Byzantine domes; for such an accolade, she would brave the Middle East anytime!

In Rome, Jed's mood darkened. He did not rest easily in the shadow of the Vatican and flaunted their illicit affair at the Hassler, presenting the passports to the concierge without a marital fiction. "Keys for Kellogg and Bernard!" the man called out when they entered the lobby after lunch. "We sound like a vaudeville team," Katherine muttered. He took her roughly as soon as they were in the room; the thrust of his hips had more vengeance in it than love. The bells of St. Peter's clanged in the distance. Ask not for whom *those* toll, she thought grimly.

Afterward, while he napped, she slipped away and ran like a truant down the wide steps of the Trinità dei Monti where young men with smoldering eyes lounged along the balustrade alone or in pairs, their summer jackets thrown over their shoulders. It was familiar ground: the mother house of the Sacred Heart Order stood at the top, and the Hassler had housed her college tour nine years before. How naïve she had been! How innocent of the dynamics of interlocking neuroses! Her reflection in a shop window revealed little change from that inexperienced girl, but she was unable to shake the sense of loss, as if a thief had broken into her house and stolen an heirloom.

Half an hour later, Jed found her wandering in via Condotti; he'd been looking for her everywhere, he said sternly. Having temporarily purged his demon, he took her by the hand and said they were dining at the most romantic restaurant in all of Rome: Santa Maria in Trastevere, near the banks of the Tiber. Romance lasted through dessert. Then, sipping his espresso in the church square, Jed narrowed his eyes at her through the flickering candle and said,

"The frivolous part of the trip is over. Tomorrow we'll find out what you're made of."

Easing toward Israel: officials of the Greek military regime looked over their passports in the Athens airport with flinty eyes and inhospitably slammed down their rubber stamps. Katherine carried apprehension onto the El Al plane like a second piece of luggage.

American tourists jammed the flight. When it landed in Tel Aviv, a plump matron bustled to the head of the line, descended the steps and, with her mink stole flapping about her like great silver wings, flung herself to the ground and kissed the tarmac.

"*Meshugginah*," Jed muttered to Katherine as he stepped around her prostrate figure. "The Israelis hate that more than anybody."

A lone baggage attendant serviced the planeload; passengers shoved each other with impunity, taxi drivers called out to prospective fares, flight personnel and tourists screamed insults at each other in democratic chaos. In Lod Airport, the Israelis had created another Tower of Babel. When Katherine opened her mouth to hail the porter, no sound emerged.

"Lost your voice, cripple?" Jed teased. "Not such a maven for once. I should bring you to Israel more often." Scrutinizing her under the bright fluorescent lights, he frowned. "Why would you be so *blond*?"

In an anteroom near the baggage corral, a large group of men was apparently segregated. Many held babies in their arms or clutched male children by the hand. Despite the steamy weather they were dressed identically in long black overcoats with large, stiff-brimmed black hats set low on their foreheads; over their ears fell soft corkscrew curls. Katherine looked through the plate-glass window, struck by the extraordinary sweetness of their expressions.

"Who are they?" she asked Jed.

"Those are the *chayehs*," he said melodramatically.

"The Orthodox from —"

"Mea She'arim."

"But they seem so gentle. Look—even the babies have those curls."

"*Peyes*. Learn the language, kid." He gave her an affectionate smile. "You like the baby *chayehs*? Feeling better?"

During the brief taxi ride to the hotel, Jed charmed the initially hostile driver into a fraternal exchange by correctly identifying him as an Iraqui. While they discussed the Six-Day War, Katherine prepared for her first moment of truth in Israel: the presentation of passports at the desk. Just ahead loomed the Tel Aviv Hilton, a concrete slab perched at the edge of the Mediterranean.

"They're very religious, you know," Jed whispered ominously as they entered the lobby. "It might be a scene because we're not married . . . they could insist on separate rooms."

From the newsstand she watched him approach the desk and heard the clerk's request for their passports. To her horror, Jed gave him a broad wink. "You'll send someone up for hers later, all right, young man?"

"Look," the clerk said patiently. "What you do when you get to your room is your business. Right now we need her passport for control."

Jed beckoned to her, shaking his head and chuckling, "It's Jewish logic—you can't beat it."

A balcony as wide as the room overlooked the sea; to the left, behind barren fields, were acres of flimsy rooftops. The city was without order or plan, as if a tyrannical child had strewn his pile of building blocks willy-nilly across the landscape. "There's only one solution," Katherine commented. "Tear it down and start over."

Jed nodded. Twilight fell and glimmering lights came on in the hills. Staring out at the phosphorescent sea, he said, "Call up and get a bottle of water, will you, kid?"

Katherine went inside and dialed the desk. "Could we have some bottled water, please?"

"What's that?" a voice barked.

"Water," she repeated distinctly. "We'd like a bottle of water."

"You want water?" came the mystified reply. "You'll go in the bathroom, you'll turn on the faucet, and you'll have water."

At midnight they walked to Dizengoff Street, where the cafés were jammed till all hours with men conversing in shouts. Katherine observed that the babble of voices, the smell of smoked fish and sauerkraut, struck a chord in Jed that went beyond the Minneapolis ghetto of his youth, back, conservatively speaking, two thousand years. Through all his mercurial moods—exuberant, maudlin, *grizhering*, celebratory, comical, affectionate, hostile, angry, joyous—she had never, until tonight, seen Jed *happy*. In Israel, he was at peace.

Gray slats of light falling through the blinds woke Katherine at dawn. Jed slumbered beside her, his hand unclenched for once. She slipped out of bed and went to the balcony to watch the sunrise. The sea was calm and blue-gray in the half-light; she turned toward Tel Aviv and saw, coming across the fields like a flock of crows in their flapping black coats and broad-brimmed hats, groups of Hasidim—the people from Mea She'arim.

Jed appeared behind her, wrapping his old beige terry cloth robe around him. "Oh, Jed, I'm so glad you're awake!" she cried. "Look at the *chayehs*! They started coming to the beach at dawn. There's an army of them."

"Crazed . . . they're all crazed," he muttered, peering down to the beach where they were settling themselves like nomads on the sand.

"Look at the way they sit—a clump, then a space, then another clump. Why do they cling together so?"

"Jews are a clannish people, my dear," he replied, a sudden coldness in his voice.

He turned and padded into the bedroom; she heard the bathroom door bang shut and sighed, mental exhaustion setting in at the thought of having to monitor everything she said. Never had she felt less capable of doing anything right.

Breakfast was an unmitigated disaster. Pronouncing the food in the Hilton dining room inedible, Jed marched Katherine through the lobby and past the swimming pool, with mumbled incantations against Jewish-American tourists, over a narrow stretch of beach to the Sheraton, a somewhat older hotel whose architect had made an attempt to reflect history in its stone facade. "I stayed here last time, but I thought I'd try the Hilton—wrong," Jed grumbled.

"Maybe I can get a Spam sandwich," Katherine ventured. "I hear they eat it in the army."

"Not in the Israeli army, you putz! I can't take you anywhere!"

"Only kidding," she said with a thin smile.

They entered the dining room and approached the kosher buffet. On one table were dairy products, on the other meat and fish. Jed looked blankly at the dairy table, passed on to the meat table and took a slice of dried-out turkey. Katherine beseeched a passing waiter for some toast and a Coke.

Several minutes later, he produced a bottle labeled Vivi-cola and a thick slab of bread that appeared to have been grilled over charcoal. Jed took a bite, frowned, and told the waiter, "Look, my friend, this is stale bread." The man looked blank. "It's not fresh," Jed said.

"What do you mean, it's not fresh? It's Friday's bread!" the waiter shouted.

"Today's Monday," Katherine pointed out; he stalked away.

"Jews are not great waiters," Jed remarked. He put down his fork and pushed his plate away, grunting, "Just shit. How's that drink?"

Katherine said, "If it's the same stuff they used to fuel the tanks, no wonder they won the war."

"You're a joy to travel with, *buktsayna*. I can't wait to take you to Turkey and watch you eat sheep's eyes."

"*You* said the food was terrible!"

"True, true. Let's take a little walk."

The foot of space between them yawned as they tramped across a field toward the Hilton. Jed talked on about Israel, his roots, Zionism. Even the ground under Katherine's feet seemed strange: black arid soil that resembled rubble after an air attack.

"It's the only place I feel completely comfortable, you know that?" Jed was saying. "No one's out to get me . . . no one's going to call me a dirty Jew. Hollywood's finished for me. This is where I belong. I'll teach at the university, travel a little. There's a sense of rightness to it." He paused as if for a response. When Katherine said nothing, he asked, "You think you could live here with me, kid?"

He doesn't mean it . . . I should just say yes, she thought. But candor crowded out the desire to please, and she shook her head. "I can understand that you feel at home here, but it's not my religion and they're not my people. I'd die of loneliness."

The line of his mouth tightened. "You're an inspiration, my dear," he said harshly. "No biblical dedication here, I see. No whither thou goest from Katherine Weyerhauser."

In silence they approached the hotel.

Had Katherine contemplated having a vision in Israel, she would have expected it to occur in Bethlehem or Nazareth or in the hills of Galilee where ancient rocks and bristling trees bore witness that the Son of God had once trod the ground in His sandals and seamless cloak. But not in Tel Aviv—not in that extended garment center, where Jews of every nationality jostled and joked in the streets;

certainly not in the Tel Aviv Hilton, whose lobby in that August of 1967 looked like a cross between the Fontainebleau and Fort Dix. Yet there, standing a few yards away at the hotel entrance, a Nikon around her neck, was her sister, Margot. The hot bright air undulated between them so that for an instant, Katherine had the impression of an apparition. But then Margot saw her and waved. Delighted as she was to see her, Katherine was baffled. That she was here with Jed was one thing, she thought, but that her sister, who had never displayed any affinity for Jews, should have trekked to Israel was quite another. Margot quickly explained that she'd been cruising the Greek Isles with friends when the war broke out.

"They went home, but I was not about to miss the opportunity to witness history in the making. I'm off to El Arish!"

"Alone?" Katherine asked.

Margot nodded, a glint of adventure in her dark eyes.

"In a *taxi?*" Jed asked as a driver waved to her from a Mercedes sedan.

"How else?" Margot grinned.

"If you come back alive, we'll take you to dinner in Jaffa tonight," Jed told her, adding to Katherine, "We can get a meal there."

With a jaunty wave, Margot was off. "That's pretty gutty of her," he commented.

"Poor Mother and Daddy," Katherine laughed. "Two daughters and both of them in Israel."

"You Winterhaus girls have got to leave the Jews *alone!*" Jed said.

Going up in the elevator, he informed her that shortly, she would meet one of the great women of the world: Leah Cafri was joining them at noon for lunch. Leah, the daughter of General Avi Shabril, who had distinguished himself in the Six-Day War, was a reporter for the *Jerusalem Press*, a young woman of twenty-four whom Jed had befriended in a kibbutz when she was a teenager. Her slanting dark eyes slid over Katherine without interest as Jed introduced them in the coffee shop; clearly there was no place for one of Jed's shiksas in her busy life. The strong bond of affection that existed between Leah and Jed was apparent as he listened to her speak about the war—tales alternately tragic, funny, profound, told in a low-pitched, hypnotic voice. What emanated from him was a feeling rare in his dealings with women—respect—yet at the same time he appeared to be immune to the exquisite Leah's sex appeal. He was the most fragmented of men, Katherine brooded, left to her own thoughts and a renewed sense of alienation as Leah made no secret of the fact that the presence of a blond Christian in Tel Aviv puzzled her.

Presently Leah rose and announced that her plane was leaving for New York in an hour. "Joshua will be waiting for you in Jerusalem," she promised, jotting down the address of the army headquarters where her husband was a commanding officer. Jed and she embraced; then she looked through Katherine and said with consummate indifference, "Good-bye, uh . . . Jed's friend."

An overwhelming compensation for the unpleasant encounter awaited Katherine that evening, when Amos Shabtai arrived to take them—along with Margot, who had returned intact from the Sinai—to dinner. He greeted Jed with a bear hug and welcomed the two women effusively. A member of the Mapai party, one of Israel's many political factions, Amos had caught some pieces of shrapnel in his right leg during the destruction of Baños, and he leaned heavily on a cane as they walked through the narrow streets of Jaffa. Kindness and wisdom shone from his eyes, belying his reputation for ruthlessness among the opposition. His air of coziness, what Jed called a *heymish* quality, made the evening a pleasure for everyone, but it was Margot who got the full benefit of his charm. After a satisfying meal in a small restaurant in the old city, while Katherine and Jed lingered behind in the street, Amos led Margot up a short flight of steps into a curio shop, where he bought a silver trinket and presented it to her. When they came out, Jed observing them from a distance, murmured to Katherine that a miracle was occurring. Katherine had been peering into an excavation: many meters below the ground where they stood, an ancient settlement of cave dwellings had recently been unearthed. "Look at your sister," Jed urged. Margot was blushing, her eyes downcast, a shy smile hovering about her lips, not her usual demeanor. "Hard to be a maven when Amos is around," Jed chuckled. "I think he likes her."

"Nobody should let his wife come to Israel alone," Katherine remarked.

"Too bad she's leaving tomorrow," said Jed.

The following morning, Margot was gone by the time they awoke at eight. Eager to be off to Jerusalem, Jed dressed in khakis and a short-sleeved shirt and strode through the lobby, indistinguishable from the military men who congregated there. Mindful of Schlomo's warnings, Katherine wore a khaki skirt that covered her knees. By nine-thirty the sun beat down with blinding fury on the silver hood of the rented Audi as Jed maneuvered through the streets of Tel Aviv, which were clogged with Volkswagens, Mercedes-Benzes, and BMWs. Rolling up the sleeves of her yellow cotton shirt, Katherine remarked, "It seems ironic that there should be so many German cars in Israel."

"Reparations," Jed replied. "It was the least the cocksuckers could do."

The heat was stifling. On the open road, a tropical wind swept through the car, puffing out their shirts and making conversation all but impossible as they sped past a barren landscape with scrubby trees pushing their way out of the earth. Now that they had left teeming, papier-mâché Tel Aviv behind, Katherine thought, they would discover the land of the Bible.

The road wound inland, past hillside settlements with blue Arabic doors, rising steadily to a crest, then falling into a valley of minarets and spires, of domes and crosses and synagogues, the meeting place and battlefield of diverse faiths, the Holy City, Jerusalem.

They left the car in a square and wandered through the Arab bazaar, where flies and beggars swarmed in dark, dusty passages and old men crouched over their backgammon boards in narrow doorways. Mendicants with their eyeballs on their cheeks held out bony hands in supplication, peddlers haggled over prices in their stalls, and the street reeked of spices and rotting fruit and sickly sweet perfume.

At noon, they drove to army headquarters to lunch with Leah's husband, Joshua. A slender young girl in uniform greeted them with a deferent air and took them into his office.

Colonel Cafri stood behind his desk in his shirtsleeves, his hand extended in greeting. He was a dashing fellow—over six feet tall, with sharply etched features—saved from all-out gorgeousness by a six-inch scar that zigzagged across his left cheek.

"Welcome, Jed. Leah has told me much about you. I'm very happy we meet at last," he said, gripping Jed's hand.

"This is my friend, Katherine Kellogg. I hope we're not disturbing you."

Joshua's smile was wide and welcoming. "Not at all. I won't be able to spend the entire day with you unfortunately, but after lunch Irith will show you around."

"It will be my pleasure," Irith said. "Joshua, the jeep is ready."

"We will go to the Old City," Joshua said. "There's a very good restaurant called El Hassam. We weren't able to go there, of course, before last month."

They piled into the jeep. As it jounced over the cobblestones, Katherine whispered to Jed in the backseat, "If you were an Arab cook and looked out and saw two Israeli army officers, wouldn't you poison the soup?"

"I myself don't plan on eating anything but pita bread," he replied.

A middle-aged Arab in a white djellaba showed them to a table beside a window covered with filmy muslin that shaded the noonday light. Joshua suggested the waiter order for them, and when the exotic feast was spread before them, he chuckled at the Americans' reticence, assuring them it was quite safe.

"There is no problem here now," he said. "Our only problem is politics. For two thousand years we have lived in this land with the Arabs. They are our cousins—Semites, after all, like us. If foreign governments would stop playing games with us, we would get along as we always have. But the Middle East is a pawn in a deadly chess game. America plays with Israel, the Russians play with the Arabs—it's very cynical. The best thing they could do for us is leave us alone. Take one message from Israel back to your President Johnson, Jed. Leave us alone."

Jed nodded in vigorous agreement, but when he extended the theory to Vietnam, Joshua demurred. "We are very sympathetic to your government there. The problem is real. There *is* a balance of power, and if Southeast Asia falls to the Russians, it will be a very dangerous situation."

"That's the first time I've heard anyone say that since I left home," Katherine said. "All over Europe there is such hostility to America's position."

"It is always fashionable in Europe to be anti-American. We think you are right to be in Vietnam. America should take heed—we are her only friends in this part of the world."

"American aid is crucial, of course," Jed said.

"Ho! Let's be honest," Joshua laughed. "Without America's money, we can close the country."

"One thing has struck me very much," Katherine said. "There seems to be a lack of militance—or perhaps I should say militarism. I haven't seen a sign of the enthusiasm for the military role that you see in other nations, particularly after a major victory."

"You are quite right," Irith said in her gentle voice. "Not when every family has suffered a loss."

"We are a very small country. There is no one who has not been hurt by the hostilities," Joshua explained. "We are not interested in fighting or in ruling . . . we just want to be left in peace. I have no desire to wear this uniform, believe me. I want to get back to my books."

As they rode back to army headquarters, Joshua told them vignettes of the first days of peace. "When we opened the Old City, the Arabs streamed into our part of town. They stood on the street corners and applauded the traffic lights; groups of them wandered through the supermarkets, gawking at frozen food. They were like children." His attitude was benign; still, Katherine wondered how it would be possible for nations with such a gulf of civilization between them ever to live in peace.

At headquarters, Joshua said good-bye to Jed and Katherine, and Irith drove them on to Mea She'arim. Here in this dilapidated quarter, life was dictated by an ancient religious zeal. Women shaved their heads and wrapped kerchiefs around them, children wore sidecurls and skullcaps. Although Irith laughed off any suggestion of menace as they walked through the narrow streets, Schlomo's warning had not been entirely in jest. Orthodox men in long coats went about their business with dour looks for modern intruders. Even Jed was not inclined to linger.

In the space of a few hours, Irith's sweetness, intelligence, and character had made a lasting impression on Katherine and Jed; their daughters could have no better role model, they agreed, and Jed vowed to send Chris to a kibbutz. They said good-bye with regret at army headquarters; then Jed drove to the Ministry of Tourism, where Sarah Raftai awaited—or lay in wait, Katherine amended presently. Dispatched by Leah to prepare an itinerary, Sarah was thirtyish, with glossy dark hair, deep-set eyes, and a voluptuous body that she brushed against Jed at the slightest opportunity. Over cups of strong coffee, she stalked him, apparently undone by his looks, his humor, and his views on Israeli politics. He's found his Ruth, Katherine thought miserably as she watched them: the woman gave every indication that she was willing to follow him anywhere.

Sarah leaned across him to trace a route to a kibbutz in the Galilee; the V of her blouse fell open. Ignoring it, she told them, "I have arranged for you to stay overnight Thursday at Ayelet Hashahar, which withstood many assaults during the war." Her eyes on Jed, she added in a low vibrato, "I will be in Tel Aviv the day you return. Perhaps we could have a drink. How shall I get in touch with you?"

"You'll leave a message at the hotel, that's what you'll do," Jed said with typical flippancy, but there was a priapic gleam in his eye. Jealousy and hurt feelings painted in bold stripes on Katherine's transparent face, they said good-bye to Sarah.

"Hurry up, kid," Jed snapped, hastening down the ministry steps. "We've got three hours. I want you to see the holy places so the trip shouldn't be a total loss."

He parked the Audi not far from the Church of the Nativity. Anyone expecting "O Little Town of Bethlehem" was in for a shock, Katherine observed with dismay. Tables of religious trinkets covered every inch of the church square: rosaries, medals, stars of David, holy pictures were jumbled together, hawked by Arab merchants. The moneylenders were back in the temple with no one to drive them away, she thought, searching in vain for some remnant of authenticity, a grain of spirituality in the great commercial desert.

"Do you want to join one of the tours?" Jed asked politely.

"God, no!"

"Whatever you say. This is your day, Eva Marie Saint."

She gave a mirthless laugh. He'd been calling her that all day.

The sun and crowd produced a furnace-like heat in the square; Jed wiped the back of his neck with a kerchief and found a small door leading to the cool dark nave of the church. As their eyes adjusted to the dim light, they wandered aimlessly in the direction of a group of tourists whose Arab guide was describing its history.

"The church was constructed over this sacred place where once there was a simple manger, to which the three Arabian kings were led by the star of Bethlehem."

On the marble floor, a medallion marked the spot where Christ was born; the dull gold star would have passed unnoticed had the guide not pointed it out. A feeling of reverence, instinctive as love or hatred or fear, overcame Katherine. "This is the actual site of the stable?" she asked in a hushed voice.

"Right here," responded the guide, pointing to the floor. "The inscription is in Aramaic."

People were prostrating themselves, touching their foreheads to the medallion and kissing it. Katherine's disillusionment faded as she edged closer. Jed was standing a few feet away, intent on lighting his pipe despite the No Smoking signs on every other pillar. Quick as lightning, she ducked and surreptitiously brushed her hand across the star.

"I saw that, Katie Winterhaus," she heard in her ear. Jed sank to one knee. "What was that, a little genuflection? You blew your whole act with that one, kid," he said with a chortle.

Flushing, she quickly inquired of the guide what evidence had led historians there.

"In *A.D.* 328," he responded by rote, "Constantine's mother, Queen Helena, came to Jerusalem. She had a dream one night and the next morning, pointed to this as the place."

Katherine's features contorted with disappointment. Jed pounced on the information. "That's right, kid," he said out of the corner of his mouth. "The queen had a little dream, turned around three times, and said, 'We'll put the stable here, boys.' " At her chagrined laugh, he said, "Had enough? Let's go to the Wailing Wall."

"Anything . . . anything," she muttered.

Outside the square, they picked up an Israeli guide named Shimon. Sexes were segregated at the Wailing wall, he explained; Katherine must stay on the right while Jed made his pilgrimage to the left. The huge square had already been bulldozed by the Israelis; where once there had been hundreds of flimsy structures, now tourists moved in a great wave across the wide, flat space toward the wall to merge with the davening Hasidim. Jed covered his head with a handkerchief and left Katherine standing with Shimon on a knoll overlooking the square. She approached the wall, but felt shunted aside with the women and, brooding about the contribution made to sexism by the Jewish religion, as well as her own, she retraced her steps. Such an observation, she imagined, Jed would consider anti-Semitic in his present frame of mind. Equal time was not allotted to the opposition; Catholicism was fair game, Judaism sacrosanct. Even Shimon, who had declared himself a devout atheist, was telling her with reverent solemnity, "Prayers written on paper and placed within crevices go directly to God."

As he spoke, she saw Jed scribble a note and tuck it between two massive stones. Tradition was exerting its hold on him, too, she thought. Despite his protestations of nonbelief he was keeping his promise to say Kaddish for his father in Israel. He stayed there for a long moment, and when he turned and walked back to the barricade, she saw that his face was streaked with tears. Only once before had Katherine known him to cry, and that was over Chris. Now he wept for Nathan Bronstein in Israel. Her arms ached to hold him, to comfort him, but Jed was not a man to accept a woman's solace. In silence they walked to the Ecce Homo Arch, through which they reached the Via Dolorosa.

The way to Golgotha. Its very name conjured up for Katherine centuries of Christian belief. As they climbed the rusticated steps, Shimon said in his offhand way, "The original road is many meters below, of course."

"You mean this isn't the actual place?" she asked in a tone of disappointment.

Shimon waved his hand vaguely. "Approximately. Like everything else, it has been paved over many times."

Pink-faced, perspiring tourists flowed around them, clutching rosaries and cameras. Souvenir shops lined both sides of the way; in the doorways Arab merchants waved scarves and postcards and Vivicola while their children roamed the street muttering entreaties. Lost in this mini bazaar, a series of signs marked historical spots: here He fell; here Veronica wiped his brow; on this step (or somewhere beneath it), He exhorted the women to weep not for Him, but for their children. A skinny boy of twelve or so plucked at Jed's sleeve suggestively. Shimon shooed him away, saying "Let's go up to the church. Peddlers are not allowed there."

Massive pillars a few feet inside the Church of the Holy Sepulchre were defaced with the markings of Crusaders left centuries before. Shimon pointed them out and he and Jed commiserated about their shared history of persecution. Following them through a small door, Katherine emerged in a small chamber with a raised stone slab. "This is where they say Jesus rose from the dead," said Shimon. Then he rolled his eyes at Jed. "I mean, if you want to believe—"

Jed laughed, but there was sympathy in his eyes when he looked

Katherine's way. Moments later when they went out into the blazing sunlight, he paid Shimon and told him they would find their way back alone. "It's not ideal to have a Jewish guide to Gethsemane," he admitted as they climbed to the top of a nearby hill, where the Mosque of Omar's golden dome glittered against a cloudless sky. Katherine replied, "My advice is, if you have one scintilla of faith left, stay away from the Holy Land." Shoes in hand, they wandered barefoot over the Persian carpets that covered the floor of the shrine, pausing to gape at the portrait of Muhammad ascending to heaven on his white horse. They smiled at something both considered a *bubbe montse*. Neutral territory at last.

Another night in Tel Aviv, then off in the morning: Herzlia, Ein Hod, Haifa, and Acco, where they explored the fortress and strolled along the sea wall. In a roadside café, Katherine saw an actual Coke bottle behind the glass case. Since their arrival in the country, she'd been experiencing withdrawal symptoms—the Coca-Cola company did not do business with Israel for fear of losing the Arab countries. "Would you take ten dollars for it?" she pleaded with the proprietor.

"I have been offered more," the woman smiled. "But it is not for sale. My son requisitioned it in the Sinai."

Hitchhikers dotted the highway. Traveling inland, they picked up a young paratrooper named Moishe. Katherine moved over to make room for him in the front seat, and they plied him with questions about the war. Moishe was no more than a boy, slight of frame, dark-skinned, with a rapid, intense manner of speech. Proudly, he declared that he was a Sabra: his parents had come to Tel Aviv from Iraq shortly before he was born. He described a battle in the Golan Heights where the Syrian army was stationed at the top of a hill with the Israelis storming them from below.

"Strategically, it was impossible," he said. "Something other than force was needed to take that hill. We were completely out-numbered, and they were shooting down into us."

"David and Goliath," Katherine said.

"Absolutely," Moishe replied. "But you saw it everywhere during those six days—the fire, the spirit to win. That was why they could not conquer us. We were fighting for our survival."

"Had you ever fought before?" Katherine asked.

"Me? No—I am eighteen."

"What was it like to go up that hill with bullets coming at you?"

"You don't think about dying. Never. If you did, you would be lost. You think only about taking the hill. We had to make short work of it."

Moishe got out at Rosh Pinna. They had been driving for another hour when Katherine began to feel sick. Nausea combined with a fever that raged through her body, leaving her weak and near delirium. Aware of Jed's voice but unable to follow his conversation, she drifted in and out of sleep, awaking to his stony silence as he steered the car doggedly into the Galilean hills. Resentment for her physical weakness seemed to burn in him with as much force as her fever. Involuntarily she moaned, leaning her head weakly against the window, nauseated as Eva Marie Saint never was. She reconciled herself to dying in Israel—and without a kind word. It was too ironic. Jed would have to call her parents and tell them. Just before they died of shock, they would stipulate that "Where did we go wrong?" should be engraved on their headstones.

Jed reached over to open the glove compartment, and cast her a malevolent glance. Why was he being so mean? she asked herself. Surely he didn't think she was faking. And what comfort lay ahead of her? A hotel room and a soft bed? A nourishing meal? No, a pallet in a kibbutz in the shadow of Syria.

At last they reached Ayelet Hashahar. A tall, silver-haired man named Dov came out to greet them. His light eyes radiated sympathy as they took in Katherine's pallor; he brought her to his office, where he gave her two mysterious brown pills and told her she would be cured in an hour. "They took them in the army for a host of ills," he said. "It was our secret weapon."

Half an hour of feverish sleep on Dov's couch, and as he promised, Katherine awoke miraculously recovered. She chatted gaily with Dov during dinner in a large, refectory-like room, while Jed observed a band of young Israelis with curiosity. Their manner was gruff, their faces unsmiling. "A whole other ball game," he repeated.

A straight-backed chair and two army cots comprised the furniture in their room. The small window between the beds looked onto a desolate plain that lay at the foot of the Golan Heights, looming dark and ominous in the distance. Long after Jed's even snoring had begun, Katherine lay awake beneath the scratchy sheet, alert for what sounded like the occasional burst of a shell.

The vulnerability of their position boggled her mind; how could he possibly sleep, she wondered, when a bomb or a grenade might be lobbed at them any minute? The specter of imminent death in Israel leered at her from the shadows again; she gathered the rough blanket and rocklike pillow and retreated to the bathroom, which, being windowless, seemed less accessible to artillery fire. Curled in a fetal position, she fell asleep in the bathtub, where, to Jed's great amusement, he found her in the morning.

A loquacious young soldier named Levi met them with a jeep after breakfast. As he steered it up into the volcanic hills, he told them about his friend, a pilot, who had been displayed on Arab television hanging upside down. "After that, we took Kuneitra," he said. When they arrived at this Syrian border village, they saw the only thing the Israelis had left standing—presumably as a joke: a hastily constructed victory gate festooned with withered flowers and multicolored Aramaic inscriptions.

Her fear had vanished with the darkness, and when they stopped at the side of the road, Katherine climbed out of the jeep, eager to explore.

"Tread carefully," Levi warned. "The fields are still mined. A random step could set off an explosion."

The fleeing Syrians had abandoned their tanks all along the roadside; when Katherine clambered over one, she found evidence that Goliath had had some hefty help—there were Russian markings on the metal. She pried a piece away and showed it to Jed and Levi. The soldier gazed northward to Mount Hermon rising above a road ironically named Mas'ada. "The blood of Israel irrigates this steep land now," he said fiercely. "And the world will tell us to give it back. I ask you, how can we be free to live and work in peace with Syrian armies sitting on top of us, looking down their gun barrels into our homes? For recreation, they used to shell us from the heights. We should politely return them this advantage and expect to survive? Never!"

It was cooler here in the north; a mild breeze rustled the palm branches. As they drove back to Ayelet Hashahar, there was a sense of peace on the plain. In a murky, ambiguous political world, the conflict of 1967 seemed biblically simple to Katherine. The good guys had mopped up the bad and gone back to their business of tilling the land. Amos, Moishe, Levi, and the abrupt young Israelis they had seen at the kibbutz made the meaning of "Sabra" come clear: hard and prickly on the outside, but tender within. At the door of Ayelet Hashahar, she kissed Dov good-bye with a sense of loss that they would never meet again; but she knew she would remember his kind, twinkling blue eyes and those miraculous pills forever. "You must hurry now," Dov told them. "It is the Sabbath, and you will find gas only in Nazareth."

On the rim of Lake Tiberias, Jed stopped the car and Katherine got out. Here at last, dipping her fingers in the water where Christ had walked, she had a sense of holiness, and as she looked back at Jed, his foot raised on the fender to fasten his sandal, the fabric of Judaism and Christianity appeared to her to be seamless, like His cloak.

They reached Tel Aviv by nightfall. After breakfast they set off in the Audi for the south, through fertile farmland that had once been an arid region inhabited by Bedouins.

"You want to know what's incredible about this country?" Jed asked. Katherine followed his gaze to a field, where a farmer was plowing. "That man is Jewish! There's never *been* such a thing!"

"Why not?"

"Because Jews were not allowed to own land! Moneylenders, merchants, Jews could be, not farmers. That's why Israel's so important."

With new eyes, she gazed on this incongruous, beautiful sight: a Jew on a tractor.

The owner of the Desert Inn, Michael Eshkol, was having an argument with a rabbi at the entrance when Katherine and Jed arrived in Beersheba. Later, over lunch, Eshkol confided, "The man is the highest-paid person on my payroll. By law, I have to give him a key to the kitchen. And you know who keeps it going? Not the Hasidim so much as the Americans! Tourists come to my hotel . . . they've never eaten kosher in their lives, but here they insist on it. They are scandalized if the food is not properly prepared."

Jed shook his head at the religious *mishegoss*, and brought up the subject of ghetto mentality, of which Eshkol professed to have no understanding. Sensing an ally, Katherine asked if he considered Judaism a religion or a race.

"Of course it is a race," he said with a smile. "Why should anyone be reluctant to say this? Who do I feel more kinship with, another hotel man in Paris, or an illiterate Iraqui or Polish immigrant who doesn't even speak my language? The latter, I assure you. I have no religion, but I am first and foremost a Jew."

Katherine flashed Jed a look of triumph, but an hour later, as they drove deeper into the Judean wilderness, she feared she had won a battle but lost the war. Resentment lurked behind his moody silence. At four-thirty, they stood beneath the fiery sun on a high plateau overlooking the Dead Sea. Love had brought her to the edge of the world, she reflected; a last outpost of civilization. Behind her were two wooden structures that comprised the new city of Arad; before her, a valley of sifting white sand, the Negev—a chasm between time and infinity. From behind dark glasses, her sunstruck eyes contemplated the desolate gulf. What the hell am I doing here? she thought; a lapsed Catholic in No Man's Land with a fifty-one-year-old Jew in search of his heritage. She squinted searchingly into the glare. There were no answers in the uncompromising Middle Eastern light.

Within minutes of their return to Tel Aviv, they came upon Sarah Raftai in the Hilton bar. Every female molecule of her extraordinary body strained toward Jed as the three sat at a tiny table in the crowded lounge. Jed responded in kind, making blatant sexual overtures, using Sarah as a club to punish Katherine for bringing up the uncomfortable subject of race with Michael Eshkol. In an insinuating tone he informed Sarah that Katherine's plane was leaving in a few hours, and Sarah made no attempt to hide her delight. Any attempt at conversation or civility was fruitless, Katherine decided; at last she rose abruptly and muttered that she was going to the room to pack. Half an hour later, Jed sauntered in, saying pleasantly, "Sarah says you're jealous."

Katherine slammed her suitcase closed. "You might at least have waited until I left the country! Would that have been too much to ask? Just three hours of patience? Or is it more fun to humiliate the shiksa in public?"

"You humiliated yourself, asshole," he snarled.

As the exchange escalated, Jed was driven to the extreme measure of speaking in an Italian dialect, which indicated to Katherine that he was in the second stage of rage. A vein in his temple jumped like a hooked bluefish. "I tella you wha I'ma no gitta married with you, baby!" he shouted. " 'Cause when you onna you deathbed, you'll call for a priest!"

"Of course I will! So what?"

"Because I'MA NO HAVE NO PRIEST INNA MY HOUSE!" he bellowed.

"Well, it's hardly an issue, is it?" she said coldly as she lugged her suitcase to the door. "Since the next Mrs. Bernard is waiting downstairs for me to get out of her way?"

Jed was a man who abhorred jealousy. He began to hop up and down, his features contorted into a samurai mask as he yelled, *"Hya! Hya! Hya!"* Katherine quailed. Japanese meant that he was in the last and most dangerous stage of wrath.

Neither of them so much as smiled at the other before she left Israel.

As her El Al plane lifted off the tarmac and was engulfed by a cloud bank, at last Katherine heard the voice of God over the Holy Land. Drowned out below by His salesmen and PR people, now it delivered an eleventh commandment: Thou shalt not intermarry. The voice was deep and rasping, with just a trace of a Minneapolis accent, and like a thunderclap it prefaced a storm. The clouds darkened. Rain lashed the aircraft as it descended over Athens. Katherine closed her eyes and thought bleakly, What a trip. She had lost ten pounds and Jed Bernard.

CHAPTER 23

The In-laws

Southern California was going through a monsoon season. This was what Jed called the dying weeks of summer when the Santa Ana winds blew, their hot breath stirring up sparks and spreading fires ignited in the parched hills, turning the sky to a glowing pink and sometimes precipitating strange behavior among the inhabitants.

In the great void created by Jed's absence, Katherine went back to books. The urge to supplement her required reading of scripts with the classics was inspired by a trip to the UCLA bookstore made shortly after registering Chryssie at the Westlake School (the Warner Avenue experiment had proved unsatisfactory scholastically, and Douglas had volunteered the tuition). They paused just inside the door, and Katherine's glance roved over books as far as the eye could see. "I wonder how long it would take me to start with A and read everything to Z," she mused aloud. "But then, Mommy," Chryssie replied, "everything would be going in and nothing coming out." "Thank you, Rabbi Goldfarb," Katherine said solemnly, making her laugh at the imitation of Jed.

They drove past his hill on the way home. The gardeners had grown careless since he'd been away, leaving the fence unmended and a pile of debris to blow about at the bottom of his driveway. The sight saddened Katherine, made her feel as vacant as the house. For close to two years her existence had been tied to Jed's; almost daily she had traveled his dirt road in the grip of a compulsion, hurling herself into the all-encompassing role of the Girlfriend, enshrining him in her mind and her daughter's as the authority figure.

("Why must I do what Jed says?" Chryssie had asked once and Katherine had replied, "Because he's the Man.") The romantic, traditional sides of her nature had hoodwinked her into believing that love gave her life purpose; her desire for male strength had caused her to subordinate her own. What must Chryssie think now? she worried, glancing over at the child. Now that Jed was gone and Mommy was at loose ends.

Without warning, in the last days of September, Jed came back from Israel. "You'll come up to the house . . . we'll go directly to Nate 'n' Al's," he told Katherine over the telephone, as if they'd been apart a day instead of more than a month.

To hear Jed tell it, had he been able to find one great delicatessen in Tel Aviv, he would have stayed. "You can't get a decent pastrami sandwich in the whole fucking country," he complained. A starving man, he drove at high speed into Beverly Hills. Nate 'n' Al's was, as usual, jammed. Jed cajoled the harassed waitress into bringing him a quick fix of lox and bagels; then he looked around the room. "It's hard to be with Jews, dollface," he said wearily. "Of course, it's hard to be with Gentiles, too."

"How's Sarah?" Katherine inquired coolly.

Buttering a bagel, he said, "I blew her off the day you left. Dark . . . aggressive . . ." He shook his head. "I missed your little blond head, *buktsayna*."

In the evening he took Chryssie with them to the movies, and even though it was *The Sorrow and the Pity*, and Jed *grizhered* throughout, mother and daughter agreed they were where they wanted to be.

That winter, Katherine nursed Jed through the flu seven times; he lived on the development money from *My Six Uncles*, which had hit a snag in the production phase, and prepared for a long visit from his sister Sonia and her husband, Arnold Greenspan, who were journeying to the West Coast to plead with their son, Alvin, to come home and lead a normal life.

Katherine's image of Sonia was still that of the young girl two years Jed's senior who had shared a room with him in the cramped apartment on Thirty-ninth Street in Minneapolis, their privacy protected only by a curtain strung between the two beds. Little Jacob would peer through the crack, spying on Sonia as she performed a ritual scrutiny of her face in the mirror, picking at spots, squeezing pimples, causing his stomach to churn. He'd left home at sixteen, telling his mother, "I can't stay around listening to Sonia scream she'll never find a husband!" But a few years later, Sonia was married well and happily to a good-natured Jewish cardiologist.

Sonia blew onto Jed's hill like a brisk wind from the Midwest. Dark-haired and attractive, chic in a navy-blue suit, she promptly put an apron over it and peered with the familiar Bronstein eyes into corners and behind doors, taking charge of the cleaning and cooking as if Jed's house, kept immaculate by his housekeeper, Birdie, were a pigsty. Her husband was a large-boned, peace-loving man, who took the first of many long naps while the others talked by the fire.

"Alvin is a great disappointment to his father," Sonia told Jed, "taking after Uncle Jed and moving to Hollywood. We needed *that*!" She plumped up the sofa cushion at her back.

Over her head, Jed rolled his eyes at Katherine, who was seated behind her on one of the barstools.

"Fortunately," Sonia continued, "your pretty niece Jill wants to go to law school, so at least one member of the family isn't into the *mishegoss* of show business."

Jed was the perfect host, funny without being "on," attentive to Sonia, exhibiting great interest in news of his nephew and niece. Only after Sonia joined Arnold in the guest room did he turn to Katherine with naked hurt in his eyes and say, "Do you believe that? She never once asked about Chris. Fuck her, I've finally had it with Sonia. After she goes home, I'm never talking to her again."

Never speaking to Sonia again, Katherine suspected, was a threat as perennial as throwing Wolf out of the house. When Alvin appeared only once during his parents' stay, Jed's sympathy for Sonia was aroused. "It's God's punishment she should have a son like that," he told Katherine. "Alvin only shows up if we're going to Matteo's or La Scala. He has no feeling for *mishpoche*—family."

Being ignored by her son turned Sonia's attention to her daughter, Jill, who, she complained to Jed and Katherine, was "still going with that Methodist, Nelson."

"But he's a nice fella, isn't he, Sonia?" Jed asked, winking at Katherine.

"What's that got to do with it?" Sonia cried. "She'll break her father's heart if she marries a *sheygets*."

"You're crazy on this subject," Jed remonstrated. "The fact that she's happy is what's important."

"Since when?" Sonia snapped.

Smiling at her similarity to Emily, Katherine said, "Sonia, if Jill were choosing between a handsome, kind, loving Gentile, and a sadistic, unattractive Jewish boy who is also a pauper, which one would you want her to marry?"

"Oh, now, Katherine, that's unfair," Sonia chided. "You've loaded the question. . ." As Katherine started to agree, Sonia concluded, "I would have to say the Jew."

Jed and Katherine yelped in unison.

Later, while Jed watched television, Katherine was alone with Sonia for the first time as they did the dishes. Vigorously scrubbing the pot that had held one of her justly famous briskets, Sonia indulged in a kind of emotional spring cleaning regarding her brother: her cheeks grew flushed and her voice higher as tales from a Minnesota youth were dusted off and held up to the strong kitchen light; childhood grudges were shaken out and aired, grievances uncovered. "Don't let her sucker you in," Jed had warned, but in the end, Katherine let down her guard and confided her frustration that the relationship was leading nowhere.

Sonia flicked soapsuds from her fingers into the sink. "But Katherine," she said with a puzzled look. "Jed had been with the most glamorous women of our time. What would make you think that you would succeed where all of them failed?"

The heat rose in Katherine's face; she turned away to cover her embarrassment, stacking plates in the cupboard. How could she have been so naïve? she asked herself. To Sonia, she was a shiksa, and that was that. For the remainder of the Greenspans' stay, she was cordial but cool.

When they were gone, she repeated the incident to Jed. "I told you, kid," he reminded her. "She takes one look at you, you're a natural enemy. But I think you changed her mind a little. Last night she said maybe I should marry you after all, because you know your way around a kitchen." Then he put his arms around her and kissed the top of her head. "My baby," he crooned. "No one's going to hurt you but me."

Not long afterward, Katherine received a letter from her mother saying that she and Douglas were coming to Los Angeles for "a nice, long visit."

Upon their arrival at the Beverly Wilshire Hotel, Emily announced, "We plan to stay for a month or two."

"We might take a run down to Palm Springs," Douglas added. "But mostly we just want to spend time with our two girls."

Katherine reconciled herself to a springtime devoted to family. After dinner one evening, Chryssie, who was a devotee of room service, asked, "Could I ever stay here at the hotel with you, Grandmommy and Granddaddy?" "You bet you can, honey," Douglas replied. Katherine smiled to herself. She might not have to neglect Jed as much as she'd thought.

Several times a week, she would leave Chryssie with her parents at the hotel after dinner, race home, take the phone off the hook, then drive up to Jed's and spend the night beside him, rigid with guilt. Brief hours of sleep were tormented by a recurring nightmare: her parents trudging up the hill and finding them *in flagrante*— "Get right out of that infidel's bed, young lady!" her father would shout, while her mother clutched her heart and cried, "Katherine . . . come home!"

But with time, the attrition of secrecy worked its way; Katherine became obsessed with the idea of her parents meeting Jed. Why she was determined to force a confrontation was a mystery; she had no illusions about altering their prejudice, and Jed was hardly eager, but she clung stubbornly to the notion that the collision of cultures would be beneficial to both sides.

Preparing the way, Chryssie announced one evening: "Mr. Bernard lives in such a beautiful house, Grandmommy and Granddaddy."

"You should see it," Katherine said.

"Who is this man, Katherine?" Emily asked suspiciously.

"A friend, Mother. He's a much older man who's been very kind to Chryssie and me."

"Well, I don't see why we should meet him. What sort of name is Bernard, anyway?"

"I don't know—Russian, I think. Come on, you'll enjoy it. He said he'd love to have you come to tea any afternoon."

Later that evening, after she had served Jed a late supper in his study, Katherine told him that her parents had accepted his invitation.

"Marvelous," he said, his head bent to the plate. "I can't wait to meet two anti-Semites at the height of my career."

"You will be polite, won't you, Jed?"

"I'll behave like a perfect gentleman, kid," he said, lifting his eyes from the spaghetti. "When I see old Dave Weyerhauser, we'll chat about the market, and your mom and I can discuss materials . . ."

"What?"

"Well for instance," said Jed, pulling his napkin from his shirt-front. "I might say . . . you see this lovely piece of Belgian lace, Mrs. Weyerhauser? My gramma left it to me. I use it to come in."

"Oh, God!" Katherine shrieked. "Jed, you wouldn't! You wouldn't, would you? I'll die!"

"Don't worry, baby. I'll say it fast—she won't get it. You can say anything. People don't listen anyway."

"Just don't call my father cripple, okay?" she asked.

Now here they were: Douglas, short of breath and hobbled with phlebitis, limping across Jed's courtyard; Emily, prim in a silk print dress with a veiled coronet of violets on her faded hair, her patent leather high heels crunching on the gravel path between the lawn and the camellia bushes; and Jed, coming out of the cool cavern of his foyer in a cashmere blazer and navy linen trousers. He had made an enormous effort, Katherine observed. His hair was freshly trimmed, a paisley silk kerchief tucked in his breast pocket, the Gucci loafers polished—the effect was stunning; at the same time, seeing him through their eyes, she realized suddenly how very *dark* he was.

Everyone behaved impeccably. Emily remarked on the lovely flowers; Douglas petted Simon; Jed engaged them in a discussion of East versus West, then took them on a tour of the house, giving short shrift to the bedroom, although not a trace of Katherine lingered there. When they had wound through the children's quarters and the guest room to Jed's office, Douglas lowered himself into the rocking chair. "Whew! This feels good. I'm bushed," he said.

Emily shifted impatiently. "Why don't we go back now, dear?"

"Let the man enjoy himself, Mrs. Winterhaus," Jed intervened. Katherine held her breath—her mother did not like being contradicted. "He works hard, poor fellow. He's got a right to relax. Can't let the women have their way all the time, can we, Mr. Winterhaus?"

"You said it, Jed!" Douglas beamed. "May I call you Jed?"

"I wish you would," Jed replied, deadpan.

Emily was studying the book titles on the shelf. Katherine ran her eye down one row: *The Rise and Fall of the Third Reich, Survival at Auschwitz, The Fixer,* and the entire works of Sholem Aleichem. Hastily she said, "Come on, Daddy, let's go to the pool—it's cooler there."

"Okay," Douglas replied. Jed gave him a hand up.

On the way into the living room, Jed said, "Would you set the table for tea outside, please, Katherine?" Automatically, she headed for the buffet. "I keep the placemats in the bottom drawer," he added pointedly.

It was a warm, bright, sunny day; not a cloud marred the blue perfection of the sky as Emily and Douglas sat beneath the olive tree at a table beside the glassy pool, looking like pilgrims who had stumbled upon an oasis in the Levant. Breathing in the scent of roses, Douglas abandoned himself to his idyllic surroundings, but the others appeared to be enacting an artificial tea party scene out of an Oscar Wilde play. Jed hovered about, pouring lemonade from a silver pitcher into four Royal Crown Derby goblets and passing a tray of cookies. Then he sat down across from Emily and inquired about their accommodations at the hotel in a strained voice. Humor had fled from him as if he were a burning building.

"Usually we stay at the Beverly Hills," Emily said, "but we thought we'd try the Beverly Wilshire this time because it's more convenient for my husband." She reached for her goblet; her hand connected with a small china vase and it toppled, shattering with an exquisite tinkle against the glass tabletop. Aghast, she stared at it and stammered an apology.

"Don't worry about it, madam," Jed said smoothly, a wicked glint in his eye. "It's nothing . . . an Egyptian relic, actually. Only one of its kind in the world."

Crimson with embarrassment, Emily responded to this with a burst of startled laughter, so Jed threw caution to the winds, looking from her to Katherine and back. "Your mother's a *shikkerer* or what? Did you come up to break everything in the little Jew's house, Mrs. Winterhaus?"

Emily's hauteur vanished; she was laughing uncontrollably, her face flushed, merriment in her eyes, an older version of the handsome woman who had bantered with Eddie Frankel. Katherine could not stop laughing. The hilarity spread to Douglas, who joined in, guffawing. Jed's timing was back; on track again, he kept them entranced for another hour with stories (hastily cleaned up) of Eddie Cantor and Bea Lillie and Bertie Hayes, a favorite of Douglas's.

Katherine looked on wonderingly: her mother appeared totally re-laxed, her father carefree. It had been years since she had seen them having such a good time.

A sunset streaked the sky behind them when they finally shook hands with Jed at the door. "Thanks very much, Jed," Douglas said heartily. "It's the best day we've had in California."

"You're leaving here a much younger man, Mr. Winterhaus," Jed told him.

"I'll say!" Douglas replied. "You've got quite a place up here all right . . . quite a place."

Emily said a gracious good-bye and Katherine drove them back to the hotel feeling positively triumphant.

Sunday was Mother's Day. After Mass and a long lunch with her parents and Chryssie at the Beverly Hills Hotel, Katherine went to a phone booth to call Jed. He was in the midst of reading a ram-bling letter from his mother detailing the sacrifices she had made on his behalf throughout the years. "You know how I'm celebrating today?" he said. "I'm suing my mother for custody of myself."

CHAPTER 24

Ma Soeur,
Mon Semblable

Douglas Winterhaus's final, most generous act before he left California was to make a down payment on a house for his daughter and granddaughter. "Chryssie's growing up, she needs stability in her life," he told Katherine sternly, adding, "I hope you aren't neglecting your Catholic crowd for these—uh, *newer* friends." Her only response was a sigh. One step forward, three steps back, she thought.

The house was a large clapboard cottage on a winding street off Mandeville Canyon, where children rode their bicycles and the loudest noise was that of a dog barking. Though it stood on almost an acre of land and had an abundance of what the real estate agent called country charm, the suburban aspect of the neighborhood made Katherine feel that she was leaving her youth behind in the little ski lodge on Beverly Glen. Moving traumatized her, the task of making the house habitable by the time Chryssie got back from school overwhelmed her; when Jed arrived, she was seated among mountains of packing crates on the living room floor, paralyzed. As he had done once before, Jed applied his keen artistic sense to the crucial area, arranging Chryssie's furniture, hanging posters on the walls, unpacking her collection of dolls and stuffed animals, which he arrayed on the bed; at three-thirty, when all else was in chaos, the child's room could have been photographed for *House and Garden*. When Chryssie walked into it, she had an indelible impression of home.

No good deed goes unpunished: the next morning Jed received a summons from Laura's attorney; she was suing him for child support during the years Chris had lived on the hill. For months his life was again dominated by a drama over which he had no control.

The summer passed in consultations with lawyers, trial dates set and rescheduled, and a final, cathartic trip to the Santa Monica courthouse, where Katherine paced the corridor with him, then waited until he emerged from the courtroom, shoulders drooping, a troubled look on his face. "There's good news and bad news," he reported. "The bad news is I've got to pay Laura twenty thousand dollars." The unfairness of the judgment brought a sound of protest from her, but Jed gave a victorious smile. "The good news is she's been ordered to allow Chris to come up to the hill on alternate weekends."

On Labor Day weekend, a subdued, rather bashful Chris came as a visitor to her father's house. She was affectionate, but unnaturally polite to Jed, making Katherine think almost wistfully of their old battles. A wall had grown up between them as a result of Laura's manipulations, and it would take more than a court order to bring it down. Once school started, Chris's life was centered in Manhattan Beach, and it was easier for Jed to drive there than insist upon her coming to him.

The sudden desperate need for money prodded him to accept a scriptwriting job from one of Hollywood's schlock producers of low-budget films. Betty Hawkins was summoned; he came up with an imaginative concept and produced an intelligent, funny first draft, only to have the producer change the hero to a heroine in order to cast his current mistress in the leading role. Jed took the money and ran.

To the outside world, Jed was an entertainer, inspiring rapt infatuations from women and men alike; to his daughter, he was a devoted, even adoring father; it was the role of lover that strained him the most. Katherine's strongest clues that he cared about her were his constant calls and the fact that he seemed to want her at his side; yet the minute she was there, more and more the mind games went on—digs, professions of indifference, indications that he resented her presence and the entire relationship. Once after Chris had canceled a Sunday outing with them, Jed sank into a black humor as he sunbathed beside his pool; coldly he informed Katherine that she should leave, take her child with her, and have a life. Two days later he called, baffled that he hadn't heard from her. "I tell the boys," he chuckled, " 'Katherine asks for impossible things—love, fidelity, kindness.' " Like Henry Higgins, he wanted to know: had he ever treated a woman any better? Why, when one of the most celebrated film queens of his day had, for love of him, slashed her wrists in his shower, his response had been: "You *dare* to bleed on the carpet, madam?" Steadfastly he refused to give Katherine the satisfaction of saying that he loved her. Reading too much or failing to complete her "chores" was sufficient to bring down his wrath on her head; should he find no immediate fault, there was always the possibility of her future anti-Semitism to enrage him, even as he himself minutely analyzed Jewish *mishegoss*.

And she, the quintessential shiksa, was incapable of ignoring the bait. A new psychological study called *The Plight of the Middle-Aged Man* gave her little insight into Jed's intricate tortures, nor did it prevent her from responding with the sensitivity of a Stradivarius when he played upon her emotions. Far from remaining passive under his abuse, she wept, argued, and fought for respect. And while she suffered, Jed's dependence on her grew so great that he took to calling her Mommy. After a particularly brutal confrontation that ended in his cold withdrawal and her hysteria, he sent her to his favorite psychiatrist, along with his own interpretations of their problems: interlocking neuroses, Sadie and Massie, Catholic nuttiness, and two thousand years of sickness.

The doctor, grown too eminent for private practice, referred her to Dr. Leonard West, a pillar of the psychoanalytic community. This rotund man with small features set in a mask of earnestness took copious notes throughout Katherine's depiction of her relationship with Jed, whose character appeared to fascinate him, but he had little success in unraveling their complicated symbiosis. When, after a few weeks, she expressed impatience with the therapeutic process, Dr. West threw up his hands and declared, "This is not some garden-variety sadist you've brought me, Mrs. Kellogg. This man has had blond women on the couch for years!"

Winter died quickly that year. A sudden profusion of blossoms, later twilights, and air heady with jasmine trumpeted the arrival of an early spring. One morning in March, Dr. West proudly announced that he'd been appointed head of the psychiatric department of a northern California college. "So I guess I'm abandoning you, too," he said with a piercing look that seemed to call for some expression of regret. Casting about in her mind for one, Katherine could come up with nothing but a relieved smile—she had been wanting to leave for weeks. When she arrived for their final session, Dr. West's last shred of viability as a therapist disintegrated in her mind; in preparation for his new life, his steel-gray hair had been dyed auburn—by his own hand and with Shinola, judging from the density of the shade. Seated across the desk from him, Katherine judiciously kept her eyes on his shirtfront. Was it a test? she wondered. How should she handle it—compliment him on the blatant dye job? "If in time you feel the need," Dr. West was saying, "my colleague, Sam Haskell, is an excellent man." What is the adult, rational thing to do? she worried. Ignore it? Be honest with him about how dreadful it looks? The hour was up before she could decide.

Since their tea at the Plaza in New York, Katherine had received numerous letters from Wilder Jergens, chronicling the progression of her romance with Manny Schwartz. Spring brought joyous news from Philadelphia.

"Manny's overcome his guilt!" Wilder wrote. "He's given his ex-wife a small fortune and assured the boys he'll take care of their mother. They finally understand he can't pass up his chance for happiness with me.

"The wedding's at Manny's apartment in Philadelphia in June. I'm converting to Judaism. Manny was just so convinced that one day I'd turn to him and call him a dirty Jew that I decided to allay his fears. It bothers me a little bit that he won't allow any child we have to be baptized, but . . . The rabbi who's instructing me is going to perform the ceremony. I hope you and Chryssie will come!"

Although Katherine was happy for Wilder, the news of the impending marriage shone a spotlight on her own ambivalent feelings. Why was she the only one incapable of resolving the dilemma, of putting her life together? Wilder's conversion she viewed with skepticism; it wouldn't really make her a Jew, she thought; yet neither of them could exactly be called normal Gentiles anymore. They were hybrids, molded from two worlds, the sort of shiksa whose condition could be classified neither as a religion, nor a race, but a special state of mind that had its own pain and rewards.

The wedding was a lavish affair, held in Manny's sumptuous penthouse overlooking Rittenhouse Square. From a corner of the living room, Katherine watched with Chryssie as her friend stood under the *chupa* with the short, dynamic, volatile groom, a yarmulka atop his curly brown hair. On one hand, Katherine was envious of the life Wilder would have with this fireball; on the other, she was aghast. How could Wilder turn her back on her religion so completely? she wondered. Like citizenship, embracing one meant renouncing the other. And how, with limbo yawning in some nether region like a mammoth gray nursery of spiritual orphans, *how* could she accede to Manny's demand that none of their offspring be baptized? Katherine's convictions about the necessity of baptism for salvation had led her once, in Jed's swimming pool, to dribble water over his head and say, only half jokingly, "I baptize thee in the name of the Father and the Son . . ." while he bellowed, "Back! Back!" raising his arms to ward off the Catholic vampire.

The wedding guests exemplified Wilder and Manny's different worlds. There were a few Main Liners, a horse trainer from Gladwyn (none of Wilder's family deigned to attend), and several of Manny's Orthodox relatives. The rabbi, a tall, gaunt man in his sixties, wandered among them at the reception, frowning and pulling on his gray beard. It took Chryssie to unbend him. As he paused in his tour of the buffet table, Chryssie came up and peered into a crystal tub of caviar, exclaiming, "Oh, look! Berries from Israel!" From on high, the rabbi peered down at the fragile blond child, then erupted in a great bellow of laughter. What had inspired Chryssie's unique expression of ecumenism was never explained; however, Katherine reflected that it spoke to the positive influence of environment over genetics.

At one point she was cornered by Manny's younger brother, Victor, a history professor engaged in a battle for custody of his daughter. His ex-wife, Alicia, was a feisty Mexican who had spirited the six-year-old off to Cuernavaca. "It's wonderful having a bilingual child," Victor remarked in his caustic voice. "The last time I had her up here, we drove by a field of cows in the country and she said, 'Oh, Daddy, look—a farmacia!' " Half an hour of little Lisa stories, amusing as they were, gave Katherine a sense of déjà vu and a suspicion that Victor, like Jed, was systematically turning his daughter into the kind of woman both men would walk away from at a cocktail party. The Jewish mother theme has been done to death, she mused. Why doesn't someone turn his pen to the divorced Jewish father?

From Philadelphia, Katherine and Chryssie flew to Rochester, where they slept in twin beds in the same plaid-curtained room where Katherine had listened to *Living with Tessie*. Although Douglas had been hospitalized with pneumonia some months before, and Emily had vowed that if God would give her one more year with him she'd never complain about anything again, he was back in his wing chair, hidden behind the paper, and she was railing at him about the dark woodwork she had never liked. Things seemed unchanged. Douglas treated his daughter and granddaughter as if they were the same age.

At the end of the week, Jed called with the triumphant announcement, "It's comeback time!" Paul Federland, an independent producer in New York, had come upon an old property of Jed's called *What a World!* and wanted him to work with a young composer to turn it into a musical. If all went well, he would hire Jed to direct the movie. "After the knibbler goes to camp," Jed said, "why don't you spend the summer with me in New York?"

The tension that had become part of her conversations with him in recent months ebbed in a tide of relief that washed over Katherine. Not once, she noted happily, had he addressed her as Mommy. Instinctively, for she was still in love, she agreed to come to New York. But she had a sense of postponement. For almost four years she had lived in Jed's shadow; two weeks apart had made her miss him as always, but her love was now undeniably leavened with a need to find her own light.

"You've just got to let me get through the scriptwriting phase," Jed told her the day she arrived in New York, and every day thereafter. They lived in a suite at the Embassy, a small residential hotel on upper Fifth Avenue. Having made a firm resolution not to jeopardize his comeback by any display of emotional need, for three weeks Katherine prepared meals in the tiny kitchenette and tried to alleviate his frustration as he labored over the script with the obnoxious young lyricist Federland had foisted upon him. The fellow had recently graduated from film school and responded to most of Jed's ideas with one disparaging word: "Boring!"

Federland turned down a dozen versions. Jed's emotional barometer bobbled like a broken spring; he lashed out at the only person he believed would not fire him—Katherine; finally he withdrew utterly, remaining prone on the couch throughout the long summer evenings, fists clenched, eyes closed or staring into space.

If she turned a page, it disturbed him; if she spoke, he answered in monosyllables; if she went out to a movie with a friend, he was resentful when she returned. Getting out of bed in the morning became an effort for her; in a private cocoon of depression, she moved through the dusty streets like a somnambulist, too dispirited even to focus on the paintings at the Metropolitan Museum, where she sought refuge from the heat. During the third week of August, there was a garbage strike. Mountains of shiny refuse bags piled up outside the buildings along Fifth Avenue; the city reeked. "New York is becoming Calcutta," she heard a man say to his companion as they hurried past the debris, their faces pinched with the effort not to breathe. There was talk of bubonic plague.

Hours of consultation on a grueling Saturday produced one altered verse from the lyricist. Throughout Sunday morning, Jed remained recumbent on the couch, his gaze fixed on the flags hanging listlessly outside the museum. The heat was equatorial; it was the worst day yet. At noon, waving a languid hand at Katherine, he asked her to get him a pastrami sandwich from the Madison Avenue Delicatessen. She complied like a coolie, running all the way, returning red-faced and breathless, hair and clothes dripping with perspiration. He reached eagerly for the sandwich and pickle. After fetching a cream soda from the kitchenette, she perched on the arm of the sofa at his feet and inquired, in the falsely chipper voice she'd been using for days, if he had everything he needed. Across a space of six feet, Jed looked at her, his features contorted into a grotesque child's mask of hatred. She recoiled as if he'd slapped her. After a long moment she said quietly, "Look, Jed, I know how difficult all this has been for you. I want to help. I'm willing to see you through this period before the shooting starts, if that's what you have in mind— if that's what the problem consists of. But I have absolutely no sense that you care about me any longer." She paused to take a breath and plunged on. "I need to know, or I have to leave. Do you love me at all?"

For the duration of this plea, his eyes had remained on her face, as if he were considering her dilemma. Motionless, he replied, "I'm here, aren't I?"

She gave a hollow laugh. "Is that *it*?"

"It's what my old man used to tell my old lady," he said with a shrug.

"Well," she said, noticing that her voice had returned to normal, "it might have been enough for your mother, but it's not enough for me."

An unfocused sense of having made a decision caused things to improve for a few days. Jed was civil, even affectionate, turning to Katherine again for advice and emotional support. She went along with it, fooling everybody—even herself a bit—that the blows dealt to their love had not been fatal. Then, the day after Labor Day, Chryssie arrived from her Colorado camp to spend three days with Christopher's parents in their town house on East Sixty-third Street. The evening before she and Katherine were scheduled to leave for Los Angeles, Jed took them to dinner at Gino's.

The restaurant was filled with Italian families, large, generous tables of six and eight, overflowing with children and grandchildren, aunts and uncles, grandparents, gesticulating, laughing as they ate, their voices racketing off the zebra-papered walls in an animated tableau of life as Katherine and Fellini thought it should be lived. In the midst of this warm archipelago, Jed brooded. He spoke only to comment on a passing woman who took his fancy, but Katherine was beyond jealousy, beyond understanding, beyond patience. After waiting on him for weeks, she fumed, devoting her life to his like some damned Nubian *slave*, for the one evening her daughter was with them he was too selfish to emerge from his preoccupation with the fucking *movie* to pay them any attention! Chryssie silently spooned in her zabaglione, sensitive as a tuning fork to the vibrations. Katherine glared at Jed. How long had she accepted the role of whipping boy for his fears and insecurities over *What a World!* On this, her last night in New York, the most he could summon was elaborate boredom, icy self-absorption?

In proportion to how we have loved, so, when the time comes, do we hate. Jewish neurotic, she raged inwardly, her shiksa eyes boring a hole through his brain with a laser beam of loathing. The table sizzled with her hatred; she was surprised the waiter braved it, coming over to ask Chryssie if she had enjoyed her zabaglione.

"See you at Christmas, knibbler," Jed said when they dropped Chryssie off at her grandmother's. In the taxi he was silent. Through the Embassy lobby he strode ahead of Katherine to the elevator, and once in the suite, closed himself in the bathroom. He came out uncharacteristically clad in pajama bottoms—like armor, she thought miserably. With a mumbled, " 'Night, kid," he went immediately to sleep.

After a restless night, Katherine awoke to his peremptory "Gotta run. I'll skip breakfast this morning." He was fully dressed, speaking from the bedroom door.

She sat up in a panic, "Would you like me to—?"

"Nope. Have a good flight, kid."

And he was gone.

It was her only day with Chryssie in New York. Determined to put on a cheerful face for it, Katherine picked her up at the Kelloggs'; they had a picnic in Carl Schurz Park, where a breeze off the river offered some relief from the stifling heat; then, for the hour that was left to them, they went to F.A.O. Schwarz. Chryssie stationed herself in front of the electric trains on the second floor. Katherine stood a few feet off, her head throbbing, feeling as if tracks had been laid in her brain for the cars to run around. Her eyes began to water. She turned aside and blindly rifled through a pile of stuffed animals on a nearby counter. Suddenly she heard a female voice calling her name. Glancing up, she saw an extremely pretty young woman in a white linen suit coming toward her.

"It's Angelica Macafee . . . remember?" the young woman said.

"Angie!" Katherine cried, embracing her.

It was Angelica's older sister, Diana, who had been Katherine's friend in college; Angelica was barely out of grade school then, but her rebellious nature, comical view of things, and an addiction to excitement had made Katherine feel a kinship with her despite their age difference.

Now, at twenty-four, Angelica's face was fresh as a Kansas milkmaid's, heart-shaped and curtained with silky, blunt-cut brown hair that was parted on the side, drawn back flat on her head, and fastened with a gold barrette, as if her mother still combed it for her. They exchanged pleasantries for a few moments, then she looked closely at Katherine. "Are you okay? You look as if you've been crying."

"Love troubles," Katherine responded with a grim laugh.

"Anyone I know?"

Katherine shook her head. "I doubt it." But the sympathy on Angelica's face was too much for her. In a convulsive rush, she began to tell her about Jed.

Angelica stopped her with an urgent look. "A writer, lives on Fifth Avenue, and Jewish? I think I had an affair with him last year. Is his name Adam Epstein?"

"No," Katherine laughed. "Do you have a thing for Jewish men, too?"

Angelica nodded. "My mother says I should go to a shrink, my friends are sick of listening to me on the subject. It's great to find a kindred spirit."

They sighed together.

"The thing everybody thinks we like them for," said Katherine, "is sex."

"Jewish men are the worst," Angelica stated flatly.

"You think so?"

"It's their mothers—they destroy them for any other woman," Angelica said, setting her bag on the counter, drawing closer to Katherine. "Adam used to take his pulse after sex. Once we were lying there afterward and he was quiet. I said in this melting voice, 'What are you thinking?' And he went, 'SHHH! I'm counting.' "

Katherine laughed wildly. "Where did you meet him?"

"Walking along Lexington Avenue."

"They're out there, prowling the streets for shiksas," Katherine said.

"It was my lunch hour and I was eating some potato chips. I saw this tall, incredibly sensitive-looking man. He came right up to me and said, 'Do you always eat out of a bag?' I said, 'Here, take one, they'll make you smart.' He said, 'I'm already smart.' "

Katherine groaned in recognition.

"I had a huge zit on my chin," Angelica continued. "I'd covered it up with makeup and was hoping no one would see it. He poked his finger directly into it and said, 'What's *that*?' "

"Why do they *do* that kind of thing?"

"Because they're always looking for what's wrong with you. 'What's the negative?' was Adam's favorite question. If you told him you'd just won the lottery, he'd say, 'What's the negative?' "

"Did you fight a lot?"

"Constantly. He was terribly judgmental. Once we went into Doubleday and I picked up a book about Bernie Cornfeld. Adam came over and asked if I didn't think he'd done a bad thing, and I said I thought the worst thing he'd done was to get caught. He went into a fit, saying he didn't see how he could think of seriously dating anyone who could say such a thing, nor in fact go out with someone who was even interested in a book about such a person as Cornfeld.

He was always complaining about my job, saying I didn't earn enough money, it wasn't prestigious enough . . ."

"What did *he* do?"

"Nothing."

Katherine laughed again. Angelica opened her shoulder bag and extracted a Milky Way, which she halved, handing a portion to Katherine. "I'm trying to give up smoking," she said as she gnawed on hers, obviously worked up by the memory of Adam. "Once I spent the evening working at his apartment. It got to be one o'clock and I was tired, so he threw me a sheet and blanket so I could sleep on the couch. I suddenly thought, I've got a couch at home that I can sleep on; why should I come all the way across town to sleep on *his* couch?"

"Why did he do that?"

"Because he didn't want me to sleep in the same bed with him on weeknights. He thought sex was a waste of time. Once he said if it were a choice between more power and fame and being a better lover, there's no contest. He was terribly withholding. Cold. He wouldn't say hello when I came in." Angelica's long fingers pushed a strand of hair away from her cheek. The more responsive Katherine's expression became, the more she wanted to talk. "After Adam and I made love the first time," she said, "he got up, put wax in his ears, put on a pair of shorts, put his head under the pillow, and tucked the sheet around his body in case, God forbid, a finger of mine should stray across the bed to touch him."

Waiting only a moment for Katherine's laughter to subside, she continued: "Adam timed sex: three minutes for foreplay, six for coitus, and three for a postcoital hug. I tried to negotiate for more: Couldn't I have a longer hug? 'Okay,' he said. 'But it'll come out of your other time.' And," she added solemnly, "it did."

Katherine realized that she was outclassed: Angelica was a regular Virgil conducting a tour through the dark wood of romantic love between Jews and shiksas. "I cannot *believe* that you went to Manhattanville," she commented.

With a knowledgeable smile, Angelica said, "There are Manhattanville girls in the lives of a lot of Jewish men in New York."

"Jed calls it Maidenville. He says Maidenville girls are crazed," Katherine told her. "Do you think you can go back to Gentile men after Adam?"

"I'm trying," Angelica said, "but it isn't easy."

"Would you have married him?"

Angelica thought it over. "No. They turn into Jewish husbands. A Jewish boyfriend is one thing, but a Jewish husband is quite another."

"But they're supposed to be the *best* husbands," Katherine protested.

"Not for us. The good things they give to Jewish wives. We'll always be considered inferior because we're not one of them." In the face of this fact, they were silent for an instant. Then Angelica's eyes lighted. "Maybe we should organize," she said.

"How do you mean?"

"Sort of a United Shiksa Appeal." Catching sight of someone over Katherine's shoulder, she muttered under her breath, "Here comes my date. My sister fixed me up with him because he belongs to Seawanakha Yacht Club." She narrowed her cat eyes in his direction. "Would you believe he hasn't asked me one personal question all day?"

A clean-cut young man in a straw boater was edging his way through the crowd around the trains; several feet away Chryssie was inspecting a rocket ship. Katherine picked up a stuffed owl from the counter, then rejected it because it reminded her of Jed, and chose a black hound with floppy brown ears. The young man was almost upon them; her time with the oracle was up. Quickly she asked, "Angelica, if you had to give one reason why you're attracted to Jewish men, what would it be?"

"You're never bored," came the immediate response.

"Right," Katherine agreed. "You're always laughing."

"Or crying," Angelica added.

CHAPTER 25

The Last Straw

The plane was thirty thousand feet over Chicago, above a bank of rain-filled clouds. Katherine stuffed a damp Kleenex into the seat pocket, adding to the collection. Now that Chryssie had her earphones on and had moved up to a front row to watch *McKenna's Gold*, Katherine was crying openly, tears that sprang not from masochism but mourning. She conceded defeat. Love had died in New York, and there was nothing anyone could do to resurrect it. The drama of being with Jed had consumed her for too long; who was she to argue with his famous two thousand years of sickness? She dried her eyes. But how was she going to go on without him? Was there life after Jed Bernard? She reached for another Kleenex. Angelica's idea about a union wasn't such a bad one. Shiksas Anonymous, she thought, emitting a laugh that came out like a hiccup. Someone to call in the middle of the night if you get a craving for a joke or an urge to take shit for something that's not your fault. What *was* her fault was allowing him to treat her so carelessly. She blew her nose. She was turning in her chips. No more Sadie and Massie. The game was over.

September is the hottest month, breeding smog out of the noxious fumes: such was Katherine's depressing, derivative train of thought as she drove home from yet another job interview at a studio in the Valley, while overhead a menacing pink haze hung over the freeway like the mantle of an avenging angel. Her telephone started to ring as she got out of her car in the driveway. Two . . . three

. . . she fumbled with her keys at the door, dropping her bag as she ran through the hall to the kitchen and snatched up the receiver. It was Birdie, Jed's housekeeper, with shocking news.

"It's Mr. Jed's house, Miz Katherine. When I come up here this mornin' . . . it was 'bout eleven . . . the front door's wide open and everythin's turned upside down. The whole place, ransacked . . . some stuff smashed . . . he told me to put most of the good stuff away, the china and those vases he's got, so they're okay, but that little statue on the coffee table's broken, and his closet's pulled apart."

"Oh, no, Birdie! Did you call the police?"

"They was already here. Seems like Mr. Bernard, he had some friend of his who's a off-duty policeman or somethin', lookin' in on it from time to time, and he saw these kids comin' out of the driveway."

"Kids? Kids did this? How old?" Katherine carried the phone to the kitchen table, where she sat with her elbows on her knees, her head lowered as she listened to Birdie's excited report, breaking in once to ask: "Does Mr. Bernard know about it?"

"That's why I'm callin' you, Miz Katherine. You gotta tell him. I ain't gonna call him with this."

Katherine made a small sound of protest and shut her eyes, wishing the task away. There had been nothing but silence from Jed since she left New York, and now she must deliver this news, be the one to revive his old nightmare: his beloved house vandalized, his precious pre-Columbian statues trashed.

"Somebody's got to ax him what to do," Birdie's urgent voice came over the line. "And you're the only one that should."

Last of all me, Katherine thought. "All right, Birdie. It's five-fifteen in New York now. I'll try to reach him and call you back. Just clean up the best you can."

From the hall floor, she gathered the strewn contents of her purse and replaced them, keeping out the address book in which she'd copied the number of the studio that he'd given her. She went into the bedroom and sat on the bed, her knees drawn up under her as she dialed. With a sense of dread, she told the technician who answered that it was an emergency. She watched the second hand sweep the clock four times before she heard Jed's impatient voice: "Yes, what is it?"

"Jed, it's Katherine. I'm sorry to—"

"What is it?" he repeated in a brusque tone that made her falter, then rush through a report of the robbery.

His response was a blast of irritation. "You call me up to tell me this? What do you expect me to do from here?"

"Well . . . well, I don't know exactly," she stammered. "But Birdie . . . I mean, the cop thought someone ought to—"

"Do you understand?" he demanded with barely controlled rage, enunciating as one would to an imbecile. "I'm . . . on . . . the . . . *SET*!"

The next thing she heard was a dial tone. She exhaled and replaced the receiver, trembling with humiliation at this fresh verbal assault. And she had invited it, put herself directly in the line of fire. Never again, she vowed. Never. She got up quickly and left the room. Though her eyes stung, she held back the tears, willing the last corner of hope that she had kept alive in her heart to go completely black.

Part Three

CHAPTER 26

The State
of Grace

"Bless me, Father, for I have sinned. It's been four years since my last confession. . . ."

Here, in this anonymous Jesuit church at the foot of the Hollywood hills, Katherine hoped to find a liberal, compassionate confessor to restore her soul to the state of grace. There was no reason not to do it, since she was no longer living in sin. But as she tried to find the voice to enumerate the sins of half a decade—all the missed Masses and neglected Easter duties, the petty jealousies, lies, and vanities—she realized that her heart was not in it: everything else dwindled in the face of four straight years of adultery. Sternly she told herself: Might as well get right to it—put Jed Bernard in your sinful past. "I'm separated from my husband, Father. For four years I've been having sexual relations with another man."

From behind the screen came a censorious voice. "How many times?"

Katherine flung an incredulous glance in his direction. How many times? In four *years*? She almost laughed aloud. I come in here, she thought, like Mary *Mag*dalene ready to wash away my sins with tears, and he wants arithmetic! For this had she driven fifteen miles out of her way to avoid the conservative parish priests in her own diocese? For this had she promoted the intellectual superiority of the Jesuit order? For "How many *times*?" Coldly, barely bothering to hide her contempt for this priest with the instincts of a CPA, she said, "I really don't know, Father," and put her hands over her face. Behind them she saw a ball of light spinning, plummeting into a void; in her ears she heard a voice louder than the priest's, bellowing, *"Bubbe montses!"* She could think of nothing but getting out of there. At last, he said, "For your penance, say ten Our Fathers and fifteen Hail Marys, and make a good Act of Contrition."

The words surfaced from her unconscious with as much significance as a nursery rhyme.

Her car was at the curb. A teenaged girl with ironed brown hair was leaning against it talking to a boy in bell-bottom jeans. They were smoking dope. The world had picked up speed in the last four years, Katherine thought; the passage of her youth had gone unremarked. As she approached, the kids slouched toward the corner; she watched them for a moment, then lifted her head and took a deep breath. The sun was shining above the palm trees, the sky was a brilliant blue. Life would go on, she thought; but oh, Jed! Jed.

From the end of a love affair, one learns nothing so much as the value of friendship. As Katherine renewed contact with people she'd neglected during the autonomous reign of Jed Bernard, she discovered that she had missed the evenings at Eve's house, the long lunches with Alison, the phone conversations with Louise. She was touched that they welcomed her back without recriminations, while expressing relief and little surprise that Jed was out of her life. All three had moved on—Eve and Alison to marriage, Louise to a production job at Paramount—while she was back to "Go." As generous as ever, and now rich in contacts and inside information, Louise gave her a tip that Artists Unlimited, a New York and Paris-based production company, was opening a West Coast branch and looking for a literary scout.

"A reader, you mean?" Katherine asked.

"Beggars can't be choosers," Louise reminded her. "If you don't stay with one thing, you'll end up on the bottom rung of a lot of ladders."

Isaac Rhodes, vice-president of Artists Unlimited, interviewed Katherine during a trip to California a week later; the next day he contacted her from New York to tell her she was hired. Once again

Louise had come to her rescue. Katherine called to thank her, and invited her to lunch at La Scala Boutique.

They sat in a corner booth opposite a wall covered with caricatures of film favorites. Louise ran her eyes over the sketches. "Except for a few classics—Garbo, Paul Newman, Donald Duck—their turnover rate is about the same as the clientele's," she said. Katherine had had a similar thought when she came in, noting a new generation of pretty girls with their heads together over the tables, probably discussing the age-old subject of the dearth of men in Los Angeles.

An aging producer festooned with gold jewelry passed the booth, eyed them briefly, and hastened toward a nubile blonde in boots and a miniskirt. "Weird how you never see men's ears anymore," Louise commented. She sighed as Katherine twirled several strands of fettucine around her fork. "If they offered me anything—Jane Fonda's legs, Liz Taylor's eyes, Raquel Welch's back—I'd say, 'All I want is Katherine Kellogg's metabolism.' You never gain an ounce."

"It's suffering. Until last week I wasn't able to get any food past the lump in my throat."

"Over Jed Bernard? You're well out of it, my dear," Louise said severely.

"Friends always tell you that when an affair breaks up. Maybe it went on too long, but I'll never regret loving Jed."

"It's a miracle to fall in love in this town. I only know one man who isn't either bitching about his ex-wife, running after teeny-boppers, or screwing a different girl every night to avoid getting involved—and *he's* engaged."

"Who's that?"

"His name's Ben Fahrengold."

For the next ten minutes, Louise gave her rapturous attention to the subject of one Benjamin Fahrengold, a young reporter for the *Examiner* whom she claimed was devoid of hostility or sexual hangups, as well as being funny and bright. "As much as I'd like him for myself, I enjoy hearing him talk about how in love he is with his fiancée," she said. "He has no interest in the singles scene. He believes in marriage, family, monogamy—"

"God, a dinosaur!" Katherine said. "I love to hear stories like that. They restore my faith in mankind."

"Actually, he's one of the few grown-up men I know."

When they came out of the restaurant, they walked down Cañon Drive to their cars in the warm afternoon sunshine. A chorus of cat-calls on the corner of Brighton Way made them both look up; at the sight of five male heads in a third-story window, their faces bisected by goofy grins, Louise waved madly, bracelets clashing. "Who's the blonde?" someone called. "Hey, Lou, bring your friend up!" another cried. "That's Ben!" Louise whispered, but to Katherine the faces were indistinguishable from one another. She said good-bye and hurried off to a meeting with a scriptwriter in Westwood, grateful that she had a professional function to perform before picking Chryssie up at school.

At four, she turned into the gate at Westlake. A gang of tall, strapping adolescents in gym suits waited outside the locker room; Chryssie circumvented them with a friend, a precocious child named Pat, who had clung to her since skipping third grade, both of them out of place among their older, rowdier classmates. The promise of beauty was there in Chryssie's corn-silk hair and deep blue eyes, but at present it was veiled by insecurity. Yanking her out of New York at an early age had not altered the fact that she was very much an eastern type, and as much as Katherine dreaded being separated from her, boarding school in the later grades would probably be a wise choice. The only thing to prevent it would be the acquisition of a stepfather, but that seemed increasingly unlikely.

Chryssie jumped in the car and propped her book bag on her knees. "Hi, Mommy."

"Hi, darling. How was school today?"

"Okay," Chryssie replied, fishing around in her book bag and coming up with a cream-colored card that announced the annual father-daughter picnic.

"Hm," said Katherine, thinking, Just what she needs.

"Too bad Jed's away. D'you think Daddy could come down?"

"Maybe. We'll ask him." Katherine made the turn onto Sunset, grateful that they were early enough to miss the rush hour, that bumper-to-bumper crop of husbands on their way home to their families. Lately, since Chryssie had joined the swelling ranks of tagged children flying to visit a divorced parent, Christopher had been functioning better in the paternal role; maybe she could get him to fly down for the picnic, she thought.

The following morning, shortly after Katherine returned from driving Chryssie to school, the telephone rang in the kitchen.

"Guess what?" came Louise's excited voice through the instrument.

"Hi, Lou. What?"

There was a portentous pause. "Ben Fahrengold wants to take you out."

"Who?" Katherine asked blankly. Then: "You don't mean . . . oh, no! Not the one who is so in love and believes in fidelity and doesn't play around?"

"Yup," Louise replied with a laugh.

"God. That is really depressing." Just outside the window, the gardener started his lawn mower; Katherine tapped on the window and mouthed a good morning, gesturing to the flower bed he was trampling underfoot. Covering her left ear with her hand, she said into the phone, "How does he know who I am?"

"He saw you with me on the street yesterday. Can I give him your number?"

Even with the lawn mower whirring in her ear, Katherine could detect the thrill of intrigue in her friend's voice. "What for, if he's engaged?" she asked.

"Don't be silly," Louise snorted. "That's *his* problem. For God's sake, Kate, he's not married. He's also not in show business, for a change. Be grateful for small favors. How can you possibly say no? He's everything you like—funny, sensitive, and Jewish."

"That's true. Well, all right. What harm can one date be?"

Usually, the first time she looked at a man, Katherine could tell. Either it was within the realm of possibility to fall in love with him. Or it was not. Benjamin Fahrengold was an exception. Just looking at him, she would never, never have known.

His voice on the telephone was low-pitched and redolent of the Bronx. Chryssie had gone to San Francisco for the weekend, and Katherine was glad not to be alone on Saturday evening, but as she was getting dressed an almost incapacitating sense of regression came over her. A blind date, of all things, at her age. The divorce epidemic was wrenching people out of time and shape; children flew alone to see an estranged parent, and people suffered growing pains into their thirties.

At the moment the doorbell rang, she was standing at her closet in her slip, ruminating. Hurriedly, she pulled on a blue wool dress, ran a brush through her hair, and went down the hall. Through a pane of glass in the door, she saw him standing with his back to her at the edge of the porch step, looking down the hill toward Mandeville Canyon. Despite the dry weather he wore a trench coat—left over from his days as a foreign correspondent, she surmised with a smile at its battered condition; his hair above the upturned collar was tousled and carroty red. She opened the door; he turned, and she was confronted with a pair of enormous hooded eyes, changeable as a cat's, their gray shade deepening to green as he moved out of the shadows into the pool of light on the porch. He was exactly her height. Freckles scattered across his nose made him look younger than he was (Louise had said thirty-three), and he had a kid's stance: head thrown back, hands jammed in the pockets of unkempt chinos, feet planted apart. He was wearing scuffed Wallabys. His outfit made her sorry she had changed out of her jeans. Louise had raved about his infectious smile, but he was not smiling now.

"Hullo, Katherine," he said in an arrogant tone, and began to move toward her so deliberately that she took a few steps backward, her coolness masking a disturbing mixture of attraction and antipathy as he followed her into the study. Feral energy radiated from him; it lingered like musk in the hall and permeated the corners of the small room. She was unreasonably nervous, she thought, as the backs of her knees struck the fire screen. One of his hands reached out to steady her. "You're even more beautiful than I remembered," he murmured. Her eyes slid to the left in search of an avenue of escape. To her astonishment he leaned forward. Could he really be trying to kiss her?

Raising her hand, she looked with comic exaggeration at her wristwatch. "This has got to be a new record! You've been in my house exactly three and a half minutes! Are you always like this?"

"Never," he answered soberly. "I'm usually quite shy. There was just something about the way you looked. I wanted to kiss you."

Katherine edged to the right. How unused to this she was—erotic playfulness was entirely foreign to her after four years of cerebral love. She grabbed her coat from the hall closet, hurried from the house, and double-locked the door behind them. His car made her smile: it was a kid's car, a snappy red MG.

The Polynesian restaurant in Beverly Hills that she ordinarily avoided was a welcome choice in this instance; sitting at the bar, surrounded by swinging singles, Katherine was reassured that no one she knew would see her with this trenchcoated thug in Wallabys.

When he removed the coat, he kept his wool scarf on.

Ben ordered a Navy Grog for himself and a Tahitian for her. The tall, glistening white concoction went down easily. With the second one, her nervousness began to evaporate. In a rich, thrilling voice that made her wonder why he wasn't an actor, Ben was talking about growing up in the Bronx. Stickball, the Grand Concourse, the High School of Science, his mother dying when he was fourteen. Unlike most men, he'd shown no interest in talking about the newspaper; he had a strict rule about not discussing work after hours, he'd responded when she'd questioned him about it.

A third Tahitian was placed in front of her. The captain appeared behind them, whisked their drinks away, and bid them follow him under hanging ferns and over a curved bridge to a small table in the back. A mossy fountain beside it trickled water. Apart from a faint purple glow from the grotto and a tiny lamp on the table, the corner was dark. Ben ordered egg rolls and spareribs, and Katherine drank her Tahitian through a straw and smiled at him crookedly in the half-light, thinking, I know all about you; after all, I've been with the master. Had not Jed Bernard taught her every nuance, led her to the bitter end of the labyrinthine ways of Jewish men and shiksas? What could this squirt from the Grand Concourse do to her?

The waitress brought two more drinks with the appetizers. "On the house," she twinkled at Ben.

"Thanks, baby," he said.

These warm Jewish men from New York, Katherine thought; they call you "baby" right away, they touch you and burn you with their eyes and rend your heart with their tales of childhood atrocities in the ghetto. All of a sudden she remembered the so-far unmentioned fiancée in Ben's life. What was he doing here if he was so in love with someone else?

"I think I'm ready for a trip east. I need New York once in a while like a fix," he said, pronouncing it Noo Yawk. Katherine's heart turned over. He sounded like Sky Masterson in *Guys and Dolls.* A picture popped into her head of Ben meeting her parents and she thought, It's just as well he's engaged. I couldn't take him anywhere.

By the time Ben launched into a reminiscence of having been a merit scholar at the High School of Science, Katherine's mind was fogged by the accumulation of alcohol, and she caught only every other sentence. A story he told about a friend who had become an avant-garde painter, and who Ben had once accompanied to Seattle in search of his runaway sister, made her murmur, "It sounds like a movie." He smiled. "It was, sort of." Loyalty and comradeship resonated in his speech. Katherine marveled at his depth of emotion and willingness to express it. This man is really a *good person*, she told herself, and I am an insufferable snob.

It was after midnight when they left the restaurant. As they crossed the footbridge to the parking lot, Ben took Katherine's arm and quizzed her about Chryssie. "It kills me not to see my son every day," he said, "but Richie and I spend every other weekend together and several evenings a week." Another devoted Jewish father, Katherine thought wistfully.

As soon as they got in the car, Ben leaned over to kiss her, but when she ducked away, he did not press the issue. Her head spun as he sped along Sunset. At the Barrington shopping center, he turned off, muttering something about cigarettes. Everything was closed. He pulled into a small cul-de-sac hidden between giant elms, and stopped in front of a miniature faux chateau. "I'll just be a minute," he said as he got out. Then he paused, apparently thinking better of the idea, and came around to her door. "You'd better not sit out here alone. It's not safe. You might be interested in the architecture of the complex, anyway. It's more southern France than Southern California," he said as he took her hand and drew her outside. She allowed herself to be led through a courtyard to a door.

The next thing she knew, Ben was kissing her in front of his fireplace. That, a bulky sofa in front of it, and a pile of newspapers in the corner were all she could make out in the pitch dark. His mouth was open; his arms pinned her to him. Katherine felt as if she were falling down a well. Her head whirled; she opened her eyes to make it stop. Ben swept her up in his arms (no mean feat, she thought, considering his stature) and carried her down a short flight of stairs to a room that was almost filled by a double bed. He lowered her onto it. Moments later she stopped struggling, as a rapid current carried them out to sea. Nothing mattered but this surge of pure lust; not the fact that he was a stranger, not his erstwhile fiancée, not even the Roman Catholic Church's threat of damnation. They ravaged one another.

Hours later Katherine awoke face down in the damp, twisted sheets with a splitting headache. Ben was sleeping soundly, his arm thrown across her back. She inched out from under him and groped among the tangle of clothes on the floor for her watch. Clutching it and her dress, she stumbled into the bathroom, closed the door noiselessly, and clicked on the light. The room was the size of a phone booth. She ran the faucet, removed a toothbrush from a glass to fill it and, taking great gulps of cold water, focused on the shelf above the sink; a paperback book was lying amid the toothbrush and shaving paraphernalia. The title read *On Becoming a Stepfather*. Shame, remorse, regret, embarrassment fused in her head, stabbing at it with little knife thrusts. So that's why he took the phone off the hook, she thought.

Ben drove Katherine home in that murderous gray light of dawn when one feels utterly debauched being out in clothes from the night before among the milkmen's trucks and clusters of maids waiting at bus stops. She racked her brain for something to say, all the frantic intimacy of a few hours before reduced to the wary formality of seatmates on a Greyhound bus. As he made the turn onto Mandeville Canyon he glanced at her. "You are incredible in bed," he said.

"So are you," she answered, her eyes averted, and having thus congratulated each other, they drove the rest of the way in silence.

Standing awkwardly on her porch, he passed a hand through his thick orangy hair and inquired if she were free on Thursday evening. Under the yellow bug light, his cat eyes look more green than gray.

"Ben, I have to be honest," she said, sober at last. "I really thought this would be one date. Louise told me you're engaged to be married. I realize that what happened was—"

"I *have* had a serious involvement recently," he broke in, his glance unwavering. "We broke up a while ago. I don't mean to be unchivalrous, but I told Louise I was engaged the way some men wear wedding rings. It makes things easier sometimes."

"I see," said Katherine, half relieved, half put off by the egotistical male presumption that all women are predators.

"Look," he said. "I'm flying up to Sacramento tomorrow to cover the governor's press conference. I'll call you when I come back."

It wasn't until the following evening that she recalled the book in his bathroom. On a suspicious impulse, she called his apartment. A woman answered; Katherine apologized for dialing the wrong number and hung up. When Ben called three days later, she refused his invitation to dinner, then asked point-blank about the woman.

"My cousin was staying at my apartment while I was away," he said.

Blushing at her admission that she'd checked up on him, chagrined at her own paranoia, Katherine agreed to a date, then cancelled it later. The appetites unleashed by Ben Fahrengold threatened her equilibrium; he repelled and attracted her at the same time. Even though she had participated fully in the act, she felt violated by it; and though she had fought him off, she had wanted him as much as he seemed to want her. Emotions too long stifled were aroused, and they frightened her.

By the time he called again, Fate had taken the matter out of their hands.

CHAPTER 27

A Lark

"How would you like to work in our Paris office for a few months?" asked Isaac Rhodes, the vice president of Artists Unlimited, bronzed from an afternoon at the pool, barking out the question in the rapid manner of speech that even in tough-talking Hollywood had earned him the nickname Motormouth.

He had flown out from New York for a few days and called Katherine, asking her to meet him at the Beverly Hills Hotel late on a Friday afternoon. Rumors about his ruthlessness and randiness had prepared her for past experiences—to be fired or propositioned—so she was rendered speechless by his offer, and stared at him in the cool green gloom of the Polo Lounge.

"Lemme tell you what the deal is," he said. "We need somebody over there who knows the language to punch up a coupla scripts we're developing—one set in New York, the other in L.A. They're interesting concepts, but the frogs don't know their ass from their elbows about America. The best they turn out is that hokey Lelouch shit. I've read your critiques—usually I like 'em better than the fucking scripts. I personally talked AU into giving you a shot at this. It shouldn't take more than six months. Think you can do it?"

In her mind, Katherine raced through a list of considerations: Chryssie, her parents, Christopher's reaction. "Starting when?" she asked.

"First of the year." Rhodes took a leather cigar case from his inside pocket and extracted a thick brown one, rolling it between

311

his thumb and forefinger. The light caught a jewel in his onyx cuff link.

The main issue was Chryssie, Katherine thought. How would she feel about leaving Westlake in the middle of fourth grade? Aloud, she said, "My daughter's—"

"In grade school, right?" Rhodes interrupted. "So vacation's coming up. You got time to make the necessary arrangements." A waiter swung through the door behind him, and he gestured to the empty guacamole dish with his unlit cigar while he continued. "It's a great opportunity for a kid. I had mine in Bi-Lingue for seventh and eighth grades. He got the best goddamned education he's ever had. How old is—?"

"Christabel. Almost nine."

"That's a hell of a name. Sounds like a mermaid. Nine, eh? Perfect time for her to pick up a second language. By thirteen, it's all over with. Does she look like you?"

"Prettier."

"Hard to believe," he said, pulling a clippers from his inside pocket. He snapped off the end of the cigar. "She'll speak the language like a native in a month and probably skip a grade when she comes home. Now, about salary. The amount won't change much, but you'll be paid in dollars, which is a big plus. And your living expenses will be taken care of, so you'll come out way ahead."

"That includes rent?"

He flicked open a gold lighter. "Up to five hundred a month."

"Can I take a few days to think it over?"

"You can, but I wouldn't—unless you want to blow the deal, Katherine," he said between puffs. "Salzman's got a man in mind for the job. If I were you, I'd make a decision in the next three minutes. Of course, if you wanna risk it . . ." With that he leaned back and surveyed the room, his glance lingering on one of the town's most durable actress-models, who was applying lip gloss with her little finger as she gazed happily into a compact and waited for the high-powered lawyer beside her in the booth to get off the phone.

It would be good to get out of California for a while, Katherine thought. Good to get Chryssie away from the insulated world of Westlake . . . good to get away from memories. . . . Her inner eye saw Citroëns circling the Rond Point, the Arc de Triomphe bathed with light against a marine blue sky, the shops along the Faubourg

St. Honoré decorated for Christmas. "I'd love to be there for the holidays," she said half to herself.

"All the better," Rhodes replied. "You've got an extra week on AU."

Katherine set down her margarita, and with the taste of salt on her lips she said, "All right. I'll do it."

"Good girl," Rhodes said, flicking the ash from his cigar. "I get over there once a month, so we'll be in constant touch. I'm gonna give Salzman a ring right away and tell him it's a go."

He snapped his fingers for the waiter to bring him a telephone. While he gave the hotel operator the New York number of Arthur Salzman, president of AU, Katherine bit into a potato chip distractedly and thought, I'll be gone before Jed comes home for the holidays.

"Paris!" Chryssie exclaimed, her eyes dancing. "No more Westlake? *Yea!*"

So caught up was the little girl in the spirit of a new adventure that when her mother had second thoughts, she talked her out of them.

When Katherine telephoned Rochester with the news, from Emily she heard a sharp intake of breath and a quavering "Oh, Katherine, no!" "The time will pass so quickly," Katherine assured her. "We'll be back in June and come straight to Rochester to see you." Finances were Douglas's main concern; he volunteered a letter of credit, an offer Katherine was grateful to be able to decline.

Christopher had gotten used to his daughter's weekend visits and was unhappy with the turn of events, but put up no resistance as long as Katherine promised an absence not longer than six months. "Why would they ask a woman to travel?" he said in a disgruntled voice as he hung up.

When Ben Fahrengold called to ask Katherine to dinner, she told him in a remote voice that she would be out of town for several months, her mood reminiscent of Jed's withdrawal before his trips. In her head, she was already in Paris.

By the twenty-second of December, she had rented the house for six months, packed their belongings into four suitcases, and picked up two first-class tickets to Paris, courtesy of Artists Unlimited.

It was the end of a decade. Katherine had survived the sixties hidden on Jed's hill, cut off from her generation by a swinging wooden gate, safe from the blunted emotions and modern flak of altered states. She had passed the Electric Kool-Aid Acid test with no more than two puffs of marijuana. The culture of Woodstock and *Hair* receded as she boarded the Air France flight with Christabel; the idea of an ancient civilization with more traditional values shimmered before her eyes like a bright promise.

The taxi puttered to a stop outside l'hôtel France et Choiseul. Under the milky arcs of light from the streetlamps, snowflakes swirled in eddies. It was twilight, that vivid, melancholy time of day the French called *l'heure bleue*; shops were closing and people streamed along the Faubourg St. Honoré. When the bellman had brought them into the airy room, clicked back the curtains on their brass rods, and withdrawn, Chryssie fell onto one of the twin beds, giggling as she was enveloped in the clouds of a feather-filled duvet. At the window, Katherine looked out at the slate rooftops slanted against a lavender sky above Place Vendôme.

"You can see Au Nain Bleu from here," she said. Chryssie tumbled off the bed and came to the window, leaning far out. Katherine grasped the ends of her long woolen scarf. "That big toy store at the beginning of the next block. First thing tomorrow, we're going to go buy you an authentic French doll."

"What'll we name her?"

"How about . . . Solange?" Katherine asked, reeling her in.

Chryssie pursed her lips and repeated the name with a melodramatic Gallic accent, then nodded approval. Brimming with excitement, she said, "It's so fun in Paris, Mommy. Aren't you glad we did it?"

The telephone buzzed and they both turned to look at it in surprise; then Katherine remembered that Alison was in Paris en route to Megève with her new husband, Bryan Draddy, a wine importer from Los Angeles. It was the concierge calling to relay the message that the Draddys expected them at the Plaza Athénée for Christmas lunch.

Christmas morning dawned gray and bitterly cold. A crust of ice made the steps of the Madeleine glisten; people climbed them quickly, bundled in furs and scarves, their heads lowered against the wind. Chryssie had come away from Daniel Hechter with a plaid wool coat and a black knit dress with collar and cuffs of white crocheted lace; she fidgeted throughout Mass, itchy to show them off. Katherine's hair was done in a new way, coiled at the nape of her neck, and for the holiday she wore a mocha velvet midi-skirt and blouse, high-heeled boots, and a brown St. Laurent cape that made her feel intimations of a more romantic era as they entered the Plaza Athénée lobby.

Among the six people already gathered at the round table in the formal dining room were Alison; Bryan, a blond, jovial man with a booming voice; and another couple, the man an Argentinian named Eduardo Schmidt who was attached to the embassy in Paris, the stunning woman next to him not his wife, as Katherine at first presumed, but a cousin en route to Gstaad with her daughter, Silvia. A few years younger than Chryssie, Silvia started babbling to her in Spanish as soon as they sat down. On Katherine's right was a boy of twelve, whom Bryan introduced as his nephew, and who whispered to her that Silvia was fluent in French as well as Spanish but spoke not a word of English.

For the better part of lunch, the grown-ups were engrossed in a trilingual discussion of the merits of various ski trails of the Western world, so Katherine concentrated on the children, finding their unselfconscious attempts to communicate in French more amusing. She translated back and forth until they were all quite giddy; once when Silvia started talking about her father, who was meeting them in Gstaad, Chryssie's giggles threatened to spill over into tears at the thought of her own absent father.

When the group dispersed after lunch, the children ran into the lobby and Eduardo Schmidt drew Katherine aside.

"I noticed your daughter had a long face for a moment," he said kindly. "Did something happen to make her unhappy?"

She felt herself blushing under his ice-blue gaze. At the table he had ignored her to the point of rudeness, oblivious to anything but the two beautiful women on either side of him, she'd thought. "Oh . . . I . . . ," she faltered, "it had to do with her father. She was worried he was missing her, I think. She's quite all right now."

"If there is anything at all I can do to help. . . . Perhaps you would consent to have supper with me tomorrow evening?" he said. "Both of you, that is, milady."

From time to time during lunch she had sneaked a cautious glance in his direction, as one might look at a too brilliant light. He was the handsomest man she had ever laid eyes on—tall and slim, with straight dark hair, piercing light eyes, a narrow nose that flared finely at the nostrils, and lips shaped like a quiver. The cleft in his chin was almost too much—the extra brushstroke of an artist who has not yet learned restraint. What little she'd heard of his conversation indicated that he was bright, witty in a low-key sort of way, and possessed of potent Old World charm.

"Why, we'd love to," she said in a dazed voice.

The following evening he took them to the Bar des Théâtres, where they ate *poulet rôti* and drank rosé next to a woman who was dining with a terrier. Eduardo was full of plans for them: "You must let me take you to La Coupole, my favorite restaurant in Paris; on Sunday we'll go to the Jardins d'Acclimatation so Christabel can see *les singes*—the monkeys—and we might all go skiing after the New Year. Have you been to Verbier?"

Her jaw working strenuously on a crust of bread, Chryssie widened her eyes at her mother. Katherine blinked back at her. Was this happening? they seemed to say to each other. Or had they died and gone to heaven?

A week of excursions with Chryssie was capped by New Year's Eve, when, after tucking her in at the hotel with her new doll, Eduardo took Katherine to a party at the embassy. There it appeared that everyone from the footmen to the ambassador, and especially the ambassador's wife, was enchanted with him. An orchestra played South American rhythms in the great marble hall; at midnight a dazzling international crowd toasted the new year with Cristal; and on the veranda, where they had gone to watch the passing of the Bateau Mouche, Eduardo bent to kiss Katherine with his perfect bowed lips. "I am madly in love with you, *mi amor*," he murmured.

"But how could you possibly be?" she responded. "We've barely known each other a week!"

"Ah, you pragmatic *gringas!*" he chided. "I fell in love the first day watching you with the children. It takes only a moment to recognize one's true destiny."

Though his words were heady stuff, it seemed likely they were romantic Latin hyperbole, she thought, and suggested as much.

"Not a drop of Latin blood flows in my veins," he informed her. "I am English and German. It's only my self-deprecating way to call myself a Chicano."

For the two years since his wife had left him for an elderly French count of enormous wealth, Eduardo had divided his living quarters between a room he let in a house in Neuilly belonging to an elderly baroness, and the flat of a Brazilian girlfriend.

"Her name is Elida," he told Katherine. "She is a stewardess, and is only in Paris once a month. That I have fallen in love will come as no great surprise—only that I have fallen in love with a *gringa*!"

A brace of white balloons were released into the air. Katherine looked up, following their ascent in the black velvet sky. One floated across the river toward the glimmering lights of Ile de la Cité. Sheltering her in his arms, his lips against her hair, Eduardo murmured, "One day we will go to Buenos Aires together, Katerina. Tonight, I have burned all my bridges. We will live together, and when the time is right, *mi amor*, we will marry."

The ambassador, a corpulent fellow with a white mustache, wandered outside with a visiting dignitary's wife. They chatted briefly, then he exchanged a few words in Spanish with Eduardo. When a tango lured the older couple back to the ballroom, Eduardo looked down at Katherine, his eyes alight. "He said it looks as though I've been caught; I replied that I am, happily so."

A daily search of the *Paris Herald-Tribune* turned up an advertisement for a four-month sublet on Ile St. Louis. The multileveled, antique-filled apartment, a fifth-floor walk-up on the quai with a balcony overlooking the Seine and the spires of Notre Dame was a miraculous find. Eager for dollars, the owner was delighted to let Katherine have it. Bi-Lingue accepted Chryssie for winter term; the Artists Unlimited offices were conveniently located near Parc Monceau; the writer to whom Katherine had been assigned was a young woman who did not seem averse to working with an American. It was an astounding run of good luck. On January third, Eduardo left for Rome on a business trip. Katherine kissed him good-bye with a sense that destiny had brought her half-way round the world to find him. "When you come back on Monday," she told him, "we'll be at Quai d'Orléans." Early Sunday morning, the telephone jangled her awake at the France et Choiseul. She threw off the duvet and sat up, then remembered where she was and said, *"Allo, oui?"* into the receiver. A low, familiar voice growled, "Cripple? Is that you? I'm at the George V. You want to have a little lunch?"

"Jed! What are you doing here?" she cried. In the bed next to her, Chryssie opened her eyes and smiled.

"It was a shock to me to discover you and the knibbler gone when I came home. Why would you leave town? I *ferpached* the movie. That cocksucker Federland's taking it apart in the cutting room but, fuck 'im. The thing's frigging brilliant no matter what he does. Even so, Hollywood's finished for me. I'm too old for that bullshit."

Katherine fell back against the pillow, laughing as she had not done for what suddenly seemed a very long time.

Promising to bring Jed there directly after lunch, Katherine dropped Chryssie off at the Plaza Athénée to see the Draddys, who were on their way home from Megève. Then she walked through side streets to the George V. The perpetual clouds of that Parisian winter were clearing, so that bright blue patches of sky showed through. As soon as she came into the lobby she saw Jed, standing at the desk, chatting with a jet-set type with pomaded hair who had a camel's hair coat slung over his shoulders.

"Hi, kid," Jed said casually, kissing her cheek. "Katherine Kellogg . . . my old friend, Guy de la Vincolioli, a principe or some fucking thing."

"Gaetano della Vincenzoni," the man murmured as his lips brushed the air above her hand. "Are you sure you won't bring your friend and come with me to Montmartre, Jed? There is a bistro there that serves the best *belons* in Paris. It's called Chez Quelqu'un . . . Mère Quelque chose—the name escapes me, but I am determined to find it."

"No thanks, Guy. Ciao."

"Ciao. Ciao, bella." The prince's coat swung around him as he swept to the door, which was opened by a bowing attendant.

"Him I don't believe altogether," Jed muttered to Katherine. "Fucking Biafra's starving to death and this putz is looking for oysters." He gave her a bemused look that made her feel too self-consciously *à la mode* in the midi-skirt and laced-up boots. "Been *reising* at Dior, I see. You look good, kid," he said.

She returned the compliment. His elegant herringbone tweed suit, striped shirt, and black knit tie were new to her. He bragged about losing ten pounds and she remarked that he fairly glowed with success, relieved to see that he no longer needed her as a nursemaid.

It was nearly two, and most of the tables in the dining room were occupied. The maître d'hôtel, whose dour face brightened at the sight of Jed, showed them to a small table beside French doors that gave onto the garden, where islands of melting snow dotted the barren flower beds. Waving the menus away, Jed requested two glasses of table wine and the fish *du jour*.

He rattled on to Katherine about *What a World!* until a waiter wheeled a service table over and uncovered a chafing dish; it simmered with a delicately sautéed sole. When he had served it and moved away, a silence fell over the table, underscored by the rapid flow of French conversation on all sides. Aware of Jed's eyes on her, Katherine lowered hers.

"So," he said after a moment. "Have you fallen in love over here?"

She sat very still, the fish blurring under her scrutiny. She *was* in love, she reminded herself. She mustn't let seeing Jed confuse her—how *could* she still be worried about hurting him? Dr. West had told her that was absurd a year ago; since then Jed had as much as abandoned her. Even so, it took all the strength she had to lift her eyes to his.

"Yes," she replied.

The color drained from his face. His skin seemed to contract over his features. Recovering quickly, he assumed an expression of polite curiosity. "A Frog?" he inquired.

"South American. He lives here, though."

"He's not in show business, right?"

"No. He's a"—she paused, thinking, This is going to kill him—"a diplomat."

Jed's face remained impassive. "Divorced?"

"Getting one. They don't have divorce in Argentina, so . . ." She trailed off as he fixed her with an owlish stare.

"Jewish?"

She shook her head.

"Catholic?"

She nodded, shredding the fish with her fork.

"But that's good, kid," he said in a false, strained voice. "It's better for you. What's his name?"

"Eduardo," she replied, the fish like sawdust in her mouth. "Eduardo Schmidt."

Jed's fork hit the plate with a clatter. "Hello, operator! Herr Schmidt from Argentina?" He leaned back in his chair, staring at her with a stricken expression. After a pause he said slowly, "I always knew you'd leave me, but I never thought you'd leave me for a Nazi."

Katherine started to laugh, and as the humor struck her with full force, she was unable to stop.

"A Nazi, do you believe that? A frigging Nazi. Well, Mrs. Himmler, how are things running at the camps?"

Oh, it was perfect material for him, she thought, tears of laughter and regret springing in her eyes. "Stop, Jed . . . stop," she begged.

Abruptly, he did.

"How long could you have known him?" he asked.

She flushed and looked away. "Ten days."

"Perfectly normal," he said snidely.

The maître d' bustled up to the table. "*Tout va bien*, Monsieur Bernard?"

"*Pas mal*," Jed shot back, and made a gruff request for the bill that sent the man scurrying to his station. After a moment, Jed said in a hard voice, "There's one thing. You could have told me *before* lunch. I need this—to sit here and watch you eat the fish and have you tell me you're in love."

"You asked," she said faintly; then resentment edged out remorse. "I don't believe this. What was I supposed to think after the way you treated me in New York? You were so cold . . . so *mean*. It took me long enough, God knows, but I finally got it through my head that you didn't love me."

"Did you ever think maybe it was because I loved you the most?" he said hoarsely.

"Well, that's just *sick*!"

"No," he said. "It's a fact of Jewish life."

"And then when I called you about the house, you were—"

"I kept telling you," he broke in. "You just had to let me get through the frigging movie."

"And the next few months and the next few years . . ."

His mouth was a stubborn line. "Ask anybody in New York. I was going to marry you, probably." Seeing her smile at the "probably," he cried, "It was in Earl Wilson's column, you putz, you!"

"I guess I missed that one."

"A little thing like that . . ." He trailed off with a helpless shrug.

The waiter presented the check on a silver plate. Jed gave it a cursory glance, snarled "For *what?*" under his breath, and scrawled his name on the bottom. "Come on, crip," he said, got up quickly, and walked out of the dining room ahead of her.

When she came into the lobby he had retrieved his British army coat from the checkroom and was standing at the door, squinting into the graying light of avenue George V. She went over to him and started to say something, but he cut her off. "Come on, I want to see the knibbler, and then I'm going straight to fucking Israel. Just do me a favor and don't speak at all, do you follow me?"

He turned up his collar and went through the doors ahead of her. They waited in the cold on opposite sides of the inner drive, looking at the ground, the barren trees lining the avenue, anything but each other while the doorman summoned a taxi. During the short ride to the Plaza Athénée, Jed sat in silence, his eyes averted, his hand clenched in a fist on the seat of the Citroën. Katherine could not see his expression, but the set of his shoulders told her enough. She reached out and touched his hand. It was ice-cold. "Jed," she said softly, "I'm so sorry."

Without turning his head, he said only, "You should have told me before the fish."

While Katherine stayed upstairs in their suite with the Draddys, Jed took Chryssie for tea at the Relais. After he left, she trudged along Rue de la Tremoille beside her mother in search of a taxi, her little face pinched with cold. In a strong, clear voice, she declared suddenly, "I'll always love Jed, no matter what anyone says."

"That's a funny way to put it, but I know what you mean. Me, too," Katherine said.

"I wish—" Chryssie said and broke off.

"What do you wish?"

"I wish we could put Jed and Eduardo together and have one man."

Katherine smiled at the recurring feminine theme of the composite husband. "Which half would Jed be?" she asked.

"The head," Chryssie replied promptly. "Where the jokes come from."

Jed left for Israel in the morning. "Don't do anything rash, kid," he cautioned Katherine when he called from Orly to say goodbye. "A man like that—a South American Nazi—he'll be at your

feet or at your throat. If you want, I'll take you both to dinner when
I come back."

"That'd be great, Jed," she replied. She felt pounds lighter,
buoyed on a cloud of gratitude and relief. To lose Jed Bernard as a
lover was bearable; to lose him altogether would have killed her.

She had gotten through it . . . things had worked out for the
best . . . Eduardo and she were the same religion . . . Jed had
mistreated her for too long, hurt her too much . . . the age difference was too great for them to survive romantically . . . friends were
what they always should have been. Like a litany Katherine repeated these phrases to herself in the days that followed; days and
nights she passed through with romantic blinders on.

While Chryssie lay sleeping in her little Parisian bedroom,
watched over by blue figures of shepherdesses on the walls, a grand
passion swept Katherine and Eduardo through the nights in a curtained bed that seemed like a galleon with its unobstructed view of
the Seine. Before dawn, at her insistence, he would creep down the
five flights of wooden stairs and past a nodding concierge, then drive
through the Bois to his room in Neuilly.

Katherine had met his titled landlady a few times; she was a
woman of ineffable chic whose opinions on spoiled, ill-mannered
American children took a nosedive when she encountered the curt-
seying Christabel. Her daughter's affinity for a foreign language and
culture astounded Katherine. Even in her sleep, the little girl spoke
in French. She quickly acquired a lusty accent as well as a different,
more self-confident manner in her foreign persona, making friends
easily at Bi-Lingue. At the beginning of March, the day before her
ninth birthday, Jed called from the George V.

"I'm on my way home, crip," he said to Katherine. "You want
to have dinner tonight, you and Edward-o?"

"Sure." Eduardo was prepared for the eventuality, and as he'd
pointed out, he was a diplomat. Now that their love was secure, she
could handle it, Katherine told herself.

"Tomorrow's the knibbler's birthday, right? We could all go to
lunch at the Plaza."

"Oh, she'd love that, Jed."

He was taking it better than anyone, she thought.

They met at Le Volga, a Russian restaurant Jed had frequented in the old days with Laura. He blinked when he saw Eduardo coming toward him, improbably handsome in a navy-blue blazer and gray trousers, his arm linked possessively through Katherine's, but they got through the introductions smoothly. Jed tailored his conversation so that the evening progressed in a civilized, amusing fashion, although his eyes tended to glaze over when Eduardo went on too long about Parisian society. An hour passed. Why, Katherine wondered nervously, did Eduardo's looks seem to be fading? Why did Jed, who was more than fifteen years older and not as classically handsome, seem so much more vital, alive, and ultimately *better* looking? Beside him, Eduardo's Old World courtliness and finesse seemed a bit pompous and ridiculous. Jed had not glanced her way for several minutes, and Eduardo, though he'd complained about the indignity of dining with her "old boyfriend," now seemed taken with Jed and oblivious to the undercurrent of tension.

The floor show began. There was violin music, and then a burly baritone in peasant garb stepped into the spotlight. Beneath the white shirt, his muscles swelled; his thighs strained against his rough trousers. When he opened his mouth to sing, his deep voice boomed through the small room like thunder over the steppes of Asia.

"Did you ever hear anything like that?" Katherine asked in an awed voice.

"Amazingly powerful," Eduardo agreed.

Jed leaned forward and confided, "The man is the *fag* of his village."

That did it. Katherine burst out laughing; Jed launched into one of his hilarious nonstop routines that had her doubled over with mirth while Eduardo veered between amusement and jealousy, an obvious outsider.

It was after midnight when their taxi drew up to the George V and Jed got out. Katherine ached with sadness as she watched him go inside alone. It seemed completely unnatural, heartless to drive away with another man. Staunchly she reminded herself of Jed's recent revelation: he had hired a pretty young secretary away from Paul Federland after the film was completed, and she was now ensconced in his house. Let someone else feed Simon, she thought, hardening her heart against the urge to cry out, to run after Jed.

As promised, he took them all to lunch at the Relais Plaza for Chryssie's birthday. For the occasion he assumed an avuncular role.

He chatted with Chryssie about her school, quizzed Eduardo about his duties at the embassy, evinced some perplexity about his living arrangements.

"It is not uncommon," Eduardo explained, "for titled Europeans to share their digs with someone who has the proper credentials."

Jed nodded, the muscles in his jaw working. Toward the end of lunch, he asked Chryssie what she wanted most for her birthday.

Without hesitation, she said, "A cake."

"Close your eyes and wish for it," Jed told her.

When she did, he motioned to a hovering waiter and a moment later she opened them to see a chocolate cake, ablaze with candles, in front of her. She did a long slow take.

Katherine looked at Jed with astonished eyes. "Excuse me, how long have you been a magician?"

A rather noisy group of South Americans entered the Relais; several of them hailed Eduardo, and when they were seated, he went over to say hello.

Jed's eyes followed him, his head moving back and forth with admiration. "The man has the best fucking table manners I've ever seen in my life. He lives with a contessa, eh?"

"A baroness," Katherine mumbled.

Rubbing the corner of his eye, Jed inquired, "When are the two of you getting married?"

Katherine raised her head and met his gaze. The subtly shifting moods of the last two days had left her feeling cornered, confused, and very defensive. "I don't know if we will, but even if we don't, it's the love story of the century!" she said fervently.

Jed looked at her deadpan. "Certainly not *this* century," he said.

For three months after Jed left Paris, Eduardo was loving, thoughtful, affectionate with Chryssie, all in all, Katherine thought, the perfect Aryan man. Then, as if Jed had cast a spell on him, his essential nature surfaced, and he alternated between being at her feet or at her throat. In public, he began to indulge in irrational fits of jealousy; in private, if their opinions clashed, he chastised her for "disobedience." When she objected to his imperious attitude, he accused her of tolerating behavior far worse from Jed Bernard. True, she thought, but to explain the difference would have been cruel.

Her introspective side, her tendency to analyze motivation, Eduardo denigrated as the American obsession with psychiatry; America, in fact, took a lot of heat for their basic incompatibility. Politics became their battleground. Newly attuned to South American culture, she started to ask probing questions about his country's record on torture and starvation. "No baby has ever died of starvation in Argentina!" he declared hotly. "How do you know?" she asked. "We have the best statistics in the world," he maintained. "Fine," she replied. "Whatever you say, Marie Antoinette." The appellation sent him into a rage. He struck her; later, tearfully, he brought her roses and begged forgiveness. The simplest meal she prepared for him at home drew extravagant praise, but while he consumed it, he watched television as if she and Chryssie were not present. A nostalgia grew in Katherine for the old days when Jed would push away the food in disgust, then talk to her by the hour. Passion, she discovered, was no substitute for warmth.

In May she assessed the pros and cons. Under Eduardo's influence, she had learned to wield a knife and fork like a queen, make love like a courtesan, and speak passable Spanish, but something was missing: the sound of her own laughter. Before long she found herself following Jewish tourists down the Champs Elysées, hoping to hear some jokes.

CHAPTER 28

Forbidden Fruit

Douglas's words were barely audible over the trans-Atlantic wire. "Mother's had a stroke, Katie," he said, a tragic quaver in his voice.

"Oh, no, Daddy," Katherine gasped.

"It happened at the end of April."

"My God! Why didn't you let me know?"

"There wasn't much you could . . ." His voice was swallowed up in static. ". . . didn't want to disrupt . . . job over there . . . Margot here for a while. . . ."

She drew the sad details from him: they had taken Aunt Doris, who was recently widowed, to the Colonial Inn for dinner on a Thursday evening; as they were ordering, Emily had suddenly started to garble her words. Now she was at St. Ann's Home, partially paralyzed, receiving speech therapy. "Your going off upset her quite a bit, you know," he said heavily, "and then . . . ." Here his voice faded out, but she knew what he'd been about to say. When she'd written to them that Eduardo wanted to marry her, his reply was: "He's a divorced man, Katie. You can't break *all* God's laws."

"Chryssie and I will take a plane the day after tomorrow," she said firmly. "Bi-Lingue's almost out anyway, and the owners of the apartment are coming back. We'll be there by the weekend."

He let out a shaky breath. "It'll be good to see you."

Katherine called Isaac Rhodes in New York and asked for a leave of absence. Then she packed their things, took Chryssie out of school a week early, and said a hasty good-by to Eduardo, giving only a vague response to his queries about when they would return.

The look in his eyes when they drove away in the taxi made her recall Jed's words: "You don't give a fellow much security, Katherine. You've always got one hand on your kid and one foot out the window."

By the time they got to Rochester, Douglas had suffered a heart attack and was recuperating in St. Mary's Hospital, across the street from Emily's convalescent home. Leaving Chryssie in the care of one of her cousins, the Stokes's eldest son, Kevin, who had a houseful of children, Katherine took a cab to see her parents.

When she'd called them from the airport to say good-bye only five months before, they'd been vital and healthy, she recalled as she walked down the corridor at St. Ann's, steeling herself for the deterioration that must have occurred in her mother. But nothing she imagined could have prepared her for the reality that awaited.

The door to Emily's room was ajar. Marooned in a wheelchair at its center, dressed in Emily's silk nightgown and bedjacket, a shriveled old woman with iron-gray hair stared at something only she could see, calling out in a piteous voice, "Mama . . . Mama . . . Mama . . ." Katherine went over and knelt before her, taking her ringless hand in hers; Emily's was limp, the nails short and unpolished. She focused on her daughter's face, but her sullen expression did not change. Her eyes were unblinking and bewildered, like those of an animal in pain. Katherine's heart contracted. As surely as if she'd delivered a blow to her mother's head, she thought, she bore the responsibility for this. The indictment was written on Emily's sunken face: by gallivanting to another continent, Katherine had put both parents away.

Since the original stroke, the speech therapist explained, a series of small strokes, like aftershocks, had aggravated Emily's condition. He illustrated how she could no longer distinguish among objects by holding up a number of flashcards; at each one, Emily pressed her lips tightly shut and shook her head. But a spark in her eye aroused Katherine's suspicions. She gripped her mother's shoulder and raised her voice. "This is costing a lot of money, Mother," she said sternly. "The least you can do is try." The therapist frowned in disapproval. Emily fingered one of the cards, pouting. On it was a large drawing of a pepper shaker. "Salt," said Emily with difficulty. "Mother," Katherine said severely. Emily shrugged and mumbled, "Pepper." The therapist flashed several more at her; she identified them all correctly.

"I had no idea she was capable of doing that," he admitted as he walked with Katherine to the elevator.

Savoring this minor triumph, she went across the street to see her father. Douglas was weak but out of danger, concerned mainly with his wife's condition. The scene with the therapist set him to chuckling merrily, but Emily's improvement was short-lived. Stubbornly she set her will against the therapist's; not even Katherine's bullying succeeded in getting her to make an effort in the physical therapy room. Finally, after two weeks, everyone agreed that she should be moved to Mapleridge, the modern, efficiently run sanitarium where Margot had arranged to have her transferred should she not recover. The house on Windsor Court was a few miles away. Katherine and Chryssie brought Douglas home shortly after Emily was installed at Mapleridge, and every afternoon they went to visit her.

One morning toward the end of June, Katherine called Isaac Rhodes in New York and asked if her job was still available in California. AU wanted her to continue in Paris, he said. Salzman had replaced her with a man in Los Angeles. Compared to the life-and-death struggle at home, doctoring screenplays in a foreign language seemed irrelevant; she told him she'd have to think it over. Eduardo's solicitous telephone calls seemed as remote as if they'd been beamed from another planet.

Only Jed's black humor cheered her up; when she first called to tell him why she'd come back to the States, he'd responded, "Ba . . . by! Mother *and* father, eh? My, my. It's not every day you meet a girl with both parents *ferpacht* at the same time. When's the reading of the will?" Irreverent he might be, but he never failed to listen, he never failed to make her laugh. He had a new girlfriend, he told her. Someone he'd met in Israel who had come to live with him on the hill. They were happy, and he didn't have to worry about her calling him a dirty Jew. Katherine felt a twinge of envy for the latest resident on the hill.

The house on Windsor Court was far too big for Douglas, the stairs impossible for him to negotiate alone. He and Katherine interviewed several nurses, and finally hired a cheerful, talkative woman in her fifties, who took immediate charge of him. With things fairly stabilized in Rochester, Katherine and Chryssie flew to Los Angeles at the beginning of August. A cable arrived before they did. Eduardo would be there at the end of the week to convince them to return with him to Paris.

The evening before he was due to arrive, Katherine and Chryssie dined on the hill with Jed and his Israeli girlfriend. Her name was Nurith, and she was like a sparrow, small-boned, delicate, with a melodic voice and a spine of steel. Chryssie took to her immediately; they had a similar childlike quality, and before supper, they stretched out side by side on the floor of the study, their faces propped in their hands to watch *The Brady Bunch*, Hollywood's latest rendition of life in the all-American family, which was equally foreign to both of them. Jed's movie, *What a World!*, was about to be released, and Nurith spent the early part of supper coaxing him to give her a private screening before the premiere. As they were having coffee, she grew insistent about Jed redoing the guest room for her. His growing irritation was obvious in his abrupt replies. She persisted nonetheless. Finally, Chryssie called a friendly warning from across the room. "You won't get to see the movie!"

"That's right!" Jed cried, a smile breaking across his face at her understanding and acceptance of the way he operated. "You're the most practical person I ever knew, Univac. If Nurith had your sense, I'd marry her immediately."

Chryssie beamed at the complicity between them. They had found their way together, Katherine thought, and in his own way Jed was as irreplaceable as Christopher in her daughter's life.

The changes that had taken place in herself, however, led Katherine to the conclusion that Sonia was right: she had tried to tackle far too much with Jed. To have known him in a lifetime was sufficient; to have married him, given their interlocking neuroses, would have been a case of wretched excess. When all was said and done, she loved him, would always love him. Ironically it had taken breaking up with him to show her how durable that love was. Whatever harm she'd once thought he'd done to her was far outweighed by the good. She liked Nurith, but she no longer envied her, and she suspected that she wouldn't last. How rare it was for love to evolve into true friendship, she reflected. It made physical obsession seem cheap—nearly, but not quite, unappealing by comparison.

The next day, Eduardo arrived in Los Angeles. Here, in the pitiless glare of the Southern California sunlight, it was even more obvious how wrong for each other they were. But both were German and stubborn. In dogged attempts to bridge their cultural-sexual gap, Katherine read passages aloud to him from *The Female Eunuch*; however, like dropping bombs on an enemy, it only made him dig in his heels. Jed's periodic telephone calls infuriated him; he began to monitor her outgoing calls as well. Once Wolf Adams answered the phone at Jed's house. "Hello, Katherine," he said pleasantly. "You're calling from a gas station, I presume?"

Was Nurith similarly irritated when they spoke? Katherine asked Jed. "It's not a discussion, Katherine," he replied. "You and Chryssie are *mishpoche*. Anyone that's with me is going to have to accept that. It goes with the black suit."

The last days of summer coincided with the end of Katherine's tolerance for Eduardo's domineering personality. He flew back to Paris vowing to find an obedient woman. Chryssie's newfound confidence made her eager to tackle Westlake again, and when Katherine confirmed that they were staying in California, she let out a whoop of joy. But then her forehead wrinkled. "What are *you* going to do, Mommy?"

"Quit Artists Unlimited. Go to school. Get my degree after all."

"That's good," Chryssie said, nodding encouragingly, as if they were the most brilliant ideas anyone ever had.

In the year that followed, Katherine remained aloof from romance while being steeped in the Romantic Age at UCLA. The usefulness of a degree escaped her, especially since earning one required a steady diet of poetry, but she had a sense of something unfinished, incomplete, and it was the first decision she could remember making in years that won her father's approval. Trips to Rochester to see her parents were increasingly painful; her mother was deteriorating at Mapleridge, speaking only in broken phrases; the last complete sentence she'd uttered to Katherine, early in the spring, was "I . . . hate . . . your . . . hair." You had to laugh, Katherine thought.

Gradually Douglas lost heart in the house on Windsor Court Road without his wife; in the spring, crippled with phlebitis, he expressed a desire to be near her, and was admitted to a private room in another wing at Mapleridge. Every afternoon, their nurses would wheel them into the solarium where they would sit side by side, dozing, their wheelchairs facing the garden, their hands clasped.

For the weeks that Chryssie was in summer camp, Katherine stayed in Rochester. When they returned to Los Angeles in the fall, having fulfilled her requirements for an English major, she decided to fill in the gaps left by a convent education, and signed up for courses in Kierkegaard and Modern Russian History.

The latter course was taught by an ex-Barnard professor named Lilian Bauer, who had recently moved to California from New York with her husband, Aaron, an attorney, and their nine-year-old daughter, Joy. On campus, Lilian was spoken of as an exciting lec- turer. She was a small, compact woman with large expressive eyes set in an angular face; a mass of crimped black hair was subdued in a ponytail during class, but often, bicycling around from one build- ing to another, she would pull off the elastic so the hair flowed down her back like an Indian's. A spirited exchange of ideas between her and Katherine began in class one December morning and continued in the Student Union over coffee. The two women became friends, partly because they were the same age amid coeds, and both had young daughters, but also because they found that the same things struck them funny. Lilian's moral support helped Katherine through the grim morning she spent in a Los Angeles courthouse, dissolving her marriage to Christopher. The difference in their religions—Lili- an's Judaism and Katherine's Catholicism—was not a factor in their friendship; only when Katherine discussed Jed did the subject arise. Then one afternoon in the spring, when they had gone to Lilian's apartment for lunch after class, she took her Scarsdale High School yearbook from the bookcase and presented it to Katherine with an enigmatic smile. "The ones circled in red were my boyfriends," she said on her way to the kitchen.

Seated on the couch with the book on her lap, Katherine began to laugh as she turned the pages. "When did you first notice this propensity for boys who look like Robert Redford?" she asked.

Lilian came to the kitchen door and leaned against it, a large wooden salad bowl propped against her hip. "I was thirteen—on the dot. I had a friend with five brothers, all of them blond, and I said to myself, 'Now this is what I like!'"

"Really?"

"Of course, I never could bring them home or invite them to a party. They were all forbidden fruit. Billy McGuire was forbidden fruit, Oliver Kirby was forbidden fruit, Jim Frye was forbidden fruit. Our neighborhood in Scarsdale was ninety percent Jewish. I just loved the way WASPs looked. Mind you, I liked Jewish boys' personalities better. I could handle them."

"And you couldn't handle WASPs?"

Lilian set the bowl on the counter and went to sit with Katherine. "You know the way Jewish men intimidate you?"

Katherine nodded.

"Well," Lilian said, "WASPs left me speechless. Tongue-tied."

"Not because you were bored?"

"What do you mean? I hung on their words! Part of the fascination was—I later figured out in analysis—if you control everything your whole life—and I could control my father, my brothers, any Jewish boy I'd ever come across—now here is a man who is not only good-looking, but I can't control him! I completely lost my personality at first. I only said, 'Yes . . . I agree . . . I see what you mean.'"

"I would venture to say that people who met me the first two years I was with Jed thought that I was unable to speak."

Lilian smiled. "I'm sure of it. My brother prefers Gentile girls because he says they're more docile. Jewish girls challenge. It's an unspoken language we all know."

"Who's 'we all'?"

"Jewish people."

"Including the women?"

"Es*pec*ially the women."

Katherine's eyes widened in surprise. "No one has ever been willing to admit that to me except you."

Lilian got up and returned the yearbook to its place on the shelf. "My guess is that my female friends would disagree with me if you were here, but when you left, they'd agree. It's like family secrets. I happen to think it would be a good idea to bring it out in the open—the truth shall set you free, and all that."

"But you do talk about it among yourselves?"

Lilian crossed her arms and leaned against the bookcase. "I would say it's almost a preoccupational discussion, particularly among my unmarried friends. It's not a myth—WASP men are treated quite differently in a sexual context. The men we marry see another side of us altogether. Gentile men were fun for me, almost like a toy. They couldn't really criticize me because they weren't one of us." Suddenly she straightened, staring at Katherine. "Why am I telling you this, you long-legged, blue-eyed blonde! You're one of those people who's been stealing our men! It's a triangle." She went back to the kitchen.

Katherine laughed and followed her. "What was it that you liked about WASP men especially?"

"Their briefcases," Lilian replied after a moment's consideration.

"What? Jews don't carry briefcases?"

"Not the monogrammed kind. They carry the ones their mothers gave them. Also, WASP boys had a certain haircut"—her hands sliced the air above her ears—"blunt. And they wore Topsiders. Jewish boys in Scarsdale had a sort of pseudo-Brooks Brothers *zhlub* look. They tried but you can't imitate the real thing."

"What do you think WASPs liked best about you? Intelligence, humor?"

"My Jewishness," Lilian said flatly. "And my sexuality. Not too hard to figure that one out—it's more exciting if it's outside the club. It was pure lust with WASPs."

"Would you have married one if you hadn't met Aaron?"

"Never," Lilian said, slicing a carrot into the salad bowl. "In the Jewish religion, sex is not grounds for marriage. What's more important is, do I want to build a family with this person? Do we share common goals? Even now, in the seventies, deep down in our cultural roots, sex is not that important."

Hearing this, Katherine smiled at the similarity to her mother's philosophy. The English sheepdog, Buber, lumbered into the kitchen; she leaned down to pet him, thinking aloud, "I never could accept that as a child . . . maybe not even now, but certainly not from my parents."

"The big difference is that Christian society is patriarchal. The father is in charge. It's a different sociological setup. With Jews, the woman is in charge."

Katherine repeated what Jed had told her about the relationship between his grandparents. "According to him," she concluded, "his grandmother never opened her mouth!"

"But the *bubbe* is still in charge," Lilian repeated adamantly. She put two plates beside the salad bowl on a tray and carried it into a small sunporch off the living room.

"Even if she's married to a rabbi?" Katherine asked as they sat down at the wicker table.

"Especially," Lilian said. "His only concern is study. Her job as the *rebbetsin* is to run everything else so he doesn't have to think about it. At a dinner table he might expound all night while she doesn't speak, but it's irrelevant. Who listens to him anyway? she thinks. She does what she wants."

Katherine propped her chin in her hand, shaking her head. "That's totally foreign to me."

Lilian smiled as she unloaded the tray. "Aaron was married before, you know, to a tall, blond, blue-eyed girl. They had screaming matches all the time." She paused and met Katherine's eyes with her large, black ones. "Joy's going to be ten next week. Our marriage works," she said. "He's like me . . . myself . . . the same thing. We speak a tacit language. You see, Kate, what you were doing with Jed was a symptom. You can't solve a sickness by identifying the symptom, you have to find the cause."

Katherine was silent. Was she being barred from the club? she thought with a quick flash of resentment. Was this wonderful life Lilian had with a man who shunned goyishe pursuits like regattas, boozing, and shooting live animals for fun unavailable to her because of her roots? She refused to accept it.

Driving home from Lilian's that afternoon, Katherine contemplated the void in her heart and acknowledged that she longed for the Jewish romantic connection, had in fact spent the last year looking for substitutes. When Eduardo was in Los Angeles, she'd taken to going into Greenburg's Dry Cleaners for a fix of humor and warmth. And in the long period of celibacy since he'd left, she could have said at any given time that she was in love with twelve Jewish men: Jed, of course, always Jed; then her internist, Dr. Hidelman; her gynecologist, Dr. Sauerstein; all the men behind the counter at Nate 'n' Al's; and Chryssie's orthodontist, Dr. Fine (never, however, her onetime shrink, Dr. West, that strange, pear-shaped man who colored his hair with shoe polish and wore a vest on the hottest days, but there was always the exception that proved the rule). No wonder Jed's a hypochondriac, she thought. With doctors like that, you pray to get sick just to see them. They keep a person going in fallow romantic periods.

The television was going full blast in the study. Chryssie and her friend, Jenny, who was in her car pool, were lying on their backs on the floor, looking a bit like Martians in their orthodontic neck gear, their respective cats on their chests, their eyes riveted on David

Cassidy in *The Partridge Family* (headed by a single mother at last, Katherine noted). Without looking up, Chryssie said, "Jed called from London—his movie's number one. And there's a message on the service. Some lady called from Rochester."

CHAPTER 29

Death and Love

"Your mom passed away last night, Kate."

The speaker was Marian, one of the battalion of nurses who had attended Emily around the clock at Mapleridge for the two years since her stroke. They fed and bathed her, turned her paralyzed body every hour, emptied the wretched catheter bag, and sat beside her night and day, soothing her with reassuring words, their fingers busy with knitting or needlepoint during the endless hours while Emily stared into space. Wheeling her mother into the solarium a few months before, Katherine had thought, The Practical Joker is at it again. Fiddling around with fearful symmetry. Loquacious Emily, to whom she'd once retorted, when accused of interrupting, "You were born talking, Mother, and according to you, anyone who's said anything since is interrupting," was unable to speak at all.

Now she was dead. Not "passed away," thought Katherine, flinching at the euphemism. Dead.

She stood very still with the telephone to her ear. It was the last thing anyone would have expected, that her mother would go first and her father would be the one left behind.

They buried Emily in the Winterhaus family plot at Holy Sepulchre Cemetery. Spring is a particularly poignant time of year for an interment, lowering a casket into the earth that all around is bursting with new life. Katherine left Chryssie in Los Angeles and came to the funeral dry-eyed, mentally braced against the horror of confrontation with mortality at the side of an open grave. It was only

later, after the reception in her father's room at Mapleridge, after
she had watched him hold his head at that straight, proud angle and
answered all his questions about what a lovely service it was and
how pleased Emily would have been at the turnout, after she had
had dinner with Margot (whose resentment of her mother appeared
unaltered by death), and was back in her room at the Country Club,
lying awake in the dark at midnight, that the tears came. She wept
for her father, for Christabel, and for Emily—not the cold, resentful
woman she had become in the last years before the stroke, and not
for the wasted, dispirited skeleton in the hospital bed; these she
blocked out as tears fell. She wept for a memory, faded as an old
snapshot: Emily, laughing at Eddie Frankel's jokes; Emily, after a
party, beautiful in a blue sequined gown, leaning over Katie's bed
at Windsor Court to kiss her good night and finding the forbidden
radio still warm; Emily, smelling of Fleurs de Rocailles and mink,
letting Katie sleep with her head on her lap on the long winter rides
back to Rock Beach; Emily, taking her to see Ginger Rogers in *Kitty
Foyle* on a school night, after a quarrel with Margot. Lines from Rupert Brooke came back to her:

> *These hearts were woven of human joys and cares . . .*
> *. . . Felt the quick touch of wonder, sat alone;*
> *Touched flowers and furs and cheeks,*
> *All this is ended.*

And the tears she shed were a child's tears; the loss not of
Emily, but of a mother.

The day after the funeral, Katherine expected to find her father steeped in grief. But when she walked into his room at ten
o'clock, she saw him sitting up as usual in the beige Naugahyde
chair, chuckling over *I Love Lucy* (And *what* a debt of gratitude America
owes Lucille Ball! she thought), the newspaper on his lap opened to
the stock quotations. In his dim blue eyes she detected unshed tears,
but something else as well: a sense of release. Not from his wife,
whom he had loved with all his heart, but from the responsibility of
making everything right for her. During Katherine's last trip two
months before, he'd sighed a great weary sigh and said, "I couldn't
die if I wanted to." Today he was like Sisyphus at the top of the
mountain, weakened, subdued, but delivered from his task. It won't
be long now, she thought, but quickly her emotions raced in to deny
it, and she contemplated bringing him to California. There was un-

questionably a touch of Oedipal victory to the plan: she would have him to herself at last. In her dreams he was well and strong; subconsciously she had accepted neither of her parents' infirmities as permanent.

But that afternoon, when he appeared still to be studying the financial page, she went around behind him and saw that he was holding the folded paper upside down. Later, when the nurse prepared to take him out for a ride around the grounds, he fell as she was getting him into the wheelchair; it took two orderlies to get him back to bed. Traveling, the doctor told her on his monthly visit, was out of the question.

"School's out in just a few weeks," Katherine told him when she left a few days later. "I'll bring Chryssie back to see you then."

She returned to Los Angeles without the sense of liberation common to adult children after the death of a parent. Where some might feel, I am finally free to do as I please, in some remote part of Katherine's brainwashed brain she believed that nothing could be hidden from her mother now; having cast off her earthly mooring, Emily would be able, after a brief sojourn in purgatory, to look down and see *every move she made.*

And that thought, in the weeks that followed, was one that would often cause her cheeks to flame.

Not long after her mother's funeral, Katherine was walking past the offices of *Newsworld* magazine on Cañon Drive when she heard her name called. Peering from the sunlight into the shadows of the doorway, she saw a flash of carroty red hair. The slight figure of Ben Fahrengold emerged, enveloped in a trench coat despite the warmth of the day. His expression was serious as he greeted her: "Hello Katherine. It's been a long time." After a brief exchange of pleasantries, he asked, "What happened to that thing you had going in Europe?"

Smiling at the jargon, she said, "It's over. What happened to your fiancée?"

"I haven't seen her for six months," he said casually, backing toward the Bistro, which was a few feet away. "Why don't we have a drink?"

She glanced at her watch: an hour until her next class; she shrugged and followed him.

At the headwaiter's urging, Ben removed his trench coat, and with a start Katherine noticed a large, unsightly scar on the back of his neck, an ancient gash with visible suture marks. What startled her was not its appearance, but the fact that she had never noticed it before, and the realization that her personal knowledge of Ben had been acquired almost entirely in the dark. The memory of that night made her flush, and when Ben turned and saw her, a shadow passed over his eyes as if he mistook her embarrassment for distaste. Self-consciously, he adjusted his scarf to conceal the scar.

Hunched over a whiskey at the bar, he quizzed her about Chryssie, her work at school, her life in Europe, her plans for the future, the latter so insistently that she felt defensive about her indecision. His own conversation was confined to an account of his eight-year-old son's accomplishments, which were considerable. According to Ben, Richie was already an expert skier, and showing signs of being a prodigy at school. The ebullient personality and humor Katherine recalled were nowhere to be seen; Ben was subdued, thoughtful, and not at all threatening, she thought. She had never quite gotten him out of her mind, even when she was with Eduardo; now the whole thing seemed an illusion.

A tall man in a tennis sweater entered the bar; Ben waved him over. "This is Katherine Kellogg, the woman I told you about," he said, causing her to turn bright red. Considering the nature of what Ben had to tell him, she thought, no wonder the man was gaping behind his glasses. "This is Peter Mandel. He's at *Newsworld* with me," Ben said quickly.

It was the first time he'd mentioned the magazine, or that he was no longer with the *Examiner*, Katherine noted. She looked at her watch again when Peter ordered a drink, and said she had to leave. Ben's gray eyes clouded. "Would you like to have dinner on Saturday?" he asked. Both men were looking at her. Without thinking, she accepted, then changed her mind and asked for Ben's number in case she had to cancel. "Oh, no," he laughed. "You're not getting out of this one. See you at eight."

There it was again—the threat. A challenge she did not comprehend.

On Saturday, Jed returned from London. He had broken up with Nurith some time before, and was going out with a Swedish model who was on location in Tahiti, so he invited Katherine and

Chryssie to dinner and a movie. With her daughter smiling eagerly in the background, she felt a rush of frustration that Ben had left her no way to contact him.

"What kind of man refuses to give you his phone number?" Jed demanded. "Write a note and put it on the door. It serves him right."

Chryssie was still looking at her hopefully; with a twinge of guilt, she scribbled an apologetic message, taped it to the front door, and drove to Jed's house with her daughter like a woman in flight from peril. Life was peaceful, calm; she liked it that way. Spring term was almost over at UCLA; soon she would have her degree. Lilian had asked her to collaborate on a screenplay about a South American revolution; romance held little allure. Her dream of the Jewish husband and father had been relegated to the closet, where she kept old snapshots and high school essays, pressed corsages, and bits of velvet from a drama school costume. Now comes along this little Jewish Lochinvar—who needs it? she thought. Who needs hope, that familiar uncomfortable feeling that he caused to stir in her breast?

"Who is this guy anyway?" Jed asked on the way in to Westwood.

Katherine described him briefly, concluding, "According to Louise, Ben Fahrengold is simply too good to be true."

Jed gave her his wise old owl look and said, "From her mouth to God's ear."

Remorse struck Katherine on Sunday morning. She told herself that she had done a rude, unkind thing. Ben called at noon; she apologized profusely, her guilt intensified by what had occurred: he had gone to the wrong house, he informed her, where a crazed neighbor had trained a shotgun on him from an upstairs window. Adventure seemed to follow Ben around, she thought, and said yes, of course she'd have dinner with him on Wednesday.

But by Wednesday, she'd flung up another wall and their conversation was strained. After two more such evenings, she wondered why he continued to call her and why she continued to go. Finally, confronted by her coldness as she said good night at her door, he said soberly, "I wish I knew how to get to you, Katherine."

You never will, she thought, flung him a cocky smile, and went inside. Having declared herself invulnerable, Katherine was lulled by a new moon and a romantic restaurant in the hills above Malibu into testing herself by going to bed with him the next time they went out. It had been no accident, she discovered; no drunken one-night stand two years before. All the remembered passion flowed between them with renewed force.

In the weeks that followed, she often had cause to recall Wilder's first description of her husband, Manny: "It's like a philosophy of life: *I want this thing.*" Ben wanted her, and he set the considerable force of his sexual energy, his intelligence, and especially, his humor to the task of getting her. He hadn't Jed's savage wit, but he had a boyish sense of fun and a great gift for mimicry that made her laugh until her sides ached. And Chryssie was incorporated into the fun at once: Ben took her along on his excursions with Richie to the go-cart ring, the miniature golf course, the bowling alley at UCLA, and the amusement parks that turn Los Angeles into a playground for children. Without reservation, Chryssie loved Ben from the start. Her daughter's growing attachment made Katherine uneasy. The involvement with Ben was temporary, she brooded, and Chryssie would be hurt when it ended. As much fun as he was, as generous, tender, unselfishly concerned about Katherine's emotions, her state of mind, anything that informed him about her, she balked at becoming seriously involved with a man who, for one thing, was short; for another, had played stickball on the Grand Concourse while she was being groomed for royalty at the Sacred Heart Convent ("New York Jews are the worst!" Jed railed. "We hated them at Michigan!"); and for another, sounded like a Damon Runyon character (even though her heart turned over every time he called her "babe"). Once, when she reprimanded Chryssie for poor table manners, Ben exclaimed, "Bushwa!" (Bronx slang for bullshit) and she cringed, thinking of Christopher. Ben's graphic descriptions of life in the ghetto seemed much rougher than Jed's.

"My nose was broken four times before I was ten," Ben related. "Later, I got a football scholarship to the Bronx High School of Science. One time after I'd made an impossible touchdown, the entire team from All Saints piled on top of me. I saved the game, but when the coach came to see me in the hospital, he said, 'We don't need no fuckin' heroes, Fahrengold. You put everybody in danger by showing off.'"

Even as Katherine's love and sympathy were aroused, tales of the ghetto revived memories of prejudice, stirring up the ghosts of snobbery that lingered in her attic. She brushed them aside like cobwebs, until the day Ben asked her to marry him. They were standing at her bedroom window, looking out over the canyon, and she went very still in his arms, stricken by a surge of fear that she identified as more than her standard reaction to commitment: it was an inability to adjust to the reality of a man who wore elasticized Jockey shorts and said things like, "I was besides myself." It was inconceivable that she should marry a man with a streets-of-New York accent—not after the great-great-great grandson of Governor Bradford; not after Jed Bernard, the toast of three continents; and certainly not after Eduardo, who was convinced that if the war had gone differently, he would have been emperor of Germany! No, Ben was only a dalliance, she told herself, warding off joy, resisting the rush of excitement, too close to the precipice of love.

But happiness moved into her heart like someone taking possession of an old house: throwing open the windows to let in fresh air, putting new paint on the walls, filling the room with flowers. Despite her attempts at emotional self-restraint, she found herself listening for the crunch of his tires on the gravel every evening, dependent as a dog going to his dish at suppertime. But she allowed him no sign of permanence. When he demanded to stay the night, she insisted he pretend to leave before Chryssie went to sleep, then move his car down the street and sneak back into the kitchen. Branding the behavior hypocrisy, he reluctantly complied.

One weekend, Ben had to fly to San Francisco. "I'm meeting with the mayor," he said. "We're doing a cover story on big city corruption." On Sunday evening he came straight to Katherine's house from the airport, vowing that he'd missed her so much, he would never go away alone again. "I love you, Katie Winterhaus," he said in a husky, tremulous voice as they embraced in her living room. "I'm so happy I'm besides myself."

"Shhh," she cautioned, repressing a rush of joy. "The gods will hear you. I have an image of Peter Pain, standing over us with his hammer, ready to strike."

Ben roared with laughter. "No one can hurt us but us," he said. "You know, when I was out at the airport, I had an itch to go up in a Piper and do some stunts. I told you, didn't I, that I used to be a test pilot in the air force? Anyway, for the first time in my life, I stopped myself from doing something dangerous because I didn't want anything to happen. It made me realize how much you and Chryssie mean to me."

Katherine closed her eyes and leaned against him. What more

could one ask for than a man with the voice of Sky Masterson, the personality of Peter Pan, and the imagination of Walter Mitty? Could it be . . . was it possible that in Ben Fahrengold, this slight, red-haired individual with the hawk nose, God had given her a second chance? A resolution to the dilemma of being a shiksa?

CHAPTER 30

Deirdre of the Sorrows

Katherine decided to give a cocktail party. In her house, with her friends and Ben's friends, and if they didn't like each other, that was *their* problem. Social opprobrium no longer concerned her in the web of happiness Ben had spun for her. Just how fragile a web it was, he understood well. Holding her close against his taut, wiry body, he would whisper, "Don't fuck it up by being crazy, Katherine." And she would think: I won't. I mustn't. Now wait a minute, what is it that I do again? Whatever it was, there was no question that she had a crazy streak, and she mustn't allow it to undermine what Ben and she were building. She might even get up the courage to marry him, in time.

The party was a huge success. Ben was in a funny, ebullient mood and charmed Katherine's friends, especially Lilian, who deemed him a "sensitive, caring person." Andrew Byrne arrived with his beautiful Jewish girlfriend of several years. *Plus ça change*, Katherine thought, when she asked him if they were going to get married. Andy hesitated, then said, "Well, we're certainly not going to *not* get married." The equivocation made her appreciate Ben even more.

To her relief, Ben was not intimidated by Jed, but chatted with him easily, joking and laughing while Jed studied him through a cloud of pipe smoke.

"Isn't he adorable, Jed?" Katherine asked happily when Ben had moved off.

"Adorable . . . adorable," Jed agreed, nodding in his Jewish grandfather persona. Then he drew on his pipe and added, "Only you can't take him anywhere."

With the righteousness of the convert, Katherine protested hotly. "What are you talking about? He went to Harvard, for heaven's sake."

"To you he may be a Harvard man. But to a Harvard man is he a Harvard man?"

"You're a snob!"

"Fine, fine, Mrs. Fahrengold, go under the *chupa*. Have you introduced him to Doug Weyerhauser yet? Or Christopher?"

"Well, no, but—"

"You can't take him anywhere," Jed repeated.

"It's not important."

With a long, hard look, Jed said, "It *is* important."

But Jed's pronouncement was blown away in a high wind of sexual rapture that night. Afterward, feeling the length of Ben's body all along her back in bed, Katherine said in an awed voice, "Just think, people used to *die* at thirty-three."

"I know, babe, I know," he answered, his face buried in her hair. "We could have a kid. Why don't we have a kid?"

A long-suppressed desire flowered in her heart. There was no better father than Benjamin Fahrengold.

At the age of eight, Richie was a freckle-faced replica of Ben, bright, obstreperous, and, Katherine had begun to see, ferociously possessive of him. Left alone with her and Chryssie, the little boy was cheerful and well-behaved, but the moment Ben arrived, he turned sullen toward them, resorting to obvious ruses to monopolize his father or, failing that, convince him to leave. Yet on the weeknights he spent with Ben, he pleaded to be taken to dinner at Katherine's house, where, if Ben spoke to her or Chryssie at the table, Richie refused to eat, or developed a stomach ache, headache, or fever, to which Ben administered with immediate concern, invariably heightening the problem and sending Chryssie into a funk, while Katherine struggled with emotions she deemed unworthy of her. The demeaning position of being in competition with a child for attention seemed to be the peculiar fate of the shiksa; Katherine doubted that Christopher's girlfriends felt a similar compulsion in Chryssie's presence. She reminded herself repeatedly that Richie was a child of divorce, even though his relationship with his mother, Anne, appeared to be devoid of neurosis, and from what little she had seen of her, Anne's placid exterior revealed little hostility toward Ben. On one occasion, when he was forced to remove Richie from the table during a temper tantrum, Katherine looked at Chryssie's frowning face and whispered, "Try and put up with it. He's only here for dinner once a week."

"But I spend six days dreading it," Chryssie whispered back. "Why doesn't Ben do something about it? Daddy would kill me if I acted like that."

Ben got the brunt of Katherine's reactions; with Richie, she gritted her teeth and suppressed her anger, which, turned inward, metamorphosed into terrible guilt: she lacked compassion, she was a monster, made selfish by her own possessiveness, she lectured herself. Then Lilian spent the afternoon with the four of them, and informed her afterward, "You're a bloody saint."

A respite came in July, when Anne took Richie to visit his maternal grandparents in Florida, and Chryssie went to tennis camp in Baltimore. With both children gone, Ben insisted on moving into Katherine's house. The fact that the idea unnerved her was a malady, a symptom of her snobbery and some unidentified fatal flaw, she told herself. In bed her qualms vanished. There they were one person, male and female completed. In the morning, she'd try out the sound: Katherine Fahrengold. It still didn't fit.

Her reticence about marriage began to preoccupy Ben. To distract him from the subject, she would unconsciously pick a quarrel, and soon discovered that unlike Jed, Ben had no use for verbal pyrotechnics—he was a street fighter. During several volatile exchanges, she worried that the neighbors would complain. Once she hit him; he promptly hit her back. Sometimes he stormed out; more often, the angry words ended in lust. Ben endured two weeks of her vacillation; then one evening he gave her a warning: "I'm taking care of number one."

Jealousy, always a factor when Katherine was in love, was exacerbated by the fact that Deirdre Brown, Ben's ex-fiancée, lived around the corner on Mandeville Canyon with her four teenage sons. He had loved her deeply and was devoted to the boys, Ben said. But Deirdre was troubled. "She's got anhedonia—she can't accept being happy."

"I hope I can," Katherine murmured.

"You're a survivor, Katie. You'll always go for life," he said with an enigmatic smile.

Incapable of making a commitment to him—even the term gave her claustrophobia—Katherine looked upon their life together as ephemeral, a wisp of smoke compared to the steady fire that had burned between him and Deirdre. On a warm summer evening, two husky boys of sixteen appeared in her driveway on bikes.

"We're here to see Ben," one announced with a hint of resentment.

"Yes . . . of course . . . hang on a minute," Katherine said, puzzled and curious, and went inside to get him. He was gone for a few minutes; when he came back he told her, "Those were the twins, Mark and Cal, Deirdre's kids. They saw my car parked outside."

"Oh, how awful for them. It never occurred to me . . ." Katherine said, the light in her eyes dimming. The Practical Joker was running amok at his chessboard, she thought. Living nearby, Ben's erstwhile stepchildren were subjected to daily evidence of having lost him. From then on, she made him park at the bottom of her driveway, behind the garage.

Deirdre Brown was a phantom around Los Angeles. Katherine had never really gotten a good look at her; twice when Ben caught sight of her—once on a street corner, another time at the movies in Pacific Palisades—he asked, "Did you see Deedee? She was there." But by the time Katherine looked, she was gone. He showed her a picture he'd taken a few years before: Deedee smiling on the deck of a Malibu restaurant, straight bangs grazing her enormous sunglasses, her upheld hand casting a shadow over her face. All Katherine could really make out was the cap of sunstreaked hair. She caught hold of her jealous nature—that familiar bull-headed spoiler would not be allowed to threaten her precarious happiness.

One evening, Ben went into the bathroom to shave, informing Katherine that they were meeting Lester Berkowitz, his oldest friend, and Lester's fiancée, Susan, for dinner at Tivoli Restaurant.

"Tivoli?" she echoed without enthusiasm.

"Tivoli," he repeated firmly. "It's the best food in L.A. Les and I have lunch there all the time. The Scandinavian waitresses are gorgeous."

"I only went there once. There were a lot of tourists," Katherine said vaguely, recalling a long, difficult dinner she'd spent with her parents on their fortieth wedding anniversary. Observing the clientele with a jaundiced eye, Emily had indulged in casual anti-Semitism, which Katherine had felt constrained to protest, thereby ruining the celebration. Ironically, when Katherine mentioned to Jed that she'd taken them there, he'd cried: "The worst! Let my people go, O Lord! Let them go from Tivoli!"

"You'll see," Ben assured her, knotting a green knit tie that turned his eyes to jade. "Deedee and I used to go there once a week."

Not to be outdone by Deedee, Katherine determined to have a good time at Tivoli.

"You should have seen Lester's last wife," Ben said as he gunned the MG down the Sunset Strip. "She was Miss Israel in 1970—a gorgeous girl. I'm not so sure I like Susan. She's very defended. But Lester's crazy about her. I've been in all his weddings. He only marries Jewish women."

Katherine was still working on "defended" as they pulled up to the restaurant.

Lester was an overgrown, unreconstituted Jewish kid from the Bronx who had come to California to practice law, not to escape his origins. Comfortable with himself and his background, he had no desire to change the pattern, only the women. He was taller than Ben, with deep-set brown eyes and the pitted complexion that gives men a rough appeal. His fiancée, Susan, was attractive but morose. After acknowledging the introduction to Katherine, she spoke to no one but Lester, in a low, inaudible voice. Ben behaved as if Susan were not there. With an arm draped around Katherine, he bantered boyishly with Lester, joking and laughing while Susan drank her sherry silently and watched them, alternately frowning under a fringe of curly brown hair, then giving a fleeting smile of forbearance. When she inquired about Ben's job at *Newsworld*, he swiftly repeated that talking about work was forbidden, and she sank into silence again.

Katherine's initial attempts at vivacity faded as she was jostled on all sides, assaulted with spilled drinks, and deafened by raucous voices in her ear. A statuesque blond hostess showed them to a booth in the dining room. The men fell into a friendly rivalry about which of them was the more expert tennis player, and Susan was incommunicado, so Katherine tuned out. Fragments of conversation filtered through her daydreaming until a change in Lester's tone jolted her to attention.

"You can't tell them apart!" he said loudly. His eyes glittered, his color was high, and although there was no particular hostility in his expression when he glanced at Katherine, there was no friendliness either. "It's a sickness," he said flatly to Ben. "The only one who was right for you was Anne, and you left her for Deedee. You think it's some kind of solution for everything you hate about your past. You call it love. I call it a syndrome, pal."

Katherine looked quickly at Susan; her head was down, her eyes hooded, but she was nodding in agreement. The dopey smile Katherine had worn throughout Lester's harangue died as his words sank in. Ben was rigid beside her.

"Where do you get off passing judgment, Bluebeard?" he snapped.

To enter the fray was pointless; to stay there while she was tacitly being insulted intolerable. Katherine excused herself and went to the ladies' room, where she telephoned Jed. His answering growl was enormously comforting. When she repeated the incident, he asked, "Why would you *be* with people like that, putz?"

By the time she got back to the table, the check had been paid. The two couples bid each other a stilted farewell. Driving home, Ben vowed not to attend his friend's forthcoming wedding and Katherine burst into tears.

"I don't want to come between you. You've been friends for life! Anyway, it's not his fault," she sobbed. "It's just what I'm afraid of—that's why it hurts so! You must see how much truth there is in what he said."

"What I see," Ben said kindly, "is that Lester's denying his own needs. Nobody's that hostile unless there's an unconscious motivation at work. I think he's jealous, and I think you're hysterical about nothing. Lester just can't deal with tall, beautiful blondes. Take it as a compliment."

"I'm surprised he doesn't get the *bends* in Tivoli from the waitresses," she said, drying her eyes.

Ben threw back his head and roared. Later, they forgot about the evening's fiasco in bed, where they always forgot about everything but each other.

In the morning, when he sat down to tie his Wallabys, he drew her onto his lap and said with a crooked smile, "You don't even know how much you love me yet."

"What does that mean?" she asked.

He did not reply.

At that moment, her father's nurse called to tell her that he was counting the days until she brought Chryssie to Rochester to see him. "We'll be there Friday," Katherine promised, realizing as she did so that the summer was almost over.

"I've got a deadline Tuesday, babe," Ben said when she hung up. "I'll be at the office late tomorrow. Maybe I should sleep at my apartment."

She nodded. It would be a good opportunity to invite Alison and Bryan to dinner, an impossibility with Ben since the two men had loathed each other on sight at her cocktail party. Never again, she thought, would she make the mistake of neglecting her friends for a man.

On Tuesday, the Draddys arrived with Bryan's brother and a case of Beaujolais nouveau from one of his latest shipments. It was a long, wine-drenched evening. Bryan's brother was a delegate to the Republican convention, and although Katherine disagreed with him in principle, they tolerated each other's opinions, which would not have been the case if Ben were there. At more than one social occasion, she had cringed as he turned political disagreements into personal insults. Around midnight, the telephone rang. As Katherine picked it up, Bryan shouted with raucous laughter at something Alison said, and after a moment's silence, Ben's voice said curtly, "I just wanted to tell you I'm home, babe." He hung up quickly, sounding tired and put off.

When her guests left a few minutes later, Katherine called him back. The line was busy. Ten minutes later, it still was. How often had he complained that it was always he who came to her? she thought. Impetuously she jumped in her car and drove to his apartment in Brentwood.

How odd, she thought as she approached—his car was parked in the street. She pulled into the garage beneath his building. A Thunderbird was in Ben's stall. It was Deirdre's. There was no mistaking it; Ben had pointed it out a dozen times driving down Mandeville Canyon. Encased in shock, Katherine got out and opened the car door to be certain. On the seat were some papers with Deirdre's name on them—escrow papers, she saw on closer examination. She stared dully at the top page. At least she's moving, she thought.

For some time Katherine stood there, leaning against the car. Then determination caught hold of her. She straightened. She would face them both, have it out here and now; it was better if all three knew what was going on. Sisterhood triumphed over jealousy as she marched to his front door; at least she could prevent him from playing one woman against another! Made rash by wine, she rang the doorbell. Silence. She rang again; the sound pierced the night air like a siren. Growing more wretched, more compulsive by the minute, she leaned on the bell. The street was dark and absolutely still. A man walked past with a dog, peering curiously at the distraught figure in a long green hostess gown. After ten minutes, she gave up and drove home, tears streaming down her face.

Throughout the long night she dialed Ben's busy number. At eight o'clock in the morning, he answered, apparently in a rush.

Her voice stringy with fatigue, Katherine said, "If you care anything at all about me, you'll come over here and tell me what's going on."

"I've got a deadline, Katherine," he said, sounding friendly and concerned. "I'll call you later and explain everything."

She waited in a frenzy of impatience. When he finally telephoned an hour later, the explanation was simple.

"I ran into Deedee when I stopped off at a coffee shop to get cigarettes on the way home last night. It's still there, Katherine. We both felt it. The best way to describe it is to say it was like an aftershock. She and I put in five years, baby. I owe it one last chance."

"At what? Marriage?"

He hesitated, "I don't know."

Aftershock, her mind echoed. Aftershock. What does that mean? Who *is* this man? His voice was that of a stranger. "Why didn't you answer the door?" she demanded. "How could you have let me stand out in the street like that?"

"I wasn't there. Deedee and I walked around all night talking. That's all we did, I swear."

"Then how did you know I was there?"

"My neighbor told me." He chuckled. "That's a pretty loud bell. Have a good trip and give my love to Chryssie."

At nine-thirty, Katherine dialed Jed's number in tears. He listened for a moment, then broke in, "I thought you were going to tell me you'd thrown *him* out. You want to come up and talk about it, kid?"

She was there in fifteen minutes. "How long has he gone with this woman?" Jed asked when they were seated in the study.

"Four . . . five years, I guess," Katherine said miserably.

"Are they getting married finally?"

"He says he doesn't know."

"Tell him if they don't, they should at least hang bells around their necks."

Katherine got up from the couch and began to pace. "She lives on my corner! Now I'll have to see his car in front of *her* house every day!"

"At least he's faithful to the street," Jed said philosophically. Her laugh came out like a sob. He fixed her with a sober gaze. "You think you're unhappy now? Marry him—then you'll know what real unhappiness is."

With the help of Jed's Valium, which ordinarily Katherine abhorred, she got to Baltimore in time for Chryssie's tennis tournament. Watching numbly from the stands, she wondered how to break the news. Late that afternoon, they sat side by side on a bunk in her room, sorting things to pack. Chryssie had been sneaking looks at her mother's ravaged face. Finally Katherine let her hands drop to her lap and said, "Ben went back to Deedee."

Chryssie stopped tightening the screw of her racquet press. Their eyes met. "What a bummer," Chryssie said.

By the time their plane landed in Rochester, the Valium had worn off, but pain deadened Katherine's senses like a massive dose of novacaine. They rented a car and drove to the Country Club, where she had booked a double room overlooking the golf course. The house on Windsor Court was on the market; she couldn't face staying there. It was early evening; the swimming pool was deserted, the grounds peaceful, the quiet interrupted only by starlings twittering in the elm trees. Outside the clubhouse, a group of women in print cotton dresses conversed in modulated tones. Katherine and Chryssie dined in the Grille on a leather banquette beneath a display of hunting rifles. Chryssie leaned across the table over her consommé. "It's really nice here, Mom," she said. "But there's something missing. I think it's Jews."

Every morning at ten, they went to Mapleridge. Douglas had

been at death's door when they arrived; after two days he was sitting up again, wan but cheerful. "It's a miracle what happens when you girls show up, Kate," the nurse told her.

In the mornings, Chryssie would comb Douglas's fine strands of silver hair back from his forehead, pat his hand, and curl up at his feet to watch comedy shows, while Gloria, the day nurse, filled Katherine in on the sanitarium gossip. One of the elderly widows, a certain Mrs. McGinnis, whose libido was in full flower now that she was in her seventies, had taken a shine to Douglas and pursued him whenever he ventured outside his room in his wheelchair. Fortunately she was nowhere in sight on the afternoon Katherine wheeled him out to the garden. He had dug out his old Panama hat from some attic cupboard; he wore it now jauntily atop his head; it gave him an oddly dignified yet comical air as he rode along. They stopped in a shaded bower near a fountain with pennies scattered over the blue painted bottom; Douglas clucked at the waste of money. A few feet away, Gloria stood making household lists, and Chryssie sat at the edge of the fountain trailing her fingers in the water.

"I hear Mrs. McGinnis has set her cap for you, Daddy," Katherine teased, sitting on the grass at his feet.

"I wouldn't marry that old bag if you paid me," Douglas grumbled.

She laughed. "What kind of woman would you marry, if you got married again?"

He turned the wristband on his watch; it was loose as a bracelet on his emaciated arm. "Oh, I dunno," he said gruffly. "Someone like you, I suppose."

Katherine's head went up; the delighted cry she uttered came from the depths of her being. "Why, Daddy! That's the nicest thing you've ever said to me!"

He shrugged his shoulders. "Well, it's true."

Chryssie turned and looked at her curiously, but in that euphoric moment the others faded from Katherine's view and she was a child again, walking with Douglas across a sunwashed brick plaza, hand in hand. Years of disapproval were canceled in one stroke. It's never too late, she thought. Everybody should get a line like that from her father before he dies.

Katherine returned to Los Angeles in a rejuvenated, hopeful mood, convinced that she and Ben belonged together. Her own insecurities, her unresolved identity, her lack of acceptance had caused him to run back to Deirdre, she was sure of it. One more chance, please, God, she prayed, and I'll make it up to him.

But on the way home from the airport, they saw a red MG parked outside Deirdre Brown's house, and Katherine's optimism faded.

Among the letters that had accumulated in their absence was one addressed to Ben. Chryssie, who had so far hidden her own feelings, picked it up and started for the door. "I'm going to take it right down there," she said fiercely, "and ring the doorbell and say, 'Here Ben. This came for you last week—when you loved us.'"

Katherine put her hands on her shoulders in a restraining embrace. "Oh, honey, you can't do that."

Chryssie's face was defiant. "Why not? Her kids came here."

The idea tempted Katherine for a moment; it seemed more honest than the conspiracy of silence civilization called for. But in the end, she forwarded the letter to the *Newsworld* office. If only for Chryssie, she had to function, she told herself, and called Lilian to set up a schedule of meetings on the screenplay. Lilian, however, was leaving for a week in Baja with her family, so the palliative of work would have to wait.

"Ben will be back," Lilian predicted on the phone. "It's a pattern of guilt with the other woman. Believe me, I know from Jewish men's guilt. He was always talking about the *work* they put in together. You and he had too much fun for him to stay with her now."

"It was my fault he left," Katherine said. "I never really accepted him. I was so self-centered, so greedy for his love that I didn't pay attention to *his* needs. I didn't really listen when he wanted to talk about himself, or the Bronx, or—"

Lilian shrieked. "You are living proof that Jewish men should be with Jewish women. They can't play on our sympathies because we've all been through the same things. My grandparents left Russia because the Cossacks were killing them. He's going to tell me that he grew up in a tenement he didn't *like*? I'm not impressed. I would know exactly how to deal with this character."

"Can you teach me?"

"Oh, God," Lilian sighed. "One look at that face and they see you coming. And then you open those blue eyes and go, 'Oh, *really*?' Well, you might get the gist if you were to do it by imitation. By instinct you couldn't. First of all, you've got to stop having all these fights with him where you scream at each other."

"I have a strange psychological quirk," Katherine said. "When a Jewish man starts to yell at me, I feel secure. Somehow I equate it with love."

"And the more he can yell at you, the less he's going to love you deep down . . . because it's so disorienting for him. Try thinking of him as a child," Lilian advised.

Katherine made a date to have lunch with her when they returned to continue the discussion. But by the time the day arrived, she no longer felt the need for Lilian's advice.

CHAPTER 31

Old Friends

Lilian was right about the guilt, Ben told Katherine. Seeing Deedee's kids had been too much for him, made him feel he was shirking his responsibilities. But after living with her again for a while, the old arguments had resumed, and this time the memory of his life with Katherine was there to remind him what happiness was.

It was everything she wanted to hear. It made sense to her the way he explained it, sitting in the Bistro bar in the middle of the afternoon, half hidden in the darkest corner behind the frosted glass partition because they couldn't risk being seen—Deirdre had yet to be informed of Ben's latest change of heart.

"I miss the laughter," he said, his eyes bright on her face. "I miss the fights. I miss feeling alive! I can't stay there any longer. I'm going to tell Deedee tonight."

Katherine had an impression of being in deep water. It threatened to engulf her; she could only stay afloat by gazing into his fathomless eyes. From a great distance, she heard her own voice asking, "Are you sure?"

"Absolutely, babe," Ben said. "I went back to my shrink to work through what I was doing. You know, I realize now that I lied to him for the entire first year of my analysis."

"What a waste of money," she murmured.

"I think we should get married before Christmas, or my birthday at the latest—January thirtieth."

"Anything—anything," she breathed, fragile as glass, his words leeching the pain from her bones. But pain, like energy, is never destroyed, only transformed. Or transferred. "What about Deirdre?" she asked. "Won't she be terribly hurt?"

In a sad voice, he said, "I think she'll be relieved. It wasn't much fun for her, living with your ghost for a month. There's one thing—no more moving the car. No more hypocrisy. Chryssie has to accept that I'm going to be her stepfather."

Three days later, Ben moved into Katherine's house, bringing a suitcase and, as a symbol of permanence, his wall clock. Katherine, who loathed the thing, joyfully hung it over the mantelpiece. Taking Chryssie into the study alone, Ben gently explained how much he loved her and her mother, and what had made him go back to Deirdre one last time. Since Chryssie had become a fan of Westerns, she'd developed a theory that if you fail to shoot the villain in the back when you have the chance, he'll come back to get you. But she wanted badly to forgive Ben and see her mother happy, so she suspended it.

Short of religious conversion, Katherine threw herself into a state of all-out acceptance. Her biggest worry was Richie, but according to Ben, the boy was delighted with the way things had turned out—he had missed Katherine and Chryssie during the weekends at Deirdre's.

Time spent watching Sonia Bronstein prepare *gedemft* meat paid off: now Katherine marinated roasts for hours, sending Ben into raptures at the pungent, familiar fragrances that wafted from the oven when he arrived home in the evenings. Jed, who called regularly to check on the progression of Katherine's romance, inquired one October afternoon, "Whatcha doin', kid?"

"Putting a brisket in the oven," she replied.

"*Again* with the cooking!" he cried. "I know I said always go against the grain, but this is ridiculous. Everybody else is coming out of the kitchen and you're going in. They'll arrest you!"

"There's a difference between oppression and love," she declared. "Ben makes it easy. He's a truly liberated man. He clears the table, he offers to help with the dishes—of course, I don't let him do that—he edits my writing—"

"Marvelous," Jed said dryly. "I wish him luck in any line of work."

"Speaking of that, he's encouraging his ex-wife to get established in a career. She's very bright and she'd like to do production work. Could you help at all?"

"Tell him as soon as I get a job myself, I'll send for her." Jed said.

"It's typical of his generosity of spirit," Katherine raved. "He's an incredibly good person. Do you know, every month he gives a pint of blood to the Red Cross?"

"Money I understand, but blood? Jews don't give away their blood."

"I actually said the word 'trust' today without stuttering."

"I gotta hang up, kid," said Jed. "Lemme give you my new number: 785396593—"

She was still chuckling over the call when Ben came home.

That night, after they had consumed the pot roast and Chryssie had gone to sleep, Katherine lay in Ben's arms in bed, his deep, thrilling voice rolling over her in sleep-inducing waves as he reminisced about Harvard Medical School.

"What made you give it up?" she murmured.

"The journalism thing took over," he said. "I got a summer job at *Life*. It was the early days of the Cuban revolution, and through a lucky break, I went along with a team of reporters to Havana. We got an exclusive interview with Fidel. He was a pure revolutionary in those days. I could see it in his eyes—a fire, a spirit of freedom for the masses."

A breeze blew the curtains away from the window, and in a stream of powdery white light, Katherine saw his jagged profile and the elongated *S* that bisected his neck from earlobe to clavicle. Up till then, his obvious hypersensitivity had made her loathe to ask about it; in any case, it had become invisible to her—she was aware of it only when he adjusted a scarf with extraordinary care or turned up the collar of his perpetual trench coat on a warm day. Now she ran her index finger tenderly over the scar.

"How did you get this?" she asked softly.

Ben reached for his pack of cigarettes on the night table. "It was in the Chad," he told her as he drew one out. "For a couple of years, I was a war correspondent, and one time I got caught in the line of fire. The *schvartze* that sewed me up didn't know what he was doing. I could've done a better job myself after one year of Harvard."

She started to say something, but he set his cigarette aside and turned back to her, stifling her words with a kiss.

The autumn evenings grew longer, and Katherine's ambition

for anything but happiness evanesced. A few hours a week she would work with Lilian on the script, but Lilian had less time now that classes had resumed, and Katherine's life revolved around Chryssie and Ben. His civic-mindedness and, most of all, his integrity continued to astound her. When he was first married to Anne, he told her, his grandfather had died and left him half a million dollars, which he'd secretly amassed over the years in the scrap-iron business in the Bronx. But Ben had refused to accept it, clinging to his ideals despite his father's outraged, "Bushwa!" In a baffled voice, Katherine asked what his reasons had been. He replied simply, "I don't believe in inherited wealth."

Late one afternoon Jed called, distraught because Chris had left her Doberman with him, and the animal had gotten past his gate and been run over on Sunset Boulevard. "I've got to take him to the vet. Could you come up here, kid, in case she gets home before I do?"

By the time Katherine arrived at his house, Jed was in tears. The dog had died on the way to the vet's and Chris was due momentarily to pick him up. "That kid never gets a break . . . she never gets a break," he repeated brokenly. "I don't want her to see the blood . . . it's all over the street."

Katherine called Ben and told him to meet her at Jed's house, then got a pail of water and carried it to the bottom of the driveway, where she dodged traffic and scrubbed at the bloodstains. When Ben arrived, Jed was in the bedroom with Chris, sobbing out the news, so obviously heartbroken that, in her concern for him, her own sorrow was alleviated. From the living room, Katherine and Ben heard her consoling him. "It's okay, Dad. He was a terrible dog anyway . . . always running out in the street. It was gonna happen sooner or later."

Ben shook his head in wonder. "Jed does everything wrong," he said. "But he does it with love, so it's okay."

Happy endings do happen, Katherine thought. Jed had his with Chris, and she hers with Ben.

That weekend, when they put Chryssie on a plane for San Francisco, security radiated in her small face, and she told Ben, "See you Sunday," in a voice so confident and trusting that Katherine felt a pang of guilt for what could only be a neurotic reluctance to marry him.

It began to rain as they drove home from the airport. By the time they turned onto Mandeville Canyon, water was running down from the hills in great sluicing mudstreams. As she poured Ben a fresh cup of coffee in the kitchen, Katherine said, "There's no way I'm going out again today."

The kitchen chair creaked as he leaned back in it, lighting a cigarette. "I've got a board meeting at the ACLU, and Monday I've got to turn in my interview with Henry Miller, but . . ." Behind him, rain lashed the windows and rattled the gutterpipe.

"Los Angeles is totally unprepared for anything but perfect weather. I've been rear-ended the last three times it rained," she said as she set down the cup at his place.

Ben gave a slow smile and encircled her wrist with his freckled hand. "That gives me a great idea, babe. I'll work on the story later. Let's go in the den and light a fire and put on the concerto I gave you."

He pulled her onto his lap. One word from him, she thought, a touch, and I go weak. It was as if he owned her, body and soul. That a man could have such power frightened her; as fierce as her desire was, the fear was stronger, and she disengaged herself with a light laugh. "Finish your coffee first."

He grinned, running his hand over her thigh. "I love you, Katie Winterhaus."

She carried a stack of plates to the sink. There must be something to this anatomy-is-destiny stuff, she thought. Here she was, preparing meals, washing dishes, making love without any desire for more, as fulfilled as the nuns and her parents and the Pope promised a woman could be as the heart of a home. She turned to look at Ben. He was blowing a smoke ring toward the ceiling.

"Did I ever tell you about the time I was sued for a quarter of a million dollars?" he asked.

She smiled indulgently. "I'm not sure."

"I was broke, so I decided to act as my own lawyer. The accident happened as I was going home to Deirdre's . . ."

Katherine turned off the faucet, pain welling up in her chest at the sound of Deirdre's name. Only a month ago, a block and a half away, another blond woman had rinsed, stacked, and put away the dishes of this little man, Ben Fahrengold, with the big eyes and the tall, tall stories.

" . . . I figured the year I had at Harvard Law was enough to—"

Katherine interrupted sharply. "I don't remember your telling me that. You said medical—"

His eyes met hers across the room. "I would have no reason to lie to you, Katherine." It was an expression he used with increasing regularity, she thought as she turned on the disposal and dropped orange peels in, listening to them being ground by the blades, the noise drowning out his words. But key phrases filtered through: ". . . the judge said . . . best presentation . . . in court . . . no way . . . insurance company settle . . ."

She clicked off the disposal. "That's terrific," she said dimly into the silence.

He was behind her now, his arms around her at the sink. She closed her eyes and let herself fall against him. "This is supposed to be a sign of how much you trust someone," she murmured, but the feeling to which she gave herself seemed more the helplessness of a swimmer, over her head and losing strength. She turned and kissed him lingeringly, delivering herself to whatever he was, whatever he wanted of her.

The morning passed with Katherine and Ben lying in each other's arms before the fire, curtains drawn, French horns playing as their bodies responded to the wax and wane of desire.

He covered her mouth with his, opening it wide so that he took in her chin and the tip of her nose, running his tongue along the underside of her parted lips until she gasped for breath. "God, we are great together," he said in a husky voice. He drew back to look into her eyes. "Sometimes I'm not sure where I leave off and you begin. We're everything a man and a woman should be together."

"Or a cat and a mouse," she said, pretending to quail at his voracious expression.

His laughter filled the room. The rain drummed on the roof. With a sigh, she buried her face in the curve of his shoulder. So what if he's making it up about law school? she thought weakly.

"Don't worry about dinner for me Monday, babe," Ben said, his lips pressed against the top of her head. "I'll be late. Richie's got an appointment for a blood test."

"Why? What's wrong with him?" she asked, looking up in alarm.

"Nothing. He has one once a month."

"Whatever for?"

"It's just a precaution."

He sat up, reaching for his Jockey shorts. Katherine glanced away. The damn things were becoming a symbol, she thought. Christopher, who scorned anything but boxer shorts of the finest cotton, had made her crazy on the subject of men's underwear. Jed wore nothing and Eduardo got away with murder in French bikinis, she recalled, but the sight of Ben in his tight Jockey shorts never failed to remind her how far afield she had strayed.

He stood, and pulled on his chinos. If only she could get him to wear them two inches longer, she thought. Even Chryssie, for whom Ben could do no wrong, had commented, "He looks as if he's expecting a flood."

"A blood test is a marvelous thing," he said. "It tells you everything. They can detect the slightest health problem."

"But he's eight years old! What could be wrong? I mean, how to turn a kid into a hypochondriac!"

"Chryssie never has blood tests?" he demanded, putting first one, then the other foot on the coffee table to tie his Wallabys.

Katherine reached over and pulled a plaid shawl off the arm of the couch. Drawing it around her, she said, "Not that I know of. Only if she's got a symptom, if something's wrong with her. Or maybe once a year . . . but not once a month! Does Richie's pediatrician recommend that?"

Ben's head had inched backward as she spoke until, seated on either side of the coffee table—he rigid on the corduroy couch, she in the overstuffed white chair, her naked vulnerability sheathed in the soft folds of the blanket—they assessed one another. That's his street stance, she thought. And Richie's got it, too. Brought to you directly from the Grand Concourse.

"I take him to Mount Sinai to get it done," he snapped. "It's more thorough."

"You're joking! That seems excessive to say the least." From a side table she picked up *Architectural Digest* and began flipping backward through its pages, her eyes sliding to his face intermittently. An absolutely irrational anger was making her hands shake. "Jews and doctors," she snorted. "God."

After a brief pause, Ben said coldly, "I don't know what your problem is, Katherine, but you're very defended."

Again with defended, she thought.

He rose. "I'm going into the office. I'm interviewing Senator Cranston next week, and I want to be prepared."

The front door slammed. Katherine closed the magazine and

stared into space, suffused with a sense of hopelessness. The day was ruined, and it was all her fault. What was *wrong* with her? She waited twenty minutes, then called Ben to apologize. He accepted gracefully.

On Sunday morning, the telephone rang early. Through a fog of sleep, they heard it. Ben flung out an arm to pick up the receiver, dropped it, swore as he retrieved it from the floor, and handed it to Katherine. They had awakened simultaneously before dawn, stirred from the depths of sleep by dreams that prodded physical urges, moving instinctively together to make love in slow motion. Now, feeling almost drugged after being jarred awake by the phone's rude ringing, she murmured a hoarse hello.

"Katherine Winterhaus? Is that you, *deah?*"

Only one person gave that particular twist to the word dear, Katherine thought, instantly awake. She sat up on one elbow, gripping the phone, clutching the sheet around her body. Ben was watching her, his curiosity piqued. "Mother . . . *Graves?*" she repeated incredulously.

A familiar, bell-like laugh tinkled along the line. "Yes, deah. I'm in Los Angeles! I imagine you're surprised to hear from me."

"You could say that," Katherine murmured with a weak laugh.

"Maggie Fraser gave me your number. She's living in London, you know, with a charming fellow."

"Yes, I know," Katherine said. "How is Maggie?"

"Maggie is fine," Mother Graves replied, and Katherine thought fondly of her beautiful, vague friend who had a fatal attraction for Arabs; she was with one now, a Saudi Arabian who imported native dress to the United Kingdom. But the reminder that she was no longer the only convent girl living in sin was small comfort to Katherine at the moment, lying with Ben a foot away from her amid the evidence of illicit sex: discarded clothes, tousled sheets, his male scent on her skin. Had God sent this woman to the phone as He'd posted Michael to the gates of Paradise? "Give me a child until he is seven," the Jesuits claim, "and he is mine for life." Until the age of *seventeen* she had inhabited convents, where the prototype of purity was Maria Goretti, up for canonization because she had allowed herself to be stabbed twenty (fifty? ninety-three?—the number rose with each telling) times rather than submit to the sexual advances of a worker in her father's field.

"I think she needs to get her life in order," Mother Graves

said briskly, "but I have faith that she will. And what about you? Who was that who—"

"What happened to your accent?" Katherine broke in quickly. "You sound different." When she was a child Mother Graves's voice had seemed as clipped as Queen Elizabeth's, or Greer Garson's at least, but what she heard over the wire now was pure Pennsylvania, except for the affected "deah."

"Not a thing, deah," the nun replied. "When am I going to see you?"

"Where are you? How long are you going to be here?"

"I'm staying at the Beverly Rodeo Hotel with a group of educators. Unfortunately I have to leave tomorrow. I'm on my way to Israel."

"Excuse me? Oh . . . Jerusalem?"

"No, Tel Aviv. Haven't you received my class letter? I've been appointed head of the Committee to Foster Jewish-Christian Relations."

"Incredible," Katherine murmured.

They made plans to meet at six that evening at the Beverly Rodeo Hotel. As she was about to hang up, Katherine said, "Wait! Will I know you? You're not wearing a habit anymore, right?"

"That's right, deah. I'll be the only lady in the lobby with red hair!"

Driving down Rodeo Drive to their meeting, Katherine wondered if she would be shocked by the sight of Mother Graves in civilian clothes; the concept struck her as similar to draping a Doric column with ruffles. A desk clerk glanced up as she entered the small hotel; the light in the lobby was dim. Two middle-aged women sat in opposite corners reading. Katherine's eyes darted from one to the other; the woman on the left rose and came toward her smiling radiantly, then kissed her on both cheeks and said her name. Katherine babbled hello and looked for a feature she recognized; what caught her eye and held it—galvanized it—was a wavy red wig. The nun wore a navy blue coat, and over one arm hung the ultimate incongruity, a patent leather purse.

They were shown to a small table in the corner of the restaurant. While Mother Graves ordered a cup of tea, Katherine tried to conjure up the image of the stark, beautiful woman she had known: "Ladyfingers," the Mistress General, standing like a black angel in the door of her office at Prince Street; or the stern warden at Manhattanville, full of regal reprimands. Where, oh where were these creatures lurking beneath the pleasant-faced, matronly suburbanite smiling at the waitress? Katherine focused on the nun's ice-blue irises; there and only there, she rediscovered the Veronica Graves of old. Depressed by her two-piece beige dress, Katherine complimented her on it.

"It's Davidow," Mother Graves informed her. "We get our clothes mostly from donations. I consider myself very fortunate that some of our contributors have such good taste. The coat is Hattie Carnegie," she added, working her arms out of the sleeves. Katherine made a move to help her but was stopped by a childhood interdiction against laying a finger on a nun.

Mother Graves inquired about her father's health, the state of Margot's soul, Chryssie; then came the remembered, habitual, unwelcome flood of personal revelations about ex-classmates. To avoid spilling any confidences of her own, Katherine steered the conversation toward world affairs. Evidently a leaning to the liberal had taken place in Mother Graves's thinking: at the mention of thalidomide, she inclined her head and said in a confidential tone, "Under certain circumstances, abortion is permissible, you know. Nuns who have been raped, for instance, are allowed to have them."

"That's the first time I ever heard that!" Katherine responded.

"It's not the sort of thing the Vatican publicizes." She sipped her tea. Here was a woman she had known her entire life, Katherine realized, yet it was the first time she had seen her ingest food or drink. The nun set down her cup with a nostalgic smile. "Whatever happened to that young man you went around with at Manhattanville? Neil, wasn't it?"

"He married a very nice girl, but they got divorced. We're still good friends, though I don't see him often." Katherine paused, screening the information, then said cautiously, "I think of Neil as sort of a precursor in my life. I seem destined to be with a Jewish man."

A beatific smile transformed the nun's face. "*Wonderful* people! The Jews in general." Two red spots of color deepened on her cheeks. "I've never laughed so much in my life as I have since I've been going to Israel. Our dear Lord was not without humor, you know. Working in this field has given me a deep, abiding love for the Hebrew religion. We're not so far apart—after all, Catholicism is just a continuation of Judaism. On my last visit, I had a most wonderful guide named Itzhak . . ."

While she raved on about Itzhak, Katherine controlled her mirth with effort. She could hardly wait to tell Jed: Mother Graves, of all people, had turned into a shiksa!

"There's a reason for my visit," the nun announced suddenly, her expression turning serious. "I want you to do something for your parents, and yourself. Get an annulment."

Katherine hesitated, struck by the timing of her mission. "I'm not averse to that," she said.

"I'm going to put you in touch with Monsignor Dowling in the Chancery office. He's a friend. Let's get this thing started."

Then Katherine's guard came down, and until it grew dark and the café filled up with noisy patrons, she talked about Ben. Mother Graves was due at a meeting at eight. They walked through the lobby to the elevator; at the door, the nun paused, her hand on Katherine's arm. The circle of gold that signified her betrothal to Christ flashed in the light.

"There's just one thing . . . if you could give up the bed par⁺ until it's settled."

Katherine felt her face redden, but she said simply, "I can't.

"Oh. You can't?" Mother Graves said in a chipper voice. "Well, let's pray you get married as soon as possible."

"Yes, Mother. I'm very glad to have seen you again," Katherine said sincerely.

"I'll always love you, dearie."

CHAPTER 32

The Annulment

True to her word, Mother Graves started the ancient wheel of canon law creaking. She had been gone one day when Katherine received a call from the Los Angeles Chancery Office saying that her annulment questionnaire was in the mail; she should complete it and make an appointment with Dr. Clement Garlock, the resident psychiatrist at St. Michael the Archangel Hospital in Pasadena

"Wouldn't you know?" she said to Ben. "Pasadena—that bastion of liberal thinkers." But he encouraged her to see it through.

Throughout the week, while Ben worked late at the magazine, Katherine complied with the Chancery Office's request for detailed responses to its queries, dredging up the past in order to have a future in the Church. A future with Ben. Three pages of questions delved into the personal histories of the applicant and spouse. "Did your parents quarrel?" canon lawyers wanted to know. "What was his relationship with his mother?" "Did he have friends?" One made her smile: "Did all conversation have to center around him?" If *that* were grounds for an annulment, Katherine thought, she could get one from every man she'd ever known, with the exception of Ben.

Jed telephoned one morning to say that Chris was spending the day with him; did Katherine want to come for a swim? She explained what she was doing.

"An annulment?" he echoed. "I'll bet that costs a few shekels."

"Not at all. You only pay for the paperwork," she assured him.

"Marvelous," he said dryly. "For twelve dollars you can start out fresh."

A perfectly normal Jewish reaction, Katherine thought; why was Ben being so understanding about it?

The next evening, Ben came home from *Newsworld* bursting with a bulletin. Peter Mandel had an article in the religion section that week about a new trend: dual religious wedding ceremonies. The subject had come to Peter's attention when his cousin married a Catholic, with a rabbi present on the altar.

Though it struck Katherine as implausible, she said, "Really? I guess it shows how things are changing."

"We could get married right away," Ben said, lifting her onto the kitchen counter.

She laughed. "As Jed would say, half of the job is done. It doesn't change the fact that you're divorced." Teasingly she added, "Of course, if you were to be baptized, it's all wiped out."

"So, why don't I get baptized?"

She stared at him in amazement. "Would you do that for me?"

He came a step closer, his eyes looking deeply into hers. "Babe, I'd be boiled in oil for you if it would help."

Later, when she repeated the conversation to Chryssie, the child commented, "I don't think he should do that, Mom. It's not really *him*, so it wouldn't be right."

The morning of her appointment with the church psychiatrist, Katherine put on a simple print skirt and blouse, and headed for the network of freeways that link Los Angeles to its many suburbs. Forty-five minutes later she emerged in Pasadena. The sunlight was glaring and a band of pink smudged the horizon. She drove past miles of opulent estates until she came to a manicured lawn, at the back of which was a turreted fortress sheltered by cypresses. Inside St. Michael the Archangel Hospital, a uniformed attendant conducted her down a long corridor to a richly appointed paneled office where Dr. Clement Garlock received private patients with varying degrees of mental disturbance.

Dr. Garlock was dressed in a gray gabardine suit that matched his hair. He had an erratic speech pattern—drawn-out phrases followed by staccato sentences—that took some getting used to. After an abrupt greeting, he handed Katherine a sheaf of papers, took her down the hall to a sterile room with bare windows and three long worktables, and withdrew. She ran her eye down the list of questions on the first page. Would it work more to her advantage to appear sane or insane in annulment proceedings? she wondered. Scrupulous honesty was the only way. There's no point in trying to fool You, she told God. Let's find out how much You intend to cooperate.

For an hour she blacked in the interminable blanks next to repetitive queries designed to ascertain the state of her mental health. Did she take drugs? (No), have physical relationships with people of the same sex? (No), feel she was preoccupied with her own feces? *(Feh!)* Did she find joy in motherhood? (Yes), enjoyment in intellectual and artistic pursuits? (Yes), and faith in a Higher Power? (Yes). For inquiries as to whether she had nightmares or guilt or had ever gotten into trouble because of sex, she filled in the Sometimes blank. One stumped her: Had she ever had a black bowel movement? A trick question, she figured; having previously denied being concerned with such matters, here she would be admitting to it on at least one occasion. The relevance escaped her. Several questions, particularly those pertaining to elimination, were posed over and over with just enough difference in phraseology to fool the feeble-minded. Either that or the author of the test was fixated in the anal phase. Father Hartigan had once told her that Rorschach tests were only as good as the individual examiner, she recalled, and decided a computer would be preferable to the SS trooper posing as a psychiatrist outside.

She turned the page. More variations on a scatological theme. For the first time in years, Katherine remembered the enemas, the ignominious ordeal to which she was subjected as a child at the instigation of her mother. Every Saturday morning, the operation took place in the kitchen of a woman dressed in starched white, like a nurse in a lunatic asylum. Flowered oilcloth curtains were drawn across the windows; a naked light bulb hung over a white sheeted cot. There, Katie was splayed on her stomach like a butterfly pinned to a mat. The room was in a squalid apartment building opposite the rear entrance to the Sagamore Hotel, where the Winterhauses had an apartment that year. How convenient that her mother had found an enema lady so close to home! They had only to walk out the back door and across Meigs Street, Emily leading a trembling, shamefaced, symptomless child, whose protestations were ignored as she was internally cleansed, flushed out, without reason or fault.

To what horrors misguided parents can submit their charges,

Katherine thought. Had the years clouded her memory, or had her mother actually *smiled* as she sat there like a jailer, urging her to relax, to hold on just a moment longer . . . just another . . . minute . . . until she was sure she would explode? Could this be the same woman who greeted her with a cup of hot chocolate on snowy days after school, who soothed her feverish brow by the hour when she was sick, who took her to see *Lady in the Dark* on the afternoon Patches was run over? Were enemas a habit, a custom, a forties fad? Was her mother deranged? What of her father—did he know, aid and abet this crime against her little person?

And how about glycerine suppositories? My God! they used to line up for them in drugstores during the war! Rationed—they were *rationed*, there was such a run on them in Rochester as bombs fell on London and Prague. For years she had thought it was part of the war effort; middle-aged America's response, possibly, to losing the flower of its youth abroad: compulsive clenching of the excretory tract.

Regularly on Saturday evenings, she recalled, the family would gather after dinner in the Stokes's cozy living room on Culver Road to listen to Uncle Fred read aloud the latest letter from one or another son, Kevin, Greg, or Tony, who were ensigns in the navy. When he broke down the letter would pass to Aunt Doris, and respectively around the circle as tears spilled over. And the next morning, off they would go clutching their coupons—the very same group—to Rexall or Cut-Rite, even the children commandeered, since the rule was one package to a customer, to procure the precious tubes that relieved their elders' apparently chronic constipation. Long ago Katherine had decided it was a family aberration, another upstate New York quirk; yet here she was almost three decades later, sitting in an exclusive loony bin in Pasadena, forced to concentrate unduly on her alimentary canal.

After another hour, groggy with ennui Katherine filled in the final blank and looked at her watch. According to the Minnesota Multiphasic Personality Board, she could have taken another forty-five minutes. Papers in hand, she walked down the corridor and knocked at Dr. Garlock's door.

He opened it a crack, frowning. "Finished?"

Katherine nodded and handed him the examination.

He brought her inside and indicated the armless chair beside his desk. "You may wait for me here," he said, then turned and went through another door leading to an anteroom.

No pictures, books, or any personal touches intruded upon the antique elegance of his office. Katherine drummed her fingers on the mahogany desk, reminding herself she must not be combative, disrespectful, or flippant. There was no point, and all she wanted was his report to the Chancery Office, not a therapy session. After a few minutes, Dr. Garlock returned with her exam booklet, placed it atop a pile of papers on his desk, and sat down facing her, his expression impenetrable.

"Do you really consider this test a reliable indication of a person's mental health?" she asked curiously.

"Ninety-nine percent accurate," he snapped.

"Really? Can you give me any idea of . . . how I did?"

Glancing at the top page in a cursory fashion, Garlock said briskly, "Your answers indicate that you do not learn from experience, and that your faith is weak."

"Really? How does it show that?" Katherine felt a flicker of annoyance, unable to recall any specific questions about faith.

"For instance," he said, drawing out his second sheet, "you answered 'Sometimes' when asked if you have ever felt a conflict between religion and science."

"Yes—"

"There is never," the doctor broke in, his lips turning white with anger, "there is *never* any contradiction between religion and science!"

She opened her mouth to retort, but the look of gathering fury on her interlocutor's face stopped her in midbreath. Uh-oh, she thought, this one is certifiable. There is no discussion with this cat! He'll tell the Chancery I'm insubordinate and I'll blow the whole annulment.

"How any girl," he was saying feverishly, "educated by the Madames of the Sacred Heart could say such a thing is beyond me. You have obviously been severely tainted by your secular associations. As for the other thing—the results are incontrovertible. You have a tendency to repeat the same mistakes over and over."

"I don't know, Doctor," she said dubiously, thinking there were no similarities between Jed and Ben, or Eduardo and anybody else. "I've made a lot of mistakes, but never the same one twice."

His eyes sizzled in their sockets. "You are wrong."

For the first time Katherine noticed the bars on the windows. She rose, smiling politely. "Yes, Doctor, I see what you mean. Thank you very much, Dr. Garlock. You'll send the results to the Chancery Office, right?"

He smiled pleasantly, suddenly calm. "Yes, with my recommendation. Now go and be a good girl."

"Thank you," she repeated. With rubbery knees she backed out of his office and walked swiftly along the labyrinthine corridors of St. Michael the Archangel, suppressing an urge to break into a run.

CHAPTER 33

The Medicine Man

A strange lassitude came over Katherine. Driving into town during the day, she would feel her eyelids growing so heavy that it became necessary to pull over to the curb to close them for a few minutes; it was a struggle to stay awake during movies or Lilian's fall course on Marx and Lenin; frequently she dozed off while Ben was talking to her in the study after dinner. Half-jokingly, she told him she had narcolepsy. It might be a potassium deficiency, he suggested. His ex-wife had once suffered from the same symptom. Finally, baffled, Katherine made an appointment with Dr. Hidelman, her internist, a legacy from Jed. "Something goes wrong," Jed always said, "you get a Jewish doctor and go to a Catholic hospital. The nuns are dedicated, they know how to take care of people. The nurses at Mount Sinai will put you away."

Dr. Erich Hidelman was tall and handsome, with a perpetual suntan that was enhanced by his white coat. Seated behind his desk after the examination, he perused Katherine's folder, shaking his head with mock disapproval. "You are disgustingly healthy, Kate. If all my patients were like you, I'd be out of business. The tests don't indicate any problems at all."

"Then why do I keep falling asleep? I can't even make it into Beverly Hills."

"Do you smoke?"

"Nope. Never have."

"Why don't you start?"

"Dr. Hidelman!"

"I get so tired of telling people to stop," he said with a sigh. Katherine laughed. He looked at her and his expression turned sober. "I think if you sit down somewhere by yourself and think about it, you'll figure it out. You're doing something you don't want to do, kid."

Apprehension backed up in her body like an engine going wrong. I don't want to think about it . . . I can't, she thought.

"If you want to talk to a pro, I'll give you a name—"

"You mean a shrink?"

His nod made her sigh. Since Dr. West had moved to Santa Clara, she had not had the faintest inclination to start over with someone new, even during the traumatic days when Ben went back to Deirdre. "Basically," she told him, "I've gone back to my original theory that psychoanalysis is a crock."

"I tend to agree with you, but when it comes down to it, Kate, it's the only game in town."

"That's how I feel about the Church."

"I think you can probably solve this one on your own, but if you want a referral, let me know."

As Katherine got up to leave, she cast an envious look at the dark-eyed, smiling woman in the photograph on Dr. Hidelman's desk. Along with everything else, she thought, he was so *sane.*

By the time she got home, drowsiness had overtaken her again; she lay down in the study to take a nap before Chryssie's car pool arrived. Dreams of Ben haunted her sleep: Ben crashing through a line of burly football players to score a touchdown while crowds cheered; Ben swooping over her house in his plane, somersaulting in the sky and smiling behind aviator glasses; Ben in Dr. Hidelman's white coat, listening to her heart with a stethoscope; Ben at Wimbledon, planting a kiss on a huge silver cup; Ben planting a kiss on—

Still straining to see the woman's face, Katherine awoke with a start. If only she knew what Deirdre looked like! Afraid to close her eyes lest the phantoms return, she stared at the dust motes in a ray of sunlight streaming through the window. Ben's wall clock chimed four. She had slept for over an hour, but she was still exhausted. How would she feel . . . how would Chryssie feel without the sound of Ben's car pulling in the driveway each evening?

When Chryssie got home from school, she found her mother in the kitchen, marinating a pot roast.

Part Four

CHAPTER 34

Absolution

"Bless me, Father, for I have sinned. It's been two years since my last confession. During that time I missed Mass frequently. I lost my temper with my daughter several times and . . . uh. . . ." (Oh Christ! Why can't I ever think of any sins besides sex?) "For three months I've been living with a man who is not my husband."

Katherine waited in the confessional, her body emaciated from missing Ben, her voice stilled to keep from crying out: Help me, Father! Do something, somebody please get him back!

The final, annihilating fight had occurred a few nights after Thanksgiving. It had started about the children. She was too strict, Ben had said, and she'd felt constrained to uphold the value of manners—of all things—and then somehow, it had gotten out of hand when he'd said something she didn't believe. It was nothing important, but when he'd looked at her with those hard, malachite eyes and repeated, "I would have no reason to lie to you, Katherine," she'd cracked. Standing over him as he sat beside the fire in the study, she'd shrieked, "You lie about your *height*, for God's sake, saying you're six feet tall as if we're all blind! You're five seven—admit it!" It was the sort of low physical blow she assiduously avoided in arguments; she couldn't believe the words had come out of her mouth. Steeped in self-hatred, she'd watched helplessly as Ben rose, brushed past her, removed his clock from the wall, and went out the door for good.

"Is this still going on?" the priest asked gently.

As long as I haven't said no, maybe it'll be all right, Katherine told herself. If I say no, it will mean it really is over. I daren't say no.

"No, Father," she said. It was a very small no.

She bowed her face into the cup of her hands. I knew I'd pay for the sex . . . I always knew it, she thought bitterly. I used to think as we lay in bed together how one day the price would be exacted for the ecstasy of loving him. While the priest gave her absolution for her sins, she dwelt upon the night Ben had made love to her on the back lawn, when his hands held her against him and her eyes, looking up, were blinded by the radiance of the moon. Afterward, she'd dreamed the police were after her, sirens blaring.

The amorphous form behind the grille raised his right hand in a blessing. They get to you all right, she thought bitterly. They get to you early enough so that the later overlay of Kierkegaard and Camus and Freud are just so many feeble waves washing against ancient, immutable rocks. She pictured her mother, robed in ethereal white, turning to God with a nod of approval as they contemplated her suffering from Above.

"I told her so," Emily said through compressed lips.

"She'll learn," rumbled God, tugging on His long white beard.

"For your penance," said the priest, "say ten Our Fathers and twenty Hail Marys and make a good Act of Contrition."

"OhmyGodIammostheartilysorry . . . ," Katherine murmured, surprised at the lightness of the sentence, having expected at least a rosary for her lapse, even from this liberal, media Paulist who hosted a popular television series. His familiar, mellifluous voice said, "Go in peace . . . pray for me."

"Yes, Father."

The wooden panel slid into place and the whisperings of another penitent began.

In the church it was dark and still. The usual Saturday evening stragglers—two women, an old man, a teenager—waited outside the confessional. Above the altar, a shaft of moonlight filtered through stained glass onto the crucifix. Katherine walked slowly down the aisle. She remembered a Jules Feiffer cartoon: "I don't believe in God. I believe in Al. Because I love him. And he'll marry me and give me a home and children . . . and . . . and play around. And break my heart. And leave me. And make me want to die. After Al—there'll be years left for God."

Dear God! My years have come too soon, she thought, kneeling before the altar. The familiarity of the place—veiled tabernacle, weeping statues, stale air tinged with the scent of incense—closed around her like strict, comforting arms, and with a sudden sense of release she watched her tears fall onto the varnished rail. She had been away such a long time.

The next day, for the first time in three years, Katherine went to Communion. It was a bittersweet reunion. She looked up at Christ on the cross and thought, What a way to get me back.

CHAPTER 35

Loss

It was three days before Christmas. Mounds of snow weighed down the branches of the maple tree outside Douglas's window. He sat a few feet from the television, drumming two fingers against his lips as he waited patiently for the morning comedy shows to begin, his milky blue eyes focused on the book Katherine had left on the tray table. For an hour the evening before, she'd read aloud to him from *The Life of George S. Kaufman*, making his bony shoulders shake with laughter at the playwright's witticisms. Later on, the night nurse, Miss Pierce, a tight-lipped woman who was never without her hair net, had scanned the flyleaf and made a disparaging remark about the Jews. "Now, now. We'll have none of that biased talk," Douglas had chastised her. With a sidelong glance at Katherine, he'd added in a gruff voice, "I've learned a lot from this young lady." A rush of emotion had sent Katherine out of the room to compose herself, suppressed tears clouding her vision so that she almost collided with a wispy old woman clunking along the corridor behind a walker.

Now, in the room next door, Mrs. Simpson started her plaintive cries for "Daddy Bill," the grandson who came to see her once every six months and who she was convinced was her husband. Chryssie sat on the floor at Douglas's feet, studying the TV schedule. It was no place for a child to spend Christmas, Katherine thought as she watched them, trying to assuage her guilt over leaving her father before the holiday. As reliable as change, Jed had come to their rescue. He was taking Chris to Aspen for a week, and had called to urge her to join them. Katherine had made plans to fly to Denver on Christmas Eve.

The agony of losing Ben blunted her pain at seeing her father so weakened. The day before they'd arrived, Anita had called a priest to give him the last rites; however, he'd seemed to revive in the presence of his daughter and granddaughter. But age was having its way with his lucidity: by the hour he would sit in his Naugahyde chair, gazing into space, counting backward aloud. "Five hundred and ten . . . five hundred and nine . . . five hundred and eight. . . ." No matter how Katherine tried to distract him, at the first opportunity he would return to the inexorable countdown, picking up precisely where he'd left off. What did it signify? she wondered. Did he believe that when he got to zero, he would die? Or was it merely the Practical Joker's final prank on the successful financier? And where was that bastard, Sol Levant? she demanded of God silently. Sunning himself on the Riviera? Getting another award from the fucking *government*? She recalled Jed's words: "Sol Levant knows what he is, dollface. Your old man's got peace of mind, and you can't buy that with any amount of money."

The next morning Douglas awoke with a start, calling out for the nurse, his eyes fixed in terror on the ceiling. Anita and Katherine ran to his bedside. While the nurse raised him against the pillows and tried to calm him, Katherine rubbed the gnarled, veined hand that lay on the sheet.

"There are crabs up there," he said in a quavering voice.

"You were dreaming, Daddy," Katherine said soothingly.

"I'm telling you I saw crabs on that ceiling. I see 'em! Don't tell me I'm dreaming!"

"They're gone now," Anita assured him in her no-nonsense way.

But Douglas was not to be talked out of the crabs. By mid-morning, imaginary lobsters had joined the platoon of shellfish invading his room, sea vultures come to bear him off with his black rosary wrapped around his fist. Although he was sitting up, calm and alert that afternoon, and the doctor assured her he might hang on for many months, Katherine could not escape her conviction that it was the last time she would see her father alive.

On the morning of their departure, she stood at the side of his bed for a long while, smoothing the thin gray strands back from his forehead, rubbing the soft place behind his ear that her childhood fingers had discovered. When the taxi honked outside, Chryssie put her arms around him and kissed his papery cheek. "I love you, Granddaddy," she said.

Smiling feebly, he mumbled, "Pretty girl . . . you're a sweetheart."

Katherine touched her shoulder. "Run out to the cab, darling. I'll be right there."

Douglas closed his eyes, but his hand still clasped Katherine's tightly, as if some mysterious breath of life passed from her to him. He looked as she remembered her grandmother had, as she herself would look one day. His lips moved laboriously but no sound came. Remember me to God, she thought. She stayed beside him until his fingers relaxed and his deep, even breathing indicated he was asleep. Then she stole to the door, where she looked back for a last glimpse of him. Without opening his eyes, he said, "So long, Skeezix."

"Merry Christmas, Daddy," she said in a breaking voice. "We'll be back soon. Before spring."

She closed the door and leaned her head against it, her body overtaken with dry, racking sobs.

The bus wound farther and farther up the mountain. In a rear window seat, Chryssie sat with her knees drawn up to her chin, braids sticking out from a ski hat, her eyes on her mother's drawn face.

"Are you upset about Granddaddy or Ben?" she asked.

"Both," Katherine said.

"One's worth it, the other isn't."

Katherine looked at her. So far the child had betrayed no sadness over Ben's second defection, nor any sense of regret for the man who had so recently announced his intention to become her stepfather. "I don't understand," Katherine burst out. "You loved him, too. You used to listen for the sound of his car just like I did, hoping it was him."

"I still listen for his car," Chryssie said gravely, "only now I dread it's him."

"Is that true?"

"It's true, Mommy," she replied with a clear, level gaze. "He's crazy. Do you want to be married to a crazy person?"

The bus driver's announcement that they were approaching the Aspen station saved Katherine from the embarrassment of a reply.

It was almost midnight. The air was thin and cold and the sky seemed closer, alight with a galaxy of stars. Waiting on the snow-covered platform was Jed in his vintage white sheepskin coat from Finland, shivering in the cold, his right hand cupped over a Christmas candle to shield its flickering flame from the wind. Chris rounded a corner in a horse-drawn sleigh; when they climbed in, Jed told the driver to take them to the nearest Catholic church. "I'm fucking outnumbered," he growled, explaining to Katherine in an undertone that Chris was going through a religious-fanatic phase (which he considered to be God's punishment for his marrying a shiksa), and was considering converting to Catholicism. All through Midnight Mass, he *grizhered*.

The sight of them at the station had filled her with love, and Katherine tried for all their sakes to emulate being part of a family, but once the children were on the slopes in the morning, she lapsed into wretched silence with Jed. He made a valiant attempt to comfort her, but she was unreachable in her anguish, which, considering the source, was incomprehensible to him. Sunk into a pit of self-castigation, she went about like a gray ghost. A solemn vow not to talk about Ben made her wonder in silence why Chryssie had said he was crazy. New Year's Day, Jed and Chris flew back to Los Angeles. Katherine and Chryssie arrived on the third.

CHAPTER 36

A Mitzvah

On the tenth of January, Anita called to say they doubted that Douglas would make it through the night. With a sense that the ground was slipping out from under her, Katherine dialed Margot's number in St. Louis. Only eight months had passed since Emily's death; their parents had not missed an anniversary together, she thought. Something inside her was unraveling; she wanted to weep with someone, to share her grief with family—what was left of it— but such luxuries are for Italians and Jews, she decided, because whatever Margot felt at the news, she did not choose to reveal it to Katherine. In a brisk, efficient voice she said that a second funeral should present no complications. Their divergent styles had sent them hurtling away from each other in the manner of like magnetic poles; the older sister Katherine had idolized as a child had for some time found her emotionality faintly embarrassing, definitely not good form. Katherine hung up without another word, angry and facing an abyss of loneliness. She went to tell Chryssie about her grandfather. Chryssie had dug out a snapshot of him in his wheelchair; she was sitting on the edge of the bed with it in her hands, her eyes starting to water. Katherine let out a breath and went to sit beside her. "Oh, honey," she said, putting an arm around her, and as they looked at the picture together, the hollow place inside her chest filled up with healing tears.

Douglas died before morning. Soon after they arrived in Rochester, Katherine and Chryssie selected a coffin lined with his favorite shade of blue; then Katherine left her at a cousin's house and went alone to Mapleridge to choose a suit in which to bury him and to collect his possessions. A huge house filled with antiques and rare books and art objects, a lifetime of acquiring things, she thought, and at the end, everything he needed fit into a shoebox.

Cosmetics were out of the question, she informed the undertaker. A tall man with protruding eyes, he offered her a choice of shoes for the corpse. God forbid he should go to *yene velt* unshod, she thought, unconsciously using Jed's terminology for the next world. The following day, she went with trepidation to view the finished product. The coffin was at the far end of a green-carpeted room that took an eternity to cross. But when she was there, looking down at her father, the burden of grief lifted. His expression was one of absolute peace; he seemed merely to be sleeping. The undertaker, however, had the last laugh: Douglas was wearing his reading glasses.

By the time she got back to the Country Club, Margot was having dinner with Chryssie in the Grille. Katherine started to describe to them the positive effects of seeing the body, but Margot interrupted. "I intend to remember Daddy as he was in that picture taken with me in Palm Beach." Turning to Chryssie, she added, "You can do what you want, but I'd advise you not to subject yourself to that."

But Chryssie insisted on going to the funeral home in the morning. As they knelt together at the side of the open casket, Katherine cast her an anxious glance. By the time she had reached Chryssie's age, she was a veteran of Catholic wakes, but this was the first dead person her daughter had encountered. For a long moment Chryssie gazed at the bespectacled corpse. Then she leaned over and said in a stage whisper, "Granddaddy looks just like Woody Allen in *Sleeper*." The undertaker, who was gliding across the room to offer his condolences, was taken aback by the sound of their muted giggles.

Tragedy comes in threes, Katherine thought on the way back to Los Angeles, mentally braced for the third. From the driveway, she could see that her front door was wide open. The house had been burglarized. The two policemen who dusted for fingerprints asked if anyone else had a key. Ben had kept his, she recalled; when the cops left, she called him at *Newsworld* to ask him to return it. Informed that he had stepped out, she left her name; a moment later Peter Mandel, whom she had not seen since Thanksgiving, got on the phone.

"How are you, honey?" he asked.

The kindness in his voice was too much for her; she broke down, blurting that her father had died and the house had been ransacked and . . .

"And Ben is back with Deedee," Peter said quietly.

When she did not reply, he said, "Why don't you let Karen and me take you to dinner on Sunday, Katherine? We've been talking about it. There are some things we think you ought to know. Ben's my friend, but you've got a right to know you're not crazy."

An hour later, Ben returned her call. He was solicitous about the burglary and assured her that no one else had had access to the key. "I'll drop it off in your mailbox," he said. Katherine took a deep breath. "Are you and Deirdre getting married?"

In a voice so falsely benevolent it made her wish for cruelty, he replied, "Yes, we are, Katherine."

"When?"

"On my birthday. January thirtieth."

"Well . . . it's all been worth something then," she said in a controlled tone.

"Yes, I think it has."

"Well," she said again. "Congratulations. I hope you'll be very happy."

She dialed Jed's number, her fingers trembling, and when he answered, she wailed, "Ben's marrying Deirdre on the same day he said we should get married."

"Perfectly normal," said Jed. "Keep the date and change the girl."

On January twenty-seventh, Katherine was dispiritedly selecting groceries at Food Giant in Pacific Palisades and almost ran into someone with her shopping cart. Without looking at him, she murmured an apology and started to move on.

"Katherine?" he said, peering at her. "Is that you? You look . . ." He trailed off, as if how she looked was too ghastly to describe. It was Lester Berkowitz, Ben's old friend, the one who had insulted her at Tivoli a few months before.

"Hello, Lester," she said, mustering a faint smile. He must be satisfied with the way things turned out, she thought, and started to push past him, but he stopped her with a hand on her arm, his eyes filled with what appeared to be genuine concern. "Are you all right?"

"I'm hanging on," she said. "Going to the wedding?"

He nodded. After a moment's hesitation, he said, "When Ben told me he was getting married, I assumed he meant to you. You know, that night at Tivoli, I was mad because I thought you were wrong for Ben. But now I see that it was the other way around. I love the guy, but sometimes I feel like I've got a juvenile delinquent kid brother or something." A woman tried to maneuver her cart around them. "Let's get out of the way," Lester said, drawing Katherine behind the wine counter.

"Did you ask him about me? About what happened?"

"Yeah," Lester acknowledged. "He said, 'Katherine was a conduit.'"

"A conduit?" she echoed dully.

"He was leading a double life, Katherine. I'm sorry you got caught in the middle."

"If I could get my hands on him, I'd break his nose for a fifth time," she said with a tired laugh.

Lester's expression was blank. "What do you mean for a fifth time?"

"Oh, he told me it looks the way it does because it got broken in fights four times when he was a kid."

"I've known Ben since first grade, Katherine. He's always had that nose."

She stared at him. "What about the scar on his neck?"

"I was with him when that happened."

"In Africa?"

"Try Southern Boulevard. Some guy hit a home run playing stickball—three sewers, at least," Lester grinned. "And Ben fell into a windshield trying to catch it. His old man's a dentist, but things weren't going so good. The guy who sewed him up did a lousy job."

Katherine gaped at him, unable to speak.

He dropped his eyes. "You've gotta understand—the ghetto can be so terrible, some guys just make up a life."

The ghetto again, she thought. The great scapegoat.

Glancing at the clock overhead, Lester said, "Look, I've got to meet a client at three, but if you ever want to have a coffee or anything, give me a ring. I'm divorced again."

"From Susan? Or Miss Israel?" Katherine asked.

"Miss Israel?" Lester repeated. "Who's that?"

"Ben said your last wife was Miss Israel."

Lester guffawed. "She was a very pretty girl, but she was never Miss Anything."

In a downpour on Sunday evening, Katherine drove into Beverly Hills to meet the Mandels, her sense of unreality growing by the minute.

An hour later, seated between them in a booth at La Scala Boutique, she felt as if she were wandering in outer space. Out of the crazy quilt they spread before her, the skein of Ben's lies, a few threads stood out like neon. Not six months but six days had passed since he'd been with Deirdre when Katherine ran into him outside the Bistro; it was merely another of their many breakups. When Katherine was about to leave town, he'd run back to Deirdre; they had been in his apartment, in bed together on that hot August night when Katherine was leaning on his doorbell.

Karen, a sunstreaked blonde with a wide smile, began to exchange horrified glances with her husband as the extent of Katherine's ignorance and distress became clear.

"What did she think I was *doing* there?"

Karen said: "Ben told her that you were always following him—that you were trying to get him to marry you."

Katherine slumped against the seat, "Has anyone told her the truth?"

"Her analyst's been telling her for years," Peter said. "She doesn't want to know."

"She's stopped going to him in order to marry Ben," Karen added.

What was she doing questioning Deirdre's awareness? Katherine asked herself. What about her own? Of course her subconscious had known all along; that was what Dr. Hidelman had been trying to tell her. And in that moment, she realized that for all the pain she had suffered since Ben had left, she had never again fallen asleep at the wheel. The mysterious potassium deficiency had disappeared with him.

"If you ask me, Deedee's a born victim," Karen said. "She's not stupid."

"Doesn't she ever get mad at him?" Katherine asked.

"Deedee never loses her temper," Peter said. "When she gets fed up, she just opens the door and tells him quietly to go."

"I guess that must work better," Katherine murmured.

"Anne got that way too," Karen said. "She was completely different when we were at City College."

"City College?" Katherine echoed. "I thought she went to Radcliffe, and Ben to Harvard."

"Is he still telling that story?" Karen asked. "The four of us met at City and went straight through together."

"How does he function as a reporter?" Katherine asked them. "The *Examiner, Newsworld*—dealing with facts all the time?"

Peter started to laugh, then caught himself at a look from his wife. "Ben's not a reporter, Katherine," he said. "He manages the office. It's a perfectly respectable, well-paid job. He had a similar one at the paper."

"Then all the stories he was writing—Henry Miller . . . the interviews with Cranston and the governor . . . flying to San Francisco to see the mayor—?"

Peter shook his head. "As far as I know, Ben hasn't been out of Los Angeles for months except for a quick trip he took to San Francisco before Christmas to settle his grandparents' estate."

The reddish light in the restaurant cast a diabolical glow over Peter's face as he nursed a Scotch and soda. Katherine had a sensation of being alone on a raft that was floating far out to sea.

"What I think," said Peter in a disgusted voice, "is that both you and Deedee should dump him. What's the guy *got* anyway?"

Katherine was silent while she considered this.

"All I can tell you," she said at last, "is that I never felt so loved before. I understand Deirdre. It's what giving up a drug must be like."

While Peter stared uncomprehendingly into his glass, Katherine pondered the mystery of why Jed hadn't seen through Ben. And Lilian. Brilliant, perceptive Lilian. What had caused her antennae to malfunction?

Karen excused herself and went to the ladies' room. His glasses flashing like windowpanes in the shadows, Peter said quietly, "The first day I saw you with Ben at the Bistro, I knew he was going to fuck it up, and I swore to myself that if he did, I'd be there to pick up the pieces. Nothing like you ever happened to him in his life. Don't you see, Katherine? You're the girl he couldn't *get* at De Witt Clinton. You're the shiksa goddess."

Katherine's responding laughter, first at the realization that the

Bronx High School of Science was yet another of Ben's myths, then at the expression shiksa goddess, verged on hysteria. The same words Andy had used, and Lester Berkowitz, and Lilian. Was her entire romantic life nothing but a cultural joke? Had God put her under a microscope to act out a compulsion? How come some Gentile women were capable of marrying a Jew and living happily ever after? Only last night, she had stared at the crawl of credits that came on after a comedy show. Writer: Al Stone; Director: Jay Gold; Story Editor: Irwin Katz. Why not one of them? she'd asked herself. They were probably all warm, funny, and smart. Why did she have to choose the Billy Liar of Jews? Or was it that he had chosen her? That her blond hair and crazed little blue eyes had acted on him as a red flag to a bull? This was absolutely *it*, she told herself. No more Jewish boyfriends. She could indulge her love of Jewish culture without marrying one. What she needed was Jewish friends, not a Jewish lover. What she needed was to talk to Jed.

Walking to her car a few minutes later, she saw Kent Forgen going into La Scala. He stopped to say hello, and as everyone had been doing, he told her how terrible she looked. "You can't be upset over that *Newsworld* fellow, Katherine," he said. "I never understood what you were doing with him. It was like *The Way We Were*, only you were Robert Redford. Go talk to Jed. There's nobody better when you're having a nervous breakdown."

At four the next afternoon, Katherine picked up Chryssie at school and drove directly to Jed's. "It's sad, Mommy. Ben's just not proud of himself," Chryssie said on the way. With enormous kindness, Jed brought them into his study, settled Katherine in his armchair beside the fire, made her a glass of tea, and went to sit behind his desk. He leaned back in his chair, his brow furrowed as he listened to the report of the Mandels' revelations, breaking in only once to say in a baffled voice, "I must say, he fooled me."

Across the room on the windowseat, Chryssie played with Kitty, who had a bag of catnip between her front paws.

"I did used to wonder," Katherine said, "how a reporter could keep such regular hours. Why would he lie about his *job*?"

Putting a match to his pipe, Jed looked at her over the flame. "Didn't you ever read the masthead?"

"Yes, but he told me it takes time to change it. And the stories were always being postponed."

"It's so easily checked," he said in a bewildered voice. "I can't believe this."

Katherine leaned her head against the back of the chair and fastened her eyes on a wooden beam, sighing. "I suppose he wasn't in Cuba with Fidel before the revolution, either."

Jed rose, put his hand to his side, and cleared his throat. "Now lemme tell you why that one's not true, kid. Castro's in the hills with twelve guys. One of them is *not* Ben Fahrengold."

Katherine started to laugh; Jed and Chryssie joined in and their hilarity grew until her daughter was holding her sides and her own eyes streamed. "It's all too ridiculous," Katherine gasped. "He must not have been a test pilot or a football hero either."

"Mommy," Chryssie said patiently, "no football coach in the country would even let him try out. He's too little!"

Katherine turned to her in mock outrage. "Wonderful! Suddenly you're a maven!" Behind her she heard Jed chuckle. "Where were you when I needed you?"

Chryssie rolled her eyes. "Well, it was just *obv*ious. I thought you were humoring him."

"God, no! I believed it all."

"Even the part about turning down the money?" Chryssie asked.

"I blocked that one out," Katherine admitted, and they all began to laugh again.

It took a long time and a lot of help to get over Ben Fahrengold. Katherine volunteered at the ACLU (where, of course, no one had ever heard of him), haunted the self-help sections of several bookstores, and looked up Dr. West's replacement, Dr. Samuel Haskell.

What fascinated Dr. Haskell, who was an attractive, fortyish, profoundly unhappy-looking man, was the fact that corporate America was manifest in Katherine's Christian ex-boyfriends; among them, they would inherit fortunes amassed from the production of soap, soup, baby food, fruit, and newspapers, as well as the ships that carried many of these items to South America. She related how, after a few weeks, her brain flattened by their earnestness, she would cross paths with the wisecracking son of a secondhand furniture-store owner, say, or a peddler's heir, or a pretender to a pushcart throne, and leaving all those worldly goods and chattels behind, follow him anywhere. What manner of madness was this? What self-destructive impulse led her again and again to that river bed where the daughters of Sion weep, presumably when they are not laughing at the gags? "Why, Dr. Haskell, WHY?" she wailed, leaning forward intently in the cracked leather armchair across from his desk.

Dr. Haskell pressed his fingers together, looked at the ceiling, and said, "Do you detect a pattern, Mrs. Kellogg?" And for Dr. Haskell, that was saying a lot.

"A pattern?" she screeched. "It's a mania! The question is, how do I break it? If I come here for five years, when I walk out, will it be like the boss saying to the secretary, 'Why, Miss Jones, I've never seen you without your glasses?' Will normal men look at me with interest again?"

Allowing himself a whisper of a smile, Dr. Haskell replied, "I think normal men look at you that way now, Mrs. Kellogg, only you don't notice them."

"How about normal Jewish men?"

"First, we need to work out what you refer to as the shiksa syndrome."

"You mean that to recognize the syndrome is to transcend it?"

"Possibly," he said in his enigmatic way.

Therapy didn't help much; in the end, Dr. Haskell's long silences led Katherine no closer to an answer than Dr. West's questions had.

That winter, Katherine spent long hours rewriting the screenplay with Lilian. As a reaction to the shallow, superficial values that even then she was convinced had played a part in destroying her relationship with Ben, she greeted with alacrity Chryssie's suggestion that she transfer from the largely Protestant Westlake to Oakwood, a small school with a predominantly Jewish enrollment; however, Katherine's enthusiasm faltered when they drove to the Valley to observe a day of classes. A dilapidated remodeled church was set on a tiny plot of land utterly lacking in physical amenities or even a blade of grass. During English class, Katherine muttered to Chryssie, "The place looks like a firetrap." Chryssie's eyes were riveted on the teacher. "That's on the outside, Mom. Don't you see how wonderful it is inside?" The truth of her words was revealed at a subsequent Parent-Teachers meeting. After the stilted, formal convocations at Westlake, the evening was a revelation. It was a free-for-all of opinions and feelings; the headmaster actually spoke of his concern for how students treated one another on a human level, and the subject of fund-raising was never mentioned. When Katherine got home, she told Chryssie, "You're right. Oakwood has a soul."

After a dozen revisions, the screenplay was completed at the end of March; Lilian submitted it to her agent, who promptly sold it to Paramount for an unconscionable amount of money. It was Passover, and she invited Katherine and Chryssie to a seder in celebration.

A light rain had fallen throughout the afternoon. Clouds scattered and the sun broke through as they drove into Westwood; in the southern sky, a rainbow looped over the freeway. While Lilian had been writing with Katherine, her apartment had been in an uproar—books and papers strewn about, her daughter's door permanently shut to hide the mess. But for this evening everything had been put in order: the table was set with woven cloth placemats and candles, the furniture gleamed with polish, even the blond wood floor had been waxed. Buber lumbered into the foyer when they arrived; behind him came Aaron Bauer, a tall, scholarly-looking man in his forties, glasses perched atop his balding head. Moments later Lilian came out of the kitchen in a pale linen dress and espadrilles.

"Schmuck!" she addressed her husband. "You forgot to pick up the wine." And this dignified man, who was held in great esteem by his colleagues and treated with near reverence by his students at UCLA Law School, smacked his forehead with his hand and hurried off to rectify his oversight, apparently unruffled by his wife's display of affectionate impatience. From her now immaculate bedroom, eleven-year-old Joy emerged; she had a helmet of black hair and a fiercely independent air. When her father returned, they brought his mother in from the library; she was ninety, Russian, and spoke not a word of English. He seated her next to Katherine at the country table outside the kitchen; then he bowed his head and said in a resonant voice: "As we gather about this festive seder table, we are uniting ourselves with our past; we are linking ourselves with our future; and we are identifying ourselves with every one of our people, everywhere in the world, who is at this moment celebrating the deathless idea of freedom, which Passover commemorates."

Chryssie's voice followed; apparently coached by Lilian, she asked a trifle self-consciously, "Why is this night different from all other nights of the year?" Katherine hid a smile, recalling Jed's childhood answer, "Because we didn't clean the windows." Eight years old and already doing jokes. After Joy had recited the next questions, Aaron filled their glasses with wine and said, "I'd like to add a quote from Voltaire, who also spoke about freedom. He said, 'Man is free at the moment he wishes to be.' "

Katherine raised her eyes and looked around the table, experiencing a sense of family such as she had not done since Sunday lunches at her grandmother's house. The paradox was that Lilian, whom she had once thought was shutting her out, now gave her the gift of belonging. And Aaron had provided her with a clue to her own feeling of freedom—not from Catholicism, which was as much a part of her as Judaism was to Jed or the Bauers, but from a heritage of provincialism and prejudice. Looking at Chryssie's face, she was confident that at least it had not been passed on to another generation.

The elder Mrs. Bauer talked in a low voice to her son and communicated with the others mainly through smiles. Aaron informed her that Katherine had a knowledge of Yiddish, so the old woman demanded a demonstration over coffee in the sitting room. The phrases *malach-hamoves* and *goy tse peygern* in the mouth of this blond Gentile set her off in a gale of laughter and spanned what had seemed an unbridgeable gap. Shortly before eleven, Katherine hugged her and called Chryssie out of Joy's bedroom, where they were engaged in a Scrabble word game. Lilian walked with them to the car. Joy had obviously decided to practice her recorder at that late hour and the high, sweet notes drifted through the open windows. Scattered with purple jacaranda blossoms, the lawn was nearly bright as day in the light of a full moon.

"I'll never forget this evening, Lilian," Katherine said. "It was a *mitzvah*."

CHAPTER 37

Ghosts in the Attic

"I'm spending the summer doing nothing," Wilder Framingham Jergens Schwartz wrote from her estate in Lower Merion. "Sometimes, when I'm reading by the pool, Manny calls from the office to ask how I'm feeling, or do I like the new material we've chosen, or how did Timmy's baseball game turn out, and after all those years of Hugo's emotional constipation, I think I've died and gone to heaven. If I sneezed, the phone would ring and it would be Manny saying God bless you! Nobody's perfect—he goes into a rage if I miss a putt on the golf course—but he gives me so much in other ways, his temper just doesn't matter much in the long run. Basically, I feel as if I've gotten my childhood dream, which was to be like Mary Magdalene, the wife of that sexy guy!

I haven't really renounced my religion as you thought. I'm just not comfortable with it. I spent so many years trying to understand transubstantiation, I think I did brain damage. The baby's due in two months. What I'm going to do is, get him baptized on the side. What they don't know can't hurt them, right?

Lots of love,
Wilder

P.S. Burn this letter!

P.P.S. Manny's brother Victor is thrilled you're bringing Chryssie to New York in the fall to look at boarding schools. Wouldn't it be fun to be sisters-in law?"

P.P.P.S. Congratulations to you and Lilian on the second screenplay! Glorious news!"

***

Labor Day at Jed's: peace, permanence, timelessness—nothing ever changed on the hill. Roses bloomed, the wooden swing hung from the branches of the olive tree, a few silvery leaves floated on the tranquil surface of the pool. Inside, the couch had been re-covered in the same plaid material, and the furniture remained where Bertie Hayes had placed it. Only Simon was missing; in his place was a russet setter, who lay a few feet from the pool table, his muzzle resting on the doorsill as he stared out at the garden. Jed stood facing away from the table, playing a difficult shot behind his back. A click was followed by two plops. "Cocksucker!" he yelled, then he growled "Your shot, knibbler," at Chryssie, who had been wait-ing patiently for twenty minutes since her last turn. "Watch the cuestick!" he warned. "You dig a hole in the table, I never speak to you again as long as I live."

Chryssie smiled and made the shot.

At the round table against the window, Chris was drawing in her sketchpad, her hair platinum in the sun-smitten light. No longer a hellion (or *choleria*), she had acquired mile-long legs and her moth-er's sensational body, but at almost eighteen had developed no in-terest in an acting career. "It makes people crazy," she confided to Katherine, who was seated across from her.

"Tell me about your boyfriend," Katherine said.

"He's okay. I'm not in love with him or anything, but I don't want to break up with him 'cause he's got great timing."

"Timing?" Katherine laughed. "Other girls are looking for a guy who's handsome, smart, successful. But what's important to Jed Bernard's daughter is timing!"

Chris laughed, smudging a charcoal outline with her finger. "Remember when you and my dad used to come pick me after school?"

"Sure I do."

"I'd see the car coming up the hill, and you were always laugh-ing."

"Again with the reminiscing!" Jed grumbled, shaking his head as Chryssie's ball sped along the baize. "Do you believe that? The kid hasn't missed a shot. I understand you're from the East, knib-bler, like your mother. You better tell those fucking boarding schools they're interviewing a pool hustler."

"SHHH! I'm concentrating," Chryssie said.

Jed gave Katherine a look. "And you were afraid she was going to be scared of me. Who else dares to say 'SHHH!' to Jed Bernard?"

Watching him stalk the table with a panther's grace, Katherine recalled how Christopher had once questioned the wisdom of providing their daughter with a surrogate father of advanced years. "What's your plan?" he'd asked. "That when she's eighteen she goes from rest home to rest home looking for him?" And she'd snapped, "Better than going from bar to bar looking for you." But things had fallen into place: Christopher had stopped drinking, and since he'd remarried, Chryssie had a real second home; and Jed, in his late fifties, looked at least a decade younger and could be counted on to show up at every important school function. Quite simply, he was their best friend.

Late that afternoon, after Chris left for Manhattan Beach and Chryssie had gone to change out of her bathing suit, Katherine and Jed strolled outside and sat beneath the sycamore tree in the courtyard. Even at that hour, the sun was still hot enough to melt trickles of tar on the driveway. A sirocco had begun to stir things up in the hills. They were silent for a while, each lost in thought.

"Jed," Katherine said at one point. "How come everybody else runs away when I explode or get hysterical, and you never did?"

He puffed on his pipe; then he looked at her and said simply, "I liked you."

She thought they were three of the most eloquent words she had ever heard.

Two weeks later, early on an autumn evening, having dropped Chryssie off at her grandparents' town house, her mind still running a film of rolling green hills and clusters of ivy-covered dormitories they'd seen in Connecticut where boys and girls milled about in noisy, cheerful chaos—a thousand light years from her own high-school experience—Katherine walked up Madison Avenue from Sixty-third Street toward the Stanhope Hotel, a good twenty blocks in which to absorb the changes that had occurred.

September is the New Year of the soul, she reflected, especially in New York, when the temperature drops suddenly and the pace in the avenues quickens, turning one's thoughts to goals and reassessments. Odd how despite years in California, New York still seemed like home; how she instinctively thought of herself here as Katherine Winterhaus. She gave a passing consideration to dropping the Kellogg, then reminded herself that the name was now linked to her professional identity, one half of the writing team of Bauer and Kellogg, who were in the midst of their third screenplay. More important, it was her daughter's name—Christabel, who was so much a part of her, who had survived the tornado of her parents' marriage and the vicissitudes of having a mother who was always in love; who, having inherited Christopher's sensitivity and been exposed at an early age to Jed's heart and humor and empathy (as well as his timing), was a fusion of the best of both worlds. The prospect of her going away to school in another year had given Katherine a strong sense of endings. As they'd flown out of Los Angeles, a verse from Cavafy had run over and over in her mind:

> *You tell yourself, I'll be gone*
> *To some other land, some other sea,*
> *To a city lovelier far than this*
> *Could ever have been or hope to be.*

When she'd looked back at the flat landscape smoldering beneath its poisonous autumnal veil, she had remembered Lot's wife. "*Macha-moves!*" she could hear Jed holler. Now, waiting for the light to change at Sixty-seventh Street, she smiled at the thought of Jed. His had been the greatest influence on her adult life; for better or worse he had taught her what it meant to be a shiksa—"There's good news and bad news!" The bad news for her was Ben. Qualities he had shared with Jed—qualities she would always search for in a man—had drawn her to him initially; then, to her astonishment and fear, she had found the object of a long search: the grail of physical and spiritual love combined. And in the end, everything but their volatile chemistry had been a lie. Was it the lie she had repudiated, or did her well of insecurity run as deeply as his? With their dual confusion about their identities (what Jed, she supposed, would call interlocking neuroses) she had been drawn further into the Jewish mystique, haunted by old ghosts, Rochester phantoms springing from a graveyard of prejudice. Once Ben had written her a note saying, "I love you for how you make my soul laugh and feel worthwhile." If only she could have done that for him. If his friends were right, what she had provoked in him was nothing more than the deep bitterness that sometimes passes for love. How ironic—the girl they couldn't get in high school had turned into the girl who couldn't get *them*. Jed had looked happier than she had seen him in

years when he'd told her, just a few days ago, that he'd finally met
the woman meant for him. She was Jewish, he said, but she wasn't
a knibbler and she never got sick. A light of understanding, of resolution had shone in his eyes as he'd admitted, "I know I used to
say the opposite, but now I think Jews should marry Jews. It's easier—you don't have all those things to fight about."

And such was the rock on which Katherine's faith was built that
neither the *mishegoss* in the confessionals, the foibles of individual
members of the clergy, nor even Mother Graves's red wig could
permanently estrange her from the Church. Catholicism was her
conduit, her way to God, even if it was often a ludicrous, tortuous,
confused, *farkrimte* way. Now that she had returned to it—Mass,
Communion, the whole thing—she could just imagine Jed's Japanese rages and her crying fits. To this day, they had heated arguments about the Messiah.

As Katherine entered the lobby of the Stanhope, a bespectacled man at the desk turned to look at her admiringly. He was tall,
blond, wore a three-piece suit, and appeared to be quite normal.
Does this mean I'm cured, Dr. Haskell? she thought. I noticed him
noticing me. No more shiksa syndrome! Then she hurried on to the
elevator, late for dinner with Manny's brother, Victor.

Not two hours later, when she was seated with Victor under a
green-shaded hanging lamp in Melon's, another ghost came out of
the past to make her sense of rediscovery come full circle. It seemed
that Victor was acquainted with her father's old nemesis, the infa-
mous Sol Levant. Their table was in the back room of the crowded
hamburger joint, jammed between two noisy foursomes, but they
might have been in a cathedral for the silence that came over Katherine at the mention of the dreaded name.

"How do you happen to know him?" she asked.

"Really it was my father who knew him at the time he, Dad,
taught history at Penn," Victor replied. "Levant was always getting
one award or another. He's got a sensational wife. His son's a problem, I understand. A dropout or some such. Lives in a commune."

"What sort of reputation does Sol have?"

"I don't know too much about it, Kate. But my recollection is
that my father spoke very highly of him."

"Really?" she asked thinly. How could that be? It haunted her
that her father's bitterness had been misplaced, or worse, a result of
anti-Semitism.

"Of course, my father thought well of anyone who was all right on the Jewish question, even if he was a mafioso," Victor said. "Would you like to meet him? I think I could arrange it. They live not far from Manny and Wilder in Lower Merion."

At sixteen, Katherine had felt disloyal at the mere thought of it; now it seemed like the missing piece of a puzzle. She said firmly, "Yes, I would."

They went back to the hotel early, so that Victor could call the Levants at home. Katherine felt her heart racing as he requested the number from Information; while he carried on a brief, cordial conversation with Sol's wife, Miranda, her mind sped backward in time, and when Sol came on the line and Victor handed her the phone, she heard in her voice the coloration, the hesitancy and shyness of a young girl.

"Of course, I remember Douglas," Sol said warmly. (Naturally, she thought, I knew he would be warm.) His voice was thin and cracked with age, but his thoughts were completely lucid as he recalled having seen Katherine in her crib, and how Westbrook Pegler had been her mother's favorite columnist. "I look forward to meeting you," he said. No reticence, not a trace of guilt, she noted. Then, after a brief pause, he blurted in a rush, "Here's what happened with your father. When I met him, I was already successful, you know. Why, Goodyear was paying me royalties of twenty thousand a month for my inventions. So Douglas saw a place where he could fit it and . . ."

Katherine's breathing was shallow; she listened, incredulous as Porfiri in the face of Raskolnikov's confession, as Sol revealed himself to her. In the background, she heard Miranda's urgent voice, but Sol plunged on compulsively: "He was a man of great stature. Everybody respected Douglas Winterhaus. He was the smartest guy in his office. I was never there, of course, in his office, but I swear to God, he was brilliant." His voice faded in and out. "It's so sad . . . even now when I remember"—he gave a little chuckle at his own emotion—"I could cry because . . . the kindness of him." He coughed. "I've been sick, you know. Let me pass the phone to Miranda. She'll set up a time."

Victor spoke with Miranda; they made a date for the week after Christmas, which Katherine and Chryssie planned to spend in New York, but Katherine conjectured that when the time came, she would be loath to keep the appointment.

Three months later, sitting in the kitchen of her house in Mandeville Canyon after Chryssie had left for Oakwood, Katherine read in *The New York Times* that Sol Levant, the noted inventor and philanthropist, had died of pulmonary heart failure. Their phone conversation had taken on an air of unreality; she had looked forward to seeing him with her own eyes. But she was to be denied that satisfaction: Fate had intervened to close the book. Suddenly a realization dawned—her eyes flicked to the obituary's dateline for confirmation. Goose bumps rose on her flesh. The Practical Joker was at it again. Sol Levant had died on Emily Winterhaus's birthday.

Katherine turned her head, staring out the window at a swallow's nest that hung among the beams of her side porch. She felt like a traveler at the end of a long road. The journey had started with Sol Levant and Eddie Frankel, with preconceptions and fears and fascination, with rebellion against parental warnings. What had she missed by being a renegade? The Country Club? Huntin', shootin', and fishin'? "The worst thing you can do is to seem different," Margot had cautioned her at Manhattanville. Sorry, Margot; might as well ask a fish to fly as a shiksa to conform to Gentile life. Neither family nor reason nor religion had affected her mania for Jewish men; what had delivered her from its hold was sheer exhaustion. They were just Too Much Trouble.

A week later, Katherine and Chryssie flew to New York. Shortly before they'd left home, Louise had called with the news that Ben and Deirdre were getting divorced. How many times had she dreamed of hearing those words? And now they meant nothing. After all the time, all the pain, all the knowledge, they left her only with a feeling of sympathy for Deirdre.

"Ben seems to be bouncing back though," Louise had said. "He told a girl I know that he expects to be made bureau chief at *Newsworld*."

"That's nice," Katherine had murmured.

They landed at Kennedy on a Friday, just ahead of a blizzard predicted for the eastern seaboard. Chryssie went directly to her grandparents, where she was to spend the first few days of vacation. On Saturday morning, when Katherine looked out the window of her room at the Stanhope, her eyes met a wall of snow. Nothing moved on the streets; a few hardy souls slipped along the sidewalks; the dots of color in the distance were people crossing the park on skis. Wilder called at ten, frustrated that Manny was snowed in in Philadelphia, while she had invited a group to dinner at their apartment at the Des Artistes.

"I'm dying to see you!" Wilder said. "We're opting for elegant dress even though there'll only be a few people, two or three couples, a business friend of Manny's—and Edward Harrow will be here! He's an entrepreneur—there's no other way to describe him. He spends a lot of time in California. Women go mad for Edward. I call him the Jewish Torturer."

"Don't look at me," Katherine said with a laugh.

"Come early so we can talk."

At seven-fifteen, Katherine stood at a double-story living room window in the Des Artistes, looking down at the lights scattered like fallen stars around Tavern on the Green. She wore an off-the-shoulder black velvet dress—a child's dream dress—and as she had done in childhood, she squinted at the lights, finding in the blur ghosts of Christmases past: Christopher backing out of their apartment; Jed *grizhering* in the light of a gaily decorated tree; Chryssie holding out her arms to receive his doll; Ben going out the door with his clock under his arm. On the stereo, the achingly romantic opening passage of Mahler's Ninth Symphony swelled. Katherine turned away from the window, banishing memories, preferring an unfettered future. The doorbell rang.

"Oh, damn! The maid's gone home," Wilder called from the bathroom. "It's bound to be Edward—he's always early!"

"Shall I answer it?"

"Do. He'd love that."

Katherine walked past the antique silvered mirror in the hallway without glancing into it. She looked beautiful and she knew it. Moreover, she felt immune. As a section of woodwinds heralded the arrival of Wilder's Jewish Torturer, she smiled to herself, thinking, What a relief not to be in love! Mildly curious, she opened the door and put out her hand. "Hello. Wilder's not quite ready. I'm Katherine Kellogg."

A slight figure seemed to hang limply in the vestibule, one shoulder raised, arms at awkward angles, hands dangling like those of a puppet in repose. In utter disbelief, she beheld all five feet six inches of him, brown hair tortured into place with brilliantine, nose reddened with cold, and ears—mastodon ears—jutting like oversized handles from the sides of his head. Oh, Wilder, no! she thought with an irrepressible smile. You can't be serious. Even for one who understands the syndrome, this is definitely going too far!

An invisible puppeteer jerked a string and the man's hand shot out, fingers splayed. The head slid forward to peer at her intently through lenses thick as binocular glass. He gave a formal little bow, grasped her hand, and held on, staring, already besotted. An ice queen, Katherine inclined her head. Blue eyes behind horn-rimmed glasses held her gaze and there, incredibly but ineluctably, she encountered her destiny. It was written on the damask walls or in the stars or anywhere else she cared to look.

"I'm Edward Harrow," he announced, clipped and courteous, a pretender, apparently, to some British lineage. Katherine had to strain to hear him over the thundering of her heart. Drawn beyond reason to this new embodiment of her childhood fantasy, she took a step toward him. Out of nowhere, a voice sounded in her ear—she would have known it anywhere: it was Dr. Garlock, that crackpot from Pasadena, saying, "The tests show you do not learn from experience."

She froze. Prickles of fear attacked the base of her skull. Oh, no. Not again, God! she pleaded. Reluctant as Christ in Gethsemane, she begged to be delivered from this scenario she knew so well—one, like His, of her own making. The passion, the laughs . . . the loss . . . the pain . . . ah, the *pain* inherent in loving this pint-sized Jewish person! Had the winter storm irrupted right through the vaulted windows to protest, she would have found it fitting. That wasn't Fate she'd glimpsed, but Folly.

On the other hand, she thought talmudically, consider the Eastern alternatives. Tally-ho and down the hatch with Christopher's blond, bland *frères semblables* from St. Grottlesex. Anyway, she reminded herself, this was not her apartment nor he her guest, but Wilder's. One must be polite. As she stepped aside to let him pass, the spirit of Jed Bernard winged a final cautionary note in her ear: "Two thousand years of sickness, Malcolm."

Katherine wavered at the threshold. This is obviously a test, she thought. I am going to be graded on my answer. What doth it profit a woman if she travels three thousand miles and makes the same mistakes all over again? Break the pattern, putz. Learn from experience for once. The hell with politeness, this is *not* for you!

Rash, inspired, she put her hand out to close the door in Kismet's face. In that instant, for no perceptible reason, Edward Harrow, né Horowitz, tripped on a Persian prayer rug in the entry. The small hands flew out. His glasses slipped to the end of his nose. Katherine's hand pressed her heart in recognition—it was Jerry Lewis's entrance in *That's My Boy*. Her own true love! Impossible that such a man could torture anyone, she scoffed. How could anybody so adorably clumsy, so boyish, so obviously vulnerable and insecure despite his wealth (ha-ha!), so physically unprepossessing (see Neil, Ben, etc.) be able to hurt her? (Shut up, Garlock.)

Edward Harrow pushed his glasses back on, darting a self-conscious glance in her direction, blinking, possibly even—could it be?—blushing.

The smile on her face started slowly and brightened. As he moved past her into the apartment, the top of his head level with her nose, she almost laughed aloud. Shorter by the minute, she thought, and possibly nuttier. And like a bolt of lightning, the last line of Cavafy's poem came back to her: "No ship exists to take you from yourself."

Edward Harrow turned and smiled at her. All at once Katherine felt as if she had sailed halfway around the world only to find herself on familiar ground. The landscape was different, the terrain rocky, but it was *home*, and worth all the *tsouris* that surely lay ahead to be back again.